Sea Change

SAUGATUCK BOOK 1

AMELIA C. GORMLEY

ACG Publications
www.ameliacgormley.com

Cover Art by Samantha Santana
https://www.amaidesigns.com/
Editor: Carrie White

ISBN: 978-1-62622-612-8

First edition
May 2014

Second edition
September 2018

ONE SUMMER CAN CHANGE
EVERYTHING...

Topher Carlisle's always been the black sheep—literally—in his middle-class family. Biracial, gay, and genderfluid, his family doesn't think he'll amount to much, and he just might believe them.

After a bout of severe depression has put both his academic and financial prospects in danger, he accepts his best friend's offer to stay in her family's summer home while he works to make up the shortfall of his athletic scholarship. But his tendency for self-sabotage is strong and soon a terrible mistake in judgment leaves him homeless.

From the moment he sees Topher, artist Jace Sieger knows that this is someone he needs to capture on canvas. He's no stranger to poor life choices, and he sees something in Topher worth nurturing.

The challenge, though, is chipping through Topher's prickly defenses to reach the sensitive, traumatized soul beneath. With the help of his friends Geoff and Robin, maybe, just maybe, they can convince Topher he's worth something after all, and that a few mistakes don't make him irredeemable.

What starts as a casual vacation fling grows into something that will change both of them forever.

(This novel is a newly-released and retitled second edition. It was previously available under the title Saugatuck Summer.*)*

ONE SUMMER CAN CHANGE
EVERYTHING...

Topher Carlisle's always been the black sheep—literally—in his middle-class family. Biracial, gay, and genderfluid, his family doesn't think he'll amount to much, and he just might believe them.

After a bout of severe depression has put both his academic and financial prospects in danger, he accepts his best friend's offer to stay in her family's summer home while he works to make up the shortfall of his athletic scholarship. But his tendency for self-sabotage is strong and soon a terrible mistake in judgment leaves him homeless.

From the moment he sees Topher, artist Jace Sieger knows that this is someone he needs to capture on canvas. He's no stranger to poor life choices, and he sees something in Topher worth nurturing.

The challenge, though, is chipping through Topher's prickly defenses to reach the sensitive, traumatized soul beneath. With the help of his friends Geoff and Robin, maybe, just maybe, they can convince Topher he's worth something after all, and that a few mistakes don't make him irredeemable.

What starts as a casual vacation fling grows into something that will change both of them forever.

(This novel is a newly-released and retitled second edition. It was previously available under the title Saugatuck Summer.)

PRAISE FOR STRAIN

…dystopian fantasy at its finest…devastatingly beautiful.

— JENNI LEA, BOY MEETS BOY REVIEWS

Strain is a well written and absorbing novel. The further into the novel the reader gets, the deeper the reader sinks emotionally. It grabs onto your heart or should I say Rhys does, and, refuses to let go. Trust me when I say you will be sobbing at certain junctures within this story. Rhys will break your heart over and over.

— MELANIE MARSHALL, SCATTERED THOUGHTS
AND ROGUE WORDS

Amelia Gormley has created a really excellently drawn post-apocalyptic world

— AUTHOR LETA BLAKE

To my Aunt Debbie (the sane one in the family).
Thank you for being the one relative I can truly share my love of writing with.

To Paul and Tristan, for understanding when I have to crawl into the writing cave and snarl at anyone who tries to drag me out.

To my cheerleading, beta, and brainstorming crew: Leta Blake, P.D. Singer, Angie Benedetti, Anne Tenino, and as always, Jenny, who is the first to read anything I write and had such lovely things to say about this book.
And finally, to the readers, especially those for whom Topher's history and family issues will resonate. You're not alone.

PART I
THE BRENDAN GARDNER AFFAIR, OR...

HERE'S TO YOU, MR. ROBINSON

You race toward something
You don't know what you'll find
But you'll notice it when you see it
You say, "there must be more
Out there waiting silently"
You know your place
But you hate it just the same

— CASEY STRATTON, "HARVEST."

CHAPTER ONE

Why must you wallow in all your delusions?
Nail yourself to the cross at least once a week
Well you've got some nerve to lay all your demons at
   my feet
Far too used to expecting so much from me

— CASEY STRATTON, "SACRIFICE"

God, the lake looked good.

No. Good didn't cover it. Awesome, amazing, some other superlative the English language hadn't invented yet. All of that. I wanted to be *in* it. I wanted to cleave through the water with distance-eating strokes. But it wasn't warm enough yet, not without a wet suit, and I didn't have one of those. I'd have to spend the next month driving to the aquatic center up in Holland to do laps. I absolutely needed to be in top shape when school started again in the fall; my swimming scholarship was hanging on the line. It might only cover half my tuition, and none of my books or living expenses, but losing it would catapult returning to school in the fall out of the realm of "difficult" and into "no fucking chance."

But if I could train here, where my eyes didn't burn from chlorine fumes and I could smell honest-to-God seaweed . . .

Jesus, I was gonna love staying with Mo and her family, especially once I could get into the water.

Speaking of Mo . . . I turned back to trudge up the beach toward the blanket she'd spread on the sand. It was sunny, but also windy and cool, especially this close to the water. We were both in long sleeves and jeans. Michigan had a way of flipping spring into summer like a light switch, so within a few weeks it could quite possibly be sweltering.

"Quit pouting," Mo said as I sighed in yearning. I dropped onto the blanket beside her and looked back at the water. "It's only a few weeks, then you can freeze your balls off to your heart's content." I gave her a dirty look. She was stretched out with a book, her freckled face covered in a sheen of SPF three gazillion. She shrugged off my glower and closed her book, grinning at me. "So, what do you think?"

"I think you lied, Mo."

"*What?*"

It was my turn to grin. "You said your family wasn't rich."

She narrowed her eyes and tossed her head, the lavender and teal chalk tones in her strawberry-blonde hair flipping like a rainbow in motion. "We're not *rich.* Just, you know, *comfortable.* We inherited the beach house from my dad's parents. I won't say we're living hand-to-mouth, but it doesn't make us wealthy."

Just wealthy enough to have two households, a vacation home, and the luxury of never wondering how they were going to pay for tuition. Her dad was a tenured professor at MSU and kept a house in Lansing. He drove to the other house in Ann Arbor to be with his wife—a pediatric surgeon at the U of M hospital—and only daughter on the weekends and during school vacations.

I didn't point that out to Mo, though. She rocked her white liberal guilt pretty hard sometimes, and got very uncomfortable thinking about the advantages she had in comparison to my clusterfuck of a family and financial situation. And hey, I certainly wasn't going to complain that my BFF's family was loaded, not when they were putting me up in their beach house for the summer so I wouldn't have to worry about rent or food. I could just concentrate on finding a job, saving for tuition, and figuring my shit out.

"I got no problem with comfortable," I said with a careless shrug.

We fell quiet then, the only sounds the wind and the waves and the screeching of seagulls. I was definitely grateful to Mo and her family for making this offer. She wouldn't be spending the whole summer here with me; she had a job counseling at a summer camp up in Traverse City, and would only be home every other weekend, but that was actually a good thing. We'd tried being roommates briefly and had discovered that we were much better friends when we weren't in each other's back pockets all the time. In the beach house up on top of the dune behind us, I'd opted for the cozy attic bedroom, with its own little three-quarters bath and huge half-moon window over-looking the lake, rather than the one on the second floor that shared a bath with Mo's room. It was perfect. We would be together, and yet not so closely or constantly that we got sick of each other.

I was looking forward to getting settled in. Maybe this evening I'd set up my keyboard and practice for a while. I knew Mo wouldn't mind if I played and sang a bit, and her dad wasn't supposed to arrive for another day or two. Of course I might have to stop playing once he got here, even if I kept it quiet in my room. My family had always complained because they could hear me through the heating vents, despite the fact that I was down in the basement.

Mo shook herself, breaking our silent camaraderie. "Oh, I almost forgot. Your phone rang when you were down by the water contemplating insanity." She pointed to the cheap Android I'd left on the blanket. I frowned at it, reluctant to pick it up. Aside from Mo, the only people to ever call me were my family, and that was rarely a good thing.

Finally I dropped onto the blanket beside her and sighed when my sister's name came up on the caller ID. Thumbing the callback button, I made a mental wager with myself as to how long it would take Colleen to disregard or casually insult me.

"Family drama incoming in three . . . two . . . one . . . Hey. You called?"

"Hey, Topher. I was wondering when we could expect you in Flint, to stay with Mom for a while."

"Hi, big sis! Nice to hear from you! College is great! Swim season went well!" That wasn't really true, but whatever. "I got great grades on all my finals." That one *was* true, but it wasn't going to change the mess I was in now. "Thanks for showing such a keen interest in my life and well-being! It's so *touching* to know you care."

"Oh. Sorry. Hi." Wow, she actually sounded embarrassed at being called out. I didn't expect it to last long, though. "So, you're doing good?"

"I'm getting by. I need to train this summer—next season is going to be important if I want to keep my scholarship—and I'm looking for a job to help cover tuition, but other than that, I'm okay."

"Oh. Good. Good. I've been working hard, too. Trying to save up for a vacation this year. My new boyfriend Terry wants to go to Hawaii, and I want to go with him."

"Hawaii sounds fun," I said noncommittally. Her duty to pretend to care about my life having been discharged, I knew exactly where this conversation was headed next.

Colleen didn't disappoint. "So, anyway, yeah. Mom. Helping. When can I expect you?"

I gripped a fold in the blanket in my fist. "Hmmm, I dunno. What's the weather in Hell looking like? Any ice storms lately?"

"Topher, don't be a dick. She's having a hard time getting around. I have to work all summer; I don't get summer break like you do, and running her errands takes up a lot of my time. You're not doing anything for almost four months. The least you could do is come help out. I would really love to take a vacation some-time this summer."

"Oh, hey, did I just do the time warp back into last year?

Because, damn girl, if this conversation isn't giving me déjà vu all over again. The answer was no then, and it's no now." I grimaced at Mo. "And I'm not *doing nothing* over the next four months, thanks. I just told you, I need to train. A lot. Not to mention get a job."

"They have a Y here in Flint, you realize."

"And yet the answer is *still* no."

"God, you're such a selfish little prick. This is family."

"*Your* family. Not mine. My association with Frederica ended when she took a truckload of pills, knowing I'd be arriving the next day to find her body."

"Not this again." I heard her growl on the other end of the line. "Right, it's *all* about you, isn't it? She can't even get sick without you trying to make yourself the victim. She had a stroke and collapsed and spent a day and a half on the floor nearly freezing to death, and you still have to make it all about you and your self-centered fucking drama."

I shook my head firmly, even if she couldn't see it. "It wasn't a stroke. I know what I saw." I rubbed my forehead, where a headache was beginning to twinge. How many times were we going to have this fucking discussion?

"It *wasn't* a suicide attempt!" Colleen practically shouted in my ear. "She's too fucking melodramatic to do it that way, okay? If she'd been planning to kill herself, there would have been notes and she would have been giving shit away left and right, writing wills, making grand gestures."

I slammed my fist down on the blanket, grateful for the sand beneath that prevented the little tantrum from hurting. "That *was* her grand gesture. You don't know the way she thinks, Colleen! She never played the head games with you like she did with me. Why would she need to leave a note when she could arrange to have her funeral while everyone home for the holidays already? She was putting on a *show*, and we were all cast in the roles of the grieving loved ones."

"She *said* she didn't try to kill herself!"

"No. She said she didn't *remember* trying to kill herself. Which is Frederica code for *Yeah, I did it, but I'm not going to cop to it, and hey, isn't brain damage a convenient fucking excuse!*" Damn it, now I was shouting.

Colleen heaved a long-suffering sigh and pitched her voice lower, adopting the tone that said she was trying to make herself the reasonable one. "There are a lot of other reasons things could have looked the way they did."

"She didn't want to be lying there alone, undiscovered, eaten by her damned cats. She knew I was coming that day." I was jabbing my finger violently in the air, like I could point it in Colleen's face, and made myself stop. "But you go ahead and pretend you're some brilliant forensic detective in your own little episode of *CSI*. Stage a recreation to prove how the way things *look* like they happened isn't the way they really happened. Convince yourself that there was some perfectly good, *completely coincidental* reason for her to have had a sixteen-ounce drinking glass full of pills spilled on the floor beside her."

I glanced over to see Mo looking at me with gentle sympathy. She knew the whole story, of course. We'd met the semester before that incident, my freshman year, and bonded pretty much instantly. When I'd held my vigil in the ICU during Christmas break, I'd spent a lot of time talking and texting with her.

". . . But you weren't *there*, Colleen," I continued, clinging to Mo's understanding gaze. "You didn't see the scene. You didn't find her lying in a pool of her own puke. You weren't the one in the ICU that first night, with the nurses telling you not to wait too long before making the decision to pull the plug. If Frederica's having trouble getting around, it's her own fucking fault. She's pulled my leash for the last fucking time."

"Topher . . ." Colleen groaned, and I could practically hear her making the effort to rein her temper in. "Even if you were right—and I lived with her four years longer than you, so maybe I know a bit more than you think about how she operates—she's sick. Okay? If she tried to kill herself, it's because she's sick. You can't hate her for that."

Oh lovely. Now it was time for a recitation from the Enabler's Handbook.

"I don't hate her." I busied my fingers trying to pick grains of sand off the dark blanket. "Hating her would require caring about her, and I don't. Not anymore. She's toxic, and I need to protect myself."

She was silent a moment. Then: "You better hope you don't ever need help from the family."

"Don't worry, sis. I learned long before puberty not to expect anything from this family." My mouth twisted bitterly, and I hung up before she could take another opportunity to tell me what an awful person I was. It was the same old refrain, and I'd heard it all before. *Topher, you're so self-centered. Topher, you're too dramatic. Topher, you just want attention.*

Feh. They used those insults to try to make me feel guilty so I would do what they wanted me to do. I had to remember that. I was doing what was healthy for me. Protecting myself. And that didn't make me a bad person.

I sat beside Mo silently, staring out at the waves crashing against the beach as I tried to convince myself of that once again.

Thanks, Colleen. Way to fuck up a nice afternoon.

Mo didn't press me to talk. She knew I'd open up in my own time. I wasn't even close to manly enough to stuff down my feelings about shit. I wore them on my sleeve, and yes, that had gotten me my ass kicked regularly throughout my school years, thanks for asking.

After a while, she asked softly, "What do you think your mom will do if you go see her?"

I scrubbed my hands down my face. "Same thing she's always done. Try to make me as sick as she is."

She tilted her head and looked at me, waiting for me to clarify.

"She just . . . ever since I was a little kid—and by that, I mean, like, six years old—my job was to comfort her and make her feel better, you know? And probably at least some of that was my fault, because I was just one of those really oversensitive, overly empathetic kids who would do stupid things like bawl in sympathy with a cartoon character who was being picked on."

I picked up a handful of cool sand and let it trickle through my fingers. "So whenever she got drunk and went on a crying jag, or just got into one of her woe-is-me-everything-is-horrible-nothing-will-ever-get-better riffs, I was the one who heard about it. I'm the one who spent hours and hours crying with her, telling her it would be all right, that she wasn't a horrible person, a horrible mother, et cetera. And eventually she'd pass out, and then it would be fine until the next time. And she'd just . . . suck me in. Every damn time. I couldn't *not* try to make her feel better. I had to try to fix it for her."

"She never got help?"

I shook my head. "Her late husband kept offering to send her to rehab, but she always refused. She doesn't get drunk anymore because she says she can't handle the hangovers, but it doesn't stop the other behaviors. She's just a bottomless pit, emotionally speaking. She doesn't want to be reassured, she just wants attention and pity." My last shrink had called that "narcissistic supply." Like I was a drug dealer helping her get her fix. It was either cut her off or stop caring about everyone and everything so I wasn't left wide open.

Mo nodded and massaged my shoulder. We fell silent again, and she drew me against her and let me rest my head on her shoulder while she rubbed my back.

"You know what *really* makes me feel like a selfish asshole?" I said at length, as the afternoon began to age toward evening. "There was a while there in the hospital when she was starting to improve . . . and I didn't want to believe it. I cried when they told me she was out of the woods, and not because I was happy. I had accepted it, you know? Years before, really. Around the time I was fifteen or so, when she made a big production of telling me she had lumps and that she *knew* it was cancer even though all the doctors told her they were just cysts, and if it was cancer, she was just going to let herself die since she couldn't stand to lose her breasts. That's when I accepted that she was going to die. I knew someday she'd drink herself to death or kill herself, and, then, once it seemed like it'd finally happened, I was okay with it. I was fucking *relieved*. I just wanted it to be over with, you know?"

"I don't think that makes you selfish, Topher." Mo's voice was gentle, and I found myself thinking, not for the first time, that she would make a damned good therapist once she finished her degrees in psychology and social work.

My eyes stung, and I wiped them on the back of my hand. "I wished her gas hadn't been shut off the week before. I wished for once she'd managed to be a responsible fucking adult and pay her bill on time. Core temp of, like, eighty degrees, can you believe that shit? If she hadn't gotten hypothermic lying there on the floor overnight, it would have been game over. That's the only thing that kept the brain damage in check, and I wished it *hadn't happened*. What do you think Colleen would say if I ever admitted *that*?"

She squeezed my hand without a word. Eventually, I laced my fingers with hers and squeezed back. After a moment I shook off my bout of self-indulgent moping and straightened up, trying to be a good guest.

"So, what's the nightlife like around here?"

She shrugged. "Well, there's a really good theater company here in town. I thought we might go see a show or two this summer. And I expect we'll head over to the club at the Dunes at least a couple times while you're here. I mean, you can't tell me you don't want to party and check out the action at a famous gay resort. Other than that, I suppose we'll drive into Grand Rapids if we want to hit some different clubs."

"Just like we do when we're at school." I chuckled. I didn't know why I had it built up in my mind that we were going *away* this summer. I knew how close Saugatuck was to the city near which I'd spent the last nine years of my life. I guess it had only felt far off and exotic because I'd never spent the summer in a beach house.

"Yeah, well, this time you'll be twenty-one, so that'll be different at least."

I snorted. "Only a week more. You know, it fuckin' *blows* that you're not going to be here to take me out on my birthday."

"Hey, the weekend I'm back after that, we'll rock the fuck out of this town. Promise."

"Sounds like a good deal." I gave her a wan smile and stood. "I think I'm gonna go lust after the lake a bit longer before we head out for dinner."

She started packing up her book. "Okay. I'm going to go up to the house and take a shower, scrape off all the sunblock. Meet you up there."

I helped her fold the blanket, then padded down the beach and stood with my sandals off while the frigid waves lapped at my feet. I imagined myself stroking out for a vigorous swim, fighting the tide. It helped lift my mood out of its abrupt downward spiral. What Colleen wanted me to do didn't matter. I wasn't going anywhere. I was here for the whole summer, and *here* was awfully damn nice. Over the next four months, I'd find a way to make money and cover the shortfall from my scholarship so I wouldn't have to deal with relying on my aunt and uncle's dubious, strings-fully-attached assistance. And in a few weeks, I'd be in the water and everything would be good again.

I turned back to head up the beach toward the house.

When I reached the bottom of the stairs that climbed the dune, a man was coming down. He was dressed preppy-sharp—stonewashed blue oxford shirt with well-fitted tan slacks—and he looked like Robert Redford in his prime. Only not quite. His bone structure had that same sort of chiseled definition, but the eyes were long-lashed and feminine, more like Tom Hiddleston. And the mouth was softer and fuller, like David Wenham.

So, okay. He was basically an amalgamation of every redheaded man to ever turn my crank (and how!). And he lived in a popular gay resort town, which meant the chances were above average that he might actually be interested. Watching him trot lightly down those stairs to the beach, I realized what my third objective this summer would be.

Agent Carlisle, your mission, should you choose to accept it, will be to find out which of these residences belongs to Mr. Strawberry-Blond Hunka Burnin' Love and convince him to do you on every horizontal surface—and against a few of the vertical ones.

I was *so* up for that gig.

He appeared to be out for a stroll, not coming down to lie around the beach. He flashed a smile at me as he reached the bottom of the stairs and slid his sunglasses down his nose, revealing eyes such a dark and sparkling blue they made sapphires turn green with envy. He had deep smile-creases in his cheeks, too long to be called dimples. Suddenly I wondered if my loose shorts were loose enough.

And he was smiling like he knew me. What—?

His hand darted out to shake mine. "Hi, you must be Topher. I'm Morgan's dad, Brendan Gardner."

Abort mission! Abort! Abort! Abort!

Seriously? Fuck my life.

CHAPTER TWO

I want you
But I can't have you
And I understand it
No one is wrong this time

— CASEY STRATTON, "CRUEL HAND OF FATE"

"You can stop drooling over my dad anytime now," Mo teased as we drove back to the beach house in Douglas after having dinner in picturesque downtown Saugatuck.

"Sorry," I muttered, slinking down in my seat a little. Good thing my complexion was dark enough that blushes never really showed.

Of course, that could also be trouble for me this summer, in a town where less than five percent of the population was non-Caucasian and only about half of one percent was black. I foresaw the possibility of being pulled over for Driving While (Half) Black in my near future. Which, really, was nothing new after living in the suburbs of Grand Rapids, where I had been one of five students of color in a graduating class of over four hundred.

But at least I wasn't blushing.

"Come on, though. Really. *Damn*, woman." I recovered and sent her a chiding look. "Give a gay boy some warning next time."

She chuckled. "Okay. Fine. If I weren't obligated by all known laws of God and man to find the subject disgusting, I could possibly admit that my dad is a bit of a hottie and—except for him, you know, being straight and married—would probably appeal to any number of gay men. So, you came, you saw, you salivated, now stop being gross."

I sniffed and lifted my nose. "I most certainly did *not* come."

"Ew! Topher! Don't you ever, *ever* link that word to my father in conversation again!" I laughed as she shuddered theatrically, then let my head roll back against the headrest and looked out the passenger-side window at the whitecaps on the waves below. It was on nights like this that I felt bad for people who went to schools with three-term years instead of semesters. Some colleges wouldn't be letting out until early June. But here we were, free for an entire month longer. It was a gorgeous May evening, still a little chilly, but mild enough that after dinner, we'd taken a quick driving tour and stopped at a coffeehouse for lattes. Then we'd gone down to the boardwalk and looked at the boats in the marina there on Kalamazoo Lake. Now we were headed home, the back seat full of groceries, a couple Redbox DVDs, and a bottle of white zinfandel.

Brendan—*Mr. Gardner. He's Mr. Gardner. Mo's dad. Mo, your BFF. Totally off limits. Straight. Married. No chance in Hell, so don't even think about getting too familiar. It's Mr. Gardner and never anything else*—was in the living room with his laptop when we got back to the house, but he closed the computer and helped us put away the groceries. Then he leaned against the island cutting block as Mo poured two glasses of wine and microwaved the popcorn.

"So what are your plans for the summer, Topher?" he asked, snagging one of the glasses of wine out of her hand. "Thanks, sweetie."

Mo rolled her eyes and poured a third.

I shrugged, pondering the question as I accepted my glass from Mo. "I'll probably try to find a job around here to save up enough money to reenroll this fall, though I imagine most of the seasonal job openings have been taken by now. It'll need to be something that still lets me swim twice a day. My scholarship isn't a full ride, and between training and classes, I don't know if I can balance having a job during the school year, too, at least not without my grades taking a nosedive."

Mr. Gardner nodded as if this were familiar information, and I wondered what all Mo had told him. Had it just been about the need to live cheap and make money, or had she told him why I was in danger of losing my scholarship? She had been the one, for over a year after my mom's suicide attempt, to drag me out of bed when I'd spiraled down too far to get myself moving. She'd been the one to convince me to finally go back to my psychiatrist and get my meds adjusted.

Did her dad know that about me? Did he know that this whole mess was almost all my fault? Well, not really—obviously I hadn't been well—but I blamed myself anyway. Would he be like my family and think the depression was a cop-out? That I was lazy? Hadn't been trying hard enough? He was a psychology professor. He'd know better, right?

It doesn't matter. We're not giving a fuck what anyone thinks of us, remember?

"Your family doesn't help?" he asked, interrupting my self-lecture.

"Don't be nosy, Dad," Mo cautioned in a singsong voice.

I pulled the popcorn out of the microwave, my determined disregard of anyone else's judgment stamped firmly into place, and tossed a snort over my shoulder. "Oh, please, girl. Like I got any secrets."

She laughed and inclined her head in a semi-bow, acknowledging the point. Twelve years of nearly nonstop psychotherapy had accustomed me to talking openly about deeply personal stuff with near strangers, which sometimes meant I lost track of boundaries and gave people more information about myself than they really wanted. Besides, if my family was going to accuse me of being a drama queen—which they'd done pretty much from the time I was able to talk—I might as well actually *be* one.

Mo handed me a large bowl and I dumped the popcorn into it, then met Mr. Gardner's eyes to answer the question he'd asked before Mo had tried to warn him off.

"My mom's sister and her husband were helping me. I lived with them from the time I was in middle school. But I'm not going to ask them for anything anymore. My family is weird about money. Anyone gives you a cent and they think they have a right to weigh in on everything you do from there on out, and I get enough of that already. I don't really want to be accountable to people who consider me an embarrassment."

"That's my girl." Mo slung an arm over my shoulder, squeezing as she dug into the popcorn with her other hand.

"Ah." To his credit, Mr. Gardner didn't look a bit put off by the turn of the discussion toward my being gay. Not just gay but *very* comfortable with my feminine side as well. "They're religious?"

"Not really, but a lot of their friends are. You know, the Grand Rapids area being the seat of the Christian Reformed Church, which is just about as conservative as it gets. I mean no shopping on Sundays, that sort of thing. I once saw a groom's family up and leave his wedding reception because there would be dancing after supper. My family attends, mostly just because it's the done thing, though. They're not so much true believers as they are very . . ." I drew a deep breath, trying to figure out how to word it politely. "Image-conscious."

It was a better word than *posers*, which wasn't a very nice thing to say. And yeah, okay, I couldn't help but be bitter about it, and I'm sure he could hear it in my voice. My senior year in high school, I'd endured a three-hour lecture about how my behavior harmed the family because I'd been seen leaning my head on my first boyfriend's shoulder. Not groping, kissing, snuggling, or even holding hands. Just a moment when I'd nudged Matt for making a bad joke.

I shrugged off the memory. "They think I draw too much attention to myself being, well, *me*. By not conforming. They think it makes *them* look bad. So, my choices are to try to pretend I'm not who I am, or find a way not to be answerable to them.

And sorry . . ." I gave him a cheeky grin, pleased that he was being so cool about it. "I just can't help it that I'm fabulous."

Mr. Gardner smiled and (*oh Jesus, don't look at the smile lines*) gestured to the Easter-egg chalk streaks in Mo's hair. "You know, I think the first time Morgan wanted to color her hair was . . . was it sixth grade, honey?" Mo nodded, smirking. "A really purple shade of burgundy. I can't say Adele and I weren't put off by the idea, and a lot of that was fear of how other people would react, whether they'd be unkind or unaccepting toward her if she deviated from the norm. But we knew we had to let her be who she was, and let her know that we loved her, no matter how she chose to express herself."

Another time, I might have taken someone down a peg for the obliviousness of comparing something as innate and ingrained as sexual orientation and gender expression to a preteen's hair-color whim, but damn it, Mr. Gardner was just too cute to snap at. Not to mention he was letting me spend the summer in his house pro bono, and from what I understood, he'd be here much of that time. Mo said he was taking a sabbatical from teaching to work on writing a textbook. So, better to play nice and not let the occasional moments of obtuseness get to me.

"Well, it's good that Mo has your support." I slipped an arm around her waist and leaned on her. "She definitely deserves it."

Mr. Gardner sipped his wine. "It's a shame you don't have the same from your family. But it's good that you respect yourself enough not to pretend to be something you're not."

Oh, Brendan, honey, Mo obviously hasn't told you nearly enough about me if you think I'm anywhere near full up on self-respect.

I gave him a slightly self-deprecating smirk and took a long drink of my zin before it got warm and bitter. "It's more just giving in to the inevitable, I guess. I mean, honestly, I sashayed before I could walk. It is what it is, you know? Might as well own it."

"It *should* be self-respect," Mo said fiercely, giving me a shake. "You've got nothing to be ashamed of."

I shrugged uncomfortably, leaning my head against hers, almost forgetting Mr. Gardner's presence as Mo and I fell into

that sort of exclusionary, near-telepathic best-friends communion. She knew that I would argue that I wasn't ashamed, but that
I hadn't quite figured out how to truly mean it when I held my
head up high. My entire life, people had been telling me to keep it
down and stop being an embarrassment. So, I was still in that
fake-it-'til-you-make-it stage, hoping genuine pride would come
if I pretended confidence long enough. For now, I was relying on
bravado and a complete lack of give-a-fuck to carry me through.

"Thanks," I murmured, squirming out from under Mo's arm. I
met Mr. Gardner's eyes as he sipped his wine, studying us. He
looked like I didn't quite make sense to him and he was trying to
figure me out.

Yeah, well, you and me both, Brendan, I sighed mentally, draining
my glass.

"So where did you live before middle school?" he asked as Mo
poured me some more.

"Jeez, Dad, what's with the Twenty Questions?" She juggled
her glass, the bowl of popcorn, and the rented DVDs out into the
living room. "*Avengers* again, Topher? I'm thinking *Avengers* again.
'Cause I'm really not in the mood to cry, so sorry girlfriend, but
Les Mis is out."

"That works. We'll do sing-along night tomorrow. I'm never
not in the mood to check out Jeremy Renner's ass."

Mr. Gardner paused in taking his own glass of wine—along
with the bottle—out to the living room, ducking his head as his
ears turned dark red. Okay, so apparently, I'd found the point at
which acceptance tipped over into discomfort for Mr. Sexy
Professor.

"Sorry, Mr. Gardner," I muttered, suppressing a smile and
slipping past him.

He waved a dismissive hand. "Call me Brendan, and don't
mind me. Will I be interrupting if I watch with the two of you, or
are there secret rituals taking place here to which I'm not
permitted entrance?"

Shit. He had to tell me to call him Brendan, didn't he?

I shrugged. "Fine by me. There's plenty of eye candy to go
around. Choose your fantasy fodder and help yourself."

"Ew. Can you *not* talk about my dad ogling people? Scarlett Johansson may be gorgeous, but still."

"It'll be a challenge, but I think I can refrain from licking the screen," Brendan deadpanned, placing the wine bottle on the coffee table next to the bowl of popcorn before settling into the chair where he'd been working on his computer earlier.

"Ew! Dad!"

I laughed so hard I had to set my wine down before flopping onto the sofa, rolling and giggling. When I caught my breath, Brendan grinned at me and dropped a conspiratorial wink.

Oh, Lord have mercy.

That was it, I decided as Mo pressed play. My *new* mission in life would be to find as many excuses as possible to stay away from the house all summer, before I embarrassed myself by giving away my cute little crush on my BFF's dad.

CHAPTER THREE

Your kindness is foreign and strange to me
In silence I lived far too long in the valley of sadness
Alone and feeling nothing
Will it be easy to need you?

— CASEY STRATTON, "IN SILENCE"

Given her druthers, Mo didn't wake up before noon. I, on the other hand, was used to getting up at the crack of dawn for swim practice. Driving up to Holland to train while Mo was still asleep would strike a good balance between my need to keep in shape and spending time with her before she had to leave.

As I came down the stairs, I heard the unmistakable high-pressure hiss of milk being steamed. I'd seen the espresso maker the day before but hadn't truly realized what it would be like to have lattes available *every morning* without leaving the house. Suddenly it felt like Christmas and my birthday all rolled into one.

"Good morning, Topher," Brendan said mildly. If I'd been slightly less groggy, I might have been self-conscious at being alone with him after stumbling out of bed, but mostly I was just waiting for my brain to get it in gear. Apparently, my little crush wasn't so all consuming that it trumped the need for caffeine. "Coffee?" he asked.

I should probably have waited until after my swim, but I was too damn tired. Last night had been one of those nights when turning my brain off to get to sleep had taken a long time. I nodded eagerly, and he slid me the first latte, then turned to make another.

"Thank you." I took a sip and closed my eyes in bliss. "Wow, this is really good. What—"

"It's the beans. I have no idea why they're so good, but they are. A few years ago, a colleague of mine let us borrow his time-share at a resort in the Cascades near Sisters, Oregon. Adele loves to golf, you see, and they have two eighteen-hole courses." Sheesh, time-share golf course condos. I gave Mo's assertion that they weren't loaded a mental side-eye. "When we got there, we just picked up whatever beans were available at the general store, which happened to be from Sisters Coffee Company." He raised his voice to be heard over the hissing of the steam wand. "This roast is called Black Butte Gold, and we all loved it. First thing we did when we got home was order more beans from their website."

I beamed and went full-on coffee nerd with him, babbling about working as a barista the summer after my freshman year at college. I think his eyes glazed over a bit, but it was nice to talk to someone who truly appreciated good coffee. Mo—the Philistine —would drink anything that was infused with caffeine, no matter how vile.

"So what are your plans for today, Topher?" he asked when he'd finished his own latte.

I cradled my cup between my hands, soaking in its warmth. "I'm going up to Holland to do my laps at the aquatic center there, then hitting some places and dropping off résumés or picking up applications. I figure I can afford the gas to commute this summer if I have to, since I won't have to worry about rent and all that; so anything between here and Holland is fair game, though I'd prefer something closer if I can find it."

Holy word vomit, Batman. I shut my mouth so hard my teeth clicked together and forced myself to stay still when the nervous energy tried to emerge as fidgeting instead.

"Do you want breakfast?" Brendan asked once I'd (finally!) quit talking.

I shook my head. "I'll just make a piece of toast. I don't like swimming when I feel too full."

He turned toward the toaster, and I hopped up from my stool. "Oh, I can get it! You don't have to—"

Brendan waved me off. "I think I can safely pop a piece of bread in the toaster without feeling overburdened by unreasonable demands."

I flushed and sat back down. "Sorry. Thanks."

"Not sure why you're apologizing, but you're welcome." He set out a butter knife and the jar of peanut butter and honey spread that Mo and I favored. He must have been familiar with Mo's tastes. "So, you didn't answer my question last night."

"Hmmm, what's that?" Wow. He had really long, gorgeous fingers, the bones and veins under the skin really well defined. From what I could tell, his physique was nothing to write home about. Middle-aged, sedentary lifestyle. He probably did enough time on the treadmill to keep his weight down and nothing more. The hands, though . . . I ripped my eyes from them.

"You said you lived with your aunt and uncle from middle school on up. Where did you live before that?"

"Oh. Grand Blanc, a bit south of Flint, with my grandmother."

His eyebrows drew down thoughtfully as he slid a piece of toast across the counter toward me on a plate. "Where are your parents?"

"My mom's around Flint, too, but I couldn't live with her."

"Should I ask why not, or would Morgan scold me for being nosy?"

I shrugged, slathering the spread on my toast. "We—my sisters and I—lived with her until I was midway through the first grade. Then one day, the cops showed up and took us away in the back of a patrol car. It was pretty upsetting. I thought we had done something wrong. We stayed overnight in a group foster home, and then my grandmother picked us up. The second time it happened, my aunt and uncle took custody of my younger sister, who was only about three at the time, while our grandmother took me and my older sister. Back then, you know, I didn't know what was going on. I thought we must have done something wrong for the police to take us away like that. But now that I'm older, I've figured it out."

I looked up as the troubled expression that had settled on Brendan's face while I related being hauled away by the cops shift to gentle curiosity.

"The neighbors reported us, see? Because we were running around the neighborhood on a school day. My mom—who's been an alcoholic my whole life—was too hungover to wake us up and get us ready for school in the morning, so we just stayed home, which got us reported for truancy." I offered him a thin smile. "After that we lived with Grandma, and I spent my weekends and vacations with my mom."

He blinked at that. Cue perfunctory apology in three . . . two . . .

"I'm sorry, Topher." He slumped against the counter on the other side of the kitchen. "That must have been very difficult."

Great. So now not only had I spewed words all over him, I'd made him uncomfortable. I hated this—hashing it over again— but there was no way around it. Not without rudely dismissing Brendan's attempts to become better acquainted. But I had spent way too many of my teenage years brooding about it all, and now I just wanted to be over it and moving on.

"I think it would have been more difficult if we *had* lived with Mom," I finally said, going for the perky *I'm over it and can now look at it philosophically* approach. "I have a rough relationship with my aunt and uncle, yeah, and let me tell you, my grandmother is so *not* the grandkid-spoiling, booty-knitting type. She's a real ballbuster. But if I'd stayed in my mom's custody, I would have wound up dropping out of some school whose diplomas aren't worth the paper they were printed on and working for minimum wage the rest of my life. And that's the best-case

scenario. But as it is, you know, I got to graduate from a top-notch school district and I'm enrolled in college, so really, I came out on top. In a lot of ways, I got lucky."

And oh, had it taken a lot of hours of therapy and Alateen to get to the point where I could see it from that angle, even if sometimes I was just giving lip service to it.

"Your father wasn't in the picture at all?"

"Nope. Never met the guy."

His eyebrows lifted at that.

I shrugged again. "My mom's first husband, the guy she married at seventeen while she was pregnant with my older sister, was in jail when I was conceived. She remarried a few years ago, but she'd been living with him for twenty years, and they were only married a few months before he died. I never lived with them, so I still think of him as my mom's boyfriend, rather than my stepdad. But my biological dad? He was just some dude she hooked up with a few times after going out to the bar."

Now Brendan was starting to look uncomfortable, as if he couldn't fathom a family who was so lower class. White trash, as it were, my own genetics notwithstanding. Knowing that seemed to make him uncertain about how to deal with me, because I might as well be from a different planet. His parents had left him a beach house. His wife had gone to med school. He was a PhD. There was no way he was the first person on his family tree to be well-off.

Maybe he was starting to think I was too trashy to be hanging around his daughter. Shit, why had I blurted out my whole life story to him? I never knew when I was turning people off, and they were too polite to be obvious about how weirded out they were by me, but I knew they must be *thinking* it, which of course made me feel paranoid because I worried that they weren't being honest with me, and that they really didn't like me that much, and and and . . .

Yanking myself out of the sudden mental flail, I sprang up from my stool and practically scurried across the kitchen to load my plate and cup in the dishwasher, not daring to look at him.

"I'd better go do my swim. Thanks for the coffee," I murmured, and beat a hasty retreat.

As I went down the driveway, I wondered when I was actually going to *mean* what I said about not caring what people thought of me.

CHAPTER FOUR

When dreams are sent into a broken sky
They've got no chance to fly
And I've dreamed away my life

— CASEY STRATTON, "BROKEN SKY"

Oh gosh. The latest coffeehouse Mo and I tried had a piano. Apparently, they had live music on the weekends. I stared at it yearningly while we waited for our coffees. Yeah, I had my cheap keyboard, but a piano was so much better.

Mo nudged me. "Why don't you go play?"

"What? No!" I cast a self-conscious look at the crowded tables. "You know I just play to mess around." Mo gave me her patented *not buying it* look, which I deserved. I didn't play to mess around. But I hadn't had a lesson since the sixth grade, and I needed practice if I wanted to remember how to play. I needed to keep teaching myself. But my own family hadn't appreciated hearing me, so I certainly wasn't going to subject a coffeehouse full of customers to it. "Besides, I don't have permission."

"So ask for it."

I shook my head and grabbed my mocha off the counter, heading for a table. Mo was always doing that—urging me to go after the things I coveted but didn't think I could have. I was way too familiar with that road, though. That way lay rejection and denial and disappointment. It was best not to encourage her.

AFTER COFFEE, we went out for a walk around downtown Saugatuck.

"Oh my God, look at that!" Mo stopped in front of the window of a body art studio. "Have you ever seen anything like that?"

"It's amazing," I agreed, giving the design she'd pointed out its due admiration. I'm not a visual person; I'm verbal and auditory, all the way. I couldn't even begin to describe *why* the design was unique, but it definitely stood out as the sort of tattoo art you didn't see often.

"Should I get inked again? I think I might get inked again." Mo didn't really require an answer, so I didn't give one. "Of course, I should probably wait until the end of summer. Do I really want to be taking care of a fresh tat up at summer camp?"

"Hmmm, good point." I linked my arm through hers and looked around highbrow downtown Saugatuck. It might be a vacation town, but it wasn't a tourist trap. Aside from its popularity with gay vacationers, Saugatuck's claim to fame was as an art colony. The clean, white buildings of downtown housed galleries, studios, and handmade-craft shops. They overlooked a boardwalk and marina loaded with pricey boats. The pristine town subliminally told its visitors to behave themselves and, please, *do* try not to be gauche.

It was more on the Martha's Vineyard end of the vacation destination spectrum, as opposed to, say, Coney Island or Myrtle Beach.

Frankly, though? For my money, Myrtle Beach was a lot more fun. I'd gone there for spring break my senior year of high school with some friends and lost my virginity to a college sophomore whose name I couldn't remember now. He'd come from Pennsylvania or Delaware or someplace like that. That had been a good fucking time in *every* sense of the phrase.

But while Saugatuck might not be a huge party spot full of carousing people, it was calm and quiet, and I guessed that had its value, too. That was one of the reasons I was hoping to find work in town, rather than having to commute up to Holland or wherever. I wanted to spend as much time here as possible. Problem was, summer jobs were prime pickings in vacation towns. I definitely wouldn't be the only one applying, and to be honest, I was late on the starting gun.

"Are you ever gonna get inked?" Mo asked, tugging on my arm to cut off my mental rabbit chasing and pulling me along to continue our stroll.

"I don't know." I frowned thoughtfully. "I definitely can't afford it right now. And, I mean, tats are really cool, but I think I'd either have to be very drunk or very turned on to cope with it. No one reputable will do it while you're drunk, and they probably won't pony up with a handjob first, either. Besides, you're not supposed to take them in the water and I can't take time off training. Coach'll have my ass if I get back to school and I'm out of form."

Assuming I can even afford to go back to school.

I didn't add that part. I didn't think it had occurred to Mo that I *really* might not be returning to GVSU with her if I couldn't hammer out the finances.

"*Topher,*" she groaned, switching gears abruptly. "I don't want to leave for Traverse City tomorrow. I want to stay here and hang out with you and—I don't know—smack you over the head when you get all defeatist and shit."

"Gee, thanks." I gave her a wry grimace. "But it's gotta happen sometime. We've had a great week, and we'll have another great weekend when you get back. It's going to be a fabulous summer." I wrapped my arm around her thick waist and squeezed, leaning my head on her shoulder. "You know you love working with those rug rats, God only knows why. So go forth and counsel. My defeatism and I will be just fine."

"You won't be bored? Or lonely?" she asked anxiously. "I feel like a bad hostess."

"Darling, who needs entertainment when I've got that lake outside the front door? And if I need human company, I'll just, you know, undress your dad with my eyes."

She slugged me on the shoulder, hard enough to make my eyes water and possibly leave a bruise, which I fucking well deserved. But it got her laughing (while cringing), enough to quit asking me what I was going to do while she was gone, because I was damned if I knew. I'd been job hunting all week and had already checked around town. The most likely suspects for jobs already had all the help they needed. I left filled-out applications with them anyway, but got mostly the "don't call us, we'll call you" brush-off.

When I stopped rubbing my shoulder and complaining to Mo about the punch, she led us down the street again, heading toward the boardwalk. She was going to treat me to a seafood dinner, since she wouldn't be there for my birthday. While we walked, she started throwing around ideas of what I could do while she was away.

"You know, you might not get paid for it, but you should see if the theater company needs any volunteer help. It would at least keep you occupied. Props, costumes, that sort of thing."

"Woman, when am I going to have time to volunteer? I plan to be working, remember?" I shook my head, frowning. "Besides, I'm too big a diva for that. If I can't be on stage, I don't want to be involved at all. I'd be miserable, sitting backstage watching others doing what I want to be doing."

"Well, find out what their production schedule is, see if they have open auditions."

"Come on, Mo. You know I wouldn't stand a chance. I'm lousy with choreography and I haven't even sung in a choir for two years." And I wasn't good enough and would never be good enough, and no one wanted to listen to me anyway. I'd certainly received that message often enough.

"I *don't* know that. What I do know is that you're very talented."

I gave her a quelling look, speaking as frankly as I could. How many times did we need to have this conversation? "No, I'm *moderately* talented. I don't have the level of talent it takes to be great without training, and I never got the training to make anything more of what I do have. So it's karaoke and shower singing for me for the rest of my life."

I knew my limitations. My family had never let me forget them. They didn't enjoy my concerts and shows, my style of music wasn't to their taste, and if I dared to feel optimistic that I might actually get the part I auditioned for, they could always be relied upon to remind me that I didn't get the part last time so why should this time be any different?

Mo sighed. "You're doing it again, you know."

"Huh?"

"Coming up with excuses to not do the things you want to do."

Oh. That. I looked back out over the harbor and didn't answer, not that Mo expected me to. There was nothing I could say, and we both knew it. Talking myself out of wanting most things that meant anything to me was less painful than being reminded that I wasn't good enough, though I could never make her understand that.

I squirmed, but we'd reached the restaurant, and the vinegary, oceanic smell of seafood surrounded us. Yay, distraction! I was off the hook.

I didn't think Mo got how anxious it made me when she kept pushing me to go after something like that. As someone who had never been denied anything in her life, she didn't understand that it was better to tell myself no than wait for someone else to do it. The pragmatic approach was definitely less disappointing, but it had taken me years to let go of my pipe dreams and get real. They say addiction runs in families. I might have dodged the bullet with drugs and alcohol, but cutting myself off cold turkey from my grandiose fantasies of ever being anything other than ordinary had been brutal.

"I'll think about it," I finally said, knowing I wouldn't. "I don't know if I'll ever go through with it. I'm just too much of a perfectionist, I guess. I'd rather be nothing than be middle-of-the-road."

She hugged me tightly. "You're not middle-of-the-road, Topher. You're fast lane, all the way. You just, you know, need to find the right car."

I squeezed her back, sighing against her shoulder. I'd miss her. Something about the upcoming summer felt off as it hadn't the day we arrived, and I couldn't figure out why. Maybe it was all the discussion this past week about my family issues and my lost opportunities and my present situation, but I was now uneasy about the months ahead, like something was bound to go wrong. I didn't know where that doomed feeling was coming from. Whatever it was, I had to find a way to stop it. I had enough to deal with this summer.

Maybe I just needed my meds adjusted again.

I pulled away, squaring my shoulders. "Come on, woman. Feed me some scallops before you dump me for two weeks."

CHAPTER FIVE

I can't keep away from you
Even though I know what I must do
The cruel hand of fate, with you
Is slowly closing around this

— CASEY STRATTON, "CRUEL HAND OF FATE"

Despite my resolution to spend as much time as possible away from Brendan and have a life, the first few days after Mo left, I really didn't get out much except to swim and look for work. I signed on with some temp services in Holland the first time I went to the pool for a long, hard swim, and drove into Saugatuck occasionally for coffee, and to check for anyplace that might be looking to hire. No one seemed to be taking applications, but temptation and the echoes of Mo's encouragement on our last visit to the coffeehouse proved too much for me. I ended up asking permission to use the piano for practice when I went in, and Aubrey, the gay and geeky manager, permitted it.

Other than that, I spent most of my time in my room, listening to music, playing my keyboard, catching up on reading, and searching for jobs online. When I made it clear that the sum total of my culinary expertise was ramen and mac & cheese (which was actually a bit of a lie, but I didn't feel like explaining that my mom had taught me to make oatmeal and fry eggs and bacon when I was six so I wouldn't have to wake her up when she was hungover), Brendan declared that he would cook if I did the grocery shopping and dishes. It was a fair deal and I jumped on it. Aside from meals, though, I was going to stick by my decision to avoid Brendan as much as possible until I got over my idiotic crush, before I did something awkward and made him uncomfortable. It wasn't that I was actually tempted to act on it (though, true confessions time: I did spend a couple nights with my hand in my shorts, having fantasies about Robert Redford in his prime. Sue me.). I was just *embarrassed* by it.

What I should probably have done was get laid, preferably by someone without red hair.

And why wasn't I out doing that, anyway, huh? Here I was, a pretty, pretty princess in full bloom, in one of the premier gay vacation destinations in the Midwest. Available gay men were practically jumping out of the water like hungry trout at sunset, and what was I doing? I was living like a monk on a private beach, nursing an awkward case of puppy love for someone upon whom I had no actual designs and who—even if he weren't straight, married, and way too old—was my best friend's father. Even if I *did* have designs on him, he was off limits on so many levels it wasn't even funny.

So, seriously, just what the fuck was that all about?

I woke up on the morning of my twenty-first birthday determined to take one day off job hunting and treat myself to an afternoon of checking out the local scene, particularly the penis-bearing portion of it. It wasn't Memorial Day yet, so tourist traffic wouldn't be all that high, but there had to be at least a few early birds and residents around, right? Mo wouldn't be home to celebrate my birthday for almost another week and a half, and I didn't really want to wait. Besides, when I went out with Mo, I couldn't really hook up with anyone without feeling like I was abandoning her. If we'd been back at school and I hadn't been her houseguest, that would have been different, but as things were, if

I wanted to get me some birthday sex, it was probably better to go out solo.

With that in mind, I packed up a beach bag.

"Going somewhere?" Brendan asked over the bowl of cereal he was eating at the counter. I decided not to eat a banana because, having psyched myself up to flirting and picking someone up, I'd probably end up deep-throating it in front of him (*but, hmmm, hey, let's pack one or two of those in the beach bag, shall we?*). I opted for a cup of yogurt for breakfast instead.

"Yeah, I thought I'd check out Oval Beach for the day."

"Oh, that sounds fun. A little cool still, but it looks like it'll be a nice afternoon. You know, I'm getting a bit of cabin fever working on this book all day every day. If you want some company . . ."

My mouth fell open and I froze for a moment, unsure how to answer that. On one hand, my inner crush-stricken schoolgirl screamed a resounding *yes!* On the other hand, doing so would not only be a Bad Fucking Idea with regard to quelling my silly infatuation, it would be completely contrary to my purpose in going out to begin with.

Unable to come up with any tactful response, I decided to go for honesty instead.

"That sounds like a lot of fun, Mr. G—Brendan. But, um . . . I'm kind of trying to get out to, you know, *meet people.*"

With my dick. I left that part unspoken.

"Meet— Oh." Enlightenment dawned. His eyes widened, and his jaw dropped a little. Then his ears turned red. "*Meet* people. Right. Yeah, you probably don't want me around for that."

I shrugged a helpless apology, unable to deny the truth of the statement. "I'm sorry. I wouldn't mind hanging out some other time, though."

"Sure." He seemed like he had to force that indulgent smile. "Have fun, Topher. Make lots of, um . . . friends."

I nodded back and shuffled out the door.

Well. That wasn't a bit awkward.

After I spread my blanket, I left my beach bag lying on it, unconcerned for my iPod and phone inside. On most public beaches, especially upscale ones like this, there was a code of honor that kept unattended possessions from walking away—or so I hoped. Besides, it was still early enough that the beach was pretty sparsely populated, especially out of season as it was. I imagined more people would show up as it got closer to afternoon.

Determined that I was done waiting to experience the water, I stripped down to my Speedo and ran out to the lake. Fuck, it was dick-shriveling cold! Seriously. My efforts to get laid just might be jeopardized by the fact that it was going to be difficult to convince the Orb Brothers to creep back down out of my abdomen. Still, I threw myself into my morning swim, stroking hard against the waves until my arms began to ache with the effort of getting back to shore. Since I wouldn't be able to time myself or track my distances on the lake, I compensated by just throwing as much speed and power into my workouts as I could. Then I staggered, shivering and no doubt purple-lipped, back up the beach to my blanket. I flopped down on it, rushing to dry off so I could pull on my shirt.

Digging in my bag for my iPod, I put in the earbuds and lay on my stomach, selecting one of my more upbeat Casey Stratton playlists—he was one of my all-time favorite singer/songwriters —to pass the time until interesting, non-redheaded people began to show up. I listened and sang along to myself, rocking out a little because I was practically alone and hell, why not? I couldn't quite match his range, but that didn't mean I wasn't determined to try.

I called up the e-reader app on my phone and scrolled through the books I'd downloaded. I'd developed a taste for erotica—porn without the pictures you wouldn't want anyone to get a glimpse of over your shoulder, what a brilliant concept!— but I wasn't going to risk a woody in a Speedo on a public beach. I finally chose the latest David Weber Honor Harrington book instead and lost myself in the diabolical machinations of the ruthless, genetic-slave-breeding Mesans as they played the behemoth Solarian League against the plucky Star Kingdom of Manticore.

The day began to grow warmer as morning aged into afternoon, and the beach became slightly more crowded. It was Friday, which meant there would be at least some vacationers arriving to begin their weekend away. I'd decided to finish my chapter and then start eyeballing the crowd for likely prospects when a shadow fell over me.

I glanced up from my phone but couldn't get a good look at the face of the person standing above me because he was backlit by the sun. He wasn't terribly tall; slender-to-medium build, too old to be a twink but not by much. His eyes and hair were dark, and tattoos were scrawled over his chest and arms. They trailed around his shoulders and ribs in a way that made me think his back would be similarly decorated. Rings and studs ran up both his ears and pierced one eyebrow.

I pulled out my earbuds to find out what he had to say.

"Sorry, I just gotta ask what made you decide on the Justin Timberlake hair. I didn't think anyone did that to themselves anymore." There was a hint of laughter in his voice, and his eyes sparkled.

I rolled onto my side and propped myself up on my elbow, trying to get a better look at him.

"Well, gorgeous, the answer depends on whether you're being bitchy or trying to genuinely strike up a conversation."

"Definitely the second one!" He dropped down to sit on my blanket without asking permission, but I didn't mind because I could finally get the whole picture. I notched my estimation of his age up by a couple years. Twenty-seven to twenty-nine, maybe. Nowhere near as femme as I was, but with a respectable amount of flash and sass. His eyes were so dark they were nearly black, with no discernible difference between iris and pupil at this range. I'd probably have to be face-to-face and up close to see that.

Which really didn't sound like a half-bad idea.

"I'm Jace."

"Topher." I held out my hand, and he shook it warmly enough, adding a nice little caress on the release.

Oh yeah, he was on the hook and I had no interest in throwing him back without weighing him first.

"Nice to meet you, Topher." He stretched out, leaning back on his elbows. "So?"

"The hair? It's natural."

"No fucking way."

"Mm-hm." I dug in my bag for my second bottle of Vitamin-water and offered it to him. Then I flipped through pictures on my phone until I got to the scan I'd had made for just this reason: the only baby picture that anyone had ever taken of me, aside from the ubiquitous just-born Polaroid from the hospital. I held it out to prove my honesty. There I was, dark skin topped with a froth of blond curls, at the age of nine months.

"Okay, so at the risk of being really tacky—and if I am, please accept my apologies and go ahead and call me on it, because I don't mean to be—how does a guy with your skin tone get that hair?" He took a closer look when I slid my sunglasses down my nose. "Not to mention—holy shit—*green eyes?*"

I chuckled, maybe a little uncomfortably. At least he understood how "clueless but well-intentioned white guy" he was being.

The brush of our fingers as he accepted the bottle had made it clear just how much darker I was than him. In fact, he was way too pale for his eyes and hair, giving the impression that he was trying for a goth look, which it was pretty obvious he *wasn't*. As for me, with my complexion somewhat darker than the white-washed version of Halle Berry you see on the cover of magazines (closer to the *real* Halle Berry, actually) I couldn't blame him for wondering, because the hair *was* incongruous—which was why I kept it. But his curiosity was just that: curiosity.

"Well, you see, when a green-eyed, blonde, white girl *really likes* a black boy with a green-eyed gene somewhere on his family tree . . ." I lifted my hand palm-up in an expansive shrug. "You kinda hit the genetic lottery. As for my hair, I suppose I could color it darker, but why?"

"Fuck yeah, why!" He waved off the idea with a flap of his hand. "Angel, you look damn fine just the way you are."

"Or at least I do now that you know I'm not ten years out of fashion."

"Oh, you looked good before that, I just couldn't come up with another line of approach that wasn't creepy or overused." He cracked open the water, and I watched his throat bob as he swallowed. I really liked the balance his slightly square build struck between being too slim and too beefy. Compact. That was a good word for it. When he put the cap back on the bottle, he looked over at me, and about the only word I could come up with to describe the way his eyes danced was "devilish." And he had enough thick, sooty lashes for any three guys. "So what brings you here?"

I shrugged, sipping my own water. "I'm staying for a while with a friend's family at their beach house down the lakeshore, in Douglas."

"But you're here alone?" He glanced around, as if looking for some unknown companion to approach.

"Yeah, my friend's working this week." I frowned, suddenly feeling lame for being on the beach alone. "*But* it's my twenty-first birthday today and I decided I didn't want to sit around the house, so here I am."

"No shit? Happy birthday!" He grinned, clearly delighted by the huge-ass opening I'd left for him. "Planning to party tonight?"

"I was if I could find some company for it."

"Consider company found. First drink's on me. A couple friends and I have a two-bedroom cottage this weekend at the Dunes. Come on over, we'll hit the nightclub."

Now it was my turn to grin. This was getting better and better. I trawled out a little more bait. "I'm in. I just need to be careful, since I won't have a designated driver when I head home."

"Stay with us if you get too smashed. There's a sofa sleeper in the living room if you need it."

I gave him my best flirty smile with a side of batting eyelashes. "Oh, please. You're just trying to get me into your room."

"Hell yeah, I am."

"Excellent."

Jace grinned and pushed himself upright, then reached over to me. His fingers trailed across my shoulder and down my arm. I didn't bother to shift to hide my reaction to that. We each knew we wanted what the other was selling.

"I gotta run, angel, but I'll be watching for you at the club tonight, whenever you decide to show."

"Oh, I'll definitely *show*." I let the dick-joke innuendo purr in my voice and he laughed, then jumped up and jogged away.

I watched his ass as he went, satisfied to discover that my assumptions about his tattoos had been correct, and tried to decide—assuming we hit it off tonight—if I wanted to bottom or top.

I WENT BACK to the house to grab a nap before going to the club, because I *really* didn't plan to sleep tonight if I could avoid it. It was too much to hope that I wouldn't bump into Brendan as I went down the stairs, dressed for clubbing. I didn't dress outrageously on a daily basis—it was my personality and mannerisms that gave me away to most people, more than my wardrobe choices—but tonight was special, so I'd gone for broke.

For all my determination to let my freak flag fly, however, I felt way too self-conscious when Brendan got a good look at me in a purple Lycra T-shirt thin enough to show my nipples, and painted-on black jeans slung so low on my hips that if they dropped a half inch more the world would know I shaved my pubes, because I damn sure wasn't wearing underwear (though I had debated on a thong for a good long while, just as a sort of Easter-egg bonus to reveal as the clothes came off). My belt and low-heeled boots both had silver accents, and I had on a number of heavy silver rings and chains.

I'd gone all out and dusted glimmer powder over my cheekbones, then added a little bit of eyeliner and the subtlest hint of iridescent gold lip gloss. I'd even borrowed some of Mo's hair chalk and added a few purple streaks to complement the shirt.

In short, I looked fucking *fine*. And with any luck, I was *so* getting laid tonight. So why was I very much Not Happy with the idea of Brendan seeing me dressed to kill?

He looked up as I passed by the living room and rubbed his neck, clearing his throat a couple times before asking, "I take it you're going out?"

"Um, yeah." I gave a bobble-head nod. "Some people invited me to meet them at a club tonight to celebrate my birthday."

"It's your birthday?" He blinked, frowning. Damn, did he look *hurt?* "You should have said something."

Ah, fuck. It never occurred to me he'd want to know. Or maybe I just hadn't allowed for the possibility. I mean, he'd been kind and friendly to me and all, but in an effort to make sure this crush didn't explode into something problematic, I was really trying not to see his interest as anything more than polite.

"Oh God, I'm sorry." I hastened to apologize and came up with the first excuse I could to try to alleviate any injured feelings or insult. "I thought Mo would've mentioned it to you. If you want to have a celebratory dinner or buy me a cupcake or something tomorrow, I've got no problem with rain checks. Well, you know, after I get past the hangover."

His frown deepened. "Will someone be driving you home?"

Once a dad, always a dad, I guess. It was kind of nice, actually. In my family, that sort of question would have been phrased in a way that assumed I would be doing the stupid or dangerous or just plain *wrong* thing.

Also, it gave me a good excuse for not coming home tonight that didn't include fucking a near stranger I'd picked up on the beach.

"If I drink too much, I've got an open invitation to use someone's couch. I'll be sa—*careful*. Promise."

"Okay." He still looked dubious, and this was getting to be more than I wanted to deal with tonight. There was an unreadable subtext to the tension here, and I didn't know if it was just my stupid crush or what. "If you do need a ride, call me. No matter what time it is. Morgan gave you her key, right?"

"Yep." Another deep nod. It was wedged in my very, very tight pocket, along with my debit card, my ID, and a strip of condoms. There sure as hell wasn't room in there for a wallet. I'd even already taken my evening meds, so I wouldn't have to bring them. Thank God my psychiatrist and I had agreed when I started college to find a cocktail of antidepressants that would keep me stable while still allowing me to drink.

"If I do come back tonight, don't worry about leaving the door unlocked. But, seriously? I'm turning twenty-one. I'd say the chances of me *not* crashing out there are pretty slim."

"Okay. Well, have fun, then." He still looked almost distressed, his brow deeply furrowed and a funny edge to his tone. "Happy birthday."

"Thanks." I almost ran for the door, eager to be free from the awkwardness. I stopped and turned with my hand on the knob. "Good night, Brendan."

"Good night, Topher."

As I shut the door, I heard him clear his throat again.

CHAPTER SIX

We were lost inside ourselves
But we didn't care to get back out
There was a light that we rushed toward
And a bright and shining silver cord

— CASEY STRATTON, "I PROMISE LOVE"

J ace broke into a wide smile when he caught sight of me
sauntering into the bar. Then his eyes raked up and down
my body and he caught his bottom lip between his teeth in
that *unf!* gesture I was pretty sure translated to: "*Damn*, you
look fine."

I definitely wasn't the only one. With his dark hair and eyes
and pale, pale skin, I would have half expected him to be wearing
all black, completing the impression that he was rocking some
goth. But his shirt was sapphire silk, unbuttoned deeply enough
to display some of that gorgeous ink on his chest, and his pants
were a dark silver-gray that took me a few (very enjoyable)
glances to identify as leather.

Well, then. Happy birthday to me and wasn't that just some
delightful gift wrapping?

His lips were so red against his light skin that you'd think he was wearing lipstick, except that they'd been every bit as red this afternoon on the beach, and his black hair didn't appear to be styled at all. It just fell loose to his collar in gentle curls, looking ridiculously touchable.

And was I going to have my fingers buried in that hair before the end of the night? If I had any say in it, you're goddamn right I was.

His hands settled on my hips the moment I got close enough, as if they belonged there, and his lips brushed mine in an undemanding kiss of greeting that nonetheless established a claim. As did the way his hand lingered just above my ass as he escorted me to the bar. Proprietary. He was letting anyone who might be checking me out tonight know that my companion for the evening was already chosen. It was a little presumptuous, and I wondered if I should be troubled by it. I mean, sure, I was into him, and fully planning to hit that if things worked out, but should I play it coy or something?

"What'll you have to drink, birthday boy?" he murmured near my ear, giving me a shiver.

"Just a beer."

He quirked an eyebrow at that. I think he'd expected me to order something really sweet and fruity (no pun intended). Which, really, I had no objection to, except that I didn't plan to end this evening puking drunk because whatever I was drinking tasted so good and went down so easy that I didn't know when to cut myself off.

His fingers played at the base of my spine as he turned to order our beers from the bartender. I'd been hard before I even walked in, just from the anticipation, but that touch was amping it up. I wondered how long he'd want to hang out with his friends and dance before we went back to his room. He scanned the crowd as he handed me a nicely chilled bottle with a lemon wedge on the rim.

"Not sure where my friends went. Probably out to the Jacuzzi. Want to have a seat or would you rather dance?"

"Let's at least find someplace to put our drinks down first." I really wanted to have both hands on him when we danced.

"Okay." His eyes had that wicked gleam again as he slid a sideways look at me, like he knew exactly what I was thinking. Expectation pulsed between us in near-palpable waves, each one making me a little more impatient. I could have suggested we go back to his room right away, but I didn't. Crazy as it was making me, there was also something delicious about it. About not acting as though it was a sure thing, making him court me a little.

I began to understand why a cat would play with a mouse for a while before eating it. Except that neither of us was exactly the cat, or exactly the mouse. Or if we were, we were mice that had run straight up to the cat and asked for a game of tag.

His hand riding the small of my back was even more sure of his claim now, and there was just a little edge to him that said if I wanted to bottom, he would take charge and rock my world in ways it had never been rocked and might never be again. But there was also something relaxed about him that said he'd be just as happy to let me pin him to the wall or throw him across a table and fuck him stupid.

The chips were in the air and I had no fucking clue where they would land. The anticipation of finding out was one amazing ride.

Then his breath was on my ear as we found a table for our beers. "You look good enough to eat."

I let my gold-sheened lips curl into a smile. "Well, that was sort of the idea. I'm glad you like it, though."

"There's nothing here not to like." His hand dropped from my back to my hips, his fingers brushing over the swell of my ass. I shivered.

"Not everyone would think so. I wasn't one hundred percent certain you'd be down with the makeup."

"Oh?" He lifted an eyebrow, propping a hip against the table to sip his beer. "Why wear it, then?"

I stepped closer, enough so that if he'd parted his knees a little bit, I could have pressed right up flush against him. I brushed my lips along his jaw, somewhere between a kiss and a nuzzle, not quite either.

"Because I didn't wear it for you."

I could swear I heard a soft groan escape his throat under the bass of the music, and then his knees did inch apart a bit more, his hands settling more firmly on my hips again to draw me closer until we were eye to eye and crotch to crotch. We gasped in unison at the friction of that first electric contact.

"And *that* is why you're so fucking hot," he rasped. Our mouths were a breath apart and he could have kissed me, or I could have kissed him. But we didn't. We just breathed together, savoring that madly intense moment of perfect wanting. After a moment he stepped back and led me to the dance floor.

I'd never felt this before, this effortless comfort and flawless understanding. In my previous experiences—which hadn't been terribly numerous, but enough so that I knew my way around the game fairly well by now—even when the hookup was good, there was usually some element of fumbling and uncertainty, questioning whether the other person wanted what I wanted, or liked what I was doing, or whatever. Not here, though. I had a weird flash of thought—*this is how adults do it*—and then it was gone.

Bottom line was, we just *clicked,* and we knew it. No questions. No doubts. No pressure. No self-consciousness to mar the excitement. I was relaxed (well, except for where there was some blatant tension going on) and sure of myself in a way I almost never was. I knew I looked good. I knew I was hot. I knew he wanted me. I knew that when he did touch me, he'd know exactly how to do it in the ways that felt the best, and I'd know the same.

It was incredibly, *incredibly* hot.

The music was a perfect club mix, fast enough to be energizing, loud enough to feel the beat vibrating in your chest, sensual enough that those who were so inclined could dance closely, grinding against one another. We were definitely so inclined. The dancing was foreplay. We used it to tease ourselves, and by the time we had to stop to catch our breaths and drink our beers, the exercise of dancing wasn't the only thing that had us sweaty and panting. My nerves were strung so taut from all his light touches that I thought I might come out of my skin, and the friction of my clothes was agonizing.

My hands already knew every contour of him. When his

clothes came off, I knew exactly what I'd find beneath. "Compact" was still a good word for him. Also "solid." By the way his weight was distributed, I bet he'd had a lot of baby chub when he was younger that had taken him a long time to shed. I also suspected it required a determined effort for him not to veer back toward the fluffy side. He'd probably lose that battle in another ten years or so.

Knowing that he'd been a chubby kid didn't make him any less sexy, but it did make him more human, as though we might understand each other beyond this mind-blowing sexual chemistry. Maybe it was because I knew it was possible that, like me, he'd struggled to get to a place where he was at home in his own body and comfortable with his appearance, surrounded by cruel and judgmental people determined to ride him down for both.

It had gotten too loud in the club for talking, and for the first time that evening, sitting there silently with our beers wasn't entirely comfortable. I should say something, strike up a conversation, get to know him better, but it was really too loud to—

"Would you like to go someplace quieter?"

I met his eyes across the table and gave an enthusiastic nod. "Yeah. Let's go."

WE WOUND up going to sit by the pool. I'd half expected him to take me back to his room, but no. We really did want to talk.

If his friends were around, Jace didn't acknowledge them. All his attention was on me, and frankly I wasn't interested in getting to know anyone but him just now.

"What do you do?" I asked, ordering another beer from a passing server.

"Art of various kinds." He leaned back in his chaise, folding his hands behind his head. I let my gaze pass up and down him, frankly admiring. Those leather pants did all the right things for him, and his shirt had come untucked (with a little assistance from my hands), revealing a slice of belly and a dark treasure trail I was *really* looking forward to tiptoeing down. "Right now I'm designing a set for a theater down in Chicago. I also do some graphic design, painting, sketching, even a bit of photography."

"Ah." My new beer arrived, cold and refreshing. I squeezed the lemon juice into the bottle and tipped it back, discarding the wedge. "A visual person."

His grin had a bit of a lopsided tilt to it. "I take it you're not?"

"Nope." I shook my head, pursing my lips. "Can't even draw a stick figure. I took an art elective in junior high once, and I don't know if I've ever been that humiliated in my life. I know what looks good to *me* but I can't begin to recreate it."

"Nothing wrong with just being an admirer." His eyes twinkled as he looked at me, and I wondered if he ever *didn't* have a good time. He gave off that vibe—that he was always having fun, no matter where he was. "So, are you in school?"

"In theory." I rolled my eyes and sighed. "Whether I'll be able to finish is another question."

"Not doing well?"

"I, um, I've had a rough time the last year and a half. Finances are an issue, and if I don't step it up, I could lose my scholarship. I'll probably have to suck it up and go into hock with student loans. I just hate to do it because right now I'm not even sure what the purpose of my being in school *is*."

He nodded, lacing his fingers across his chest and tapping his thumbs together. "You're having trouble settling on a major you actually like." He didn't phrase it as a question, because it wasn't. He just *knew* what the issue was.

"Exactly."

"What would you be doing if you could study anything you wanted, no matter how impractical?"

"Musical theater." No hesitation there.

"Your school doesn't have a program for it?"

"They have a theater program, but not specifically musical theater. I auditioned for the program at Western but I didn't get in." I shrugged. "It was a long shot from the beginning. I knew that, I just had to try. I'm okay, but not good enough for that. When it comes to talent—except in the visual arts—I'm kind of in the jack-of-all-trades-master-of-none class, you know? Meh, okay singer, okay actor, okay dancer. I think I've gotten to the point where I've accepted my limitations, but I'm having a hard time letting go of the pipe dream and settling on something more grown-up to do."

He frowned. "Twenty-one is a bit young to be talking about accepting limitations. The sky should be the limit for you right now, angel."

Shit. Just what had convinced me that sitting down to talk was a good idea?

I smiled, shrugging it off. I would *not* go down that spiral again, not now, just a few days after Mo had brought it all up. "There are circumstances, and trust me, it's better for me to be practical here. I just can't seem to find anything else I actually *care* about."

"Well, is there anything else you're good at?"

There was swimming, but I was never going to be Olympic class, so once I was done competing in college, I was going to hit the end of the road there, unless I wanted to coach. Which I *really* didn't. In my experience, coaches came in two varieties: Those who had made it and settled into coaching afterward to rest on their laurels, and those who weren't good enough to make it and bitterly resigned themselves to coaching as their Plan B.

"Not anything I think I could really make a career out of. Let's talk about something else, because I'm feeling pretty fucking good tonight and I want to keep it that way."

"Okay." Jace set his empty bottle aside, and his gaze swept over me with intent. Just like that, we were back to the sexy. My pulse leapt and my jeans got tighter. "Tell me why you're feeling good tonight."

I flashed him a flirty grin, drawling out my words ponderously. "Wellll . . . I'm feeling good because . . . I'm twenty-one, and I'm damn fine to look at, and there's a sexy guy across from me waiting for the right moment to take me to his room and blow my mind."

His smile broadened. "Setting your expectations a little high, aren't you? How do you know you won't be disappointed?"

"The same way you know." I wasn't smiling now. I was deadly

earnest, needing to know if this synergy going on was all in my mind, or if he was feeling it, too.

His own smile faded a little as well, and he dipped his head in acknowledgment of the point. "So, do you think the right moment might be soon?" he asked softly.

I swallowed hard, my heart beating so fast in my chest that I could barely breathe. "God, I hope so."

He stared at me a moment longer, and then he moved. Slowly. Giving me plenty of time to back away. He shifted up and left his chaise, stepping over to mine, and caught my hand, lacing our fingers together. His other hand slid along my jaw, drawing my face up for a kiss.

It started as the same gentle brush with which he'd greeted me, but this time it felt like he was asking permission. His tongue stroked my bottom lip and I opened to it, inviting it inside. We sort of . . . sank into each other. My hands gripped his waist and bunched in the silk of his shirt, tugging him closer. He tasted better than anyone who'd been drinking beer ought to, and he smelled amazing. Like . . . I don't know . . . cinnamon and wood smoke, and maybe a little like the stuff from the fog machines alongside the dance floor. It was all subtle, so I was having a hard time figuring out exactly what it was, but it definitely worked for him.

We were both shaking with arousal, but he kissed me like we had all the time in the world. Which really, I suppose we did, since it was still pretty early, but God I felt like we'd been teasing ourselves with this for hours.

When he pulled away, his eyes no longer danced wickedly. They burned, dark and intent.

"Come on."

CHAPTER SEVEN

Gone is the sense of safety
I'm on the edge of a cliff
I'm tossing my love over
Listening for the sound of impact

— CASEY STRATTON, "PROJECTOR"

I flowed to my feet without any conscious effort, drawn inexorably by the pressure of his gentle tug on my hand. He led me away from the pool, weaving through the crowds to one of the larger cottages. Unlocking the door, he gestured me inside and pointed to the apartment-sized fridge in the kitchenette.

"Another beer?"

I shook my head, then stepped close to him and pressed him back against the wall for another kiss. Not forcefully—just enough to give us something to lean on if our knees weakened. If we'd been asking permission before, this time we were stating intent. A little rougher, a little less patient, a little more demanding. We groped and grasped for handholds on each other's hips or ass or back. Whatever we could reach.

I kissed my way past the start of his tattoos to the point where they disappeared under the collar of his shirt. He moaned and went pliant for a moment, letting me explore. The sweat-damp skin of his neck was rich and salty and spicy under my tongue.

"Can I ask a favor of you before we go any further?" he managed after a moment.

"Hmmm?" There was salt in the hollow above his collarbone, warm on my tongue.

"May I take your picture?"

Like a needle scratching along a record, I zipped to a halt. "What?"

He licked his lips, smiling at my sudden unease, his eyes dancing again. "I swear to God it's not as sleazy as it sounds. I think I might like to paint you sometime, but obviously you won't be able to model for me. So I wondered if I could take some photos to use as references."

I chuckled uneasily. "Is this how you start all your hookups?"

"No, I promise it's not." His head rocked toward his shoulder, tilting enticingly. "So?"

"Okay . . ." I answered slowly, still thrown off my stride. "Um . . . where?"

"In here." He took me by the hand and led me into one of the two bedrooms. A suitcase was open on the luggage rack, camera gear was spread out on the dresser, and a sketch pad occupied the middle of the bed. I barely had time to do more than glance at the pencil drawings on it before he flipped it shut and moved to the desk.

Seeing it reassured me a bit. It looked like he really was an artist.

"I'd like to do two sets, if you don't mind. One nude before we fuck, and another when we're done." He pressed close, brushing his lips along my jaw until I turned to welcome the kiss. His voice dropped to a sexy murmur. "I want to capture the look in your eyes, before and after. Hungry, then satisfied."

I shuddered, clearing my throat. "Okay. I just, um . . . Hey, look, I know some scary-ass leather daddies, you hear me? If these end up on some internet porn site, I'm sending them after you."

He laughed at that, and Jesus, how were his lips so incredibly red?

"No. No one will see the photos but me. I'll even print them myself. The painting, however, might find its way to some art blogs, or maybe a gallery."

"Okay." I nodded just a little nervously and he kissed me again, hard this time, demanding. And then there was no room for nervousness. There were just lips and hands and his body firm against mine and *Gawdalmighty* had I ever been this hot for anyone in my life?

"God, you're gorgeous," he whispered, tonguing my earlobe as he pulled up the hem of my skintight shirt. He rucked it up to my armpits and glanced down, then smiled. "I knew it. You're a swimmer, aren't you?"

I gasped as his hands splayed over my abdomen, mine working their way under the silk of his shirt. "Yeah. It's that obvious?"

"I thought you might be when I saw you on the beach this afternoon, but you were wearing a shirt so I couldn't be sure. I *love* swimmers' bodies." He made an appreciative sound, groping my abs with frank admiration. "Angel, you are just hitting my buttons on *every* level."

Maybe I should have gotten bashful or demurred or something, but the lavish praise felt good. This hookup wasn't just because I was some random body available at an indiscriminate moment when he was horny. He wanted *me*, and I wasn't really certain I'd ever had that before.

I got to discover that his hair was every bit as soft and touchable as I'd thought it would be. Then my hands flew down the buttons of his shirt, pushing it off his shoulders before I ducked to let him drag mine over my head. And there was *skin*, his against mine, warm and alive, smooth beneath my fingertips when my eyes conspired with his tattoos to trick me into thinking there should be texture. I brushed my thumbs across his nipples, making him shiver.

"Given the amount of hardware above your shoulders, I half expected these to be pierced," I murmured against his lips. Our tongues stroked against each other in that breath of space between our mouths, not close enough to seal the kiss and delve deep.

I felt his smile. "They were, but it drew the eye away from the ink, so I got rid of them."

His hand tried to wedge between my jeans and my skin, but there just wasn't room for it. Only his fingertips managed to brush the root of my dick, but it was enough to make my eyes roll up in my head and my hips buck forward, seeking more. While he freed me from my fly, I dug the strip of condoms out of my pocket and threw them on the bed.

"Nice," he hummed when I'd toed off my boots and kicked my jeans across the floor. He sank to his knees with a slight creak of leather, licking the just slightly stubbly skin around the base of my cock. "I adore this effect."

"Hmmm?" Concentrating on the sweet nothings was getting harder, especially with his hand stroking like that, the fingers of the other teasing my balls and taint.

"Skinny boy. Shaved. Makes the cock seem very . . . commanding. Catches the eye."

I was about to burble something amused about him being a *really* visual person, but then his lips were sliding along the side of my dick, his hand gliding up and down. Everything pulled up with high-wire tension and I had to catch his head, uncertain whether he meant to take me in his mouth or not.

"*Don't.* Not unless you want to miss that first photo op."

"Ah." He drew away, his hands no longer arousing, simply stroking my hips and thighs, slow and soothing. "Need to back off a minute?"

I gave a jerky nod, licking my lips, trying to find my way free of the throbbing ache of being that close and then stopping.

"Lay down," he whispered, placing a kiss on the hollow of my hip. He rose and peeled the bedspread back, bunching up the top sheet down at the foot. I stretched out and let him position me on my side, propped up on my elbow, with one knee hooked forward. He draped the sheet in artful folds over my hip and thigh. Not covering my dick, no. Framing it, more like. Drawing attention to it by coming so close yet *not* covering it.

The whole thing said *come hither*.

While he arranged me, he spoke. "You can tell me to stop at any time. If you're not comfortable, or whatever. I'll even let you wipe the memory card yourself if you need to make sure no one sees the pictures. You don't have to do anything you don't want to, okay?"

I nodded, relaxing a little more at his obvious sensitivity to the fact that I might be worried.

"Good." He kissed me slowly, caressing my shoulder and back. "Now just lay there and think about how bad you want what we're going to do when I'm done with the camera."

I watched the soft, round bubble of his ass move beneath the silver-gray leather as he crossed to the equipment on the dresser and fitted a lens on the camera. I thought perhaps he did some weight training to keep in shape, because his back was solid and well defined under the red-gold spires of his tattoos, which looked like desert rock formations. When he turned around, he took a couple shots. By the time the light of the flash stopped strobing in my eyes, he had set the camera up on a tripod, and was spending some time focusing it while I watched, trying not to lose the mood.

Then he stepped back and faced me, commanding my gaze. His hands went down to his fly and slowly, *slowly*, dragged it open. I looked on raptly, swallowing hard before I wet my lips.

Click.

Startled, I looked back at the camera, which he hadn't touched. Then I realized he must have programmed it, or maybe he had a little remote, or—

"Don't worry about that. If you need to stop, say the word and we'll stop. If not, then just look at me, Topher. Look right at me. Watch *me*."

My eyes flew back to his, and the leather slithered down his hips. I let myself relax again. He wasn't trying to con me into making porn for him. Nothing about this felt skeevy; every inch of him exuded honesty. He just wanted to paint me. That was flattering, really. And the whole picture thing? Kind of hot.

Another *click* punctuated my soft groan as a dark nest of hair came into view. Then his cock sprang free, thick and dark red and beautiful, and my breath caught in my chest.

Click.

I couldn't have torn my eyes away from that if I'd wanted to, especially not when his fingers wrapped around it, stroking slowly. More clicks followed, but I barely heard them, barely registered the flashes. I was sweating, shaking. I could hardly breathe. My hips shifted and rocked just the smallest bit in time with each caress he gave himself, as if subconsciously begging his hand to surround my cock instead.

And then the clicking stopped, and his pants dropped the rest of the way to the floor, and Jace strode over to the bed, coming at me hard and fast. He covered me, devouring my lips, plunging his tongue into my mouth like he wanted me to try to deep-throat it.

I grasped him, clung to him, mashed my mouth against his with equal violence. There was nothing in me but *wanting*. I burned for him, had to have him now, right now. His hand fumbled blindly with the drawer of the bedside table, locating the lube just before I pushed him onto his back and wedged myself between his thighs, taking over the kiss.

He groaned and gave over, going pliant beneath me. I rutted against him, our cocks sliding together, our moans filling each other's mouths. I hooked an arm under his thigh, pushing his knee up, seeking his crack with my fingers as he made sharp, urgent, encouraging sounds, finally wrenching his mouth away from mine to gasp, "Yes."

I'd barely worked some of the lube into his hole when he shoved the condoms at me. "Hurry."

"Seriously?" I lifted my head, gazing at him wide-eyed.

He nodded eagerly. "I like it rough. Do it."

My hands shook as I rolled the rubber on, and then he was grasping my shoulders, pulling me to him with a bruising grip. I pushed into him and his spine arched. His head rolled back, a growling moan escaping his throat—all details that were nearly lost in how tight and hot he was, gripping my dick.

"Oh, fuck yeah," he gasped when I paused for a moment,

waiting for his body to unwind, for some of the tension to ebb. "Keep going. Do it. Hard."

Fuck, I just about came at his words alone. But I did what he asked, driving into him, listening to his howl, underpinned by my own desperate moan. My hips snapped against his, the impact jarring us both, and then I had to stop for *my* sake or I was going to lose it completely. I buried my hands in his silky, sweat-damp hair and kissed him like I meant to suck his soul out through his lips. I kissed him until he began to wriggle restlessly beneath me, making plaintive sounds.

"Go, Topher. Please. Go. Go."

Then there was no holding back. Just a headlong charge for the finish line. Just skin slapping against skin, explosive pants and gasps erupting between us, grunts and growls and groans that sounded more animal than human. Our hands scrabbled for purchase on skin too slick with sweat to grasp. Somewhere along the way I reared up, lifting my body off his to drive deeper, ramming into him, keening my imminent loss of control. I barely felt the movements when he grabbed his cock and started stroking, but I sure as fuck felt the spasms gripping me. They dragged me over that breathless edge into a blinding white abyss.

IT TOOK us a few minutes to come back to ourselves. Jace didn't seem to mind my weight above him, and I certainly had no objections to using him as a pillow, nuzzling his throat, caressing him as the sweat cooled on his skin.

Finally he rolled me off him, onto my back.

"Stay there," he murmured, removing and discarding the condom for me. I twitched as he arranged my softened cock to lie on my hip, and then bunched the sheet up. No artistic peekaboo drape now. This time it was rumpled and messy, heaped around me.

Another bead of sweat trickled out of my hairline and down my temple, reminding me of one detail.

"My eyeliner—" I lifted my hand to try to wipe away what I

was sure was a massive case of raccoon-eye, but he caught my fingers.

"Smudged and perfect, just like it should be after that."

He curled one of my arms up onto the pillow, beneath my head, and turned my face toward the camera, then rose and stepped behind it. He didn't do anything to try to make me react this time. He just let me drift in post-coital relaxation, my eyes half-lidded. No doubt I looked completely sex-drunk.

When the clicking stopped, he caught his tongue between his teeth, scanning through the pictures on the view screen before he returned to bed. Then he curled around me, snuggling, kissing my shoulder.

"Did they come out okay?" I suppose I should have been embarrassed by how vain I sounded, but I wasn't. I liked his obvious admiration. It felt good.

"They're absolutely gorgeous, even if they're not *quite* what I had in mind when I envisioned doing it."

"Oh?" A little bit of energy must have been returning, because I could lift my head again to peer down at him.

"Mm-hm." He chuckled softly. "When the idea first occurred to me, I assumed I'd be topping, so I imagined for the second set, you'd have that completely wrung-out look exclusive to someone who's been well and truly fucked . . . the way I probably appeared a few minutes ago." He kissed my shoulder, ending with a nip on the muscle there. "You took me by surprise, there. And that's *so* not a complaint, by the way."

I smiled, stroking fingers up and down his spine as he continued to pepper my shoulder and chest with soft kisses.

"Well." I hummed thoughtfully when I could move again, rolling onto my stomach and turning my face to peer at him through my smudged eyes. "You could always take a third set."

His eyes danced again as he grinned at me. He growled and lunged up, pushing his face into the curve of my neck and sucking hard on the skin there as his weight settled on my back, his cock beginning to firm up against the crack of my ass.

"Oh, fuck yeah."

CHAPTER EIGHT

Something's got to get me through
I can't take another disappointment
Still I return to you with my arms open
With my heart stolen

— CASEY STRATTON, "CRUEL HAND OF FATE"

The hangover excuse didn't float quite as well around noon the next day when I returned home, no doubt still looking very sex-drunk and sporting an impressive array of hickeys (turned out Jace liked to suck on my neck. A lot.). I was tired and sated and so fucked out I could barely drag my exhausted—and delightfully sore—ass up the stairs, much less squirm uncomfortably when Brendan's eyes widened. Then his face shut down, going carefully blank.

I barely managed to keep my eyes open as I showered, washing away the scent of amazing sex with a considerable amount of regret. Still, even blissed out in the aftermath of an all-night sex-a-thon that truly *did* rock my world, it bothered me more than I liked that Brendan might think badly of me for the way I'd chosen to spend my time.

I sighed as I finally began to drift off. *And that is the great hypocrisy of my existence.*

Despite my protestations, I still had fucks left to give about what people thought of me after all.

I FINALLY DRAGGED myself out of bed around dinnertime. When I shuffled down the stairs, Brendan looked up from tossing a salad. "Evening, Topher. Hungry?"

"Starved." I nodded enthusiastically, grabbing a bottle of water out of the fridge and then working around him to unload the dishwasher and do the other cleaning-up chores I hadn't done in two days, despite our agreement. "Sorry, I should've found out if you needed me to pick anything up on my way home."

Brendan waved me off, laughing softly. "Don't worry about it. In our family, birthday celebrations come complete with chore amnesty."

I smiled, grabbing the dishes to lay out place settings at the breakfast bar, where we'd taken to having our meals. With just the two of us, it didn't seem worth it to set the table.

Thanks to Brendan's easygoing attitude, the self-consciousness of this morning was evaporating. If he was offended by anything I'd done, it didn't show. And more importantly, if he was, I didn't seem to care as much as I had when I'd arrived home. Maybe lack of sleep and the intensity of the sex the night before had just left me feeling raw-edged and vulnerable when I'd walked in and assumed he was put off. Now that I'd rested, I was calmer.

So calm, in fact, that it seemed like getting laid might have done what I'd intended it to do. I didn't feel like I was in danger of slipping and getting all awkward and bumbling and puppy-dog smitten with Brendan tonight. I could look at him as just Mo's dad and a nice guy I was rooming with for the summer, without that undercurrent of attraction constantly threatening to embarrass me.

"That smells delicious. What are you cooking?" I asked, opening the refrigerator. "Water, tonight? Beer? Soda?"

"Lasagna, so open that bottle of red on the wine rack. Unless, of course, you're too hungover for wine."

I chuckled, glad I didn't blush discernibly. "No, I think I'm actually okay. And lasagna? Seriously? Wow."

"Well, a birthday dinner calls for a little effort, I think." He shrugged, bending down to pull out a bubbling pan overflowing with dripping cheese.

"Birthday—" I cringed self-consciously. "Oh God, you didn't have to."

He shrugged again and tossed a foil-wrapped loaf of what smelled like garlic bread into the oven. "I didn't get a chance to find out what your preference might be, so I just went with Morgan's usual choice in birthday dinners. Hopefully you like it."

"Ooh, yeah. Mo has good taste. Thank you." I stared at it almost lustfully, and my stomach started grumbling, reminding me that I hadn't eaten much in the last two days. The day before, I'd been too focused on getting out of the house for a day to stop and eat, and today I'd been pretty much unconscious the whole time. I located the corkscrew and began to work it into the wine bottle. "Wow. No way am I going for my swim tonight."

"You're welcome." He set the salad on the breakfast bar between our plates. An honest-to-God Caesar salad, all garlicky, with croutons and flakes of Parmesan and the leafy kind of lettuce that had some actual flavor. "I figured someone should make you a birthday dinner, since I assumed you weren't going to see your family."

"Oh. Yeah." I smiled awkwardly, pouring the wine and then slipping onto one of the barstools. We dug into the salad while we waited for the garlic bread to cook and the lasagna to set. "They sent me a card, left a message on my phone. That's no big deal but thank you anyway."

"I suppose I'm just trying to understand how your family could be so rigid that you think you have to cut yourself off from them just to be yourself." Brendan hitched himself up on the barstool beside me. "Is this a recent thing? Did they think you'd outgrow your orientation, gender expression, whatever it all is—you'll have to forgive me if I don't quite understand the nuances and issues at play here. Sexuality and gender identity aren't my field."

I sighed, spearing shreds of romaine lettuce. "I don't think I realized how much pressure they were putting on me to conform until recently, but it's been there all along. I just wasn't . . . aware enough to pick up on it."

"Like what?"

"Like they kept trying to steer me away from my own interests. Not blatantly. It wasn't like, 'you can't do that, it's a sissy thing and you need to be a boy.' It was more like . . . they'd find excuses not to support me in the things I tried to do, or convince me it wasn't worthwhile. I remember when I was in the eighth grade, I was accepted into a very exclusive regional choir. It was a big accomplishment. But rather than being proud of me, all I heard for the whole year was how much of an *inconvenience* it was for them to take me to rehearsals once a week, and if I wanted to do an extracurricular activity, why didn't I try out for sports instead?"

A crouton crunched and crumbled on the tip of my fork as Brendan regarded me, his brow drawn down. "How could they not have been proud of you?"

I shrugged. "They didn't like it when I drew attention to myself. That, and they'd just . . . try to strip away my enjoyment in things by making them seem warped. Like, one time my choir director worked one-on-one with me after school to prepare my selection for state Solo & Ensemble Festival. But then I got a long lecture about how I shouldn't do that anymore or people might get the wrong idea, and then his career would be ruined. Like they thought I'd, I don't know, seduce him or something. Same thing when I got accepted to work with one of the best vocal coaches in the city for private lessons. Not only was it a waste of money and an inconvenience to drive me to the lessons, but once they found out I'd be working alone with him, they started insinuating all sorts of Bad Touch shit, if you know what I mean. Making it into something dirty. Because, you know, kids don't work alone with their music teachers without creating a scandal. But I was queer, so obviously he was going to molest me or I was going to molest him or . . . I don't even know."

I dropped my fork in disgust and took a long drink of my wine. My palate wasn't nearly educated enough to tell if it was a good wine or not, but it tasted okay to me. Brendan watched me soberly, nodding encouragement.

"Getting involved in swimming was something I started to get them off my back about sports; it just turned out I actually liked it. But it still wasn't enough."

Brendan squeezed my shoulder in passing as he rose to pull the garlic bread out of the oven. "Go on. I'm listening."

"I remember one time, I kind of passed out in the kitchen. I'd been working really hard because I had the lead in the musical, see, and with my job and trying to keep up with schoolwork, I hadn't been eating or sleeping much. So, I got dizzy and just . . . dropped. Hit the floor, just for a couple seconds. And when my head stopped buzzing, my uncle was *yelling* at me, as if I'd done something to piss him off. He said if I couldn't even set the table without keeling over, I should be getting more exercise instead of wasting my time in choir and theater. Because dancing three hours a night, five nights a week totally doesn't count as *exercise*, right?"

Brendan sighed, sliced off a few pieces of garlic bread, and brought them to the counter in a basket covered by a napkin, then returned to scoop squares of lasagna onto plates. "Could it be he was just frightened at you fainting, and handled it badly? I know I'd be terrified if Morgan did that in front of me."

That was the sort of thing my shrink always said. Nice and neutral. I shrugged. "Yeah, maybe."

"Still," Brendan murmured. "It wasn't fair for him to react that way."

Something in my chest lurched, and it had nothing whatsoever to do with my attraction to Brendan. He believed me. He didn't assume that I must have been wrong and my aunt and uncle must have been justified in whatever they did, which is what everyone else I knew had done whenever I'd tried to explain. In my family, my aunt and uncle could do no wrong. Hell, the closest I'd ever come to someone believing me was my therapist, who listened but never offered opinions about the situation, so I never knew if she agreed that it was wrong or not.

But Brendan . . . Brendan was just like them. Well educated. Well-off financially. Successful. Prosperous. Intelligent. He was in their league, the kind of person they'd respect, and *he was on my side.*

My eyes began to burn, and I scrubbed my hands down my face. "Sorry. I'm not trying to throw myself a pity party, here, really I'm not. It's just hard to stop once the subject comes up, because taken by themselves, the individual scenes don't really demonstrate anything except a moment of questionable parenting, but—"

"Taken together, it becomes a pattern. A very large, complex pattern of them penalizing you for so-called feminine pursuits and pressuring you toward things that would be considered more masculine."

"Yeah. That. Thank you. They just . . . they couldn't let me be myself, you know? They had to try to force me to be who they wanted me to be." Fuck, I was getting mopey again. I dug into the plate of lasagna he set before me, then smiled with delight at the first bite. Nothing like good food to flip a mood around. "This is delicious. Oh God, you put spinach in here! *Yes!*"

He laughed and, *goddamn,* his teeth were amazingly straight and white and helllllooo to the smile lines and whoops, there went my schoolgirl crush again. I felt like Hermione in the presence of Gilderoy Lockhart.

"I'm glad you like it." We ate in silence for a moment, and then his hand settled very lightly on my forearm. "They were wrong, Topher. You know that, right?"

I do, I thought, paused in winding a long string of mozzarella around my fork.

Except when I didn't. Except when I looked at all the times that everyone I knew—every relative, every friend of the family— believed my aunt and uncle were blameless because they seemed so damn kind and reasonable and *perfect* to the outsider. High school sweethearts, homecoming queen and king, graduated *summa* and *magna cum laude* from college, respectively, in addition to being the first college graduates from their families. Successful careers, beautiful children, gorgeous home, lots of friends. Clearly they were doing everything right, so if there had been a problem, it must have been totally on my end. They were right and I was wrong. Full stop.

"Well, yeah, I know. That's why I'm having my birthday dinner here tonight instead of with them." I smiled bravely at Brendan and began turning my fork again, trying to break that gentle, lingering touch on my arm that meant nothing but kindness and quasi-paternal support from him but sent all the wrong misguided, self-serving signals to me. "I think I came to that conclusion—that they were wrong, I mean—somewhere in high school. I won't say I was an easy kid to live with; I know I wasn't. I had plenty of damage from my mom's alcoholism and my unstable early childhood, not to mention bullying and puberty on top of that. They put me in therapy again to fix me, but eventually I realized I wasn't the only one who needed fixing. *We* needed fixing, but they wouldn't own their share of that."

"Were they ever physically abusive?"

I shrugged, squirming at the word choice. "No. *No.* Not— No. I mean . . . I— I got my face slapped once in a while, and my aunt had this habit of digging her nails in when she grabbed my arm or my jaw. But not like . . . *you know* . . ."

He didn't say anything, but merely watched me, and for some reason—probably that gentle understanding of his—I kept on stammering even when I probably should have shut up.

"I started feeling really anxious when they did that, and when I was about seventeen, my therapist suggested I choose a nonconfrontational moment to calmly and rationally explain to them how it made me feel when they grabbed me, and ask them not to do it anymore."

"Did you?"

I nodded, my mouth pulling down. "I waited for a calm moment and asked my aunt if they could please not do that anymore because it freaked me out. I told my therapist I'd done it and she thought I'd done a really good job."

"Did they respect that?"

"No." I shook my head, my eyes beginning to burn again. I was too humiliated by what had happened then to even tell the rest of the tale—how, the next time they were yelling at me, my aunt *had* grabbed my arm. I had jerked it out of her grasp and said, *Don't touch me*, but she grabbed me again, digging her nails in. And I jerked away again and said, *Don't touch me!*

Jesus. My heart was racing even at the memory. My hands shook so hard that my fork clattered against my plate and I had to put it down.

Next thing I had known, my aunt had me by my hair, on my knees—I wasn't fighting back, I was just curled in a ball trying to protect myself as she pounded on my back with her fist. With me screaming, *Don't touch me! Don't touch me!* over and over. Finally my uncle had intervened. He'd tossed me over his shoulder and carried me to my room, thrown me inside and slammed the door, all while I was screaming for them not to touch me.

The recollections were so vivid I might as well have been there on that floor again. It kept playing on instant repeat in my mind, the cringing and shouting and hitting. I wiped away a tear I didn't even realize I'd spilled, and turned my attention back to my lasagna, picking at it listlessly. I couldn't tell Brendan any of that. "No, they ignored my request and it led to a really bad scene. That's what I got when I tried to reason with them like an adult and asked them to treat me with respect. But, I mean, did they abuse me? No. No. They didn't, like, beat me or anything. Not, like, you know . . . *real* abuse."

Brendan sagged a little, pushing away his plate as if he'd lost his appetite. So had I, for that matter.

"Topher. Abuse doesn't have to leave black eyes and welts to qualify."

My throat closed up and my heart began to race even faster. My breath came short and shallow, like there wasn't enough air in the room. "*Don't*. Please. Just . . . I can't go there."

He was right, and I knew he was right, but the sound of *that word* made me feel like I was on the verge of majorly wigging out. It brought up all sorts of knee-jerk denials. I just couldn't cope with the concept. They were perfect, right? Nice, successful, popular, educated people with a beautiful home and tons of friends. They couldn't have been abusive. It didn't compute.

I'd probably have to work with my therapist on that once I got settled somewhere and started seeing one again.

"All right. It's all right." Brendan rubbed his hand soothingly back and forth across my shoulders, just offering comfort and support while I pulled myself together. After a moment, he drew away and ruffled my hair. "Here. I've got one more thing for you."

He went back into the kitchen and rummaged around in a cupboard I couldn't see. Then I heard the burring *snick* of a lighter, and he turned to reveal a plate with two gorgeously decorated cupcakes on it, each with a candle—one shaped like a two and the other like a one so that it read twenty-one.

I burst into watery laughter. "Oh jeez, I didn't mean for you to *really* get me cupcakes!"

He shrugged, setting them down before me and smiling brilliantly. "There needed to be something to put the candles on. I imagine Morgan is going to want to get you a cake or something when she's here next, but for now this will have to do."

I tried to stop giggling long enough to catch my breath and blow them out. It took two tries, but then I pulled off the candles to lick the frosting from their bases. We peeled the paper cups off the cupcakes in companionable silence, humming appreciatively with the first bites. As I chewed, his hand returned to my shoulder.

"You're a bright, beautiful young man, Christopher Carlisle. And it's their loss they drove you away. But I'm glad you see that you deserve better than that. Don't give in on that, okay? Demand that people respect you, no matter who you are or choose to be. You're worth respecting."

He slid his arm around my shoulders in one of those half-hug/squeeze things. Platonic. Nothing inappropriate about it at all, except for that teeny-tiny flare in the screwed-up wiring of my brain that didn't know how to respond to kindness from a gorgeous man except with attraction. It wasn't a come-on. He wasn't trying to get into my pants and, truly, I didn't *want* him to. He was just comforting and encouraging me. Which was, frankly, better than his coming on to me ever could be. So much better.

After a moment, I told that fucked-up part of my brain that confused affection with lust to cool it and leaned against him, accepting what he offered.

"So," he said when we were licking the last crumbs of our cupcakes off our fingers. "Would you like to go out for coffee or something? My treat."

"Actually, would you mind if we just hung out here? Watched a movie, maybe? I don't really need to go out again tonight."

"Okay. Let's get the dinner dishes cleaned up and we'll do that."

We chose *The Hobbit* this time, which Brendan hadn't seen. I was only too happy to gush fanboyishly about it to him. We sat at opposite ends of the sofa and lost ourselves in Middle Earth. When he laid his arm across the back of the sofa, stretching, I made myself ignore the fact that it was nearly within touching distance, and refused to read more into it than there was.

CHAPTER NINE

Maybe your saving grace will be yourself
You know better than anyone else

— CASEY STRATTON, "THE WINDOW WILL CLOSE"

"Okay." Mo took a sip of her mocha, leaning on the piano as the keys tinkled out lazy scales under my fingers. "That sounds amazingly hot."

"Mm, girl, you have no idea." I sighed, closing my eyes. The hickeys from my night with Jace had faded. The afterglow had . . . well, it had mostly faded, except for the occasional ripple that snuck up to goose me at odd moments.

Like just now, describing it to Mo.

"So where's this guy from? Any chance of you seeing him again?" Her eyes were avid, making it clear what she hoped the answer would be. It wasn't that Mo had to get her vicarious thrills off my sex life; she had one of her own, occasionally, and didn't need mine. But comparing notes—or war stories—was always a favorite pastime. Honestly, though, I think some part of her hoped I would find a steady, though I wasn't sure why. She was always asking me if I'd be seeing my hookups again.

I shook my head, trying (and as always, completely failing) to figure out the fingering of the intensely complicated bridge from the concert version of "Opaline."

"Nah, he was a vacationer. From Chicago, I think he said. Not that I wouldn't do it again, given the chance, but yeah, it was a one-off."

"Chicago's not that far." Mo shrugged, frowning.

I gave her A Look and changed songs, returning to fingering a gentle melody on the keys. "We didn't even exchange numbers. Or email addresses. Hell, Mo, I don't even know his last name . . . and I'm pretty sure he doesn't know mine either. So, yeah, that's not gonna happen. It was a good time, now it's done and I need to get back to figuring my shit out." I hadn't had a lot of luck with that in the weeks since she had left. I'd gotten a call from a temp agency for a two-day reception job at a company that designed business forms, and a half-day gig just sitting in the office of the temp agency doing some filing while waiting to see if an emergency "need someone *right now*" call came in, but other than that, nothing. The local restaurants weren't even hiring bussers or wait staff, thanks to the glut of college kids like me on summer break. I was getting worried enough that I was almost ready to bite the bullet and start applying for fast food jobs, though I knew that was a dead-end road that would exhaust me, keep me from finding a better job, and pay me less than I needed for tuition anyway. Or (*shudder*) telemarketing. "What about you? Any raunchy deep-woods hookups with the other camp counselors you'd like to dish about?"

"Not unless I want to get fired," she snorted. "Though, I tell you, there's an archery instructor I would do at the crook of a finger. OhmyGawwwd the arms . . . !"

"Ooh, sounds intriguing! What about the rest? Are we talking Legolas or Hawkeye?"

She smiled, laying her chin in her hand. "The ass is *completely* Hawkeye, but he's definitely closer to the Legolas end of the spectrum when it comes to pretty faces."

"And just where does our pretty archer live?"

"Big Rapids." She smiled slowly. "He goes to Ferris, so . . . not impossibly far. We've talked a few times. There's a chance I may give him a call, drive up on one of our weekends off, if you won't be too disappointed in me neglecting you for a day . . . or more, if things go well."

"Pfft!" I flapped a hand at her, waving her off. "I'll be just fine."

I fell silent, playing softly as Mo finished her coffee. There. I was pretty sure I had "Congratulations" down. Just to test it, I sang softly under my breath. As I was finishing, a woman walked toward the piano, pulling a bill from her wallet and looking around. It took me a moment to realize she was searching for a tip jar.

I quickly waved her off. "Oh, no, no ma'am. I'm just borrowing the piano for practice. Thanks, though."

When I looked back at Mo, her eyes were alight.

"That's it!"

"What?" I missed a chord and backtracked, beginning the measure over again. Some of Casey Stratton's piano lines were incredibly difficult to emulate by ear, and he didn't publish his sheet music. I was having to make do with trying to recreate the brilliance of my singing/songwriting idol by guesswork.

"They might not need baristas here, but why don't you talk to the manager about playing on the afternoons or evenings when they don't have live music booked?"

"Oh, please." I rolled my eyes and closed the piano cover abruptly, suddenly feeling too self-conscious to continue. "I'm not good enough for that."

"That woman obviously thought so."

"She was being polite."

Mo scowled at me and stalked away to take her cup to the bus bins. I shrugged and gathered up my backpack, futilely checking my cell phone for messages from prospective employers. When Mo returned, though, she had geeky Aubrey the shift manager with her.

"Hey." He smiled warmly. "You know, your friend has a good idea, here. There's no reason why you couldn't play a little louder, make your selections into more of a formal set. I don't know if I can get the owners to sign off on hiring you, but I think it'd be okay to set out a tip jar."

"Oh, well—" I stammered to a halt, giving Mo an irritated look. "I'm really not that good, I just wanted to practice."

"You're fine. And you can still call it practice, if you want. You'll just be, well, practicing *louder*."

"He can sing, too, you know," Mo prompted.

"Mo—" My voice dropped in warning.

"It's cool, whatever you're comfortable with. Here—" He thrust his cell phone at me. "Put your number in and I'll let you know what the owners say."

Five minutes later, Mo was dragging my bewildered ass out of the coffeehouse, looking very smug.

"Did he just scam your digits?" she asked slyly. "I think he just scammed your digits."

"No," I said quickly, firmly. I would *definitely* have picked up on that. Aubrey was nice, but he wasn't giving off that vibe at all. He might become a friend at some point, though. "You got your signals crossed there, girlfriend. And quit matchmaking. Remember how well that turned out last semester?"

I gave her a repressive look and she had the courtesy to look abashed as we headed down the street. I fell quiet, trying to sort through the jumble of emotions the incident in the coffeehouse had left me with. I mean, on one hand it was hugely flattering for someone to be willing to pay me for just tinkling around on the piano, especially after so many years of being told I wasn't good enough. On the other hand, I needed to maintain a realistic assessment of my abilities and the prospects they provided me with. No pie-in-the-sky dreams of stardom, of being "discovered" and signing a record deal in the coffeehouse of some quaint, two-stoplight beach town.

Twenty-one is a bit young to be talking about accepting limitations. The sky should be the limit for you right now, angel.

I hushed Jace's voice in my head. He didn't know me. He didn't know anything about me. He didn't know how much rejection I'd already faced and why it hurt less to accept reality rather than put myself out there.

Back to the coffeehouse gig. On the *other* other hand, Mo had a point. It was an awfully tidy solution to my money problems, at least until something more stable came along. But on the other other *other* hand, tips probably weren't going to be nearly enough, and yeah, some money was better than no money, but the same logic that applied to fast food applied here. How was I going to search for a job if I spent enough time doing this to make any money?

And I was way the fuck out of hands.

"You okay, Topher?" Mo asked when the silence stretched on too long.

"Sure. Why wouldn't I be?"

"I don't know. You seem . . . subdued."

I shrugged, but I couldn't really argue the point. The whole music thing—and the money I *wasn't* saving—definitely had me distracted. My mind kept turning the problem over, looking for some solution I hadn't seen yet. But beyond that, I'd been *feeling* subdued since that night with Jace . . . or maybe it'd been the next evening, when I'd talked with Brendan. I hadn't meant to spill my guts to him the way I had, but he was so damned earnest about wanting to hear about me, it had all just poured out. He was comforting and reassuring and it felt good to have someone like him think good things about me. Until him, no one but Mo (or my therapists) had ever asked me about myself like that, or if they did, they got uncomfortable when I answered honestly. No one wanted to hear about that shit. Hell, even *I* didn't want to hear about it.

At any rate, between Jace and Brendan, two layers of purging had happened in that twenty-four-hour stretch which had left me very tranquil: one relieving my physical needs, and the other my emotional.

I wouldn't be exaggerating to call the night with Jace my lifetime best (to date). It made every other sexual encounter I'd ever had seem like backseat fumbling in comparison. It had set the bar for my future experiences; I'd be expecting a lot more out of future partners, and myself as well. From here on out, I didn't think I'd be going home with random guys I wasn't really all that attracted to or interested in, just to have a piece of ass. There would have to be something approaching that incredible chemistry I'd had with Jace.

As for the emotional stuff . . . since that night of the belated birthday dinner, Brendan and I had been spending a lot of time talking and hanging out together when he wasn't working on his book. He was nice. He was funny. He was downright mischievous in a very sneaky, understated way. He *listened,* and he was interested and concerned with me. I hadn't had a lot of that in my life, at least not without co-payments attached.

So, yeah, I was subdued. But it wasn't because I was down. It was because—for the first time in as long as I could remember—I was calm. Bordering on content, in those moments when I managed to stop obsessing about the money situation.

The matter of getting a job aside, I felt more emotionally stable than I had in the year and a half since my mother's suicide attempt. Not merely grudgingly functional but driven enough to really try to make things work. Whatever foreboding I'd dealt with at the beginning of the summer had faded away, and I had hope.

Hell, I was even looking forward to Brendan's return, because I wanted to spend more time with him, and had my crush under control enough that I could do so safely. We were becoming friends, he and I. That had happened before; I'd always related to adults better than people my own age, ever since I was a kid. It was why my teachers had adored me and my peers had loathed me. Being with Brendan was sort of the way things had been with my choir director in high school, at least until my family had insinuated that it was inappropriate for me to spend time with him. This time, though, there was no danger of anyone interfering. I could be friends with him without anyone spoiling it for me.

"Topher?" Mo was staring at me now, and I realized I still hadn't answered.

"Sorry." I shook myself, linking my arm with hers. "If I am, it's not a bad thing. I'm actually feeling all right at the moment. Better than I have for a long time. If I'm quiet, I guess it's just because I'm spending a lot of time in my head. In a good way."

"Okay. If so, I'm glad." She leaned her head on my shoulder, and we strolled along in comfortable silence until we passed the tattoo and piercing parlor whose designs we'd admired the last time we were in town.

"He got them here," I blurted before I even knew I'd meant to speak.

"What?"

"Jace. His tattoos. They were amazing. I think he got them here. The designs . . . well, they're not the same, but they're familiar. Similar."

She stopped walking and admired the sketches and snapshots in the window again. The diamond stud in the side of her nostril caught little glints of the setting sun. "You think he comes here often?"

"I don't know. He had a lot of ink, so maybe in the past he did? But if he's done, he wouldn't necessarily have to come back."

"True." Mo sighed, one corner of her mouth drawn down. Then she nodded once, more to herself than me, I think. "I'm gonna do it. I'm gonna get another one."

"What? Now?"

She shrugged. "Why not, if there's an opening? If I do it now, I'll have a few days to heal up before I have to go back to camp."

If the tattoo shop was a surprise—so clean and upscale looking that it didn't appear out of place on the pretty streets of Saugatuck—the tattoo artist inside was even more so. No bears inked head to toe or heavily pierced goth girls here. Thin and bespectacled, he could have been a banker, a lawyer, or some sort of businessman who went to work in three-piece suits and had teleconferences. He wasn't *actually* wearing a suit, but he just looked so . . . *clean-cut* compared to what you'd normally envision in a tattoo artist that it was a little jarring.

He was good-looking, maybe in his early thirties, and he didn't have a bit of ink on him. At least, not any that could be seen outside his clothing. I was pretty sure that violated some sort of cardinal rule of tattoo artists.

He greeted us like we were the only customers he'd ever had, his attention perfectly zeroed in on Mo when she started asking questions. He introduced himself as Geoffrey Gilchrest and sat her down with a bottle of water while he gave her his credentials, which included a master's degree from the New England Institute of Art and a three-year apprenticeship with a Hollywood tattoo artist who inked A-list celebs. By the time he was done, Mo was wide-eyed and practically panting to get started, but they took their time, flipping through portfolios as I examined the snapshots on the walls, looking for one that might be Jace.

I was a little surprised by the scope of the design Mo chose. Her other tattoos were small and isolated: one on each ankle and one on the left shoulder just above her breast. I'd pegged her for a tramp stamp this time around, and when she stripped off her shirt and bra and leaned over the padded rest, presenting her back, I thought I'd guessed correctly.

But no. The design was only anchored at the small of her back. From there, runners of gorgeous ivy crept up her back toward her right shoulder, while another tendril wrapped around her waist and climbed her ribs like a trellis.

The longer he worked, the more discomfort she evidenced. I admit, a few of those sounds reminded me a lot of that moment when Jace had demanded I fuck him with hardly any prep— pained in the very best possible way. If Mo had been a guy, I probably would have gotten really turned on by the whole thing.

Instead, I just let her crush my knuckles and watched as the design she'd chosen blossomed into being on her skin. The most amazing thing about it was the variety of shades he used. This wasn't just a uniform green ivy, it was marbled, shot through with stripes of green so pale they might have been white, speckles and veins so dark they were nearly black, and everything in between. This ivy had depth and texture. It looked like it was in 3D, growing out of Mo's freckled skin, or possibly simply growing up around her, crawling up her body and surrounding it. As he worked, they talked about the possibility of someday adding more vines or perhaps blossoms of some sort.

Some of the detail work, they decided to leave until Mo was home for the Fourth of July because Geoff had another appointment coming in. When it was over, Mo sat there a while, catching her breath while I returned to browsing the designs, trying to decide whether or not my intuition that Jace had gotten his ink here was on the money.

Geoffrey covered Mo's tats in petroleum jelly and bandages, then began cleaning up. "What about you?" he asked me with a smile and a wink. "Are you considering a tattoo?"

I sighed and shook my head. "Not just now, thanks." It was tempting, but the swimming thing really was an issue, as I'd told Mo the last time she'd asked. I braced myself for the sort of pressure Mo usually laid on me, but Geoff just shrugged and accepted it, and Mo was too distracted with her new ink to try to sway me. She wasn't even pushing me to ask about Jace, which was a minor miracle.

Note to self: when Mo pushes, take her to get inked.

We left with Geoffrey's card in our wallets and an offer to call him anytime to consult or make an appointment.

Mo and I spent the remainder of the weekend lazing about as she waited for her tattoo to heal. It was a good thing Brendan had left to spend the week in Ann Arbor with Mo's mom; it meant Mo could go around topless to avoid anything chafing. Which I really couldn't have cared less about, but it was fun to tease her about flashing her rack all over anyway.

She left on Sunday, and I spent the day rattling around the empty house, unaccountably lonely for just having spent the weekend with my BFF. I'd been in Saugatuck for four weeks now, and still hadn't found a job or figured out what I was going to do about school in the fall. That calm contentment Mo had noticed was nice, but if I didn't get a move on, it was going to leave me stranded, the summer wasted and nothing to show for it.

Sighing, I grabbed my laptop and started searching for job prospects again. I was still at it when Mo texted from somewhere along the way up to Traverse City.

Forgot to mention one of the art galleries in town has a help wanted sign. You should check it out.

I scoffed as I reread the message.

What would I do at an art gallery?

I was expanding my job search to Holland when the next text came.

Well duh. work. who cares? just ask. Also ask if jace is a regular at the tattoo shop I forgot when we were there.

I chuckled again.

OK. I'll check art gallery just for you. Pass on the tattoo parlor. Stop by Big Rapids on the way home next time and get laid so you're not trying to run my life, k?

She must have been on the road again because I didn't get a response until after I'd gone to bed in the eerily quiet house.

stfu you know I'll run your life whether I get laid or not. deal w/it.

I decided not to dignify that one with a response.

CHAPTER TEN

We were two people with good intent
But our execution was painfully bad
And I know we loved the best we could
We tried to make it all okay
We tried to make it all go away

Brendan returned on Monday while I was down at the lake for my afternoon swim. With it being Memorial Day, even the private beach was busy. The local residents were all hosting parties and guests. It was a gorgeous, warm day, the water temperature finally approaching endurable on a regular basis, and I was happy to quit driving in to Holland to swim.

After I'd exhausted myself, I lay on my blanket, toasting my chilled skin under the brilliant sun. I wished Mo could've stayed another day, but of course she had to be back before the next camp session began. Being there by myself was lonely, though I went swimming on my own all the time. On this particular day, I wanted company. Or maybe I was just missing Mo. I was surrounded by people, but I wasn't *with* them, and I'd already had a couple encounters with nearby residents who didn't believe that, yes, I was staying on one of the properties that gave me rightful access to the beach. It made me leery of trying to strike up any conversations. I was debating packing up my towel and returning to the house to scare up some lunch when I glanced at the stairs to see Brendan coming down the dune.

I couldn't help it; I smiled. I'd missed his company, and now that I had a grip on my silly infatuation, I could just be happy to see him without worrying about the rest.

"Hey there!" I called as he caught sight of me and crossed the sand. "Just get back?"

He nodded, giving me a friendly smile in return, and sat on the blanket beside me as I rolled to my side to face him. "Yeah. Adele had an emergency at the hospital, so I thought I'd head back early. She says to tell you hi, by the way, and she's looking forward to meeting you on the weekend of the Fourth."

The thought of meeting his wife made me cringe in embarrassment. *Oh, hi, Mrs. G. Glad to meet you. I'm the weird gay boy who's been ogling your husband for the past couple months.*

"Oh, she's coming over for the Fourth?"

He nodded, looking out over the lake. "Yeah, that's when she scheduled her vacation. For three weeks, actually, so she'll get to spend some time with Morgan, too."

"That's cool." I smiled and dug in my bag for another water bottle. "Did you get a lot of work done in Ann Arbor?"

He chuckled, accepting the bottle when I offered it. "Thank you. Yeah, actually, I did. Adele works a lot of long shifts at the hospital, so I was alone a lot. I had plenty of free time to work."

I blinked, frowning. "I'm sorry. Is my being here keeping you from working?"

"What?" He looked taken aback by the question. "No, of course not."

I nodded, still feeling a little troubled by the idea. "Okay. Because I'm still trying to find a job. Mo said she saw a job advertisement at an art gallery, though I don't know what sort of qualifications I'd have. I've got an offer to play for tips at the coffeehouse, too. If you need me to get out so you can have some quiet . . ."

"Topher." His hand came to rest on my bare, sun-warmed

upper arm. "You don't disturb me. At least not any more than I want to be disturbed. I enjoy your company."

I think I must have given him a really sappy, smitten smile at that. I don't know. All I know is something shifted in the next instant, that companionable moment suddenly growing tense and awkward. His hand dropped from my arm like he'd been burned, and his eyes darted around in an almost furtive way. After a second, I dared to sneak a glance in the direction he'd been looking to see a woman seated on a nearby blanket watching us over the top of her book without trying to seem obvious about it. She was a neighbor; I'd seen her around a few times before while I was swimming. She was one of those who'd challenged my right to be on the private beach, until I'd called Mo to have her come down and verify that I was indeed a guest of hers.

I didn't like the speculative way she was looking at us, the obviously gay boy and the middle-aged man. Suddenly it was like my family and my high school choir teacher all over again; he'd been nice, and I'd loved working with him. He'd been a *mentor*, but their insinuations had made it into something dirty, to the point where I never felt comfortable working with him after that.

My harmless little crush was nowhere near as filthy as whatever that woman was imagining; I knew that without a doubt.

"Well, Topher." Brendan cleared his throat, and his voice was a little louder, a little more proper and paternalistic. "I think I'll go back up to the house and fire up the grill for dinner. I grabbed ribs on the way through town, if that's okay with you?"

"Sure, Mr. Gardner." I nodded agreeably, disgusted to realize I was doing it too. Speaking loudly enough so she could overhear just how innocuous our interaction was. No hanky-panky going on here, no ma'am!

Fucking filthy-minded busybody bitch. And here we were, placating her, trying to defend ourselves against silent intimations of vile things we hadn't even done.

"If you don't mind, sir, I'm going to read a while longer. I'll be up for dinner later."

Brendan nearly winced at my formal tone. He darted another glance at the woman, and his ears began to turn red.

"Sounds good, Topher. Enjoy your afternoon." He gave me a stilted smile and pushed himself up off the blanket, trying to look unconcerned as he made his way back up the stairs.

I spent the next hour trying not to feel the woman practically leering at me until I finally assumed I'd proven that I wasn't rushing up to the house to be banged by my host.

I SUPPOSE for Brendan it was a little like encountering the serpent in the Garden of Eden; there was no sin until someone *told* him there was.

Then he couldn't ever be clean of it.

If he'd ever given me a moment's thought outside the context of his daughter's friend and a kid he liked and wanted to help, he'd kept it so under wraps I never got so much as a whiff of it. I didn't believe he had, I really didn't. I was pretty good at picking up the vibes of sexual interest, no matter how well disguised, and he had never put any off. But after that moment, when he realized what people might think of us, it was clear he couldn't consign me to that safe, neat, mental box anymore. Suddenly I was something else. Something dirty and scandalous, something he needed to avoid.

At first, I didn't get it. I resented the hell out of that evil-minded bitch for soiling our easy camaraderie and so, in a gesture of defiance, I tried to act like nothing had changed. Like we were still pals, harmless and platonic. But Brendan couldn't do it. Once you're made aware of something, you can never become *unaware*, no matter how hard you try. Over the next few days, everything began to unravel. He wouldn't talk to me, would barely acknowledge me. He skirted around me whenever we were in proximity to one another as though I had some contagious illness he didn't want to catch by accidentally brushing against me.

That's when *I* began to feel unclean, and I hated it. I hadn't done anything *wrong*! I'd behaved myself. I wanted to throw an epic tantrum and rail at the injustice of it. It was like it had been with my family all over again. Just because I was who I was, everything I did had to be wrong or dirty by default, right? But all I had done was indulged, in the privacy of *my own mind*, a benign crush that I knew would never, *ever* go anywhere. I hadn't set out to seduce him, or even to tease him into the sort of awareness that dried up old cunt with her prurient mind and salacious gaze had forced on him. But now I was losing someone I'd begun to feel close to, someone I'd begun to trust. Someone who seemed to care.

With a single speculative look, she'd stolen a friend from me.

Once I realized Brendan couldn't shake it off and be comfortable around me anymore, I began avoiding meals when he was in the kitchen and tried to stay out of the house or up in my room as much as possible. At least Mo got her way. I spent a lot of time at the coffeehouse. Aubrey said the owners would consider paying me a wage if I appeared to have an impact on business, otherwise I was just welcome to whatever tips I made. It wasn't much, but I didn't care about the money, so long as it got me out of the house.

We went nearly a week without speaking a word to one another beyond the barest civilities. I admit I spent a good few hours in my room—not to mention the lake or my car or wherever—crying and feeling sorry for myself. I was mourning, as though something had died.

Perhaps something had.

After listening to Brendan pace restlessly around the house for four nights in a row, I admitted defeat.

"Brendan?" I caught him at the top of the stairs, apparently heading back to his room.

"Yes, Topher, what is it?" His voice sounded tense. Strained. I could barely see his face in the darkened hallway, but he sounded reluctant even to speak with me. I decided to get this done with as quickly as possible.

"I have some friends who live off-campus up in Allendale," I lied. "I think I'll see if they can let me crash out on their couch.

Maybe I can find a job around there, near campus. I'll call them tomorrow and leave this weekend."

He hung his head. "You don't have to do that."

"Yeah, I do." My voice cracked, and I swallowed hard. And under the hurt, I was so fucking *angry*. Was it *really* too much to ask to be left in peace so I could benignly co-opt my best friend's family for the summer because my own sucked? It might be pathetic, but who was I harming? "Look, it was really generous of you and Mo to offer me a place to stay, but I don't want to make trouble for you or give people the wrong idea. Small town gossip and all that. So I should go somewhere else. If I can't stay with my friends, maybe I'll go over to Flint, score some brownie points with my family by helping to take care of my mom for a while."

"Topher . . ." That seemed to shock him out of his numbed detachment. I'd told him weeks ago about my mom's (theoretical) suicide attempt and the resulting decision to cut her out of my life. "Don't do that. Don't go back into a situation that's not healthy for you just because people are foolish. Because *I'm* foolish."

"You're not." I shook my head in reflexive denial, trying to figure out how to reassure him. "You can't help it if it bothers you to know people think things about you that aren't true. Hell, it bothers me no matter how hard I try to convince myself it doesn't."

I stepped closer to him, putting on a brave smile. He smelled like red wine, and I wondered just how heavily he'd been drinking, though he didn't *seem* drunk. I reached out to pat his shoulder encouragingly, like he'd done for me many times since we'd gotten to know each other.

"It's okay to mind what other people think. I don't blame you. At least you and I know what's true. We haven't done anything wrong. So—"

Brendan's head came up at that, his eyes glittering in the thin moonlight coming in from the massive window in his bedroom just a few steps down the hall. His gaze riveted me, pinned me down, even as I staggered a step backward.

Everything I'd sworn he didn't—*couldn't*—feel for me was in his eyes.

"Oh, *no* . . ." I breathed, horrified and fascinated and, God help me, exultant in the same instant.

He *wanted* me.

It could never happen. *It could never happen.* I couldn't hurt Mo like that, couldn't betray her kindness, *his* kindness. I couldn't encourage him to do something he would regret for the rest of his life, however much a part of me yearned for it.

But sweet baby Jesus save me, I was responding to the heat in that look he fixed on me, growing hard and aching despite my terror and confusion. I'd spent the week feeling alone and unwanted and cut adrift, and he looked like an anchor. The fact that he wanted me made me feel less alone.

Now, more than ever, I needed to man up and walk away. What had been a harmless situation had just become even more fucked up. By several orders of magnitude.

He caught my hand as I tried to snatch it from his shoulder, where I'd rested it when I'd tried so innocuously to offer him comfort and reassurance. Now that small contact seared me, and his hand around mine felt like a band of fire, his skin blazing.

His eyes were so hungry and his face so tormented. He didn't *want* to want this, no more than I'd wanted my infatuation with him. I'd been so, *so* wrong in my analysis of the situation. The awareness that had been thrust upon him wasn't of the potential scandal we might stir up, however innocently. It was of all the non-innocent things we could do to fully warrant that scandal.

Oh shit, oh shit, oh shit. Walk away, Topher. Walk away now while you still can.

Why wasn't *he* walking away?

He wasn't. He stepped closer.

"Topher . . ." he whispered, just that soft brush of my name filled with anguish and need. He didn't really want to do this, except he did, and his hand around mine shook so fucking hard.

Why couldn't I pull away? Why couldn't he? It was every imaginable sort of wrong and we both knew it and why wasn't that enough to stop us? I don't know, and then it didn't matter.

One of us took that final step forward—I truly have no idea who —and our lips pressed together. We exhaled in the same instant, our breath exploding between us.

I was shaking too, I realized at that first tentative touch. Yet my mouth opened without any forethought and my tongue stroked his bottom lip. That was the moment *I* escalated things. I didn't mean to do it. I would hate myself forever for it, but I did it. I upped the ante.

Are we really doing this? some appalled part of my brain asked. My conscience said *no*, but my body—and perhaps some confused part of my heart that wanted to take all the kindness and understanding he'd offered me these last few weeks and make it into something more—said *yes*.

Why *shouldn't* I have this? If the world was going to damn me and think awful things about me anyway, no matter how good I was, why *shouldn't* I have at least one thing, one moment, I wanted?

Still, perhaps my conscience would have won out in that final standoff if his lips hadn't parted, if his tongue hadn't met mine, if his hands hadn't drawn me close and pressed me against the erection beneath his flannel pajama bottoms.

If he hadn't taken control of that kiss and turned fear and hesitation into demand and hunger.

Once he did that, there was no going back.

CHAPTER ELEVEN

When the shaking stopped
We were left in dust and flames
Buried our heads in shame
How did we let it come to this?

— CASEY STRATTON, "NAILED TO THE CROSS"

It was wrong. It was *wrong*. Wrong in every possible, conceivable way.

It was wrong, and it would always be wrong, and we needed to stop because Mo and Brendan's wife and . . .

At that point, the appalled part of my brain just up and dissociated, looking on in horror and revulsion at what we were doing. But it was drowned out by an unreasoning, unfathomable *need* that just didn't give a Technicolor fuck about right or wrong.

So there I was, naked on Brendan's bed, with the light of the moon riding over the waves of Lake Michigan spilling across my skin, and Brendan's fevered body bearing down on me.

I could have opened my mouth and said something. He would stop, I knew he would, if I told him to. And if I had, we could have backed off, found sanity again, ended this before it went from unwise to completely fucking disastrous.

I could have said *stop*. But I didn't.

"Topher . . ." he panted against my jaw, his lips and hands trying to cover every square inch of skin. He was maddened, totally beyond restraint. Sucking, biting, gripping, groping. His breath was a little sour with wine, but I didn't care. I didn't fucking care. I met those crazed kisses with equal madness, my mouth clashing against his, my fingers raking down his back. I gripped his ass and jerked him closer and spread my thighs to let the flannel covering his cock rub against mine.

My conscience screamed hysterically at me, but I tuned it out and lifted my hips, grinding against him.

His hands abandoned me to shove his pajamas and boxers down his hips with frantic pushes. And he was hard and thick and silky and slick and perfect, rutting against my belly, sliding alongside my cock in the sweaty space between us.

"Topher, please . . . I want . . . I want . . ." His groan sounded agonized, near tears. He might have been, for all I knew. God knew I was. But he was straight. He'd never been with a guy, had no clue what he was doing.

We didn't have any condoms or lube. They were upstairs in my room. If I stopped to go get them, which I knew I should do, it would have been over, and that was unacceptable. I could have given him a handjob, sucked him off, frotted against him until we both came. But I didn't want that. Because he was Brendan and he was sweet and kind and he treated me well and made me feel good, made me feel like I had value.

I wanted him within me. And it was stupid, but then, this whole goddamn thing was far beyond idiotic so, really, what did one more gargantuan mistake matter? If we were going to be wrong, then we might as well be fucking *wrong*. I was already so deep in reckless disregard for everything I knew to be right and intelligent that seriously, who the hell could keep count of all the errors?

I pushed him away and rolled to my hands and knees, then I spat on my fingers and thrust them inside myself. I'd never done it that way, the way Jace had liked it, with no prep. I'd certainly never done it with so little lube. It was going to hurt like fire, which—frankly—was a pretty damned appropriate metaphor for this whole fucked-up situation, wasn't it? He was going to split me open and it was going to hurt and *I didn't fucking care.*

"Brendan . . . please . . ." I panted, groping blindly behind me, trying to find him and guide him to me. And then he was there and he didn't know to go slow and *fuck* it hurt. I bit the pillow, keening into it, my body racked with shudders and tears springing to the corners of my eyes. The sweat on my skin prickled and turned cold when he went still, bending forward and pressing his forehead against my back.

"Topher?" There. There was a shred of sanity, at last. Concern. Worry. Joined so intimately together that I imagined I could feel his heartbeat pulsing inside me, the need seemed to abate long enough to allow us to *think.*

"I'm okay," I gasped, still shuddering but beginning to adjust, the rending ache becoming something manageable. Starting to carry a little undercurrent of pleasure, even. I reached down between my legs and began to stroke back to life the erection that had flagged with the onslaught of pain. Pleasure helped to hurry the discomfort on its way. "I'm okay."

Still, he remained immobile, though his body trembled. His hips brushed my ass and his hands rested on my ribs. And it seemed he was withdrawing mentally, gathering himself, maybe even on the verge of letting conscience and reason take control again.

No. *No.* Yeah, I knew we should stop, but here we were already, what the ever-loving *fuck* did it matter if we stopped now? The damage was done. We'd already gone beyond the point where we could say we'd stopped ourselves in time. Way beyond.

Fuck it. Might as well finish. Might as well at least have what we'd thrown everything to the wind to have.

"Please . . . Brendan . . ." I arched my back, opening myself to him a bit more. And yes it still ached, but it was getting better all the time. "Please don't stop."

The noise he made against my back sounded suspiciously like a sob.

"Don't stop." I stroked myself faster, growing hard in my

hand, so hard. I pushed back against him, urging him deeper. "Don't stop. Don't stop. Please . . ."

Drawing a shuddering breath, he lifted himself off my back and *moved*. We yelled together at the first wave of pleasure, and then that moment of sanity was gone.

We didn't last long. Despite the discomfort—or perhaps because of it; was this what Jace had been after?—it didn't take long for me to spurt over my fist. Just a few thrusts of Brendan's dick gliding past my prostate. And it didn't take him much longer. He jerked, pumping when I came down. Another spasm of pleasure hit me just from the thought of him coming inside me, which was something I'd never allowed anyone to do before.

Only for him, only for Brendan with all his kindness and understanding and comfort, would I be so fucking colossally stupid. I knew I'd been safe, and I'd been tested, so I couldn't harm him. I hoped he'd been faithful to his wife until now, and she to him. If not, I might regret this the rest of my life.

Who the fuck was I kidding? Of course I'd regret this the rest of my life, whether he was disease-free or not.

I collapsed beneath him onto the wet sheets, and he pulled out of me and rolled off to the side, not touching me. My ass burned and I was cold in the air-conditioned bedroom, the sweat chilling on my skin.

I wished he'd hold me.

He lay there silent, distant, as moments ticked by. Finally I couldn't take it anymore.

"If you ask me to go right now, or if you run away, or treat me like you don't want anything to do with me, I'll hate you forever."

I hated myself for being close to crying at the thought of it. I knew my voice sounded choked, but at this moment, Brendan rejecting me was about the only thing I could think of that would make everything that had happened tonight feel worse. To be discarded, tossed aside like he didn't even want to know me now that he'd gotten it out of his system. I was probably being melodramatic to think that I'd just go throw myself in the lake if he treated me that way and went back to his straight, white, wealthy life like it had never happened, like *I* had never happened. I knew I really wouldn't, but the temptation would definitely be there.

After a moment of silence, I felt his fingertips on my spine. Gentle. So gentle. Concerned. Caring. I was glad I'd faced away from him, because two tears spilled onto the pillow beneath my face.

"I don't know what to do, Topher," he whispered brokenly. "We shouldn't have done this."

"No, we shouldn't have. But we did." I found the courage to turn and face him. "Look, I don't expect anything more here. I'm not going to ask you for any promises or turn into an idiot and imagine we're going to live happily ever after. This is fucked up and we both know it. The only thing I'm going to ask is that, whatever happens, you level with me. Respect me enough to be honest. Don't do anything to demean me, okay? Can you do that?"

"Of course." His hand came up and cupped my face. "I wouldn't do that to you, Topher. This may be a mistake, but it's not your fault it happened."

"It's at least partly my fault," I said firmly. "I could have stopped. I knew I should have stopped. I *decided* not to. Don't try to make me a victim here."

"No." He closed his eyes, looking unspeakably tired. "No, there's blame to go around, I guess. I'm certainly no victim, either."

Even now, looking weary and drawn, he was beautiful. His hand on my face felt good, and I turned into it, nuzzled his palm, enjoying the moment of tenderness.

Kissed it.

His eyes opened at that. "I still don't know what to do right this minute," he murmured.

I swallowed hard, wondering if it was wise to make myself any more vulnerable. But that was already a done deal, so why not?

"Do you . . . do you think you could hold me while we get some sleep? Deal with the rest tomorrow?"

His face tightened, nearly a wince, but he whispered, "Of

course," and drew the down comforter up over both of us. I gave him my back, and his arms closed around me, his body spooning against mine.

Jesus, I was sore. I closed my eyes with a tired sigh and tried to feel warm again.

Before I fell asleep, the back of my neck grew wet. I laced my fingers with his and squeezed, and his arms tightened around me as he grieved over the mistake we'd made.

CHAPTER TWELVE

Floating down the river with you
I could tell there would be trouble ahead
But it felt so good next to you
That I risked it
I wished for it

— CASEY STRATTON, "CRUEL HAND OF FATE"

How was it possible for everything to feel great and wrong in the same exact instant?

I woke up with Brendan pressed against me in a bed I had no business being in. His arms around me felt good, even though my mind took up the obsessive chant, *wrong, wrong, wrong.*

I knew what I had to do. I had to find some way to make us not hate ourselves or each other for what we'd done. If we slunk away, miserable and ashamed, the wrong was all we would remember for the rest of our lives. We would never remember the kindness and gentle affection of those first few weeks of slowly building friendship that had sprung up between us, and suddenly it seemed imperative that we not lose sight of that. We, together, were more than this one mistake. Yes, this was a category-5 shitstorm, a disaster of behemoth proportions, and it was going to leave a metric fuck-ton of emotional debris scattered in its wake, but before everything had gone off the rails, there had been some good, too, and I didn't want that obliterated by the bad. I already had too many relationships in my life where what hurt about them far outweighed anything good.

Or maybe I just decided I might as well be hanged for a sheep as a lamb. In for a penny, in for a pound. Choose your cliché. I'd take what I could get while I could get it.

Either way, instead of trying to make a discreet exit that would have allowed us to try to pretend nothing had ever happened until the awkwardness became unbearable and we each ran away, I rolled over and kissed him.

He shuddered awake, startling. He didn't pull away, but neither did he respond for a moment. Then he sighed, and his hand grasped my arm and his lips softened against mine. Just for a moment. It wasn't chaste, but it wasn't passionate either. Sad, rather. Needy. Confused. Seeking comfort.

Then he drew back and searched my face, those red-rimmed eyes concerned.

"Are you okay?"

The tender brush of his knuckles against my cheek nearly undid me. I nodded.

"Yeah. I'm okay. You?"

He huffed a bitter laugh, rolling onto his back and covering his eyes with his hand.

"I don't know, Topher. I don't know why I'm lying here when I know this can't happen again. I should be up and running away and I'm not. I should be telling you all the reasons you should get as far away from me as humanly possible for your own sake, and I'm not. What do you do when you discover you're not the person you thought you were, when you realize you're far, far worse? Horrible, even?"

"You're not horrible," I murmured, hugging myself and curling up a bit because for some reason it was fucking cold in this room. Was the air conditioning set to "meat locker" or something? "If you were horrible, you wouldn't feel bad right now."

He sighed and rocked his head to the left, meeting my eyes. "I do feel bad. And yet that isn't stopping me from . . ."

"Relishing the memory?" I supplied for him, trying for perky. I hoped he did. That's what I'd wanted when I'd kissed him awake, to cement the good. I'd wanted to salvage one positive feeling out of the wreckage. Something we could look back on someday and say, *It was almost worth it.*

"Wanting it again," he rasped, drawing in on himself when my eyes widened. "*Now* tell me I'm not horrible."

. . . Oh.

I hadn't let myself even consider that possibility. It wasn't that I didn't—or wouldn't—want it, so much as I'd never even thought of it, certain that after this one time, we'd try to put the pieces of our worlds back to rights and repair the damage as best we could.

I shouldn't say yes, and I didn't want to say no, which left me wondering what I *could* say. But it was okay. I realized after a moment that it hadn't been a request. He made no effort to go for another round. He was just explaining another part of what made this so awful and confusing for him.

I floundered for something else to say, desperate not to let this end with us fleeing from one another in panic and revulsion, hating ourselves. Desperate to make us okay.

"How long— I mean, when— Why— *Fuck.*" I sighed, frustrated with myself. "When did this happen?"

I wondered if he understood what I meant. I couldn't put words to whatever he felt for me, to ask when it began.

He shook his head, shrugging, echoing my sigh. "I, um, I know that night you went out for your birthday, and the next morning when you came back, I was . . . uncomfortable. I didn't consider that it might be attraction, at first. I figured I was just uneasy with you being so open about your sexuality. I think I convinced myself that maybe I had a little homophobia lurking somewhere inside, so I made the decision to get to know you better, become more comfortable with you. I just didn't want to be yet another person to make you feel you couldn't be yourself. I wanted to be someone you could trust."

I nodded slowly. "So it did begin with that woman on the beach."

"No. The week before, actually. While I was in Ann Arbor. I, um, I dreamed about you. And I was so appalled afterward, just disgusted with myself. But I didn't want to . . . to be awkward with you or avoid you. I feared you'd think you'd done something wrong if I did that, and *damn it*, I didn't want to make you feel that way. So when I came back on Monday, I was determined that I was going to work on that friendship we'd established, reinforce those boundaries, keep that going until I was just comfortable with you again. But . . . I must have given something away there on the beach. She must have seen something I didn't want to show, and she made you uncomfortable and I was afraid you'd think I was going to try something with you and—" He sighed again. "I didn't know what to do, Topher. I didn't know how to make it right. And now . . ."

"Have there been others?" I could barely raise my voice above a whisper, terrified of the answer.

"What? No," he said emphatically. "In twenty-five years I've never once been unfaithful to my wife."

"What about before? Were there other guys, or have you never—?"

He sighed again. "There was some experimentation with one of my roommates in college. I . . . didn't treat him well."

"Why not?"

"Well, thirty years ago, coming out wasn't nearly as easy as it is today. I'm not saying it's a picnic now, but back then . . . I buried my moments of attraction to men, and since I was never going to be unfaithful to Adele anyway, what did it matter how I identified myself?"

"And you're sure there hasn't been anyone else?"

"No!" He frowned, sounding annoyed. "I think I'd remember. Why—?"

"We didn't use a condom last night." Shit. If my math was right, he'd been *experimenting* right around the time the AIDS epidemic had first hit the headlines. "I know *I'm* safe, I get tested and I don't take risks—at least I never have before. But—"

"Oh." His brow unfurrowed, his expression smoothing. He nodded his understanding. "Um, aside from being monogamous, an HIV test was a part of my last life insurance physical, about five years ago. I swear, unless Adele has cheated on me—and I really have no reason to think she has—you have nothing to worry about. At least, not on that subject."

I nodded, swallowing hard. "Okay."

The silence that fell then was awful, filled with guilt and uncertainty, neither of us knowing what to say. I caved first, rolling away from him, huddled in on myself. Cold. So damned cold.

"I, um . . . I should go back to my room," I murmured finally, though I made no effort to move. I guess I was still waiting for a Hail Mary play, some magical moment that would make us both comfortable and make this all right.

He moved behind me and I flinched when his hand landed on my shoulder, stroking down my bare arm. "Please don't go," he whispered, and then his breath and lips brushed along my chilled shoulder blades, and his body pressed warm and hard—very hard—against mine. "I have no right to ask, and I know we shouldn't, but please . . ."

God help me, it felt good. My nerve endings awoke like a choir gestured to life by the conductor's baton, drawing that first, deep, unified breath before beginning to sing.

He felt good, and why shouldn't he? None of the reasons why we shouldn't changed the fact that he was a warm, attractive man who'd been kind and even, I think, cared for me. Just because it was wrong didn't mean his hands weren't smooth and soft and stroking my skin with not-inconsiderable skill.

And then his kisses moved up to that sensitive place where back and shoulder and neck all meet. The rigid length of his cock rocked against the crack of my ass and . . .

I drew in a hissing, alarmed breath. That was *so* not happening.

"Too sore," I whispered, lifting my upper leg. "Here."

I reached between my legs and found his dick as he nudged

me with it. I guided it into the space between my thighs and closed them, squeezing.

"There." I gave a slight wriggle, feeling him pressed against my taint and balls. He didn't move at first, so I did it for him. Just a fraction of an inch, not enough to dislodge him. Just enough to give him a hint of what he should do. I tightened my thighs as hard as I could and he grunted behind me, thrusting into that improvised cleft.

"Topher . . ." he breathed, searching for a rhythm. His arm was tight around me, clasping me intimately close. His face pressed into the curve of my neck, the susurration of his breath warm and moist on my skin.

He whispered my name again and I felt cherished. This might be wrong, but he wasn't treating me like *I* was wrong. I twisted, turning my upper body toward him, seeking a kiss. The angle was bad, but he gave it to me, our tongues sliding together between the imperfect fastening of our lips and my hand coming up to hold the back of his head, my fingers weaving into the hair at the base of his skull.

His hand on my chest traveled lower as he picked up the pace, moving faster between my thighs as they grew slick with sweat.

"Topher, may I—"

"*Please.*" I was hard and aching when those gorgeous long fingers I'd once admired wrapped around my cock. My spine arched and I thrust into his grasp, my head tipping back to rest against his shoulder. His hand knew its way around a dick— probably from playing bachelor Monday through Friday for years, or so I was really hoping—and he gripped with just the right pressure, twisted and curled in just the right places. He slicked his palm with my pre-cum and found a rhythm that would send me over the top fast and hard.

"*Fuck.* Brendan . . ." The tympanic bass line of *wrong, wrong, wrong* that rumbled with every beat decrescendoed. A chorus of pleasure rose up high and clear on the descant, trilling above that dire thrumming, pushing it to the background.

It was wrong, but it was *good* and just now the good mattered more. I kept my arm hooked back, holding him with my fingers tangled in his hair, writhing between his body and his fist as he fucked into the gap between my legs. Our breaths erupted in sharp bursts. I finished first, pulsing over his fist, dripping down his fingers, then I clung to him, panting and shuddering for breathless moments as he gasped and groaned and strove for his own release.

When it was over, we lay entangled limply together, sticky with each other's cum and earthy with sweat and musk. And, God help me, for those few minutes of afterglow, lying there with his arms around me, his heartbeat drumming against my back, it didn't *feel* wrong.

I GOT MY WISH, at least. When we finally parted to go shower and dress, it wasn't a shamefaced slink. Brendan kissed me one last time, almost chastely, and urged me up with gentle hands. Then he helped me gather my scattered clothes.

"We'll talk later, Topher," he murmured, and I nodded mutely and left.

I don't think it's fair to say we avoided each other the rest of the day, but we stayed apart, gave each other space. It probably wasn't safe for me to go swimming today, as exhausted and confused as I was, but I did it anyway, punishing my body by driving it against the choppy waves. I swam until every muscle in me ached with fatigue, then stumbled ashore and collapsed onto my blanket, almost literally burying my head in the sand. I napped there for some time, catching up on days' worth of lost sleep. Then I threw myself at the lake for another desperate swim before the clouds started to darken and the wind picked up.

When I returned to the house, Brendan had made dinner and eaten already, leaving the leftovers out for me to help myself. That's when I did start to feel like he was avoiding me.

I did the dishes and went up to my cozy dormer bedroom for a shower, then wrapped myself in my plush microfiber robe and sat on my bed with my knees drawn up to my chest and my arms around them. I looked through that half-moon window above my headboard, out at the sky as the clouds went from steely to black, and wondered if Brendan was in his room directly below me, staring at the same vista.

I might have thought Brendan had left the house if the car hadn't been in the garage, that's how quiet it was. There were no sounds except for my own breath and the ominous growls of thunder beginning to rumble across the water.

Now I understood what people meant when they said the silence was deafening.

It was better this way, I told myself. We'd done what we'd done, and we'd managed to make it out of that situation without the sort of shame or resentment I'd been afraid of. Where we'd left things this morning had been as good a place as possible, given the circumstances. Now we could step back, cool off, and figure out how to fix this without destroying Mo, her mother, and ourselves. If that was even possible.

It was finished. So why did my chest ache at the continued silence? I was drowning in the open air.

It got worse when I tried to imagine what I'd say to Mo, how she'd feel, what she'd do. I couldn't imagine confessing this to her, but I couldn't imagine pretending to be her friend while knowing what I'd done, either. If and when she found out, it would probably destroy the best relationship—the only good, true relationship, really—in my life.

And yet, when I thought of losing her, I wanted *him* more than ever.

The first flicker of lightning appeared over the lake, and I could hear the waves crashing even through the walls. The more I thought about it all, the lonelier and more hopeless I felt. I was going to lose them both, I was sure of it. All I could do now was cherish what time I had left with them until it all came apart.

Wiping my eyes, I pushed myself off the bed and rummaged in my bags. I dropped the lube in the pocket of my robe when I found it and descended the stairs with calm, deliberate steps.

Brendan's bedroom door was open, and he was sitting on the side of his bed in just his pajama bottoms, gripping the edge of the mattress, his knuckles white. He wasn't at all surprised to see me, like he'd been expecting me to come to him—or perhaps trying to talk himself out of going to me.

I hesitated in the doorway for one silent, uncertain moment. Lightning flashed again, illuminating us in startling white light, and a moment later, thunder cracked like a shotgun blast.

Each time I stood on this precipice, it seemed a little easier to jump. I think he must have felt the same, because after a long, solemn stare, he held his hand out to me.

I closed the door behind me and took it.

CHAPTER THIRTEEN

Tired of waiting
So tired of all this waiting
So long I've been here hating
What I've become and hating
What doesn't change
And more what does
I cannot change what I am now

— CASEY STRATTON, "WAITING"

F ortune was with us, it seemed. Mo decided to spend her next weekend off in Big Rapids with her pretty archery instructor.

"You sure you don't hate me for not coming down?" her voice asked over my phone as I searched town for the art gallery she'd mentioned. "I can swing by there for a day, then come back up to Big Rapids . . ."

"No, no!" I was probably a little too quick to assure her that wasn't necessary. Fate, or whatever higher power you chose to believe in, had granted me a reprieve. I wouldn't have to face her and confess yet, or perhaps worse, try to hide what Brendan and

I had done while pretending everything was normal, going back to sleep in my attic room alone while she was in the house. "Are you kidding? If Archer McLovelyArms wants you to spend the whole weekend, you go, girl. Get you some."

She snorted. "His name's Cody Rey."

I quirked an eyebrow, even though she wasn't here, and for the first time in the entire conversation, banter didn't feel forced.

"You sure he's an archer? Sounds more like a gunslinger. Just what exactly is he packing?"

It took Mo a few minutes to stop laughing and catch her breath. "I'll let you know next week." We giggled together for a moment longer, then: "Did you stop by the art gallery?"

"I'm actually on my way there now, if I can locate the damn place."

"Oh good! Yay!" She sounded far too delighted by this information and proceeded to give me directions.

"Okay, I gotta go," I said, spotting the gallery ahead. "Call me next week, give me all the gory details."

She said good-bye, and I tucked away my phone before walking into the gallery.

The first thing I noticed was that there was no Help Wanted sign in the window. Well, great. I'd waited too long and the position had already been filled. There went the best chance I'd had at finding a job here in town. The tips at the coffeehouse and the occasional one- or two-day temp jobs weren't nearly enough. I *needed* something steady.

Guess that's what I got for spending a week doing the nasty with a man I shouldn't have even considered touching. I should probably have counted on a lot of karmic kicks in the teeth in the foreseeable future.

A bell chimed as I walked in, and after a moment, a heavily pregnant woman of Asian descent waddled from the back room. She gave me a scrutinizing once-over, discerning immediately that I wasn't there to shop for paintings.

"Can I help you?"

"Um, maybe?" I bit my lip for a moment, suddenly unsure. "A

friend of mine told me she saw a Help Wanted sign here a couple weeks back, but I guess the position has already been filled? If it has, then perhaps I can put in a résumé in case you need any more help in the future?"

The woman looked at me again and began to smile, tapping two fingertips to her curving lips.

"I think your friend was trying to matchmake. There hasn't been a Help Wanted sign in the window here in two years."

I blinked in confusion, looking her over, because hello? Woman. Definitely not anyone Mo would ever try to match me up with.

"Um, no. No no no. My friend wouldn't . . . She knows that I'm . . ."

"Oh, not with me." The woman's eyes sparkled with more amusement. "With the gallery owner, Robin Brady. He's gay, and very good-looking, and, sorry to say, one hundred percent taken."

"Ah. *And that, Your Honor, is when I snapped and strangled my best friend.*" I closed my eyes and gritted my teeth for a moment. "Yeah, um. Mo probably meant well, but . . . yeah. Sorry for taking up your time."

Thank God no one could tell I was blushing. I turned on my heel, prepared to try to beat as dignified a retreat as I could manage.

"Though now that you mention it—" Her voice stopped me with my hand on the door. "I start my maternity leave in a few weeks, and Robin *will* be looking for help, though I doubt he's actually realized that yet. He's still taken, but if you'd like to leave that résumé, I'll recommend he call you to set up an interview."

"Great!" I nodded eagerly, extending my hand. "By the way, hi. I'm Topher Carlisle."

"I'm Ling Gilchrest, Robin's sister-in— well, not-quite-law." She shook my hand and accepted the résumé I pulled out of a portfolio in my backpack, promising Robin would call me when he got back from a buying trip to Chicago.

"Thank you." I smiled at her, pleased to have found something resembling an opportunity. "If you find out about anywhere else hiring, you know, just some general help, feel free to pass my number along to them, too."

"I'll do that." She grunted, laying one hand over her huge abdomen and taking a moment to compose herself before smiling again. "Take care, Topher. We'll be in touch."

On the way back through town, I walked again past the tattoo parlor where Mo had gotten inked. I was so not going to inquire about Jace like she had pushed me to do. However, seized by a momentary flash of inspiration, I went inside.

Geoffrey was there, just as incongruously clean-cut as ever. "Good afternoon. Topher, wasn't it?"

"Yeah, hi." I shook his hand again, smiling nervously.

"Thinking of having something done?"

I chuckled, feeling my face heat up for the second time that day. "No, not at the moment. I, um, I'm here in town for the rest of the summer, and I don't know any local people. I've been looking for work, but it seems like all the summer positions are filled already. And I know sometimes in a small town like this, if you know people who know people, you can find stuff that never gets listed in the classifieds. So I thought, if you didn't mind, I'd just give you my name and number. Then, if you heard of anyone needing help, you might let me know, or give them my information?"

"Didn't I see you playing piano at the coffeehouse last week?"

"Oh, that's just an informal thing for tips. I need something that actually pays a wage. If you'd like, I could bring by a résumé, too, or email one. I still have your card."

"Ah, okay. The networking approach is a pretty clever idea, actually. Good thinking." He pursed his lips thoughtfully. "Have you been to the art gallery down the street? Ling is—"

"Yeah, I just came from there, actually. She promised to have the owner call me, but I don't really know anything about art, so in case that falls through, I thought I'd put out feelers in a couple other directions."

"That's good. I'll put in a word for you with Robin." He winked at me. "I have just a little pull there."

"You— Oh!" For the first time, I noticed the band on his left ring finger, and remembered Ling mentioning that this Robin guy was gay and off the market. And her sort-of brother-in-law. I grinned, ridiculously pleased by the symmetry of the whole thing. "Right. Ling *Gilchrest*. She's your sister. Cool! She seemed really nice." Wow. I would never have guessed it, seeing as how she was Asian, and Geoff was about the WASPiest WASP ever to WASP. Of course, considering that I'd had more Asian classmates than black because of the number of families in the area who adopted Asian children, I probably shouldn't have been surprised.

So, Ling was (probably) adopted, and Geoff was with Robin. Got it.

"Nice doesn't begin to cover it. She's amazing." He cleared his throat and shook himself. "Anyway. The position at the gallery will only be part-time, but I can use some help here if you need more hours. Mostly cleaning, sanitizing, and janitorial stuff. All extremely important for obvious reasons. I might also need you to help with the appointment schedule, answer the phone, greet clients, take care of them while they wait or decide on designs. Having someone else to do the grunt work frees me up to take a few more appointments or get home a little earlier. Tourist season gets pretty busy, which means I have to spend a lot more hours at work to keep everything up to standard, but in another month or so I'm going to want all the free time I can get."

I nodded eagerly. "You'll have to teach me how, but I learn really quickly. Which I know probably everyone says, but it's true."

He gave me a kind smile. "I believe you. I'll talk it over with Robin tonight when he calls, and we'll decide on a wage and see if we can figure out a schedule for you."

"Thank you." I bobbed another nod. I don't know why his kindness made me feel a little emotional, but it did. Maybe because of all the turmoil of the last couple weeks, and the uncertainty of the weeks to come. I might very well lose the last stable thing in my life soon, which made every smile and friendly gesture more precious to me.

Of course, the emotion could have been coming from the fact

that I *finally* had a solid offer of steady, paying work, assuming I didn't manage to screw it up somehow. If the wage they decided on was sufficient, then one of my two major worries for the summer would be a thing of the past. And regarding the other worry, the distinct *lack* of karmic kick-in-the-teeth inherent in finding a job at last almost felt like a pardon.

Now if only the situation with Brendan could come to such a clean resolution.

Geoff held out his hand. "You're welcome. I'll call you tomorrow."

I shook his hand and left, heading for the coffeehouse to play for a couple hours. I felt lighter than I had in days, relieved of at least one burden. The other—namely Brendan—was going to be a whole lot harder to sort out.

I wished I could say that the affair with Brendan made me happy, but it really didn't. Being his friend had made me happy. This just made me confused. But there were moments of tenderness and kindness that verged really close on joy, and sometimes even laughter, as we rediscovered how much we liked each other's company, even in this new context. But mostly it was just angst. Hot, sweaty, frequently sexy angst, but still angst. And fear. And dread of the day when we'd have to account for what we'd done.

When I got home, Brendan wasn't at work on his laptop for once. He was sprawled out idly on the sofa, and there was a freshly delivered pizza box on the breakfast bar.

"Done with work for the day?" I asked, grabbing a bottle of beer out of the fridge for myself and a fresh one for him. Because, pizza.

"Well, I had to send some stuff to my editor and I'm waiting for feedback that I probably won't get until Monday, so it seemed a good time to take a break from working on it twelve to fourteen hours a day."

"Ah." I set the beers down on the coffee table before him and he twisted off the caps while I grabbed plates and napkins for both of us. I slid a hesitant glance at him under my lashes. "Did Mo call you?"

He nodded, his expression sobering. "Yeah." He blew out a slow sigh. "We dodged the bullet there, I guess."

"Guess so." I handed him his plate and sat beside him.

We fell silent, eating our pizza and sipping our beers. I wondered if Brendan was pondering the same question I was: when and if we'd finally find the strength to stop this insanity the way we should have done a week ago when it'd first started. That was the worst part of it. He wasn't using me. He wasn't taking advantage of me. If he had been, I'd like to think that something would have pinged me the wrong way and I'd have been able to pull back and call a halt to it. But he genuinely did like me. Care about me. He didn't want to hurt me; he just didn't know how to stop, and neither did I. Every time it looked like one of us might be almost ready to try, the other pulled him back in.

That sounded stupid, didn't it? I always thought so, whenever I watched a movie or read a book that had someone committing infidelity, miserable because they didn't know how to stop. I'd scream at the character to *just fucking stop* already. I didn't understand how two people could meet such a deep-seated need within one another that they kind of became addicted, contrary to all reason, no matter how destructive the situation.

I think for Brendan, I satisfied that long-suppressed aspect of his sexuality that he'd never allowed himself to experience. I didn't know how to put into words what need Brendan fulfilled for me. It was his kindness and understanding and acceptance— things I'd never had before. At least not from someone like him.

But moments like this, when we couldn't ignore that this was an awful thing we were doing and it was destined to end in misery, not just for us but for people we loved, were why the affair couldn't ever make us happy. It might meet certain needs within us, but joy would never be one of them.

When the pizza was gone and the dishes put away, we sat side by side on the sofa and I told him about the possibility that I'd found an actual job in town. As we spoke, his hand drifted closer to me, his fingers brushing up and down my neck and jaw until I forgot what I was speaking about and began to grow warm, pliant, *hard*. My eyes turned to him, asking the question we asked ourselves every single time.

Are we really going to do this?

Accepting the answer was easy, now. Too damn easy.

Yes.

Someday the answer would be *no* and that would be the end of it. But not yet.

Not yet.

CHAPTER FOURTEEN

Pulled to you like waves to the coastline
I can let you go, I'm sure I'll be fine
I keep telling myself those comforting lies
To get through the longest night

— CASEY STRATTON, "CRUEL HAND OF FATE"

I could smell coffee and toast as I emerged from the shower after my swim a couple days later, and heard water running in Brendan's bathroom. Since I didn't have to be in town to start work for Geoffrey until noon, I let myself into his bedroom and watched from the bathroom doorway as he shut off the water. He turned to see me standing there, and a smile spread over his face. I just couldn't help it; I stepped into the bathroom to greet him as he emerged from behind the glass slider.

"Good morning." There was an invitation in his eyes and he drew me in, leaning close to claim my mouth.

I sank into the kiss, humming, letting my hand trail down his body—still dripping wet from the shower—to his groin. Here, Brendan's age sometimes told; he was still soft. Quickly, I pulled my hand back up, pressing my clothed body closer, creating some friction, waiting for him to firm up a bit.

His hand captured mine and urged it down again.

"Touch me, Topher," he whispered against my neck, his hair dripping on my shoulder. I tried to flinch out of his grasp, but his hand tightened on mine, pushing harder. "Please . . ."

Suddenly my heart was racing and I couldn't breathe. My hand was getting closer to that wet, malleable flesh and my stomach started to twist, sending up a wave of nausea.

"No," I gasped, pulling away as much as his arm around my back would allow. I tugged, trying to reclaim my hand, but he wasn't getting the hint.

"Damn it, let go!" I snapped, twisting my wrist and jerking away hard. I nearly stumbled when he released me in his surprise, his deep blue eyes astonished.

"What is it?"

"Nothing." I was shaking, still queasy. The skin around my wrist stung. I looked anywhere but at his body. If he was still soft, I didn't want to see it. But then, considering what had just happened, I wasn't sure I wanted to know if he was hard, either. "I need to get ready for work."

I spun on my heel and raced for the stairs. Brendan charged after me, snatching a towel around his hips.

"Christopher, wait!"

Fuck. He had to use my full name, didn't he? Had to invoke that instinctive, bred-in-the-bone obedience toward older authority figures. I stopped with my hand on the banister, tipping my head back and fighting to limit the expression of my frustration to an irritated groan.

I flinched at the first brush of his fingers on my shoulder.

"Don't touch me," I rasped. "Not right now."

"Okay." The hand disappeared. "I won't. But . . . will you just sit down with me? Tell me what just happened?"

"You're not my fucking therapist, Professor." I tried to make the dismissal scathing, but instead it just sounded weary. "I don't need to sit on your couch and work out my issues with you."

"I'd like to know what's going on, so I can avoid it happening again." He sounded a little hurt, and I sighed, turning to face him. He looked so confused and concerned. Jesus. When was the last time anyone but Mo had cared about my feelings, unless they were being paid by the session?

I wanted to crawl into his lap and hide in him until all the bad feelings went away, and wasn't that just fucked up beyond belief? The last thing I needed was to start thinking of him as the daddy figure I'd never had.

"You really, *really* don't want me to read you another chapter of Topher's Pity-Poor-Me Drama." I rolled my eyes. "How about we leave it at 'Topher's turned off by flaccid dicks'? So, I'll go have some coffee, you haul out some porn and get it up, then when I come back upstairs I promise to be in a better mood, and we can pick up where we left off."

"Jesus, Topher." He scraped his wet hair back from his face. Beads of water collected on his temples and neck from where the ends were still saturated and dripping. "Do you really think I'd consider going to bed with you when you're like this?"

"Yeah, I know, the freaking out is super-unattractive." I grimaced. Why wouldn't he just walk away? "Sorry. I'll try to keep that under control in the future."

I wasn't being fair to him and I knew it, but this was what I did when threatened. When I was backed into a corner, I came out swinging.

"Goddamn it, that's not what I meant!" The corners of his mouth and eyes grew white as he scowled. "Give me some credit for not being quite that shallow, would you? You look like you're ready to fall apart, and I'm worried, okay? I'd like to know what the fuck just triggered you so I can avoid doing it again."

My gaze darted away from his, scurrying around the hallway and down the stairs, looking for something, anything else to focus on. In my peripheral vision, his hand stretched out again, but he stopped short of touching me. Smart man.

"Topher, please?"

My throat aching, I shuddered and laid my hand in his. He squeezed it, his thumb rubbing across my knuckles.

"I need to go get dressed. If you want, you can go sit down-stairs, have some coffee. I'll be down in a minute. Or if you don't want to be alone, you can come with me. I'll keep my hands off. No expectations just because you're in my bedroom."

Suddenly I very much did *not* want to be alone. If I was going to get into this—and I really didn't see how I could avoid it now, because I owed him an explanation—I didn't want to be alone in my own head for any length of time before it all came out. I wanted to get it over and done with.

"I'll go with you," I whispered, and let him guide me back to the bedroom.

While he dressed, I sat on the edge of the unmade bed where I now slept with him every night, wringing my hands in my lap and trying to find words. Once he had his underwear and jeans on, he offered me a prompt.

"Was it . . . an ex? A former partner? Did they do something—?"

I shook my head, finding some of my attitude again. "Not exactly. *Fuck.* Okay, fine. Whatever. The story goes something like this: The week school let out for summer vacation between second and third grade"—he sucked in a horrified breath and I offered him a grim nod, taking a bit of malicious satisfaction in narrowing my eyes to give him a *you asked for it, bucko* glower —"my mom—I told you once I spent weekends and summer vacation with her, right?—decided to go down to Alabama for a few months to hang with her father and cousins. Now, Grandpa had a brother and sister-in-law who adored children and never had kids of their own. They always loved having everyone's kids come stay with them. It was a *thing* in the family; everyone did it. Whenever you visited, you left your kids to stay with them for at least a day or two. So Mom let them keep me for the summer. Let the weird, hyperactive kid who liked to play princess be someone else's problem for a few months, right? Aunt Pearl and Uncle Jim would get to have a kid visit, Mom would get to party and not worry about having to make anyone a meal once or twice a day, so it was wins all around—except, of course, for the eight-year-old kid, who got to spend the next two months with a seventy-something-year-old man's hand down his pants, and being forced to shove his hand down the old man's pants in return."

"Jesus." Brendan wiped a hand down his face, pulling at the corners of his mouth, and sank onto a chair across from the bed. He looked like he might throw up. I didn't blame him, though I just felt numb. Hollow. I was inured to it and could recite the facts with detachment. It wasn't the first time I'd told this story. My therapist in high school had eventually coaxed it out of me. She'd then promptly broken confidentiality and told my aunt and uncle about it. The only reason I knew she'd done so was because she told me herself; my aunt and uncle never brought the subject up. It had just hung there, ignored. I never knew if they believed me, if they blamed me, if they hated him, or what.

"I don't know why he bothered," I said, strangely warmed up to the subject now and unwilling to stop until I'd gotten it all out. "He never got hard, not once in the whole time. He would just make me . . . *squeeze* that goddamn, clammy, disgusting thing until he finally got frustrated that he couldn't get it up. Then he'd blame me. But he'd take me out fishing, buy me toys and treats, do all sorts of nice things for me. He called me his little buddy and I loved the attention, but it came with a price tag, you know? The one time I tried to passively resist by positioning myself in a way that he couldn't grope me when he snuck into my room at night, he said, 'Oh, I guess you don't want to go fishing tomorrow, after all,' and I just rolled over and let him do it. Never even considered telling. I guess those fishing trips and gifts were more important than refusing to do something I knew was wrong."

"Topher—" Brendan was wearing a sympathetic but detached face. A therapist's face. I'd spent a lot of time looking at exactly that sort of face since that summer. "It's not uncommon for victims to cooperate with their abusers. Especially when they're kids getting the first positive attention—or any attention, really— they've received in their entire lives. It's why abusers often target neglected kids. They'll go along, no matter how much it hurts or how much they hate what's being done to them, or what they're being forced to do."

"I didn't hate it." Oh look, there were the tears. Weird, how sometimes I began crying while not actually *feeling* anything. My last therapist had called me on that all the time.

Something's coming up, she'd say when I'd start blinking fast out of the blue. *What is it?*

I don't know, I'd answer. Because I didn't. I never did. I couldn't even begin to name what was causing the tears or what emotion I was experiencing.

I wiped them away as they spilled from my lashes.

Brendan's expression became even more gentle and sympathetic as he drew on his shirt. "It's not uncommon to respond physically, either. Even to feel pleasure . . ."

"No. You don't get it. I didn't *feel* anything when he was touching me. It didn't feel good. It didn't hurt. There was just . . . nothing. I never felt *anything* when he had his hand on my dick."

"Blocking out the memory of the sensations is a pretty typical response as well. Bad or good."

"Couldya quit analyzing me, Professor?" I snapped. "I've been over all that with my shrink, thanks. I mean, who *doesn't* feel anything when someone's hand is on their junk?"

"You're right. I'm sorry." He bowed his head, bending over to pull on his socks. "That's not who you need me to be for you right now. Guess I was just trying to distance myself."

I shrugged. Whatever. This wasn't about him. "Okay, look. I don't know. Maybe I got hard. Maybe he hurt me. Maybe I came. Maybe he did other things to me that I can't even remember. Worse things. Maybe it was all of the above. But I don't remember feeling any of that. Just . . . nothing. All I remember is what *he* felt like when he made me touch that . . . that *thing*. I don't know what he would have done if he had been able to get it up, but when he couldn't, it was my fault, you know? My failure. I couldn't even do the one thing he asked in exchange for all he did for me. I wasn't his little buddy, then. I was that little nigger sissy-boy who was too useless to do even the one thing nigger sissy-boys are good for."

"Oh, *Topher*." His own eyes were wet now, and his face positively anguished. He was aching for me. Not pitying, just hurting because he cared and it hurt him to know this. More tears spilled down my face. When was the last time someone had cared enough about me to feel my pain?

"Where was your mother in all this?"

"She stayed with other relatives. I only saw her once or twice. Around the beginning of August, I don't know, I-I-I think I must have started acting out or something. By that time I was really starting to hate Uncle Jim, and he wasn't paying all that special attention to me anymore. Anyway, they decided I should go back to my mother. So, they called her one night and told her they would be dropping me off where she was staying—which they did. And then they drove off as I knocked on the door. No one answered. So I knocked again, louder, and there still wasn't an answer. I was used to her being hungover, so I played in the yard for a while, probably until early afternoon. Tried to entertain myself, but I got lonely and I missed her. I wanted my momma and she knew I was coming, so why wasn't she there? What would I do if she never came back? They'd left me on the doorstep like unwanted baggage, you know?"

Tears kept pouring down my cheeks, and Brendan looked ill again.

"So I started pounding on the door and screaming for her and no one came, so I went around to the back door of the trailer and pounded and screamed there, and finally her cousin's ex-husband opened it, really angrily, and he was nude. She was rolling out of bed behind him, dragging a sheet around her. And there I was, sobbing, and he was yelling at *me* for waking them up and bawling on his doorstep. And she didn't stop him. She just told me to hush and sat me down in front of the TV with a bowl of cereal, then went back to bed with him while I tried not to hear them fucking in the next room."

I wiped away the last of those strangely emotionless tears, feeling hollow. Finally, I lay down on the bed and curled up on my side. "You know, I'm mostly okay with it, really. I started therapy the year after that. I don't remember what my behavior must have been like once I got home, but obviously it was a problem because suddenly there were social workers and psychologists and behavioral therapists, and they were taking me off sugar and caffeine and putting me on a special diet for some reason. So I've dealt with it, put in a lot of work."

I don't know why I didn't tell him that I hadn't told a single therapist about it until I was sixteen, and then only because she was the first one to ask the goddamn question. How had none of them ever guessed?

"Until this morning I never even knew I was capable of freaking out like that about it. So I guess, just . . . don't ever make me touch you if I don't want to, okay? And don't take it personally if I don't want anything to do with it when it's soft."

"Of course not." He looked down at his folded hands, his eyes troubled, and I knew, somehow I just *knew*, that the next words out of his mouth were going to be the long-delayed suggestion that we stop.

I didn't want to hear that. At this moment they'd feel like rejection and I couldn't cope with that.

"Can you come lay down with me? Please?"

His face was conflicted as he looked over at me, but finally he sagged in defeat and crawled onto the bed behind me, spooning me. His arms were tight and warm, and I was chilled even though it was almost mid-June. I wish I could say it felt safe, but I don't think anything could have made me feel safe just now, raw and exposed the way I was. But at least I wasn't alone. At least someone cared for once.

There was more to the story that I was just too exhausted now to tell. Like going back to Alabama when I was nineteen, when my grandfather passed away. Aunt Pearl and Uncle Jim had been there at the funeral, and even though my family knew what he'd done to me, no one stepped in when Uncle Jim opened his arms and expected a hug. Aunt Blythe had just watched me cautiously, like she was waiting for me to make a scene.

I'd let that fucker hug me rather than make the rest of them uncomfortable with my drama.

I still had a couple hours until I needed to be at the body art studio, so we lay there for a while. Not speaking. Not moving. Lost in our thoughts. Well, I was lost in memories, really. As always, once they came up, it was hard to shut them off again. They replayed obsessively, like an old record skipping over and over. Maybe I dozed a bit, but if I did, it wasn't deeply or for long.

Our stomachs were starting to rumble their displeasure over having delayed breakfast when Brendan finally spoke again.

"I've lost count of the number of ways this is wrong, Topher."

"I know."

"We need to stop."

"I know."

"I'm being selfish."

"We both are."

And we were. We were both betraying people we loved. We were destroying each other.

His lips touched my shoulder, followed by a breathy sigh. "The difference is, I'm supposed to know better."

That was true, too. I could chalk all this up to youth and impetuosity. I had far less to lose, though it killed me to think what would happen if we broke Mo's heart. He didn't have that excuse. He was supposed to be the mature one, the responsible one, the wiser one.

The faithful one.

He was supposed to be the one with the self-control to not let this happen. And *that* was how I was destroying him. Because I knew he was too weak to stop, and I played on it, abetted it, even though it made him feel worse about himself. It wasn't deliberate. I didn't mean to do it, but somehow, I ended up doing it anyway. I was strong enough to walk away. I knew that without question. I had it in me to do what he couldn't, but instead I drew him in. All the reasons he was bad for me were plain as day. But I was bad for him, too. I was Kryptonite to his willpower.

We would stop. We would. But not before it hurt a lot more. I knew it was coming, it had to be, and I didn't care.

I turned and slipped my thigh between his, rubbing it back and forth against his crotch until his fly began to swell.

"Know better tomorrow," I murmured, and kissed him.

For a moment, his hands tightened on my shoulders, like he might push me away, like he might *finally* find the strength to stop after all. And then he groaned and slid them around me instead. His mouth slanted across mine, hard and hungry, and he rolled me over onto my back, his weight settling upon me.

CHAPTER FIFTEEN

Without you I think I could be
Happier than with you, maybe
You would finally learn to stop avoiding

— CASEY STRATTON, "THE HARDEST PART"

I'd been working for Geoffrey for a week when he informed me that Robin would have some work for me today down at the art gallery. So after lunch, I walked down the street to find Ling in the front of the gallery, moving around paintings that looked much too large for her to be lifting in her condition.

"Here, let me help you with that!" I dropped my backpack and rushed over to try to take the large canvas from her, only to find that it was a lot lighter than the size would indicate.

She smirked at me. "You notice I'm not moving any of the framed ones."

"Right. Sorry." I stepped back and ducked my head, my face warm. "How are you, Ling?"

"The size of a house and very, very ready to take some time off, put my feet up, and spend my days eating bonbons while oiled cabana boys fan me with palm fronds."

119

I laughed. "They have oiled cabana boys with palm fans in this town? Awesome! Where do I sign up?"

She chuckled and hung the painting on another wall. I noticed that around the shop, there were a number of empty display easels and wall mounts. "We're rearranging some stock, setting out some of the new inventory Robin picked up in Chicago. You're here today to get familiar with things, since I'll be leaving in a couple of weeks. And to move the heavier pieces."

"Okay." I nodded briskly. "Just tell me where to start."

It turned out that Ling was actually willing to let me do all the lifting, light or heavy, while she sat on a stool and directed traffic. She instructed me about how to move the canvases and framed works without (hopefully) damaging them, and started teaching me a little bit about how the inventory was cataloged so that they knew what they had sold and when. I'd nearly finished moving the last piece she wanted moved when jogging footsteps drummed down the stairs in the back of the shop.

My first sight of Robin said that he and Geoffrey had obviously cast themselves in the wrong roles. Geoff, the clean-cut one, should be running the art gallery, while Robin, with tattoos starting at his temples and twining down both sides of his neck to disappear under his shirt, was obviously meant to be doing body art. If not for the ink, he would have looked like a Ken-doll clone: tanned, blond, and muscular. He should have been slathered in baby oil lifting weights on Muscle Beach or something. I stared at him for a moment, and he stared back.

"Robin," Ling said, "this is Topher. Topher, Robin."

"Hi." I gave him a friendly smile, sticking my hand out.

He shook it, blinking at me, then shook his head. "Well, I'll be fucked sideways and backwards."

I frowned, feeling hugely self-conscious. "It's the hair, right? People always wonder about the hair."

"Nope. Actually I've seen *that* before."

My eyebrows rose. "You have?"

"Mm-hm." He crooked a finger, a smile flirting at his lips. "Come back to the storeroom. I want to show you something."

That could have been interpreted in some really filthy ways, but he wouldn't do that in front of his not-quite sister-in-law, right? Ling merely watched us with wry amusement. "Don't worry about me. I'll just mind the store."

Confused, I followed Robin into the back room, where he began sorting through carefully wrapped canvases that hadn't been stored in the vertical racks lining the wall yet. Finally he located three large portrait-sized ones and propped them against a wall, lined up in a row like a triptych. Then he stripped off the coverings.

"Holy shit," I breathed, staring at myself.

Well, it was me, yet not really. I mean, clearly it was, but not anything like I'd ever seen myself.

The first one, with a wispy background that suggested feathers, gave the impression of an angelic figure with my face, dark skin contrasting with the soft, golden lighting. I gleamed with a subtle gilt shimmer and my eyes both laughed and burned. I looked eager and innocent, and maybe a little nervous, as I lay on the bed awaiting an unknown lover.

The second was darker, as though hours had passed since the first and the sun had set. I looked lazy, heavy-lidded, debauched. A slightly smug smile tugged at the corners of my mouth. One very satisfied fallen angel.

The last one made my throat ache a little. The background was lighter again, this time touched with pink over the gold, as if the night was over and an unseen sun was rising. I was sprawled on the bed like I was near collapse, limp, dazed, exhausted. Love bites speckled my throat and finger-shaped bruises darkened my wrists and hips. Not only had the angel fallen, he'd been utterly and completely wrecked in the best possible way.

If I ignored the eyes, I would think the subject of the painting was ready to fall into a contented sleep. But the eyes ruined that illusion. They were wide open, and too old, too deep, too *knowing* for the age of the angel. They were the eyes of someone who'd seen way too much pain and ugliness. Cautious. Vulnerable. Soft. Sad. Full of wistful yearning.

It wasn't the narrative of that carefree and passionate night I'd spent with Jace, not as I recalled it. And yet it was, from sundown to sunrise, told in stages.

They were gorgeous paintings, but what sort of impression must I have left on Jace for him to see me like that? They weren't me. Not me *at all*. The semi-angelic young man in those paintings was idealized beyond all recognition, someone mythical and amazing, and that *wasn't me*. I was just Topher, the fucked-up kid who was betraying his best friend by making her dad an adulterer, the kid who would probably never finish college and who couldn't seem to achieve anything more than mediocrity in anything he pursued. Not because he didn't want more, but because something seemed to block him every time he tried to strive for it. In fact, it seemed like the only amazing thing I'd ever done was that night with Jace.

I wished Robin weren't standing there, a complete stranger. The sight of those paintings was too intimate. It left me exposed, stripped bare, and not in the sense of nudity. His seeing them—or perhaps just my reaction to them—was an invasion of privacy way beyond the physical stuff.

"You do good modeling work," he said kindly as I took it all in. "There are a lot of local artists around here. I'm sure you could get more gigs."

I shook my head quickly in refusal of that notion, still unable to form any coherent sentences.

"Do you want to sit down, have some tea? We can get to know each other."

Finally I swallowed and found my voice again. "Yeah," I whispered. "Please."

"So, you buy a lot of art from Jace?" I managed to ask, trying to figure out *something* to say to cover my confusion. Why did it bother me so much to see myself portrayed that way? It wasn't me; it was just some random guy's imagination, using me as a model. It shouldn't have mattered.

Robin nodded, sticking a cup of orange and cinnamon–

scented tea in front of me. I sipped it and suppressed a shudder. I've never quite understood herbal teas, at least not without a truckload of sugar. They smelled pretty, but never seemed to have any flavor. Might as well be drinking plain hot water.

"He usually does at least one show a year here. Joscelin Sieger originals sell well for me, and I usually get first pick of his new pieces because he and Geoff went to art school together. Those paintings I just showed you are some of his best work yet."

Don't ask about Jace. Don't ask about Jace. Don't—

"Is he local?"

Shit. Thanks, mouth.

"No, he's based out of Chicago. He only comes up for shows and to visit me and Geoff."

I nodded, trying to convince myself that I was relieved to hear that. I'd probably be long gone before Jace ever came back. That was a good thing, right?

Right?

Robin leaned back in his chair as I made myself take another sip of the tea, trying to pretend I liked it.

"So, we never got a chance to do an interview. Tell me a little about yourself, Topher."

It was hard to make my brain jump tracks away from Jace and those paintings, and I stammered for a moment.

"Um, well, I'm a competitive swimmer up at Grand Valley, still trying to decide on my major. Geoff probably already told you that I really have no experience with art—or body art, really—but I've got no problem doing grunt work."

"You'll be here through almost the end of August?" Robin gave me an assessing look and stood, crossing to the fridge in the office and grabbing a bottle of water for me, then taking away the flavorless tea.

"Um . . ." I looked away, kicking myself. Fuck, why hadn't I thought of this before I told them I'd be available for employment? "I, uh . . . I've been staying at my friend's family's house in Douglas since the semester ended, and I was supposed to be there for the summer but that's probably going to change soon. In a couple weeks I don't think I'll be able to stay there anymore. But as long as I can find someplace not too far away, I can commute. I've got a car. It's kinda on its last legs, but it's holding up for now, and it doesn't look too beat-up to park around here. My sister used to drive it for work, so it's clean and looks good, and . . ." Robin blinked at me and I trailed off, realizing I'd been babbling. "So, uh, yeah. I can be here through the end of the summer."

Except, of course, that finding someplace to live was going to eat up the money I was supposed to be saving, which meant I wasn't really going to be any better off.

Maybe I could sleep in my car, drive up to the aquatic center in Holland to shower. Or maybe they had showers at one of the public beaches, so I could save gas . . .

Robin tilted his head. "Your friend's family had a change of plans?"

"Yeah. Something like that." I didn't dare meet his eyes, because I was pretty sure my guilt and misery were written all over my face, and after the shock of seeing those paintings, I was just too raw to be able to hide it.

Sometime in the next two weeks, Brendan and I would *have* to end things. We'd have to. This mess definitely had an expiration date, and the clock was running down. In two weeks, Mo and her mom would be coming. Mo would only be there one week, but Brendan's wife—and for the life of me, I couldn't make myself think of her by name—would be there for three. There was no way I could stay in the house for that time, pretending nothing had ever happened. Maybe for a week, while Mo was there—though that would be miserable, and Mo would see right through it and it would all go up in flames anyway—but definitely not for three weeks. I couldn't sleep in that dormer bedroom with him below me in bed with his wife. I'd screw up. I'd give it away. And if Brendan decided to come clean, I *definitely* couldn't stay there anymore.

So either way, I was pretty much screwed where the housing situation was concerned.

I was screwed on a lot of other fronts, too. But focusing on the most immediate one at least kept my mind occupied and kept me from bursting into tears every time I thought of the colossal fuck-up I'd committed.

"Your family's out of the picture, I'm guessing." Robin's gaze had sharpened. It was less assessing and more dissecting now. And not in the easy, comfortable way with which Jace had just looked at me and understood me, either. No. Robin was cutting deep, with a dull scalpel and a blunt probe. Which was pretty fitting since I'd felt like a frog stretched out and pinned down belly-up on a wax slab from the moment I'd seen those damned paintings.

"Yeah." Robin nodded, murmuring to himself rather than me, answering his own question. "Estranged from your family, almost no friends because you're from someplace where they don't particularly welcome your skin color or orientation. Afraid to really open up to new people because somewhere along the way you learned just about everyone's out to hurt you. You're pretty much all alone, aren't you?"

I stared at him wide-eyed, my breath coming quick and shallow, and tried to blink away the burning in my eyes and the tension in my throat. Fuck it all, why did I always have to wear my emotions on my sleeve? How did people suss me out so fast?

"That's not really your business, is it?" I snapped, doing that going-on-the-offense thing I do when I panic. "I'm not sure what this has to do with me working for you."

Bravado for the win.

He crossed his arms over his chest, and one corner of his mouth lifted. "You think you're the only young gay man who's ever been there?"

I scoffed, looking pointedly around the pretty, expensive art gallery perfectly suited to this well-heeled vacation town. "You're doing okay for yourself."

"Yeah, I am. I got fucking lucky. Some of my friends didn't, though, and they're dead now. Killed by fag bashers, overdoses, or suicide. Infected with HIV they got peddling their asses on the streets. You don't know me, Topher, and you don't know what I've seen in the years it took me to become the man I am now. But I know you. You might be all alone, but you're sure as fuck not unique. And right now, I think I'm looking at you standing on life's big old chess board, and you're about two moves in any direction from being one of the ones who ends up in a bad place."

I scowled. "What's it to you, anyhow?"

Robin gave a negligent shrug. "Call it a pay-it-forward thing. See, I've been on chat with my husband every night for the last week, and he's been telling me about this kid he hired on a whim and gut instinct to help us out. Sweet guy, funny, hard worker, polite, eager to learn, and scared as fuck about something."

I flinched. I couldn't help it. "Oh, great, so while I've been working for him, Geoff has been taking notes and gossiping with you about me?"

Robin shook his head, still looking amused. "I love Geoff to death, but he and I both know that when someone's in trouble, I'm the better guy to handle it, so he's been waiting for me to get here." He sighed. "Then of course, I meet you and I realize you're the same guy in those paintings, and that young man in the paintings is a *lot* of things, but scared isn't one of them. So I'm guessing whatever it is, it's a recent thing. Maybe something going on right now. And I'm guessing you've never had a gay adult in your life—someone who's seen a lot of what we face and the sorts of mistakes we make because of it, and knows how to navigate it all. At least, not one who went that extra step and took you in hand and said, *you're not alone.*"

Fuck, fuck, *fuck!* I was *not* going to start bawling in front of this nosy, presumptuous asshole. I *wasn't.*

So I blew up instead.

"Well, kum-ba-fucking-yah!" I flung myself up from the table, beyond caring that I was pretty much torpedoing my only chance at employment. This chucklenuts had started it. "Great! I'm not alone. Except maybe I want to be alone, hmmm? Maybe I *should* be alone, didya think of that when you were looking in your crystal ball, Madame Sees-All-Knows-All? Maybe I've done something so monumentally fucking *stupid* that the only possible outcome is for me to wind up alone because that's *exactly* what I fucking deserve."

Of course, to my utter mortification, he looked amused. I half expected him to start golf clapping.

"Ooh, epic bitch fit! I give it five stars. Haven't seen one that good in forever, and I live in a town full of queens, so that's saying something. Now, if you've got that out of your system, sit your ass down and let's talk."

I groaned and sank back into my chair, dropping my forehead to the surface of the table. "I'm sorry."

When I looked up again, he just shrugged at me, as if my tantrum had barely even registered. Or perhaps he'd been expecting it. "I've seen worse. I used to counsel LGBT street kids at a shelter. So, what's this tragically idiotic thing you've done that's going to leave you homeless and alone?"

A fucking counselor. Great. It seemed to be my destiny to be surrounded by shrinks and social workers. My forehead hit the table again with a thud. *Ow.* The words left me in a rush.

"I'm-fucking-the-married-closeted-father-of-my-only-close-friend-in-the-entire-world-and-his-wife-is-going-to-be-here-in-two-weeks."

I heard the hiss as Robin sucked his breath in between his teeth. "Ouch."

"Yeah." I sighed, my forehead rubbing against the table as I nodded miserably. At least he didn't try to deny the idiotic part.

"You know there's *absolutely* no way that can end well."

"Duh."

"So what are you going to do?"

I shrugged, sitting up. I actually felt a little better, having confessed my secret to someone. It didn't improve the situation, but at least someone knew and maybe even understood.

"Well, it can't go on. Whether we confess or not, we need to stop. We're just . . . dragging our feet doing it."

Robin nodded, looking relieved. "Okay. Good. At least you're not in love with him."

"No." I dropped my gaze to my hands, folded on my lap. "I'm not sure if that makes it better or worse. If I were in love with him, at least I'd have something resembling a worthwhile excuse for doing it. 'Sorry I destroyed your family, Mo, but, you know, it was just a fling.' *Ugh*."

"Is he in love with you?"

I shook my head, not looking up. "I really doubt it. I think mostly he feels sorry for me. I don't mean in a pity-fuck kind of way. I mean, he sees me as someone he just wants to help, someone he likes and feels bad for, but there's nothing he can do about shit that happened years before he came along, so he just gives me what he can."

"Somehow I doubt it's as selfless as all that." I looked up to catch a wry twist pulling at Robin's lips.

"Maybe not, but he's not the bad guy here. Or at least not the only one." I shrugged helplessly. "I knew what I was doing. We both know we're wrong, but we keep going anyway. He's not pressuring me or taking advantage of me. He promised that whatever happens, he'll treat me with respect. So, now it's just a matter of finding the right moment to end it and moving out. And praying that we don't completely destroy the people we care about."

"Hmmm." Robin didn't seem convinced, and I gave him a questioning look. "Sounds like you're thinking of spilling your guts."

"What else can I do? I can't keep this a secret. Especially from Mo. She's— She'll know I'm hiding something."

"I can't tell you what to do there, but look. Before you go making any confessions, be sure you've got your head on right about why you're doing it and what the consequences will be."

"I know what the consequences will be. I'm going to lose my best friend, not to mention the rent-free room for the summer, which means I'm not going to be able to save enough money to go back to school in the fall."

"I meant for your friend. I get that you're in a bad spot and it's hard to see outside that, but think what the consequences will be for her. Are you thinking of confessing just to make yourself feel better? Is it going to improve your friend's life in any way? Will it improve yours? His? *Who* will be helped if you tell the truth?" I met Robin's eyes and must have looked unconvinced. Keep it a secret? Live with that lie? *Really?* "I'm not saying don't confess, but ask yourself those questions before you do. You won't be confessing just an affair, you'll be outing someone who maybe isn't willing to come out yet, and I really hope I don't need to tell you how catastrophic that can be for some people. Don't charge into it because you feel guilty and you're hoping for absolution."

I bowed my head and nodded. "Okay. Yeah. I get what you're saying."

"As for finding a place to stay, unfortunately I don't know you well enough to offer you a key so you can crash out on the sofa in the office upstairs. Now, that's no reflection on *you* personally; I wouldn't allow anyone I didn't know *extremely* well to have unsupervised access to a building with this much valuable inventory in it. I will, however, give you our home and cell numbers. If you get stuck with nowhere to go, call us. We've got a sofa at our house, too. We also have a guest bedroom, but it's occupied for the next few months."

I frowned, caught squirming somewhere between relief and pride. "Thanks, but I need to stop relying on others to bail me out."

"It's up to you, but there's nothing wrong with accepting help for a while when you need it, until you can get on your feet. As long as you *are* trying to get on your feet, which I don't think is a problem here. You just need an opportunity." He chuckled softly. "Which we can give you. I can also offer you an absolutely ironclad guarantee that neither of us will try to fuck you. What I *can't* guarantee is an uninterrupted night's sleep. That is, unless you have a magical ability to tune out babies crying."

My head came up. "Ling's staying with you?"

"She'll be with us for the first three to six months after the baby is born." He smiled softly. "She's our surrogate, and she's going to stay on for a while to breastfeed. Then, once Zhen is sleeping through the night, Ling will go back to her own apartment."

"Wow. That's amazing." I blinked, touched by this for some reason I couldn't really name. The idea that Ling would do something like that for her adopted brother and his husband was astonishing.

Maybe because I couldn't see one of my own sisters doing anything of the sort for me. I was lucky if they remembered to call me on my birthday.

Was this how family was supposed to do things? The question lingered with me as I thanked Robin again for his offer and returned to work.

CHAPTER SIXTEEN

I predicted this
Saw where I could bleed the whole time
Tried to hide every knife
Should have known you'd find a way to strike

— CASEY STRATTON, "NAILED TO THE CROSS"

Brendan and I didn't even make it two more weeks.

At the beginning of the last week of June, I came home from playing at the coffeehouse to find Brendan asleep on the sofa, his laptop still running on the coffee table beside him and his reading glasses askew on his face. I looked at him for a long, wistful moment, taking in how beautiful I found him and how much I'd come to enjoy being with him.

I didn't love him, but I would sure as hell miss him.

Something pulsed in my chest; I thought it was surety. I stripped off my shirt and kicked off my shoes, knowing as I did so that this would be the last time. A good-bye. Tomorrow morning I would end it.

He came awake as I crawled half-nude over his body, giving me a drowsy, dopey smile.

"Hi."

"Hi." I smiled back, letting myself be happy at the sight of him. Not sad. Sad would come later. For now I just wanted to enjoy him one final time.

I carefully pulled his glasses off his face and set them on his laptop, dipping for a slow kiss. His arms came around me, pulling me flush atop him, and I ground my hips down as my tongue slipped into his mouth, using my body to jumpstart his arousal.

"Topher . . ." he groaned, his voice full of longing. He cupped a hand to the back of my head and took charge of the kiss, tipping my head to angle my mouth against his, thrusting his tongue demandingly into my mouth. His fingers dug into my back, hands sliding over my skin. Beneath the rocking of my pelvis, he swelled, thick and eager.

We didn't make it up the stairs. At least not right away.

I don't know if I did something to clue him in that this was the last night or what, but suddenly we were desperate, needy, clothes flying and hands grasping with bruising force. It was a bookend to the insanity of our first night together, heedless and rough.

We didn't have lube down here, but that was okay. Appropriate, even. Again with the symmetry. We would end the same way we'd begun, with hurt and wild need. I thrust spit-slicked fingers into my ass, taking only a little more care than I had that first night. I wanted to ache the next day, to feel it in every muscle and nerve. In all honesty, I'd discovered I kind of enjoyed the feeling, the merciless burn as unready muscles fought against what I was trying to force them to accept when I pushed myself onto his cock.

I tipped my head back and yelled up into the vaulted ceiling, momentarily overcome. Once I sank down on him fully, I paused, panting softly, waiting to relax before I moved. And then I rode him, staring down at his enraptured face. He looked up at me like I was something wonderful, something miraculous, and that look threatened to make me sad again. So I closed my eyes and blocked it out, focusing on lust and pleasure, on the feel of his hands riding my hips, helping me move, on his grunts and sighs and, finally, whispered pleas.

When it was over, I sank down against him, limp and sweating, my cum growing sticky between our chests. His arms surrounded me, and I felt cared for. As if maybe there were a sliver of right in it to offset just a little bit of all the wrong.

Maybe if I'd ended it then, the whole disastrous next morning wouldn't have happened. But the tenderness felt too good, so I lingered in it. I let Brendan lead me up the stairs by the hand, and into the shower, and then I curled up in his bed with him wrapped around me. And when he woke me up early the next morning, hard and ready and rocking against me, I decided the night wasn't *quite* over yet.

I NEEDED to get up and do my morning swim so I could get to work, but first we had to talk. I was trying to come up with the words to tell Brendan we were done when his sigh ruffled my hair.

"Adele and Morgan will be here this weekend."

"Yeah." My finger traced lazy patterns on his chest.

"It's . . ." Another sigh. "I don't know how to say this without sounding crass, which really isn't how I mean it, but you know it's probably not a good idea for you to be here while they're here."

"Yeah, I know. I've been trying to figure out my options there."

"I'll call around today, see if any of the local B&Bs have a vacancy for the next few weeks. If not, then I'll get you a room at a motel, or maybe the Dunes. I'll come see you when I can get away."

Everything within me went tight and cold, hurting like I'd just been impaled on a shard of ice. I jerked my head off his chest.

"What?"

I stared at him in disbelief, adrenaline kicking in. My breath came short and shallow, my heart racing with the sickening flood of anxiety that always preceded a confrontation.

"I know it's not ideal, but it's better than running the risk of letting something slip . . ."

I would not cry. I *would not* cry. I rolled out of his arms and off the bed, storming out of the bedroom and down the stairs to gather up the clothes I'd left scattered around the living room the night before.

"Topher!" Brendan came hopping out on one foot, nearly tripping as he hastily pulled on a pair of pajama bottoms. "Come on, Topher. I'm doing the best I can, here. It's only for a few weeks. I don't know what you—"

"Get out of my way," I snarled when he stood on the stairs one rise above me, blocking my progress. I clutched my clothes in front of my nude body like a shield, trying to hide the way I was shaking.

The best thing I could say about the morning was that he did as I demanded, standing aside to let me pass. But he chased after me as I rushed for my room in the attic.

"Topher, just stop. What is it?"

"What is it? *What is it?*" I began dumping clothes out of the dresser drawers, snatching them on as quickly as I could before hauling my suitcase and large duffel out of the closet. I would not cry. I *would not* cry! "Brendan, what was the *only* fucking thing I asked from you that first night? Do you remember?"

He blinked, scrubbing a hand through his tousled hair. "You . . . you asked me to respect you. Which I do, I'm just trying to—"

"Oh really?" I gave him a derisive sneer as I threw wadded clothes into my bags and began slamming about, looking for odds and ends I might have missed. "That's what you call this? You offer to put me up like your personal rentboy in some no-tell motel and promise to drop by every few days for a booty call while your wife's in town, and you think that's not *demeaning*? Well, fuck you."

"What do you expect me to do? Toss you out on your ass?"

I paused to give him a long, injured look. "At least that would have been honest."

"So, according to you, discarding you like I don't give a shit is less demeaning than trying to take care of you."

He folded his arms across his chest, leaning a bare shoulder against the door jamb. He was positioning himself like he was looking down at me, like he was the only reasonable one, patiently and maturely waiting out my tantrum, and I fucking *hated* him for it. Condescending jackass.

"I never asked you to take care of me! This? This is exactly what I *didn't* want. You *promised* me . . ." I shook my head, my eyes burning as I turned my attention back to packing. I jerked the zipper of my suitcase so hard I'm surprised I didn't pull the damn tab off. "Let's be honest, hmmm? You're not trying to take care of me, you're trying to take care of *you*. You want to have your respectable, white-bread, married, *straight* family life as well as your faggy brown boy toy on the side, and seriously? Fuck that shit. I *trusted* you, Brendan! I trusted you to respect me enough not to pull something like this, not to try to keep me dangling along so you could have it both ways without giving up anything."

He gave me an incredulous look. "You want me to give up my *family*?"

"*No*! But you don't get to have it all. None of us do. We agreed that this was wrong. We agreed that we needed to stop. We've been clear on that from the very beginning. Why couldn't you just have *left* it at that?"

"So you're upset that I didn't dump you?"

Fucking hell, how did this once-intelligent man become so damned clueless?

"Oh, for fuck's sake, get over yourself! Hate to break it to you, boyfriend, but you are *not* all that. I'm upset because you think you can play games with me, and that is *so* not going to happen. I'm fucking *better* than that!"

He rubbed his forehead as though he had a headache brewing. "I don't understand you, Topher. I don't get why you'd think I was doing that."

"Yeah, well there's your first problem. *You don't get it.* You can't even see what you did. You're going to sit here today and you're going to convince yourself that you were right, and I was unreasonable, and you won't even *think* about what you just tried to make me into." I hauled my backpack over my shoulder, then the strap of my laptop case. The strap of my duffel bag hung over those two and *fuck* did all that weight on my shoulder hurt. I wheeled my suitcase behind me, my progress awkward, bulky, and off-balance, and glared at Brendan until he stepped aside to let me bump down the stairs. I'd have to make another trip for my keyboard, damn it. "But hey, it's not my problem, now. You think what you want. I'm gone."

He sighed and reached for my suitcase. "Will you at least let me help you down the stairs?"

"Fuck off." I'd rather break my neck than let him give me a second of assistance.

"Topher, come on!" Now he sounded annoyed, and seriously, fuck him, he didn't get to be pissy over this. I turned around and gave him a withering look.

"Be sure you clear the lube out of the bedside table before you bang your wife in that room. It's a dead giveaway."

I knew he must have been watching me from the house as I stacked my shit in my car, but he didn't try to talk to me again when I made my second trip to get my keyboard. Feeling his gaze on me, I kept my head down and refused to wipe my eyes until after I'd driven away.

CHAPTER SEVENTEEN

Give me one good reason
That I should let you stay
That I shouldn't walk away
And cry me a fucking river
You can't deliver anything but pain

— CASEY STRATTON, "CONGRATULATIONS"

"Well, look at it this way," Robin reasoned as I sat with him and Geoff at their kitchen table that night, half-plastered from the pitcher of margarita they'd blended up. Was I going to have a tequila hangover in the morning? Oh, honey, you bet your sweet ass I was. And how many fucks did I give?

Not a one.

"Even if you *were* overreacting to read what you read into this guy's offer—which I don't think you were, though I doubt he actually thought it through enough to intend it to be read that way—you still have to ask yourself: What's in it for *you*, hanging around some motel room waiting for a married man to make a booty call? What benefit would *you* get out of that situation, or out of prolonging your relationship with him? He might not have meant it to be an *insulting* offer, but it was absolutely a one hundred percent *selfish* offer. There was no upside for you whatsoever, unless the sex really was just that amazing."

I shook my head before taking another drink, then shrugged morosely as more lime-flavored bliss washed over my tongue. "Eh. It was good, but not good enough for that."

"Well. There you have it."

I wasn't sure what to make of the fact that Robin was quickly becoming a sort of mentor-confidant for me. Geoff was a little more reserved, though he was kind. I didn't know what to make of him, yet, either. He sat beside me, considerably less wasted than I was, nodding calm agreement to Robin's assessment of the situation.

The fact was, Robin kind of had a point that I'd never had another gay friend, much less one who might be older and wiser. I'd hooked up with guys on campus, but never hung out with them. The only friend I'd ever had that I could turn to for relationship advice was Mo. Before her, the one person I'd had to talk to about my sexuality was my therapist, who really was no expert, even if she hadn't been quite as bad as the guy I'd been seeing before I moved away from Flint. He'd spent my sixth-grade year trying to coax me out of my "confusion" about sexuality and gender.

"Yeah, you're right. I know you're right." I sighed as Geoff refilled my glass, God bless him. "I guess I just thought better of him than that. I would have been fine with breaking it off. I was *prepared* for that. I mean, it would have sucked because if Mo finds out, it will ruin our friendship and I won't even have anything worthwhile to show for it. But to hang around waiting for a married man to make up his mind? Even *I* know that's a dead end."

What really stung, though, was the fact that Brendan hadn't been concerned enough for me to think of it from that perspective, to ask himself what he could offer that would make it worthwhile. And I didn't mean materially—I didn't want a single fucking thing from him, materially—I meant emotionally. What could he put on the table that would make that sort of arrangement anything but damaging for me?

I'd known from the start that I wasn't good for him, but he'd never bothered to ask himself if he was good for me.

That's the part that made me want to curl up and cry. I'd thought we each had something the other needed. But from his perspective, it had been all about him from the beginning. All the trust I'd put in him, all the things I'd shared with him, and it was all about him.

When I was well and truly shit-faced, Geoff forced two Tylenol and a large glass of water down my throat, and they poured me onto their sofa with a pillow and blanket. They had a nice house with good furniture, so at least it was a comfortable sofa.

The room was doing that spinny thing it does when you're drunk and it feels like the surface you're lying on won't stop moving. It actually took me a while to fall asleep because of that, and just as I was nodding off, a thought jerked me awake.

Even if Brendan decided not to tell Mo and his wife about the affair, how would I explain no longer staying at the house?

Digging for my phone, I quickly fumbled out an email.

Mo,
Too drunk to type much. Finally making some friends here in town. Might be hanging out with them a lot more in the next few weeks, staying at their place so I'm not underfoot all the time, so don't freak if I'm not at the house when you get back. See you soon. <3
T

She would never buy it, but at least it would give Brendan a chance to figure out what he was going to tell her before she demanded a better explanation from me.

Setting the phone back on the floor, I finally passed out.

THAT FRIDAY WAS the day before Mo and her mom were due to arrive for the week of the Fourth. At that point I'd been staying with Robin and Geoff for four days. Brendan had tried calling me a number of times, but I always ignored the calls, and deleted the messages without listening to them.

I'd worked this morning doing inventory at the art gallery, and now I had the afternoon to myself before heading to the tattoo parlor in the evening to help clean everything up. Feeling flush with my second paycheck deposited in my bank account, I treated myself to lunch and went for a walk around town. I was turning off Culver Street to pass through Coghlin Park, heading down to the boardwalk, when Brendan jogged up behind me.

"Hey. The guy you work for at the art gallery said you were out and about. I'm glad I found you."

"Gee, that makes exactly one of us." I didn't bother looking at him. "Say, don't you have a wife to go bone?"

"You knew I was married all along, Topher." He sounded weary, as though I was being *bothersome*. Jackass.

"Yeah, I did. Trust me, I'm fully fucking aware of my own stupidity."

"You couldn't have thought I'd break up my marriage for this."

"You have no idea what I thought, because you never bothered to ask me." I tried to throw as much scorn as I could into the glance I tossed over my shoulder at him. I also walked faster, trying to keep him behind me. I wanted him to have to trot to keep up, like I was too busy to stop for him. "Dirty little secrets apparently don't get consulted on that sort of thing."

He groaned, and it was gratifying to hear him puffing to keep up the pace. Guess all that easy living in academia had made him a bit soft.

"Okay, so if you didn't think I was going to—I don't know— leave my wife for you, or whatever, then what are you so pissed about? I've already risked way too much here as it is. If anyone finds out, my marriage is over and my daughter will probably never speak to me again. I went out on a limb to be with you. What do you want?"

I whirled on him. "How about some human fucking dignity,

you piece of shit! Just because I knew all that doesn't mean it's not completely degrading to just be swept under the rug—or should I say, into the closet?—the second your *real life* shows up."

I growled and stalked away, muttering a rapid-fire rant to myself. "I should just start screwing women; at least they set aside a drawer for their sex toys when they want to keep them out of sight. Of course, they don't actually offer to get their toys a room at a B&B, so maybe I should be flattered."

"Oh, now you're just being dramatic." He had to jog to catch up.

"Well, duh! Hello! Drama queen here!"

"For Christ's sake, Topher, will you slow down so I can talk to you?"

I dropped my voice a little; the boardwalk was crowded today. "I don't know what you think we have to say to each other, but I'd really rather not." The grass underneath my feet gave way to the weathered planks, each footstep making more noise.

"Topher. I want you to apply to State for next year. You can stay with me, and I could help with your tuition . . ."

I turned to stare at him incredulously. "Oh, so much for not risking your marriage. Brilliant. So now you want me to be your fucking *houseboy?*"

Brenden shrugged uncomfortably. "You're Morgan's best friend. It wouldn't be hard to sell it as an 'honorary family member' type of arrangement. Adele and Morgan would approve. No one would need to know about the rest of it."

Wow. Talk about adding insult to injury. I let every ounce of bitter derision I could muster drip from my next words. "And what would my senior thesis be about? The texture of your bedroom ceiling? I imagine I'd be getting some good, long looks at it. That *would* be the price for this act of charity, yes?"

"Please, can you just stop being such a bitch for two fucking minutes? Jesus." He ran his hand through his hair, clenching his fingers near his scalp.

I gave him a scathing look and turned away again. "Fuck you. You're not queer enough to call me a bitch."

"Oh, what? So, because I'm not going to leave my wife for you, I don't even qualify as bisexual?"

"You could, but you're not." The only thing that kept me from trying to outpace him again was the crowd and the fact that I was afraid someone would overhear.

"And just why is that?"

"Because to call a spineless, wishy-washy closet case like you 'bi' would be an insult to bifolk everywhere." I shook my head in disgust. "You're a fucking stereotype, you know that? Bisexuals are fighting to get rid of the misperception of themselves as being greedy or on the fence, and here you are undoing all that."

"Shit. Topher, come on!" He grabbed my biceps and I turned, looking at his hand with as much haughty disdain as I could manage.

The worst part was, he actually did sound genuinely distressed.

"I'll give you what I can, but you can't ask me to completely turn my life upside down for you. That would be selfish of both of us. If it were just me, it'd be one thing, but we're talking about Morgan's life, too. It wouldn't be fair—"

"Let go of me right now or I swear I'll shove your flabby white ass right in the fucking lake," I snarled. Shit. Now people were beginning to stare. "Let's get one thing straight—pun fully intended. I'm not asking for a *fucking thing* from you. I didn't cut myself off from my family's attempts to control me with money just to become your piece of ass with an allowance on the side. You had your chance to at least treat me with the respect due someone you actually care about, and you blew it. You don't have anything I want. Go away."

He sighed and dropped his hand, bowing his head. "I *do* care about you. I *miss* you, Topher. We can work something out. Just think about it, please?"

My eyes began to burn. Goddamn it. I blinked, trying to push back the urge to cry. "No. There's nothing to think about. God knows I'm pretty much a black hole where self-respect is concerned, but I think I can manage at least this much. I wanted to think I was special enough for you to *respect* me, not just want me. But all you can do is make me hate myself, and what fucking pisses me off the most is that you're so goddamned self-absorbed, that thought never even *occurred* to you. That's why there is no way this is happening."

"You *are* special." Jesus, I wish he'd stop using that tender tone, the one he'd used in bed on too many dark nights. The one that had sometimes made me think maybe he'd fallen a little bit in love with me. "I wish things were different, or that I could offer you more, but I can't."

"And you *still* think this is about what you can offer me! That's why there's nothing left to say." My voice and throat were tight. "Thanks for letting me stay at your beach house this summer, but it's time I found someplace of my own."

He looked like he wanted to argue again, but finally his shoulders dropped in defeat. He reached for his back pocket and pulled out his wallet.

"Will you do me a favor? At least take this and use it for tuition." He held out a personal check. "Re-enroll at GVSU or wherever you want to go. Just . . . call me sometime if you change your mind."

Just like that, the grief and remorse were gone, and I was back to rage. I snatched the check from his hand, sneering at a dollar figure large enough to cover two years' worth of books and tuition.

"So, is this hush money? A payoff? An attempt to show me what you can 'offer'? Or is it *payment for services rendered?*" I asked bitterly, glaring at him a moment before I began to shred the damn thing with jerky pulls. "Fuck you. It was *never* about money. I'll be your dirty secret. I'll even do it for free. But I won't be your whore."

I threw the scraps in the lake and ran from him. It was too clumsy and stumbling to be an actual flounce, because now I was *hurt* rather than pissed. I probably looked every bit as tragically dramatic as a heroine of the silver screen, fleeing the scene in tears. Except I wasn't crying, just running as fast as I possibly could until I finally reached the art gallery and dashed inside. Robin looked up in alarm from where he was talking about a painting with a tourist, but I just kept running into the store-room, practically hiding behind the vertical racks.

I held it together until Robin bade the potential customer farewell and came back five minutes later. Then I burst into tears while he held me and let me cry.

CHAPTER EIGHTEEN

Tired of waiting
So tired of all this waiting
And still I'm contemplating
What I can do to save me
Is there a chance
To bring this back
To where I can care again?

— CASEY STRATTON, "WAITING"

Mo spent Saturday and Sunday catching up with her mom and dad, so I didn't see her until Monday. The moment I met her at the coffeehouse, she started grilling me.

"So what is all this? Are you *shacking up* with these guys?"

"What?" Startled, I nearly dropped my latte. "No! No, it's not like that. Robin and Geoff are *together.* They have a baby on the way, for God's sake. I'm just crashing out with them for a bit."

"What, because you don't see enough of them every day at work?"

I shrugged, refusing to meet her eyes. "That's different. I don't really get to talk to them, then."

"Talk about what?" She frowned, sipping her chai carefully.

"Just . . . stuff. You know, I haven't had many gay friends, especially ones who weren't clueless college kids just like me. These guys are nice. They've got their shit together, they know what it's like to be where I am, or at least they know people who have been. It's a good idea, getting to know them."

"Okay, I can see that, but why can't you just hang out with them after work or something?"

I forced a smile. "Because sometimes talking involves a few margaritas." She chuckled, and I slipped through the opening to change the subject. "Plus, it saves on gas. So, how is the archer-slash-gunslinger in Big Rapids?"

"Cody. His name is Cody. And he's fine." A slow smile spread across her freckled face. "Really, really, *really* fine."

"Aww yeah, girl." I grinned and breathed a silent sigh of relief as Mo allowed herself to be distracted. She happily chattered on about her archer and his sexy arms while I mentally tied myself in knots about whether I should confess to her. I wouldn't say my evasion to that point wasn't at least somewhat selfish; I was relieved not to have to lose her just yet. But if that had been the only problem, I would have come clean anyway, because here she was still thinking she could trust me, behaving as if she could trust me, and the plain fact was, she *couldn't*. I sickened myself for misleading her like that. How dare I look her in the eye and act like I still deserved her friendship?

But at the same time, I wasn't sure it was right to take the choice out of Brendan's hands, because Robin was right. Confessing would effectively be outing him. Which, as a matter of principle, wasn't a cool thing to do. At all.

Being in the closet had never really been an option from me. I had a brief period around the seventh- and eighth-grade years, still settling in to my new (very white, very conservative) school district, where I tried denying that I was gay, but when it came down to it, I could never have passed convincingly. At best, people would have just rolled their eyes at my attempts and said I was in denial. My orientation and gender-nonconformity was obvious in everything I did, every gesture, every lilt of my voice, and it had been since I was a child.

But if I could have passed, would I have tried to? Whatever Brendan had done, however insensitive he'd been there at the end, did I have the right to make the decision about whether or not he should come out for him?

It wasn't as simple as coming clean so that there was no deception in my relationship with Mo. I wished it were. If it had been, the decision would have been, if not easy, then at least straightforward. But there were other issues involved here, some of which—as Robin and Geoff had reminded me—I needed to be sensitive to as a member of the gay community. They'd made sure I considered all the angles before I decided.

People's lives could be ruined by being outed. And maybe popular opinion was that they deserved it for cheating—or being gay or bi in the first place—but I didn't think anyone who believed that considered the complete potential cost. People could lose not just their spouses and families, but their jobs, their livelihoods, their friends, their homes. They faced discrimination and homophobic violence and sometimes they even ended up killing themselves.

What Brendan and I had done was wrong, without a doubt. We both knew that, though I think maybe toward the end there he'd started to lose sight of why. But was all that shit I'd just listed a proportional consequence for it?

In the end, I kept quiet. It ate at me, but I supposed that's what Robin had meant when he'd said not to confess just to make myself feel better. I decided to put off making the decision for the time being. I could always do it later, see if I could get some hint of how Brendan was going to handle things.

"Hey! Topher!" Mo snapped her fingers in front of my face. "You in there, girlfriend?"

"Yeah, sorry." I shook myself. "Got distracted."

"That's okay. I was making sure you were coming to the fireworks with us on Thursday. We're cooking out beforehand, and I'd like you to meet my mom. This may be your only chance this summer. She works a lot."

Oh, *fuck*.

"Um." I took a sip of my cooling latte and choked, coughing. "Well. Uh, I should probably see what Robin and Geoff have planned."

She set her cup down with a thump and pinned me with a hard stare. "Topher, what the fuck is with you? We were supposed to spend as much of this summer together as we could when I wasn't working, and now you've got new friends and you're just off and away. I'm starting to feel a little dumped here."

"No! No, it's not like that. It's just . . . I need to get a life, you know? I want to spend time with you, but it's lame spending most of my summer—when I'm twenty-one, and pretty as fuck, and in a freaking *gay vacation town*—rattling around that big old beach house while your dad works downstairs. You've got Mr. Big Rapids now, and that's terrific. I'm glad. I don't mind that a bit. I love you, Mo, but I need to have something that's mine, too. New friends. New hobbies. I don't know. Something."

"Okay." She dropped her gaze to the tabletop, sighing. "That makes sense, I suppose. Um, why don't you invite them along, if they don't have other plans? It would be cool to get to know them better. We can make extra food, and there's plenty of room on the deck."

That wasn't optimal. Optimal would have been not having to meet Brendan's wife at all. But if I had to do it, I supposed having some moral support there to keep me from acting crazy wasn't a half-bad idea.

"Okay, let's ask," I said, nodding resolutely. "Why don't you come down to the gallery with me right now, we'll talk to Robin, see if he and Geoff and Ling already have plans. Oh shit. Oh. No. Wait. We'll go to the studio. Talk to Geoff instead."

Her eyebrows crept up. "'Oh shit?' Why is going to the gallery a bad thing?"

I threw my head back and cursed my life. "You remember that guy I had the one-off with back on my birthday? The one who took the pictures?"

Mo nodded. "Yeah, what about him?"

I cleared my throat nervously. "Well, it just so happens that Robin is selling the paintings Jace made using those pictures."

For a best friend whom I loved dearly, Mo could be fucking diabolical when she wanted to make me squirm, and the grin she flashed told me I was in trouble.

"This I *have* to see."

"I'd really rather you didn't. Please."

"Oh no. You're not getting out of this. Let's go."

As Mo grabbed my hand and jerked me to my feet and practically dashed through town toward the art gallery, I thought, for all that I still felt weird about them, those paintings at least provided me with a perfect distraction. Mo would think of nothing else for days.

SINCE THE FOURTH was on a Thursday, there would be a lot of tourist traffic from vacationers taking long weekends. Like most Saugatuck businesspeople, Robin and Geoff would have their shops open until midafternoon, after which they would close up and come out to the Gardners' beach house for the cookout. I'd been hoping Robin would come up with some sort of brilliant idea to get me off the hook, but he just shrugged and said that if I had decided to hold off on telling Mo what had happened, the only thing I could do was try to behave as normally as possible. Mo already knew I didn't have to work that day, so there was no avoiding the expectation to show up a little earlier and hang out with her mom. I delayed as long as I could by inviting Mo to hang with me down at the beach after my morning swim, but eventually there was nothing left to do except trudge up to the house.

I'm pretty sure condemned prisoners have mounted the steps to their gallows with more enthusiasm than I climbed that stairway up the dune.

Sad to say, it might have made me feel less guilty if I could have found something to dislike about Adele, but I couldn't. She had that gentle sweetness you see a lot in people who work with children. Her hair was darker than Mo and Brendan's, but it was easy to see where Mo had gotten her tall, broad-shouldered, thick-waisted figure. Like Mo, Adele carried it well and un-self-consciously. She didn't try to make herself smaller or more graceful. It elevated my opinion of Brendan that she wasn't a perfect little Barbie-doll cheerleader type. He might be an insensitive, selfish jerk for trying to turn me into his kept boy, but he wasn't so clueless that he couldn't see the beauty in a woman a lot of guys would have overlooked, enough to have remained committed to her for twenty-five years.

In the face of Adele's complete likability, though, the weight of my guilt sat even more heavily on me. She didn't deserve anything Brendan and I had done, and if she ever found out, some part of her might always wonder if it had been something to do with *her*. Because of course, in our society, if a husband strays, it must be due to some shortcoming on the part of the wife, right?

Adele was sure of herself and straightforward, but also a little awkward at making casual conversation, as if she talked to kids so much that she didn't quite know how to talk to adults. Which was, to be quite honest, probably the only thing that saved my ass.

That, and Mo. Mo was perfectly willing to carry on the majority of the conversation, regaling her mother with stories of things the two of us got up to at school. All I needed to do was throw in the occasional agreement or answer a few simple questions. Unlike Brendan, Adele didn't start out asking the hard stuff and keep digging deeper. She limited it to small talk and nonintrusive inquiries, so I wasn't obliged to either spill my life story with my customary candor or evade the questions entirely. But she was nice, and since I didn't have to try to ignore or act nonchalant around Brendan, it wasn't that hard to behave as though everything was fine.

And why didn't I have to worry about Brendan? Because he'd told Adele that he needed to work and would be hiding out upstairs with his computer until it was time to fire up the grill.

Maybe God didn't hate me after all.

The afternoon wore on, and it got late enough that Mo decided to haul out the beer. As much as I wanted to get tipsy and relax, I didn't dare. Not when a single careless word would fuck up absolutely *everything*.

Brendan came out of his bedroom at last, murmuring a polite and perfectly proper greeting as he passed by me. Mo and Adele and I sat around under the patio table umbrella with our beers, while they playfully demanded that Brendan do all the work since he'd been absent all day. Under any other circumstances, I would have taken pity on my host and volunteered to help.

That was so not happening today.

Brendan was just about to lay the franks and burgers on the grill when we heard the sound of a car in the driveway. Mo jumped excitedly to her feet.

"Robin and Geoffrey must be here!" she chirped, rushing for the stairs.

Oh, thank you, Jesus.

I followed at a more sedate pace, both to greet them and to see if they'd brought any snacks or beverages that needed carrying. At the least, I could help Ling up the stairs onto the deck, if she'd come with them.

Robin was hidden behind the open trunk of the car. Geoff was standing next to it, asking Mo how her tattoo was doing. Ling was beside him, looking bigger than ever. The July heat and sun were obviously not doing her any favors, and by now I'd heard her complaining often enough about wanting the kid to be born already that I decided the first order of business was getting her seated in the shade with something cool to drink.

"Hey, Ling. Come on. I'll help you up the stairs and introduce you to Mrs. Gardner."

I got Ling up onto the deck, and Adele quickly stepped into action, all solicitous maternal warmth. She escorted Ling to the shadiest seat and offered her a glass of iced tea. Confident that no disaster would befall her, I jogged back down the stairs just as the trunk slammed shut.

Robin's arms were full of a large cooler that looked almost too big and heavy for one man to handle, even a guy his size. And behind what appeared to be a veggie platter and several bags of potato chips was another guest. He glanced up as soon as I came around the back corner of the house, and his dark brown eyes danced with a devilment I knew way too well.

"Hey, Topher. Good to see you again."

Oh, fuck my life. Seriously. Just fuck it.

PART II
THE FUCK-UP ARTIST, OR...

HOW I LEARNED TO STOP ANGSTING AND EMBRACE THE IDIOT WITHIN

Complacency has wrapped you inside a sheet
You wish for someone to come
And save you
But no one comes
You must take care of yourself
We all learn that
We all learn that

— CASEY STRATTON, "HARVEST"

CHAPTER NINETEEN

Take the pause
But don't stop too long
There is so much here to mend

— CASEY STRATTON, "THE BITTER TRUTH"

"Hi, Jace," I managed to croak through a throat gone suddenly dry with absolute mortification.

Mo's head snapped up like a predator scenting prey.

"Jace? Oh! You're the *painter*!" Oh fuck, oh fuck, oh fuck. She was just *way* too delighted by this development.

He chuckled and tipped his head. "Sometimes."

Robin propped the cooler on the bumper to conduct the introductions. "Morgan, this is Joscelin Sieger. He's a friend of Geoff's from art school, and as you've seen, I often carry his work in the gallery. Jace, you already know Topher, and this is Topher's friend, Morgan."

Mo shook his hand enthusiastically, examining the inked length of arm exposed by his red tank top.

"Pleased to meet you. So, was Topher right? Did Geoff do your tats?"

Geoff chuckled. "I did, but Jace designed them. He did a number of the designs you see in my shop."

"Oh, that is *too cool*." Mo practically dragged Jace and his armful of snacks to the back of the house. "Come on, I want to know *all* about your art."

As her voice faded away, I looked at Robin, trying to squash something very close to betrayal. I was breathing so fast I thought I might hyperventilate.

"Seriously, dudes? What the *fuck*?" I hissed, glancing back and forth between them. Robin's mouth opened in a surprised O and Geoff looked at the ground, then tried to take the cooler from Robin. Robin wouldn't let him, though, so Geoff walked away, leaving the two of us behind. By which I took it to mean this was all Robin's doing and I should just deal with him.

Robin sucked on the inside of his cheek. "Ah. So, you slept with Jace. Okay, that was probably information I should have had. Topher, I had no idea, or I would never have—"

"*What?*" I had to force myself to pull my voice back down. "You *saw* those paintings! You've got them on display! Half the people who pass through Saugatuck know I slept with him!"

He gave me a look that said I was being silly. "Sweetie, artists do erotic paintings of models they've never touched all the time. All I knew was that you'd modeled for him."

Given the fact that he'd seen how I'd reacted to the paintings, I wasn't sure I believed him, but I couldn't exactly accuse him of lying. I braced my back against the side of their car and ground the heels of my hands into my eyes.

Robin leaned against the car beside me, laying an arm across my shoulders. "I'm sorry. I thought it would help."

"Help how? What's he even doing in town?"

Robin shrugged. "I really don't know. He just breezed into the gallery this morning, said he'd made a reservation at the Dunes months ago for the holiday weekend, and wanted to say hi. I invited him here today thinking that with more people around, there would be more distractions from possibly uncomfortable moments that could draw attention. That way the conversation would be more widely distributed, so you'd be less obligated to talk to people who might ask awkward questions."

"Right." I sighed heavily, wishing the ground would just open up and swallow me. "So now I've got to make small talk and play catch up with my one-night stand in front of the married guy I just spent almost a month sleeping with, as well as his wife and daughter. No, no, that's not going to be awkward at all."

"Well, if you get cozy with Jace, Brendan should stay the fuck away and you won't have to deal with him, and his wife will have even less reason to think anything untoward ever happened. Just make sure Jace knows what you're doing so you're not leading him on."

I stared at Robin, wondering how he came up with all this social maneuvering off the top of his head.

"Alternatively, I can pull Jace aside and ask him to fake not feeling well so I have an excuse to get him out of here. In which case, really, you're probably going to owe him an explanation and an apology later."

I ran a hand through my hair and closed my eyes, trying to rein my brain into thinking rationally for a moment. "No. No. I'll pull on my big-girl panties and deal with it. Jace and I don't need to be weird around each other. It was a one-night stand, we had a good time, no reason why we can't just hang out with friends."

Robin's mouth opened as if he were about to say something, but he pulled it back. "Okay. If things get too uncomfortable, let me know, I'll run interference."

"Right." I drew a deep breath and nodded. "Cool. Come on, let's go. I'll introduce you to everyone."

IN OTHER CIRCUMSTANCES, running into Jace again would probably have been a lot of fun. If I had been relaxed and enjoying myself, we could have fallen back into that natural-as-breathing rapport we'd had the first time. And, to be quite honest, *had* it been other circumstances, I would totally have been up for a repeat of that whole night. Even now, there was a pull in my body that *wanted* to flirt and build up that incredible sexual tension we'd had all over again, but there was just no way that was happening.

"He's *cyooot!*" Mo singsonged in the kitchen as I filled glasses with ice. The cooler, it turned out, contained several lidded pitchers of sangria packed in ice. There was even some virgin sangria for Ling. It was a great choice for a humid and blazingly hot afternoon, and everyone pretty much loved Robin and Geoff for bringing it.

Except Brendan, who was busying himself at the grill, a polite —if somewhat distant—host. So far, though, the only weirdness had been in my mind.

"Girl, don't even." I spoke without thinking, shaking my head and grabbing a fresh pitcher to replace the empty one out on the patio table.

"What? Why not?" Mo gave me an utterly bewildered look, and only then did I realize what I'd done. I was so used to Mo knowing everything about me that I forgot she had no reason to know why right now was *so* not a good time for me to flirt with Jace, much less score an invitation back to his room.

Fuck.

Her smile faded, and her eyes dimmed. "Topher, what's going on?"

"I'm just—" I sighed heavily, closing my eyes and gripping the edge of the counter for support. "I'm just trying to work some things out in my head right now, you know? I'm a mess, and I have no idea where I'm going or what I'm doing, so now probably isn't a good time for me to be hooking up with anyone."

"Okay, who the fuck are you and what have you done with Topher?" she demanded sharply. "Girlfriend, you've had *issues* since the day we met, and that never seemed to stop you before. Last time I checked, inner turmoil didn't prevent someone from enjoying the occasional orgasm. I mean, if it was a relationship or something, and it was going to screw with you working things out, then yeah, I could see that. But he'll be back off to Chicago in a few days and you can return to figuring out your shit. I'm not seeing how enjoying his company would fuck any of that up."

"Mo—" I swallowed hard, shaking with fear. I *had* to find some way to stop her asking questions, because she wasn't going to let me get away with dodging them forever, and refusing to answer outright would just make her push harder. If she kept poking, sooner or later I was going to crack under pressure and blurt out *everything*. But for the life of me I could not come up with a lie that wasn't going to unravel under just the slightest scrutiny, and Mo wasn't stupid. She'd scrutinize. Panicking, I seized upon the truth, or at least as close as I could come to it without outing Brendan.

"Okay, look. I'm not going to go into a lot of details here because it's something I'm really still confused and ashamed about. That's why I didn't tell you to begin with, but last month I was . . . *involved*, I guess? Kind of? . . . with someone. More than a one-off, but it could never be a relationship, either. Short-term thing, it wasn't going to work, it really should never have happened to begin with. It was a bad idea on every possible level. And it's over now, way, *way* over, but I'm still a little messed up, you know?"

"Oh my God." Mo blinked at me. Then she grabbed my arm and dragged me bodily into the laundry room/half-bath off the kitchen, closing the door and pitching her voice low. "Topher, did you fuck a *married man?*"

Shit shit shit! She knew me too fucking well.

Still, I thought, trying to swallow back my panic, she had absolutely no reason to think it was her father, right? That would be inconceivable to her, because while he might have been married, she had no idea he had even the slightest interest in men. I could still do this "tell part of the truth" thing, however cowardly it might be and however much I might feel like a complete sack of shit for doing it. Maybe it would be enough to convince her not to ask for more details.

"Yeah. Okay? Yeah, I did. Married, closeted guy. Bad, bad, *bad* fucking idea. It wasn't anything I ever meant to do or set out to do. I'm not a home wrecker. I mean, hell, how many times did we have that conversation when we went clubbing? Those were always the two kinds of guys I swore I'd never touch, right?

Married and in the closet. And I swear, I didn't flirt with the guy or set out to seduce him. It just . . . happened. It's over, I'm not seeing him anymore, it's never going to happen again, but I still feel awful it happened in the first place. So, I fucked up. Maybe I shouldn't be thinking of sleeping with anyone—even someone who will be gone in a few days, someone who could never be a relationship—until I get my head right."

"Wow. Topher . . . wow."

Mo leaned against the door, staring at me as though trying to figure out who I was.

I wished her luck.

"I know," I murmured, tracing a finger along the edge of washing machine. "I don't blame you for thinking I'm awful. I *know* I'm awful."

She sighed and stepped forward to wrap me in a hug. "Aw, honey, I don't think you're awful. You messed up. I can't say it's fine, because, I mean, seriously? Topher? Not cool. But it happened and it's over. I'm not going to beat you up over it."

My eyes burned as I muffled a sob in her shoulder. I hated myself even more, now. Hated myself for coming this close to the truth and still leaving her room to trust and forgive and comfort me when I didn't deserve it. She wouldn't have been hugging me or telling me it was okay if she *knew*.

I wanted to give her the rest of the story just so this hug and her love wouldn't be based on a lie. She deserved that. But I couldn't. Not here. Not with all these people around. Not when Brendan still hadn't made the choice to come out.

Fuck.

I pulled away, denying myself her comfort and wiping my eyes. "Don't, um . . . don't do that. It's okay to beat up on me. I've earned it, I really, *really* have. And I'm not saying that to passive-aggressively try to make you work harder at reassuring me. Don't tell me it's okay. Really. Just don't. You have every right in the world to be disappointed in me. I fucked up in a really rotten way that's probably going to end up hurting people I never wanted to hurt. I know it, and I deserve the consequences. So don't comfort me about it or try to absolve me, please? I just want you to see why I'm not really at my, you know, sexy best with Jace here today."

Mo cleared her throat, watching me with gentle concern, but she stood back, no longer trying to embrace me. "Okay. When you're ready to forgive yourself, I'll be here and we can talk."

"Thanks." I wiped my face again. The tears really did not want to stop.

"That's why you're staying with Robin and Geoff, isn't it?"

Horror punched me in the gut like a fist.

"Wh-what do you mean?"

"He lives around here somewhere, doesn't he? That's why you moved."

Relief washed over me, leaving me feeling almost light-headed. She hadn't put the rest of it together, after all. "Oh, yeah. Yeah, that's it." I took a few calming breaths, trying to pick my way through all the emotional extremes to find a coherent thought. "Look, can we just not talk about this anymore right now? I just . . . can't."

"Sure." She offered me a sober smile. "I think I might head up to Big Rapids tomorrow, for the rest of the weekend. I don't think having me around pushing you to be happy is doing you any favors just now. If you need me, call. You know that."

I nodded, my throat too tight for speech. I didn't deserve her. I didn't. I wished I could tell her everything, so she could hate me and quit offering me love I hadn't earned.

She ran a hand over her pastel-streaked hair. "Before I leave, I *will* suggest that you set a limit on how long you're going to punish yourself. Why not have fun for a night or two? Is it some sort of penance? Why? Do you really think that man's wife and/or family will feel better about things if you never get laid again?"

I gave a miserable, watery chuckle. "No, I guess not. I'll think about it, okay? Just . . . don't push me at anything today. Please?"

"Okay." She sighed, shaking her head at me and opening the door. "Come on. People are waiting for their drinks."

I nodded, then stopped in my tracks at the laundry room door.

"I love you, Mo."

She smiled back at me. "I know. I love you, too. Even when you're a fuck-up."

Resisting the urge to burst into tears again, I followed her back out to the kitchen.

CHAPTER TWENTY

I get so tired of unraveling
Nothing ever working
So I face what I was hiding all along

— CASEY STRATTON, "THE HARDEST PART"

I was just about to grab the pitcher of sangria off the island counter when the French doors leading out to the deck opened and Jace stepped in, squinting as his eyes.

"Hi, Jace!" Mo beamed at him, obviously still delighted he was here, despite my ambivalence. "Need anything?"

"Directions to the washroom?" he replied with that omnipresent grin. He really didn't know how to *not* have a good time, did he?

Mo pointed. "Around the corner, there." She snagged the pitcher of sangria almost out from under my hand. "Can you get the fruit plate out of the fridge, Topher? It's kinda packed in there; you might need to dig pretty deep for the fruit dip."

"Sure." I was still too grateful for her love and friendship, however unworthy I was of it, to smell the obvious setup until after she was gone.

I smiled tremulously at Jace and then hid in the refrigerator,

163

hauling out the platter of berries and sliced fruit before diving back in to find the fruit dip. What kind of fruit dip, anyway? Did she mean the store-bought caramel kind for apples, or a bowl of homemade whipped-cream-based fluff, or something else entirely?

I knew the hand on the small of my back instantly, like it was the most familiar thing in the world. It might have been a high-voltage wire for the way electricity shot through me.

"Dollars to doughnuts there's no fruit dip," he murmured behind me.

Would Mo do that to me not five minutes after I'd asked her not to push me at anything?

Fucking A. Of course she would. *I* was the fruit dip, apparently.

I backed out of the fridge, hanging my head with a sigh. "For Mo, that was extremely subtle."

"She's got a gift." Jace leaned against the counter beside the fridge with his arms across his chest, looking me over. "How are you, Topher?"

"Good. Good. Fine. How have you been?" I retreated a few paces, mirroring his posture against the island chopping block opposite him.

"I've been good. Really good, in fact, though I'm wondering if you would rather I wasn't here."

"What?" I blinked rapidly. "Why would I— Why would you think that?"

The corner of his mouth quirked up in a wry smile. "Because this is the first time you've met my eyes since I arrived, and if I were a vampire, you'd be thrusting garlic and a cross at me right now."

He didn't look offended or insulted. As always, he looked amused. So much so that I couldn't help but hang my head and chuckle a little.

"I'm sorry. I just wasn't expecting to ever see you again. I assumed you were some tourist passing through, not a regular visitor."

He shrugged. "I pretty much thought the same about you.

That doesn't explain why you're so flinchy, though. Are you involved with someone now? Do you have a policy of not doing repeat engagements? One-night stands aren't welcomed back?"

"What? No!" Jesus, did he really think I was so crass?

"If you do, that's cool. People have their boundaries. I won't step on them; I just need to know what they are."

"It's nothing like that," I quickly assured him, unfolding my arms to rest my hands on the counter on either side of my hips. "*I'm* not like that."

He let his posture relax, too. "Good. Because I'm glad to see you again. I'd been wondering how you were."

"I'm . . . um . . ." I hummed thoughtfully, tipping my head back and closing my eyes. "To be honest, and for reasons I *really* don't want to get into, I'm not doing quite as well as I was last time you were here."

"I can tell." I opened one eye to peer across at him. "If I met you on the beach today, I wouldn't try to pick you up."

"Ouch." That stung my vanity a bit. I might be having issues, but that didn't mean I wasn't still pretty.

He gave an unapologetic shrug. "That isn't the same as saying I wouldn't try to convince you to have a cup of coffee with me and get to know you, see what's eating you."

"Wow. First Robin, now you." I shook my head. "Don't worry. I'm hoping for an improvement."

"Actually, Robin's saved me the effort of worrying." That ready grin made another appearance. "Knowing him, he has the sympathetic ear and well-meaning advice angle covered, so maybe I can just coax you to let it go and have fun with me for an evening."

I couldn't help but grin back. "That sounds awesome, but I'm kind of already committed. Barbecue. Fireworks. You know."

"I wasn't inviting you back to my room." He cocked his head in a quick, offhand shrug. "Yet. But that guy at the beach? The one I danced with? The one I spoke to by the pool? You think he might want to come out and play for a bit?"

God, that sounded good. Jace and I had fallen into such easy, effortless sync that night of my birthday. Flirting. Teasing.

Talking with the sort of comfort that came with much longer acquaintance. I would love to feel that way again—alive and wild and carefree. I didn't think I'd relaxed completely since Memorial Day, when everything had gone crazy.

If not for Brendan, I would do it.

"I can try." I ducked my head. "Things are a little weird for me today, so I might get tense once in a while, but I can try."

"Excellent." He grabbed the fruit platter and tipped his head toward the French doors. "Let's take this outside. I think the burgers are ready. Then I can tell you all about me until you're ready to talk about yourself again."

IT WAS A PARADOX. Is that what it's called? A no-win situation when the thing that is supposed to solve a problem turns out to be impossible due to other complications arising from the original problem, leaving you back at the beginning with the problem unsolved?

So, for those of you keeping score at home:

The point of all this—the problem—was to behave as normally as I could so that Adele and Mo wouldn't clue in to the fact that anything had happened between Brendan and me. The way to solve that problem was for me to actually behave as though nothing *had* happened. But if I did *that*, I would be flirting with Jace like no one's business.

Now, however, even if I could have relaxed enough to flirt with Jace, the overly empathetic part of me cringed at the idea of Brendan's feelings being hurt by seeing it (after all, the guy *had* liked me enough to make some rather impressive offers, no matter how insulting they had been). I was afraid that it would come off as petty, as though I were trying to rub his face in it or something. So I *couldn't* flirt with Jace, at least not with as much conviction as I would otherwise have had. Therefore I couldn't behave as though nothing had ever happened between me and Brendan, which meant I was still in danger of doing something to trigger weirdness that would give the whole damn thing away.

Exhausting, right? This was what it's like to be in my head. All the damn time.

Unfortunately—or perhaps fortunately—Jace didn't get the memo that there was a paradox-like thing twisting itself into knots around us. He was determined to drag the playful, flirty, slightly slutty Topher he'd once met out onto the dance floor, so to speak. Since I'd promised to try to relax and enjoy things a little, I couldn't exactly tell him to cool it. And frankly, I didn't *want* to. Damn it, Mo might not know the whole story, but she had a point about punishing myself. Was I supposed to take vows of chastity and self-denial to atone for my affair with Brendan? Just how long did I have to keep to myself in order to prove (to who? Who was going to care, anyway?) that I was really, really sorry for what had happened?

Still, I pitied Brendan. He really didn't look like he was enjoying the party. I knew Robin, Geoff, and Ling had all tried to engage him in conversation, but he always ended up sitting quietly, sipping his drink, listening to the conversation but not talking to anyone.

"Don't worry about Dad," Mo murmured, catching me darting another concerned glance at him. On the other side of me, Jace and Geoff were regaling the rest of us with art school stories. "He's really introverted. He doesn't like crowds to begin with, so he gets pretty burned out during the school year and basically becomes a hermit in the summer if he doesn't have any courses to teach. If I'd realized how much he was counting on not having to deal with people this summer, I probably wouldn't have suggested making this a party today."

I wished I could believe that was all. Maybe it was self-absorbed of me to assume his reticence had to do with me. So far, he hadn't done a single thing to indicate he was even aware of me in any unusual way. At least his introversion gave him the perfect cover. If he wasn't normally outgoing, no one would think it strange if he was withdrawn today.

So that left only my behavior in question.

I nodded and went back to listening to stories about Jace trolling his roommates with sculptures of "*ahem*, questionable artistic value" in embarrassing places, and afterward we got a story about Geoff trying to find an apprenticeship with a tattoo artist, which was right about the time Jace's hand brush the small of my back again.

"My designs were fine," Geoff was saying, "but the big problem was that I didn't have any tats myself. It's a *thing* in the tattoo community, it shows you know what it's like on the other end, and it also demonstrates commitment. So no one would take me seriously."

"Why is that?" I asked, blurting out the somewhat tasteless question I'd been sitting on for weeks. It was a graceless interruption, because those fingers were sending shivers of awareness through me, making my thoughts trip over each other. "That you don't have any tattoos, I mean."

Geoff smiled slightly, and flicked a glance at Robin, who looked a little smug to my eyes. "I could say it's because I have a bleeding disorder and I have to be careful about anything that could result in bleeding or infection. I've known about it since I was a kid, of course, but what did I do? I grew up to be absolutely, insanely in love with body art. And lots of us hemophiliacs have tats, but my mom was one of *those* moms, and if I got one, it would have sent her into a panic because of my disorder."

Ling nodded silently, confirming this.

"Okay, that really blows." I gave him a sympathetic smile and he nodded.

"It did. But after she passed on, well . . . by then I had other things I wanted more." He and Robin exchanged another glance that obviously communicated things the rest of us had no part in. Robin smiled into his drink.

"Anyway, like I was saying, I finally found an artist willing to take me on as an apprentice. And I have Robin and Jace to do my most elaborate work on, so basically at this point it's just a personal choice."

I nodded, thinking it was obvious there was more to it than Geoff was saying, but before I could ask any more questions, Jace's fingers began skating lightly up and down my spine from mid-back to sacrum, and I forgot how to do words.

Thank God Brendan was on the other side of the table where he couldn't see what was going on. Still, it was all I could do to try to remain unaffected, not to arch into the touch. I couldn't help growing hard under the table, but luckily no one could see that, either.

The conversation moved on. Jace's hand didn't, except to widen the range of its roaming. Each pass brought it a little higher up my spine, a little closer to the point of being conspicuous. When it reached my neck I nearly jumped out of my chair.

"Hey, it's getting late. I should go for my evening swim before we head down to the fireworks." Yeah. Hopefully Lake Michigan would be cool enough to take care of this boner, even in July. "Maybe all of you should go on ahead, stake out a good spot, and I'll join you when I'm done."

The plan was met with general agreement, and I thanked God that I'd been smart enough not to drink a lot, so no one could suggest I shouldn't swim or drive. Ling and Brendan were the only others who had limited themselves, and I imagined they'd be designated drivers, so there was no chance of Brendan opting to remain behind.

I refused to meet Jace's eyes as I scurried away to change into my suit and grab my towel, but merely gave them all a hurried wave as I retreated down to the beach, which was—thankfully—emptying out as everyone else decided to head to the fireworks display as well. It was still light, of course, but prime spaces to sit would disappear quickly.

Congratulating myself on winning an hour of much-needed solitude, I stripped off my shirt and tossed it carelessly onto the sand with my towel. Then I sprinted into the lake and plunged beneath the waves.

CHAPTER TWENTY-ONE

No one said it would be easy
Take off that blindfold that you hide behind
Nowhere to run to when the end arrives
We will be left to justify our own lives

— CASEY STRATTON, "WHEN THE END ARRIVES"

It was only when I looked back to shore to see Jace standing by my towel that I realized I might as well have issued an engraved invitation.

He liked swimmers. Duh.

Maybe it *had* been an invitation. God knew I wanted him so bad I was vibrating with it, even with all the weirdness.

And, oh, hey! Lake Michigan in July was not, in fact, cool enough to get rid of my wood. I supposed that shouldn't have been a surprise to me, considering I'd heard people talk about fucking in the lake. Thank God I'd worn trunks rather than the Speedo.

Not that it wasn't still going to be very, very obvious.

I could at least delay things awhile by getting my workout. I did several laps in toward shore and back out, working on different strokes, getting a little more winded each time I had to fight the waves. Finally, my arms aching, I swam to shore.

He was watching me with a very satisfied smile that grew even broader when I emerged from the water, his appreciative gaze dropping without shame to my abs.

"Fuck, that's hot," he murmured, handing me my towel. I barely bothered drying my shoulders and hair, more concerned with draping it strategically in front of me.

I cleared my throat. "You're not going to the fireworks?"

Teeth flashed. Eyes twinkled. "I thought I'd catch a ride with you."

"Wow, that's subtle." I whistled between my teeth.

"Are we being secretive for some reason?" His head rocked toward his shoulder curiously.

"Oh. No, I guess not." I shook my head. "Sorry. I don't know why I'm feeling self-conscious today."

I *so* did, but I sure as hell wasn't going to tell him that.

"Well, let's figure it out in the car. They're waiting for us."

I shook the sand from my shirt and pulled it on, then gave in to the inevitable and draped my towel around my neck rather than trying to hide my crotch. If he copped a look, I missed it, and seriously, why did I care anyway? Why should I be ashamed that he turned me on like a light switch, or mind that he knew it? I hadn't minded that night at the Dunes. We'd both known what we'd wanted from each other, and we'd reveled in it.

That's what he wanted again. That's what he'd been requesting when he'd asked me to let the guy he'd met that night off the leash. We'd been so free and comfortable and uninhibited; that was why it had been so amazing.

I couldn't seem to get that back, though. Everything in my head was jumbled, and the silence between us as we climbed the stairs up the dune bypassed uncomfortable and made a beeline for excruciating. What the fuck was I doing?

W HEN I CAME BACK out of the house after changing, Jace was leaning on my car, looking patient and amused.

And hot. Always so fucking hot.

Fuck it. Flinging the bag with my wet suit and towel into the back seat, I pinned him against the car and kissed him hard. Just like before, we simply melted into each other. He tugged on my hips, drawing me closer, rubbing our bodies together as I slipped my hands into his soft black curls to grasp the back of his head, and drove my tongue deep into his mouth.

I was shaking when we separated, resting forehead to forehead. So was he, panting as if we'd run a marathon.

"This is more like it," he rasped, nuzzling my ear. "You know, I lied when I said I wasn't inviting you back to my room tonight."

"Good. I wanted you to." I moaned softly as his lips moved down my neck. "I don't know if I can, but I want to."

"Why can't you?"

"Fireworks, remember?"

"After."

My thumbs traced the bumps of his nipples through his shirt. "It'll be late."

"I've got nowhere I need to be. Not for the whole weekend. Do you have to work?"

"No, not until the afternoon."

"Then why not?"

I couldn't think of a single reason, at least not one that didn't begin and end with guilt and self-consciousness about Brendan.

"Yeah, why not?" I breathed against his mouth, my lips brushing his before sealing the kiss. Jesus, my body was on fire. Every nerve was alive, every sense full of him. It had never been like this with Brendan, not even at its most desperate. What had happened with Brendan had been about a whole other set of needs, all of them very messy and complicated.

This was simple. Even pure. I wanted Jace. I just did.

He gentled the kiss, drawing away. "We'd better go, or I'm going to fuck you right here over the hood of your car."

"Fireworks first," I reminded him.

"Of course." His dark eyes danced again. "Wouldn't miss it for the world."

I THOUGHT we'd be conspicuous by our absence if we skipped the fireworks—though I knew Mo wouldn't have minded—but I almost regretted my insistence on going when I realized Jace *still* didn't see any need for discretion. Instead of jostling for position somewhere on the lawns near the harbor, Robin had a better offer for us to view the fireworks. He had a boat at the marina, and though there wouldn't be enough room for all of us on the boat itself, there was plenty of space on the private dock along the slip where it was anchored. So we had prime seats. Jace sat beside me on one of the quilts on the dock, and immediately began doing what he'd done earlier at the patio table, and that night in the club. His hand was always on me somewhere, again with that proprietary edge, though tonight I couldn't figure out exactly why.

Was it because, once again, the deal was all but sealed? We knew how this night would end. Everything leading up to that point was just foreplay.

His fingers brushed my neck, and I couldn't help by shiver. I stole a glance at Brendan, who was sitting with Adele and Mo on the other side of Robin, Geoff, and Ling (who was sitting in the only lawn chair). I bet Robin had arranged that division, or maybe Mo, to give me and Jace some relative seclusion with one another. Brendan was looking anywhere except at us. I didn't know if he was avoiding looking at me, or if he just didn't care. Still, I was once again off-kilter and self-conscious, so much so that I half figured Jace would pick up on my discomfort and back off.

He didn't. If anything, he kept pushing harder, getting more handsy.

"What are you doing?" I murmured, turning my head toward him.

His mouth opened, but then I could see a flippant answer die unspoken upon his lips. His eyes sobered and he leaned close, pitching his voice low.

"I don't like the way that married guy keeps looking at you whenever he thinks no one is paying attention. It creeps me out."

"Oh." I tensed and pulled away from his caressing hand. "Don't—don't do anything to make a scene, okay? Just play it low-key and we can talk about it later."

His eyebrows shot up, and then his expressive face shuttered slightly. "O-kay. Sure."

"Thank you," I whispered, pleading for forgiveness and understanding with my eyes.

After a moment, he nodded, looking annoyed, and then I was let off the hook as the Powers That Be decided it was dark enough to cue up the national anthem as a prelude to starting the show. I stood with everyone else and sang along, and Jace was smiling again when we sat back down.

"You lied to me," he murmured in my ear, so close his lips brushed my earlobe. He scooted closer to me on the blanket, so much so that his body pressed flush alongside mine.

"I did?"

"You said you were just an 'okay' singer." His arm slipped around my waist, and he positioned himself slightly behind me, so that all I would have to do was relax to lean back against him. "And I'm beginning to suspect you're a better actor than you cop to, as well."

I ducked my head and therefore almost missed the first rocket. It erupted above us in a shower of green and white sparkles, the boom concussing our eardrums.

"Lean back on me," Jace said in the silence afterward, barely doing more than whispering against my earlobe. "And pull your right knee up. Otherwise we might *make a scene.*"

"Wha—" My voice rose in alarm, but it was drowned out by the next explosion. I obeyed without thinking, leaning against the arm he had planted on the blanket behind my ass. Then I drew my right knee up toward my chest, creating a barrier between us and the rest of our party.

The deafening report of the next rocket to go up masked my squeak when his hand slipped into my lap.

"Oh God." I gasped, trying to pretend nothing was happening. Nope, absolutely nothing weird about cuddling with a near stranger in the presence of my secret ex-lover. The pace of the detonations picked up, cloaking my gasps as the flat of his finger and then his palm rubbed up and down the crotch-seam of my jeans.

He brought me right to the quivering brink of blowing my load in my pants, then backed off, cupping his hand almost protectively over the bulge there, covering but not trying to stimulate.

"Here's how it's gonna be," he growled in my ear between booms. "When this is over, we're going back to my room, and I'm going to fuck you until you can't remember your own name. Then, when you can form words of more than one syllable again and string them reliably together into sentences, you're going to tell me what the hell is going on here. But get this straight in your head: I. Don't. Hide. Not from anyone, not for any reason. I don't care what's going on; if you expect me to be with you, don't even think of asking me to pretend I'm not. Got it?"

I nodded quickly, looking at him in some distress at the thought that he might believe I was asking him to be my secret. I hadn't meant to do that. Had I? Or had I been putting my worry about Brendan's theoretical hurt feelings at seeing us together above any consideration that *Jace's* feelings might be hurt?

Fuck, I was an idiot. I hadn't even put the words "Jace" and "feelings" in the same thought. I'd been treating Jace like a good-time guy with no real depth.

"I'm sorry," I whispered, feeling very, very small under a massive wave of remorse. I knew then that if I pulled away from that arm he'd told me to lean on, we'd be done. He'd go back to Chicago and I'd never see him again. So instead I turned my face in toward him, letting my head rest against his shoulder.

After a moment, the arm behind me slipped around my waist, drawing me against him more fully.

Holding me.

I didn't deserve it, just as I didn't deserve Mo's affection. But here we were, and I liked it, and there was nothing deceitful about accepting it from Jace, at least, because I knew I wasn't going to mislead him like I was doing to Mo. I'd tell him everything.

Somehow, I kept slipping a little lower every couple minutes, until by the time the fireworks display hit its grand finale, I was lying with my head on Jace's thigh and his fingertips gently scritching my scalp. Each explosion vibrated in his quadriceps. I still didn't want Brendan to be hurt, but the fact was, Brendan's feelings needed to stop being a variable in the calculus of my decision-making. He'd chosen his path just as I had mine, and I wasn't responsible for rectifying everything for him any more than I was responsible for doing it for my mother. I wasn't with him anymore and I would never, ever be with him again. I had to move past thinking of him as a part of my life. I still wouldn't out him unless I had no other choice, but beyond that, he was on his own.

After the thunderous grand finale, we got up and folded the blankets for Robin to take back onto his boat. While we packed up our things, Ling complained good-naturedly that the baby had gone out of her mind with each and every mortar that burst, and she would never get any sleep tonight with Zhen so worked up. Despite their dutiful sympathy for Ling's plight, Robin and Geoff couldn't help but beam proudly and pat the visibly shifting lump while Adele commiserated and shared war stories from her own pregnancy with Mo.

When we reached the cars, I hugged Mo tightly and said good-bye, since she'd be leaving for Big Rapids in the morning. While I did that, Robin turned to Jace.

"We have some wine left over from making the sangria. Wanna come to our house for a drink before you head back to your room?"

Jace hesitated, and I—excruciatingly aware of Brendan's presence behind us as he loaded a cooler into the back of their SUV—said softly, "I need to grab some clothes first, anyway."

If Brendan reacted, I didn't turn around to see it.

Mo squeezed me in adamant approval of this development, and Jace smiled, looking slightly taken aback. "Sure."

Brendan muttered something about having a headache and needing to get home, giving everyone a general and understated good-night before shutting himself in the driver's side of the SUV.

I flinched when the door slammed, but I didn't let my smile falter.

CHAPTER TWENTY-TWO

You know I don't know the way
To find where my love is
I weave a twisted story
Of what I feel, of what is real

— CASEY STRATTON, "MAYBE FOR A MINUTE"

Ling went straight to bed, while Jace had a glass of wine with Robin and Geoff in the dining room. I packed a change of clothes for the next day, not even bothering to pretend I was going to have time to come back here to shower and get ready for work before I had to be at the tattoo parlor.

I hadn't eaten much at the cookout because of my discomfort, so after I packed my bag, I ducked into the kitchen, offering to make a sandwich for anybody who wanted one. They all declined, but Jace followed me anyway. As I worked on piling smoked turkey deep on whole wheat, one of his hands settled on the small of my back and the other on my shoulder, drawing me close as he kissed my neck. I sighed and closed my eyes, becoming a mass of nerve endings in one split second, all of them yearning for him.

After a moment I cleared my throat and turned my attention back to my sandwich.

"This isn't a complaint, but I have to ask why you do that."

"Do what?"

"Touch me like you have every right in the world to. You do it even before it's a sure thing that I'll sleep with you."

"I don't know." His voice lifted, sounding slightly puzzled. "I think because whenever you're within arm's reach, it seems like my hands would feel more natural on you than they would hanging at my sides."

"Okay." I nodded, accepting that without question, because it sounded just about right. I could be ridiculously protective of my personal space at times, especially with people I didn't know well, but when Jace was near me, it was like he belonged within my bubble.

We said good-night to Robin and Geoff as soon as I had finished scarfing down my sandwich, and I don't think I was imagining the urgency on Jace's part when he hurried me down the driveway toward his car.

I smiled when I saw his room at the Dunes.

"What, no huge-ass cottage this time?"

He looked at me out of the corner of his eye, leading me up the stairs of the hotel portion of the resort. "It was a last-minute cancellation. I'm lucky I even got it on a holiday weekend."

My eyebrows shot up as he slid the card key in the door. "You told Robin you booked it months ago."

Holy shit, was he blushing?

He ducked his head. "Yeah, well, I thought it would be too creepy to admit that I decided on an impromptu visit the moment Geoff mentioned during an email exchange that the guy who had modeled for those paintings was in town full-time and working for them."

I froze just inside the doorway. "Seriously?"

"Seriously." He tugged me into the room, far enough to close and bolt the door, then rubbed the back of his neck, glancing at me from under his lashes. "I don't know why, but I've thought about you a lot. Especially while I was painting you. You . . .

struck a chord, I guess. I've never turned out anything as good as those paintings in such a short amount of time."

"Wow." I swallowed hard, unsure of what to make of that revelation. I let the strap of my duffel bag slide off my shoulder onto the floor of the open closet, and glanced around, feeling at loose ends. Then his hand captured mine and he pulled me close, until he was sandwiched between my body and the door.

"Don't worry about it," he murmured, and kissed me.

For all that alpha-male crap he'd pulled at the fireworks display, he started off incredibly gently. His hands framed my face, tilting my head into the kiss, the brushes of his lips becoming strokes. He captured my bottom lip between his and sucked on it, making no effort to open my mouth or thrust within. Just those light kisses, punctuated by flicks of his tongue against the edges of my lips, and careful nibbles.

Amazing. Best kissing technique ever. Seriously. He didn't mash his mouth against mine, he just took his time, until my lips were so sensitive I couldn't bear it. We groaned together when my tongue slipped out to meet his in the space between our mouths, and *that's* when it intensified. His hands tightened on me, moving down my shoulders and back to clasp me closer, his tongue sliding into my mouth and staking a claim. My knees weakened, and suddenly I really wished I was the one leaning on the door, because I was going to be hanging from his arms soon if I didn't find something to support me or get horizontal.

My lips tingled as I pulled away from him. They were puffing up, filling with blood. I touched my tongue to my upper lip while I kicked off my shoes and jerked my shirt over my head, walking backward toward the bed. Jace followed, stripping a lot more impatiently, throwing his clothes aside. He shoved me back so that I fell onto the bed, and peeled off my jeans and underwear himself.

Then he planted his face in my groin, licking and breathing deep, inhaling the scent of me. I wanted his red, red mouth around my cock so fucking bad, but he gave me everything except that. His tongue stroked the crease of my thigh where it met my torso. He sucked and licked my balls with such attention and enthusiasm that he had me arching off the bed, writhing and groaning before he finally moved on to my taint. I drew my knees up, hoping he might rim me, but after only a teasing stroke at my entrance, he nibbled his way down my inner thigh and calf to my foot.

Holy fucking hell, who knew having your toes sucked felt that good? It was like they were wired directly to my groin, each *almost*-ticklish nibble and pull sending a small shock wave of tension through my cock and balls.

"Please!" I panted, twisting on the bedspread and lifting my head to stare at him in desperation. Pre-cum dripped from the head of my cock to cool on the sweaty skin of my belly. "Come on, Jace. Just fuck me already."

That diabolical grin flashed as he turned his face away from nuzzling the arch of my foot.

"Oh, *nonono*, angel." He *tsk*ed, licking the hollow behind my anklebone before nibbling on my Achilles tendon and, ohmygod seriously, how the ever-loving *fuck* was that even erogenous? "I'm going to take my own sweet time with you."

And I'd be damned if he didn't. He worked my other foot over, then went back up my leg, lingering to torment the sensitive skin of my inner thigh. I was going to have a mass of hickeys there for a few days. Then my hips. My abs. My nipples got special attention, because once he got to my chest he started sucking and biting again, leaving marks all over the damned place. He pinched my nipple until I cried out, then sucked on it until the ache faded, then did it all over again on the other side. My collarbones and neck definitely weren't spared, nor were my shoulders or armpits, and especially not the delicate skin of my inner arm.

He'd left a few respectable hickeys that first night we spent together, but I was pretty sure this time he was going for a record. By the time he stretched his nude body out on top of mine, I was absolutely *quivering*. I was so hard I thought even the pressure of his cock nestling alongside mine would make me come, and my skin was slick with sweat. My breaths came in desperate gasps until he swallowed them, plunging his tongue into my mouth, his lips grinding against mine so damn hard it hurt.

"Oh God, please," I whimpered when he drew away to bite my earlobe almost to the point of pain. "Please. Please. Jace. Want you. Want you so fuckin' bad . . ."

"Roll over." He didn't have to tell me twice. With unaccustomed passivity, I flipped to my hands and knees the moment his weight left me, only moving to let him rip the covers out from underneath me and fling them to the foot of the bed. I heard the sound of a luggage zipper and some rustling on the other side of the room, but I couldn't see far enough over my shoulder to watch him. A moment later, condoms and lube landed on the bed beside me, and then his hands seized my ankles, yanking them out from underneath me until I dropped down flat onto the mattress.

"Good. Stay there," he muttered, straddling my thighs. I just about cried when I realized he wasn't going to fuck me yet, humping against the sheet in desperation until his hand cracked lightly on my ass—just a warning, with no real pain.

"Don't even think about it."

"*Jace* . . ." I nearly whined, clenching my fists beside my head on the pillows. "Come on already."

His fingers wound in my hair and pulled my head back a little, his other hand wedging under my chest to twist my already sensitive nipple.

"What did I promise you tonight, hmmm?" Even now he was just chilling out, having a good time, while I was ready to vibrate completely apart into a formless blur of component atoms. "I said I was going to fuck you until you couldn't remember your own name. If you're still talking, I'm not done yet."

He released my hair and let my head fall back to the pillow.

I tossed a baleful look over my shoulder. "Yeah, well, I'm not feeling much fucking going on here, so as far as I can tell, you haven't even started."

He just grinned, goddamn him. Fucking bastard.

"This is just the warm-up act."

Then his lips and teeth and tongue were on my neck again,

my shoulders and back. Rougher now than they had been before. More biting, less sucking, more squeezing and groping, less caressing. His fingers dug so hard into my lats I thought he'd leave bruises as he worked his way down to nibble on the slope where my back flared into my ass.

He gripped my cheeks, kneading hard, spreading them then pushing them back together as his tongue swept down along my sacrum.

"Oh God. Yes, please," I panted, trying to lift my ass up and offer it to him. Tongue, fingers, dick, I really didn't much care, as long as he was inside me. He shoved my cheeks apart, and his breath caressed my twitching hole.

Mouth it is, then.

I admit, I hadn't been rimmed much. It was one of those finesse things that you didn't often get when picking from the grab bag of college-aged hookups. But in my limited experience with it, Jace was definitely champion-class. No tentative, perfunctory strokes here, no sirree. He nibbled and tickled and blew against wet skin and muscle until it prickled and clenched, then warmed it back up with his tongue. He began to spread me open with his thumbs on either side of my crack, his tongue flicking and probing deeper, then withdrawing to circle and sooth.

When he thrust it into me, I nearly came up off the bed. Then I just writhed, trying to hump the mattress until he swatted me again.

"So help me God, Topher, if you come before I've got my dick in you, I *will* make you regret it."

I was panting too hard to even argue or talk back, so he returned to fucking me with his tongue. He wasn't hesitant or careful about it, either. Hell no. He used that thing like a cock, wriggling and driving it into my asshole as it relaxed.

If I'd been capable of catching my breath, I would have burst into a round of the "Hallelujah Chorus" when he finally reached for the damned lube and slipped two fingers deep inside.

"Fuck! Yeah . . ." I hissed at the burn. He nibbled my ass

cheeks, working his fingers in and out only long enough to distribute the lube before pulling his weight up off me entirely.

I heard the noise of the condom going on and wriggled my ass impatiently.

"Please. Jace, *please.*"

"Okay, angel. I'm done playing now." He kissed the back of my neck, draping his weight over me, and eased inside as I lay there flat.

I liked to think his groan of relief as the clenching muscles of my ass gripped him was no less desperate than mine.

It was incredibly intimate, covered like that, his body flush against my back. His lips moved slowly and gently over the back of my shoulders and his hands soothed up and down my arms. He began to rock into me with small rolls of his hips. Not hard, not deep, not nearly enough to drive me to the edge. Leisurely. Like he had all the time in the world to just be there, on me and in me.

I felt *protected.*

That thought scared me; I'm not sure why. Suddenly I was trying to buck underneath him, to lift my hips and thrust back, maybe even get to my hands and knees so he'd have to move off me.

"Shh. Take it easy. We're not in any hurry."

"*You* might not be," I choked. "Fuck me, damn it."

"When it's time," he said patiently. No matter what I did, he refused to be rushed. Eventually my only choice was make him stop or go quiet beneath him and let him do it his way. Once I'd gone still, he began to pull his hips back a bit more, sliding in a little deeper and harder each time, though he kept up the undemanding pace.

"You don't have to rush, Topher." His voice was soft and hypnotic, barely more than a whisper, and so tender. His breath warmed the back of my neck. "Not with me. You don't have to settle for getting off and getting gone, or think a quick, barely satisfactory fuck with someone who doesn't give a shit is the best you're entitled to. You're better than that."

I whimpered, rolling my face against the pillow in wordless denial.

"I don't know your story, and I'm not going to ask for any more than you want to give. But I know, I can just tell from the way you act, that people have tried to take things from you, tried to take *you* from you. They tried to take away something amazing, something that deserves more, something that wants to *shine*. I see it. I see the part they never managed to steal, no matter how hard they tried."

I was beyond words. I trembled beneath him, less from desire now as from something deeper and far scarier. I think I made a questioning sound, asking him to complete the thought even as it terrified me.

"*Your soul*," he whispered, answering the unspoken inquiry.

A ragged half sob burst from my lips, bit off at the last instant, and I realized the pillow was damp beneath my cheek. What the fuck was this? What was he doing? Part of me wanted to throw him off and storm out, and part of me felt anchored in place, mesmerized. I kept trying to convince myself he was being creepy, but it didn't feel that way. He saw so far into me it was terrifying.

"*Please*," I whimpered, frozen with fear and filled with unspeakable need, both to deny what he'd said and to give in to it, to let him get that deep into my head.

Jace drew back, out of me. I moaned when the pressure of his cock filling me was gone, nearly sobbing again with frustration. But he just grabbed a thick pillow and put it next to my hip, then rolled me onto my back with my ass on it. I can't even imagine what I must have looked like to him—dazed, lost, so damned confused and needy. If he minded, it didn't show. He just guided my knees up and apart and slid into me again, much more forcefully this time, his hips bumping hard into the backs of my thighs.

"Oh God!" I flung my head back, shouting, but he caught my hair and pulled me into a fierce kiss. For someone who said he'd ask nothing of me, that kiss seemed to demand everything, and I gave it. I gave it all.

He covered me again, his mouth hungry on mine, his hips pistoning, slamming against my ass. His weight pinned me down and kept me trapped while his tongue fucked my mouth as urgently as his cock was fucking my ass. I clung to him, overwrought, overwhelmed, my fingers scrabbling on the sweaty skin of his shoulders until he drew off me far enough that I had to grip his forearms instead. He bent me in half and he *fucked* me. Hard. Like he wanted to come out the other side. His skin slapped against mine and his grunts underscored my wails. He felt *so fucking good* inside me, but the pleasure was almost an afterthought in comparison to the way my thoughts and emotions short-circuited, spitting dangerous sparks, threatening a full-on inferno.

My cries became near screams and still he pounded me, until it ached, until I spewed hot, thick cum all over my stomach. I was so lost in it, I didn't even feel how tight the grip of his hands had become, nor did I hear his low howl, or feel him pulsing. He collapsed onto me, quaking as I wrapped my limbs around him and whimpered into the curve of his neck. A final spasm rippled through me, leaving me wrung out and stunned in its wake.

I stared up at the ceiling, still gasping and shaking.

What the fuck had just happened?

CHAPTER TWENTY-THREE

You are stronger than your agony
Give it time and I know you'll see
Everything I can see

— CASEY STRATTON, "HIGHWAY"

I sort of drifted, lost in the afterglow, while Jace cleaned us up. Then he slipped into bed behind me and drew the covers up over us, wrapping himself around me and kissing the back of my neck, right on the knob of my spine above my shoulders, in a spot that I was starting to think of as *his*.

He was silent, but he wasn't sleeping. I knew he was waiting, because his plans weren't fulfilled for the night. He didn't ask, though, and I didn't make him.

Sighing, I began to talk. I told him all about Brendan. Everything. More than I'd even confided to Robin and Geoff. I couldn't see if he was appalled, but his arms never withdrew from around me and there was no judgment in his voice when the tale wound to a close.

"Well. I'm trying to decide if that's better or worse than I'd originally assumed, which was that it was all one-sided on his part. You asked me what I was doing earlier, and the fact is I was trying to warn him off. I thought he might try pushing you into something you didn't want."

I rolled to my back, turning my head to look at him. "Why would you think that?"

"Bad experiences." He shrugged. "Let's just say I didn't have a great track record with married men by the time I was done with art school. Bad experiences beyond a few creeps trawling the club scene while their wives were out of town, and the instructor who tried to sell me a spot in a show, with the currency being favors performed on my knees."

"Ah." I shook my head. "No. I don't think he's like that."

He nodded against the back of my shoulder. "Okay. Were you careful?"

"No." I flinched, shuddering.

His tongue clicked against his teeth. "Okay, here's the thing about married men, Topher: If they'll cheat once, they'll cheat again, and something about being in the closet that deep just makes them desperate. More prone to taking risks."

"I'm pretty sure this was his first time. He felt just as awful about it as I did, and he was just as scared. I really hope he's not that good a liar. But yeah, it was dumb. Really, really, incredibly dumb. I'll get tested next month."

He kissed the point of my shoulder. "I think being twenty-one is all about the dumb. At least it was for me. Try to be smarter, but don't beat yourself up too hard. It's done. Move on."

I nodded, taking his hand as it rested on my stomach and playing with it, sliding my fingers in and out between his. "I guess I just still don't get *why* it happened. I mean sure, he's hot, but I find a lot of guys hot and I don't end up fucking them. We were friendly, and I could talk to him and then suddenly everything just went *insane*. Like we both just lost our minds."

"What did you talk to him about?"

"My issues, mostly." I snorted softly. "He was a good listener. You know, the first day I met Robin, he said something about me not letting people in easily, but it's really not true. I'm more likely to dump my baggage in someone's lap than try to hide it away, because I apparently can't resist a pity party. And, wow, from the very first conversation I ever had with Brendan, I just unloaded. He made it easy. He kept asking for more. I don't know. Maybe it has something to do with him being a psychology professor. I'm used to talking to shrinks."

His breath ruffled my hair. "Well, dumping your baggage on someone isn't the same as letting them in. Some people use candor as a shield. Best defense is a good offense, right? You blurt it all out and then you wait for the inevitable revulsion when the other person just walks away from it. The ones you really want to keep around are the ones you hide the bad stuff from until you feel safe."

I swallowed against a knot in my throat. "I guess that's true. But it was different with him. I couldn't keep my mouth shut about all of it, even though I didn't want to turn him off."

"Did it *feel* like talking to a shrink? That sort of thing?"

I shook my head. "No. Freaky as this sounds, I think maybe it's because he's a father—and according to Mo, a pretty good one. I needed someone like him to agree that the things that happened to me weren't okay. That it wasn't me who was always wrong."

"That makes a lot of sense."

"But of course, I can't be around someone like that without getting my signals crossed. All my interactions with parental-type authority figures have been sexualized one way or the other, ever since I was a little kid. Either they were being inappropriate with me, or they had . . . they were, like, prurient. You know? Like they spent way too much time thinking about the dirty things I could get up to, and then they'd accuse me of doing it even when I hadn't, and it was just *creepy*, like they were getting off on making up fantasies about me."

He went a little still when I mentioned the kid part, but I so didn't want to tell that particular story now. And I didn't really feel it was necessary. I think Jace already knew. Not the specifics, but he knew that people had done awful things to me. I didn't need to say it.

"Maybe I'm just not capable of being with an adult—fuck, I say that like I'm *not* an adult, but you know what I mean?

Someone that much *older*, with that sort of authority or vibe or whatever—without getting what is and isn't appropriate mixed up in my head. It has to be about sex because I don't know how else to interact with someone in that role."

"I think I know what you mean." His hand closed firmly around mine. "It's a fucking good thing I'm not any older, or I'd start to feel very, very wrong about this."

I dipped my head, kissing him softly. "No. I think you're just right. Old enough to be a little wiser and less confused than I am just now, but not so old that you scramble my radar."

He pulled me down so that I rested with my head on his shoulder, tucked under his chin. I could hear his heartbeat and feel the light stroking of his fingertips against my scalp. The warmth of his arms around me was amazing. Again, the only word I could come up with for it was *protected*. Fuck, that word was terrifying. I didn't try to throw him off and get away this time, but it took an effort not to.

"I don't know you all that well, but I know you're an amazing guy, Topher," he whispered against my hair. I shook my head in denial, but he wouldn't stop. "Maybe you're confused now. Maybe you make mistakes, and you're not sure where you're going or what you're doing, but you give off this vibe that tells me . . . Well, I would bet anything I own that you've been through things that would send most people into booze or drugs or cutting or suicide or just being so sick and fucked up that they can't function. Don't you see, angel?"

His arms tightened around me. "*You're still on your feet.* You may hate yourself for every little mistake you make, but the fact that you've survived means you've come out on top. It might not be a perfect victory, but those are really, really rare. Every day you stand up and face life again is a win."

"I wish you wouldn't do that," I murmured, hiding my face against his shoulder.

"Do what?"

"Idealize me. Those paintings you did were pretty, but they weren't *me*."

I wasn't exactly expecting him to laugh at that. My head came up, indignation ready to boil from my lips, but he just pushed me back down.

"One of the first things you learn as an artist, Topher, is that you have to stand back from something to see all of it." He kissed the top of my head again. "I've got perspective you don't. Trust me on this."

THANK God I didn't have to work early the next morning. Jace and I didn't go for the all-night marathon sex we'd had our first time together, but we woke each other up a couple times. By the time we staggered out of the shower to tumble—hard, groping, and dripping wet—onto the bed for another round, I was already in danger of being late. Considering the circumstances, I suspected Geoff wouldn't mind, but it still wasn't a good precedent to set.

About the only thing that saved me from tardiness was a text message on my phone, which I managed to hold out of the way, evading Jace's efforts to lob it across the room.

"Mm, get off," I moaned when I was done reading it. Jace's mouth was busy at my neck, determined to add to my collection of hickeys.

"That's the plan, yes." He snatched the phone out of my hand and tossed it onto the nightstand.

"I need to go. Ling's not feeling well so I have to fill in at the gallery instead of just cleaning up at the tattoo parlor. Which means I'm already late."

"Shit," Jace groaned, rolling off of me. He took his cock in hand, stroking slowly, not so much jerking off as trying to soothe himself. "This is gonna be one brutal case of blue balls."

I snorted, climbing off the bed and hauling my duffel out of the closet.

"Hey, if you want to rub one out while I'm getting dressed, at least one of us won't be limping." I dragged my boxer briefs—which I'm not at all ashamed to say do *marvelous* things for my ass, though it was Jace's ass I was particularly interested in this time around—over my aching hard-on.

"If I do that, you may as well join me, because I have to drive you back into town." He sat up, glowering, and started gathering up his clothes.

"Damn, that's right. Sorry."

"It's okay. I'll drop you off at the gallery and go get some coffee and breakfast for you, since we kind of missed that part of the morning here."

My stomach grumbled at the reminder. "Good thought. Of course, I missed my morning swim, too. I need to be extra sure to get a swim on my dinner break."

"Tell me you're coming back here again tonight." He tugged a tight polo down over his solid torso. It displayed the ink on his arms beautifully.

"If you want me to." I sat down to tie my shoes, using it as an excuse to duck my head against a sudden bout of bashfulness. After that first time, he'd toned down the psychological intensity, but my emotions were scoured raw. He'd stripped me bare last night, ripped away all my boundaries. Now I felt exposed and skittish in the aftermath.

"Of course I do." He prowled toward me with his jeans still unbuttoned, tempting me to pull his shirt up and follow his trea-sure trail all the way down. "I'm here for the weekend, Topher, and I think I'd like to spend as much of that time with you as I can. See if . . . if maybe there's something here worth spending other weekends on? If that's okay with you?"

Just like that, I was scared again. Because I wanted what he was offering, to see what this might turn into. I didn't like the thought of him leaving in a couple days and just disappearing, possibly never to be seen or heard from again. But the voice of my guilt whispered insidiously that I didn't deserve this after what I had done. Didn't deserve to be happy. Didn't deserve to try to build something new—something potentially amazing—and move on with my life.

Of course, it could also be that I didn't really feel safe letting anyone else get close just now. Not after the way Brendan had reneged on his promise to treat me with respect. Not when I was facing the prospect of losing Mo if she ever found out. Making myself vulnerable to another person was not high on my list of Good Ideas at the moment.

"Topher?" His head rocked to the side, looking at me from an angle, and he sucked on his cheeks uncertainly.

"Yeah. That's okay with me." I pushed that voice aside, knowing it would be back. "More than okay."

CHAPTER TWENTY-FOUR

Our sea change it may be slow in coming
At least we've been dealt back in the game

— CASEY STRATTON, "SEA CHANGE"

I f Robin minded that I was rather dreamy and distracted at the gallery that afternoon, he didn't say anything. I floated, drifting from task to task, lost in my own thoughts. Every once in a while, a memory would creep up on me and crash over my brain like a tidal wave, stopping me in my tracks, like I was experiencing that moment all over again. If there was a completely positive, sex-related equivalent to an acid trip, I was *definitely* tripping.

Robin just endured my moments of absentmindedness without asking too many questions and sent me off for my swim and dinner break after we'd locked up.

Jace was waiting for me outside the gallery.

"Hey. Want a ride down to the beach?"

I grinned, my eyes passing down his body to take in his swim trunks and sandals.

"Sure. But just so you know, I will *not* have time to have sex with you in the water unless I plan on skipping dinner."

His eyes danced as he opened the passenger-side door of his car for me. "I'll keep it limited to foreplay."

I laughed as he shut the door behind me, waiting for him to hop in the driver's side and take off.

"I don't wanna hear a damn word about blue balls if you do."

He actually limited himself to a few gropes inside my Speedo. He didn't swim out as far as I did, but he held his own for a while, then floated on the waves and groped me some more when I came back. I admit, I liked trying to keep us afloat through each wave while he wrapped his legs around my waist and ground against me, thrusting his tongue down my throat. If I hadn't needed my arms to keep our heads above water, I totally would have snuck a hand down the back of his swim trunks and finger-fucked him right there.

Then he took me out to dinner and smirked while I adjusted myself under the table because that hard-on did *not* want to go away.

I'd figured Jace would go do something to entertain himself while I worked at the tattoo parlor, cleaning surfaces and sterilizing Geoff's equipment as he inked the last clients of the day. Instead, he just hung out on the sofa in the waiting area with his sketch pad, doodling designs and talking to Geoff and the customers about body art stuff that didn't really apply to me. I tuned out and lost myself in my own thoughts until I heard my name.

"Huh?" My head came up as Geoff was finishing with his final client, putting a bandage over a tramp stamp for some tourist passing through town.

Geoff nodded to Jace. "I was just telling him you weren't interested in having anything done."

"Oh. It's not that I'm not interested. It just never seems to be a good time."

"Well, what are you thinking of?" Jace asked while Geoff ran the client's credit card and escorted her to the door. "I bet between Geoff and me, we could design something really gorgeous for you."

I sighed as Geoff locked the door and turned out the lights in the windows. "I'm sure you could, but the problem is my swimming. I can't take the time to wait for something to heal."

"That's a good point," Geoff acknowledged, grabbing the bottle of disinfectant spray from me. "I really wouldn't recommend a tattoo unless you can give it a few weeks before going into a lake or pool. A piercing would be different, of course."

Something in my stomach flipped. "How would that be different?"

"It would be small enough to cover with a Tegaderm patch." He opened a drawer and tossed a flat packet at me. "It's the thin, second-skin kind of tape they put over an IV catheter when you're in the hospital. It's waterproof, so you could put it over a piercing before you went swimming, take it off after."

"Oh." I stared at the Tegaderm wrapper, my pulse beating harder. Why the fuck was I feeling so jittery?

A piercing—and yes, it would definitely have to be a piercing, not only for practical reasons, but because everything inside me had clenched into a big ball of *want* at the discovery that it might be possible—seemed so intimate. Maybe even a little kinky, because I didn't want some pedestrian facial piercing, I wanted it on my body. And the thought was an extremely sexy one. Until this moment, I hadn't imagined I could have any trouble being frank about my desires, especially with Jace. But I felt incredibly shy as I stood there, with his eyes on me.

Maybe it was just the attention. Suddenly the focus of everyone in the room was on me and my issues, making it all about me. I was the center of attention and that was never a safe place to be.

Maybe that was why I was hemming and hawing still, torn between wanting to do it and feeling I shouldn't. Body art was meant to be seen, shown off, admired—even if only by select individuals who got to see you with your clothes off—and I could never do anything that would attract that sort of notice without expecting someone to put me in my place. I could just imagine the eye-rolling that would take place if I showed up at a family gathering with a tattoo or piercing. They'd assume I was doing it to put myself on display.

If it's someplace private, the way you want it to be, then they don't ever need to know, and they can't accuse you of being an attention whore, the rational part of my brain whispered. But my emotional programming tended to ignore the rational part of my brain.

I set the packet on the counter and went back to disinfecting every surface. "I guess I just don't know what I want to have done," I mumbled, not meeting their eyes.

Jace bit his thumbnail and stared at me.

"Yeah, you do."

"Huh?" I snapped around to look at him.

"You know perfectly fucking well what you want to have done. You just can't make yourself say it, for some reason."

"Okay, that's just creepy." Heat flooded my skin, and my stomach twisted nervously. Holy Christ, how did he see into me like that? I was embarrassed by my own transparency, and it was annoying to realize how easily he read me. Though, admittedly, I was somewhat turned on, as well. See also: scared.

Backed into a corner, I did what I always did and went on the offensive. I narrowed my eyes almost defiantly.

"Fine. My nipples. I want to have my nipples done." I threw the statement down like a gauntlet.

Geoff's eyebrows crept up, but he stayed out of the conversation. Jace just shrugged.

"Okay then. So have them done."

"What, now?" My voice didn't squeak at all there, nope, nu-uh. All macho-manly stoicism here.

He shrugged again. "If you're ready. If not, whenever. Or never. No one's saying you have to, but if you want to do it, do it."

I stared at him, completely forgetting what I was in the middle of doing, only vaguely aware of the sounds of Geoff working the autoclave.

Then I had a mental picture of fucking Jace that night with my nipples still aching, the new barbells in them shining. It was so powerful and erotic, my knees nearly buckled with it.

"Okay," I rasped.

BY THE TIME I was standing shirtless beside the chair at Geoff's workstation, my lips were swollen and bruised from the kiss Jace had given me after I'd announced my decision, and my entire body was hard, aching with arousal. I'd never been so fucking aware of the nearly invisible hairs on my skin as when Geoff's gloved hands swabbed cool antiseptic over and around my nipples. I clutched Jace's hand like a lifeline, crushing his fingers from fear alone.

"Relax, angel," he murmured right next to my ear. "I'm here with you, and I'll take care of you when it's all done."

"Not on your life." I gritted my teeth at him in an approximation of a tight smile. "If I'm butch enough to still be conscious when this is over, we're going back to your room and I'm gonna fuck you into the mattress."

"Ooh, that works, too."

Geoff chuckled softly as he marked my nipples on either side with a pen and then clamped forceps on one before I sat down. I waffled between curiosity and dread, unsure of whether to close my eyes and wait for it to be over, or open them and watch it happen. Curiosity won, though I was on the verge of hyperventilating as I watched Geoff bring the hollow needle up and push it through the holes in the forceps. I almost didn't feel it until it came out the other side—that's when it got intense enough for me to grunt sharply. Then he inserted a titanium bar into the needle and guided it through, screwing the bead onto the other side with practiced ease. Small traces of blood welled on either side, hardly enough to notice.

Panting, sweat beading on my brow, I tipped my head back and stared at the ceiling until I got my bearings. The initial surge of pain as the needle had pushed out of my nipple was gone, but it'd been replaced by a constant, throbbing, red-hot ache.

Jace moaned softly. "Damn, that looks good. How you holding up?"

"I'm okay," I whispered, though I knew I was shaking.

"Still good for the other one, or do you want to stop there?" Geoff asked briskly. We might have been laying the foundations of a solid friendship, but he was one hundred percent business right now.

I drew a deep breath and blew it out, acclimating to that burning, pulsating pain enough to feel capable of moving on.

"Still good," I said, and watched as he clamped the forceps on the other side.

I don't know why the second one hurt worse, but fucking hell, did it ever. I groaned as the needle went in and shouted, *"Fuck!"* when it seemed to take forever punching through the other side. If there had been other clients in the shop, I would have been humiliated to show myself as such a wuss, but only Jace and Geoff were there to see it. I screwed my eyes shut and endured the tugging as he threaded the bar through.

Afterward I sat there trembling, waiting for the pain to recede to something manageable.

"Sorry," I gasped after a moment of trying to remember how to breathe.

"For what?" Jace stroked my hair soothingly.

"Screaming like that. Guess I'm not as butch as I thought."

Geoff laughed at me. "Topher, I've had three-hundred-pound leather daddies burst into tears having that done. Trust me, you did just fine."

Well, gee. That made me feel good. I grinned, stupidly proud of myself.

"Oh. Okay. Here, let me get up and I'll finish helping you clean."

He flapped a dismissive hand at me. "Don't bother. We're almost done anyway. Take it easy, or take Jace, or whatever you have planned. Don't forget the cleanser, the Tegaderm patches when you swim, and the saline soak. I'll see you tomorrow."

I nodded, gathering up the supplies he'd laid out for me before we'd started, when he'd gone over all the details of the aftercare. Jace didn't even offer me my shirt, just draped it over his arm while I waited to see if my legs would work.

My nipples throbbed as I sat in the passenger seat of his car on the way back to the Dunes. It was a cloudy, temperate night and Jace rolled the windows down to catch the gusty breeze off the lake. I wasn't sure if the cool air helped the pain any, because it made my bare nipples tighten up. Underneath the unrelenting ache, the arousal that had gotten me into that chair to begin with had made a healthy recovery. All day, I had been itching for Jace —and he for me, if his handsiness was any indication—and now we could finally do something about that.

The door had barely shut behind us before I shoved him roughly toward the bed. Not even so much as a kiss was exchanged; I didn't dare get my fevered nipples close enough to him for that.

"Pants. Off," I growled, working my own belt, skinning my jeans and underwear down my hips just enough to let my cock bob free. He had only kicked off his shoes and worked his pants down to his knees by the time I was suited up and slicking lube over the condom. I planted my other hand between his shoulder blades and bent him forward over the bed while he was still on his feet.

"Oh, *fuck* yeah." He groaned when I thrust my lubed fingers into him. He was tighter in this position, and God I couldn't wait to feel that around my dick.

"You like it rough, right?" I taunted, pulling my fingers out and swiping the rest of the lube along his crack.

"Yeah." He braced his hands on the mattress. "Fuck, Topher. Give it to me."

I did. I echoed his groan as I pushed into him, fast and hard, knowing now that we were both burning, burning, my nipples and his ass, and Jesus, wasn't *that* a metaphor for whatever was happening between us? I was on fire for him, in a way I'd never been before, for his pale skin and dark hair and red lips, for both the fucking *incendiary* raunch and the heartbreaking sensitivity that came in turns from his brilliant artist's mind.

And I knew it was the same for him. I knew it the same way he'd known I was holding back on admitting to wanting to have my nipples pierced. I didn't buy into all that mystical soulmates crap, but I couldn't deny that we had amazing chemistry and we just *understood* one another, instinctively, resonating together like the multilayered harmonics of a perfectly tuned chord. We just clicked.

I held his hips and cut loose, not holding a single thing back. Hard, so hard, and fast, skin slapping against skin in a nonstop patter until I was sure my hips would be bruised from banging against his ass, soft and round as it was. His voice rose and fell in a near-constant ululation, and sometimes I couldn't tell from the tone whether it was pleasure or pain driving his cries, but since the words mostly consisted of encouragement, I threw everything I had into it.

He took his weight on one hand to jerk off with the other, and then he *clenched*, gripping so hard I thought he might injure me. Only a few more strokes into that clamping, shuddering tightness and I was over the top, groaning desperately, spending every last drop of cum in my balls into the tip of the condom, calling his name.

We were both sore and moving painfully when we parted and collapsed in a breathless heap. I managed to fumble around until the condom hit the trash and we were both arranged more or less comfortably on the bed. I wanted to hold him but couldn't quite figure out how to manage it without irritating my nipples, so he ended up spooning me instead, which caused me to give a grunt of dissatisfaction. Some weird, persnickety voice inside me fussed and tutted.

"What?" he murmured against the back of my neck, sounding sleepy and satisfied.

"I'm pretty sure it's a rule somewhere that whoever tops should be the big spoon." Seriously! We were going against the natural order, doing it this way.

His body shook with a near-silent chuckle. "I say we make our own rules." His hand slid up my chest, his finger circling, but not touching, my pierced nipples. "You don't know how bad I want to play with these."

"Hmph. Do it and draw back a nub."

He laughed harder. "They just look *so fucking sexy*. And watching you get them . . . oh, my God. You have no idea. I've never seen anything so hot. I can't wait to see how you respond when I touch them." He sighed in contentment, his voice drifting off to a drowsy slur. "Mm. I'm going to have a lot of fun with those when they're healed."

He was already asleep, and I was too fucked out to make much of the implications of that statement. Then I thought about the papers Geoff had sent home with me saying it could take months for them to heal, and I smiled.

SOMETIME IN THE MORNING, I woke up to thunder crashing around us, rain driving hard against the patio door. The light creeping in around the edge of the blackout curtains was gray, suggesting it was sometime after dawn, though I wasn't sure how much after because of the storm.

Jace was rocking against my ass. How long he'd been awake and getting worked up, I didn't know, but I was perfectly willing to push back against him, generating more friction as he reached for my cock and rutted against the small of my back.

We were both moaning so loudly we nearly missed the chime of a text message arriving on his cell phone.

"Ignore it," I panted when it disrupted his rhythm. I closed my hand over his around my cock, intent on finding it again. Then *my* phone chimed.

With a mutter, he rolled away from me to grab his phone off the bedside table. "It has to be Robin or Geoff." Mine was in my jeans on the other side of the room, but when I dragged myself out of bed to grab it, his hand closed over my wrist. "I'm pretty sure I already know what yours says."

There was humor in his voice, and he offered his phone to me. Geoff's name was at the top of the screen.

@hospital. Lings in labor. Topher has wknd off paid. Prob open shops Tues or Weds Will txt later.

I burst into excited laughter. "Oh my God. Awesome! What

should we do? Do we, like, buy cigars? Go sit in the waiting room with them?"

Jace shook his head, chuckling, and rolled out of bed to grab his laptop case.

"Right now it should be just family there. They're great friends, but it's not *quite* at that level, you know?"

"Ah, yeah." I nodded, embarrassed at having gotten carried away. "Me either."

"I'm going to send a balloon bouquet. You want your name on the card?"

"Yeah, please!" I couldn't help but smile. It wasn't my family or my baby, but I was still overjoyed for them. While Jace shopped for the balloon arrangement, I grabbed my phone and responded to the text message they'd sent. I congratulated them and wished them luck, then grabbed the supplies Geoff had sent home with me the night before and went into the bathroom to run through the piercing care regimen he'd prescribed.

When I came out, Jace had set his laptop aside. He lay on the bed, sucking on his cheek thoughtfully. I peered outside, around the curtain, at the driving rain.

"Guess I won't have to worry about swimming today. At least not unless I want to drag myself up to Holland." Guilt tried to creep in about that, especially since I'd missed my morning workout the day before, but I stomped on it ruthlessly. Most of my teammates wouldn't put any more effort into swimming over the summer than it took to dunk their friends in a pool. I was the one pushing myself to be in shape for the upcoming season, and missing a day or two wasn't a catastrophe. It was just the critical voices of the past—the ones that told me I never tried hard enough—that made me feel like I was being insufferably lazy.

"I guess not." He caught my hand, tugging me down onto the bed beside him. I tried to be careful of my nipples, but they were already aching a little less, so I decided to dare curling up against him. "So. You have at least three days off."

"Yeah, I do. Why?" I flashed him a flirty grin, rubbing my groin against his thigh. I was perfectly willing to pick up where we'd left off before the texts had arrived. "Thinking of staying in town a couple days longer?"

"Actually"—he flipped, rolling me onto my back and lying above me, careful to keep any weight off my chest—"I had a different idea. Wanna spend a few days in Chicago?"

I blinked at him. Then I threw my head back and laughed with the sort of delight known only to adventure-seeking, small-city suburbanites faced with the opportunity to visit a *real* city.

"Oh, fuck yeah."

CHAPTER TWENTY-FIVE

I'm almost sick of trying to wade through this
I should be fine and over it

— CASEY STRATTON, "YOU WERE MY RELIGION"

It took us a while to get on the road. First because we had sex again, then because we fell asleep, and then because the whole shower and clothes and breakfast ritual had to take place. The thunderstorm had passed by the time we were finally in the car, and as we drove along Lakeshore Drive, Lake Michigan was that hazy, tranquil gray-blue it only seems to be after the rain. I leaned my head against the headrest and closed my eyes with a sigh. I wasn't quite tired enough to fall asleep, but relaxing during the nearly three-hour drive sounded like a nifty idea because I had no idea what we'd be doing once we arrived in Chicago.

Interestingly, I didn't feel the need to fill the silence in the car with chatter, and wasn't that strange? No awkward silence; it was completely comfortable for me and Jace. After he merged onto the Gerald R. Ford, his hand landed on my knee, caressing just for the sake of touching me. As if, like he'd said, it felt more natural to have his hands on me than to keep them to himself.

"If you want music, feel free to play with the radio." There was something satisfied and affectionate in his voice, as though he was really, truly happy to have me there with him. "There's a plug-in for your iPod if you want it."

I grinned, reaching into the rear seat for my backpack and trying not to whimper as the movement tugged at my new piercings. "Oh, you're so gonna regret that offer."

"Yeah? Why's that?"

"Because I'm one of those obnoxious people who *has* to have music on a road trip, and because the selections tend to be more along the lines of show tunes and indie artists no one has heard of than anything most people would rock out to in the car."

"Go ahead, do your worst."

I plugged in my iPod and browsed through the menus for a moment, then leaned back again when a tinkling piano line swelled into the oceanic melody of "For Reasons Unexplained." It rose and fell gently, flooding from the speakers to swirl around us. A moment later, an androgynous voice with a soaring vibrato joined it.

Jace listened attentively for a moment, his eyes widening. "Holy shit. What is this?"

I smiled, pleased with his reaction. "My idol. Casey Stratton."

He shook his head, his eyes on the road. "I've never heard of him."

"Not many people have. He's been mostly indie his whole career."

"How did *you* discover him?"

I sighed wistfully. "He went to my high school about twenty years ago. Which is, of course, why he's my idol."

"He does mostly alternative stuff?"

"Yeah. Think Tori Amos with a dick. Angsty, introspective, sometimes pissed off. That's when things get fun." As if to prove my point, the next track on the playlist was "You Were My Religion," with its driving beat and power chords. That one had always resonated with me because of the anger and defiance in the lyrics. We were listening to *Signs of Life*—my favorite album— and I had plans to move on to *The Crossing*. Jace had no idea what he was in for.

I caught myself singing along and stopped before I got lost in it. "If you think he sounds good recorded, you should hear him live. You don't really get the full impact of just how talented he is until it's just him and a keyboard, no processing. Brilliant piano. Gorgeous voice. He's just amazing."

Jace flicked that perceptive gaze at me for a second. "You wish you were him."

"Yeah." I nodded, suppressing another sigh. Listening to someone that good was a bit of an exercise in masochism, really. Casey had done what I would have sold my soul to be able to do. It didn't matter that he wasn't a household name with millions of dollars and a shit-ton of Grammys; it wasn't about being famous. Casey had made that clear by his choice to go indie, even though it meant he'd never get the exposure a major label could provide, and I felt the same. It was about being good, being able to make music and give the finger to all the people who'd ever told me I wasn't good enough or mocked me for dreaming I ever would be. Casey had done that. And as much as I loved his music, at times it made me ache with envy. "But, he was, like, you know, a *prodigy*. Mostly self-taught and just, you know, one of those guys that gets clobbered over the head by the Talent Fairy until they have the stuff coming out their ears. I'm slightly above average, but not anywhere close to that." I laughed softly at myself. "He still lives in Grand Rapids. When I was in high school, I used to imagine contacting him through his website and . . . I don't know . . . asking him to meet for coffee, beg him to be my Yoda. Something. Ask him to tell me how to survive that fucking little narrow-minded 'burb and get out and rise above it all."

"Well, why didn't you?"

I shrugged, ducking my head. "Because that's just stupid fanboy shit. I don't have what he has, talent-wise. I can't do what he did."

Ouch. There was that stab of envy and hopelessness again.

Jace grimaced but said nothing. We fell silent again, the music surrounding us. It soothed me and lifted me up out of my readiness to feel sorry for myself. It didn't take me long to forget myself and begin singing along again, transported by piano, strings, and soaring high notes.

"You're really better than you give yourself credit for," Jace said after a few minutes.

"People keep saying that, but it's not true." I gave him a frank look. "That's not false modesty or self-denigration, either. I know I'm good; what I'm *not* is great. I don't have that level of natural talent, and I know it. With the right training, I could have made up the difference, but I missed that window, so all I'm ever going to be is a gifted amateur."

It was way too emo to say aloud, but sometimes in my melo-dramatic moments, it felt like—barring some divine revelation—the only thing at which I'd ever *truly* excel was fucking up. Fucked up my relationship with my family, fucked up my oppor-tunity for a good education, fucked up my best friend's family and, by extension, my friendship with her.

That's me. Christopher Carlisle: Professional Fuck-Up Artist.

And that was quite enough with the pity-poor-me bullshit, thank you very much. I wasn't going to fuck up this weekend with Jace, too, by going down that spiral. I jerked myself out of it and smiled, ready to change the subject.

But Jace wasn't done with it. "I think you give up too easily."

I rubbed my forehead. "Didn't we have this conversation by the pool the first time we slept together?"

"Yeah, well I guess I've got more to say still. You compare your worst to some genius's best and decide you're not good enough? How the fuck are you ever supposed to win that game? It's still possible to find some way to do what you love and feel like you're successful at it. You just need to find out what your options are."

"And do *what*? Be told that I'm not good enough? *Again*? Because, you know, I haven't heard *that* message thousands of times already."

It was hard not to sound as frustrated and inadequate as the subject sometimes made me feel. "Do you know how *hard* I worked back before I stopped doing choir and plays? Every single conductor and director I had agreed on one point: I had an amazing work ethic. I was always at rehearsal, always ready to put in one hundred and twenty percent, always had my part memorized well before it was necessary. But no matter what I did, it was never enough to get me solos, and the only time I got the lead in a musical, it was because I was right for the part physically, not because I was the best option vocally. What I needed was training, and my family wouldn't let me have that. I can't afford it now, even if it weren't too late. So I mean, really, how many times do I have to be told I'll never be more than mediocre before it stops being worth the effort?"

His mouth twisted. "Do you want to know how many times I had to apply to get accepted to a decent art school? How long it took me to start getting shows? Fact is, if Robin hadn't opened his gallery around the same time he hooked up with my best friend, I'd probably still be eating ramen noodles twice a day. I got lucky. But that's the *point.*" His eyes shifted to me briefly before he looked back to the road. "Sooner or later, the opportunity to shine comes along, angel, and *that's* when you get the chance to show people what you really have inside, show them the stuff that might not be obvious in a thirty-second audition. And you'll never be in the right place at the right time if you don't keep trying, no matter how many times you get rejected."

"That sounds swell, but there's a little problem with trying to feed myself until that magical day arrives."

Fuck, when had I become so cynical?

"What about teaching? Or conducting?"

"You know how many schools are slashing art and music programs completely right now because of the economy? If I were to teach, it would need to be math or science."

Jace's knuckles whitened where he gripped the wheel, and his voice became a little sharper, more impatient. "Okay, you know what I think? I think somewhere along the way, someone hammered into you over and over that making a living was more important than *actually* living, and you finally bought into it."

"Well, if I'd done that, I wouldn't be sleeping on Robin and Geoff's sofa like some hobo off the streets, would I? I'd be trying to make myself more masculine and understated so my family would keep bankrolling my education without trying to use it to pressure me to be what I'm not."

I thought that would annoy Jace further—and really, *why* the fuck was I arguing about this with him instead of enjoying our trip?—but he just smiled, a tiny curve at the corner of his mouth.

"See, that's what makes me think it's not anywhere near too late for you, Topher. You've stepped one foot outside that cage, but you just can't quite drag the other one out. You're not mediocre. You're not anywhere close to it. Mediocrity has been wrapped around you like bandages until you don't know how to unwind yourself from it. You can still be brilliant. You can do what you love. You can *live* and make a living. You just need to work your way through all the conflicting messages you've been given."

He reached for my knee again, and I slipped my fingers through his, clinging. Something knotted and ached inside my chest, yearning to believe him. But I was so fucking scared of disappointment again. I'd had enough of that for one lifetime.

"What messages?"

"They—and I don't know who *they* are, family, teachers, peers, it doesn't matter—told you perfection was absolutely paramount and that nothing less was even worth doing, while simultaneously telling you that you could never be perfect. It left you wondering why you should bother trying, even though your heart keeps telling you to do what you love. They told you success was more important than the endeavor, while convincing you it was impossible for you to succeed."

Annnd once again he had me ready to just lay my head in his lap and fucking cry like a lost little kid. I didn't know what scared me more—that he saw into me with such complete clarity, or that he was trying to give me hope when I'd fought so hard and so long to kill it.

"How do you do that?" I whispered, swallowing thickly.

"Do what?"

"Know me so well."

"You're not the only one to have a shitty upbringing, Topher."

My eyes widened at that. I'd assumed that, like Robin, he was one of those privileged guys from a liberal family who'd supported him wholeheartedly.

"What was your family like?"

His hand tightened on mine. "They put me in conversion therapy when I was fourteen, including two trips to residence facilities—one of which was pretty much a psychiatric hospital, and the other more along the lines of juvenile detention disguised as a summer camp. When I was sixteen—by which time I'd already tried to commit suicide once and nearly attempted it again but chickened out, which is a damn good thing because I'm pretty sure I would have gotten it right that time—I started pretending to be 'cured.' I had to give up studying art for the last two years of high school and managed to fuck up my knees playing football to keep up the charade."

His face tightened, and I fell silent, not daring to interrupt.

"The day I graduated high school, I withdrew every dollar I'd earned or received as a birthday or Christmas gift from the bank. The account had their names on it alongside mine, see, so they could cut me off from my money if I looked like I might rebel. Then I gathered up every drawing and painting I'd managed to hide away. I went downstairs to my graduation party and smiled while I opened my cards to collect all the cash and checks. Then, in front of everyone they knew, I looked them in the eye and told them I was gay, I would always be gay, and that I was an adult now, so they could accept it or they could lose their son." He shrugged. "They chose option B."

"Shit." I didn't even think about it. I just lifted his hand to my face and kissed it. "I'm sorry."

"I'm not."

"How—" I frowned, stroking his hand. "How did you survive? How did you get through art school?"

"Honestly?" He gave me a wry smile. "I found a sugar daddy."

My eyes widened at that and he gave me a nod as if to say that yes, he absolutely was serious.

"After I left my family behind in Nebraska, I bought a bus ticket for Boston, and lived in hostels and bathhouses while I placed discreetly worded personal ads and trawled gay chat rooms until I finally found a taker. I didn't like him much, but I could fake it. Definitely not how I would have chosen to lose my virginity under optimal circumstances, but I had my eye on the prize. And yes, before you ask, he was married and in the closet. For five years he helped with my bills and tuition, and in exchange I went along with whatever he wanted to do in bed when he 'worked late' three or four nights a week. Anything except barebacking, that is. That was my hard limit."

"Wow," I breathed, doing some mental math to readjust my thinking toward the arrangement Brendan had offered me. Things could have been a lot worse than what I'd turned my nose up at.

Jace shrugged. "By the way, PSA time: It's a damn good thing I stuck to that limit, because by the time I graduated, I'd discovered the guy had also been indulging in anonymous hookups on Craigslist. He had HIV. When I found that out, I told him not to touch me again. Not because he was infected, but because he'd cared so little about my well-being that he'd been trying to pressure me into unprotected sex while he was taking those other risks. Anyway, he disappeared, but by then I'd gotten what I needed from him. I'm just lucky I dodged the bullet with regard to oral transmission of any number of things. We didn't use condoms when I went down on him, but then, I didn't let him come in my mouth, either."

I nodded, processing this for a moment, then looked over at him. "Is *that* why you've never given me a blowjob?" That little act was becoming conspicuous by its absence from our sexual repertoire since we'd met up again. He hadn't had an issue going down on me that first time together, but since he'd learned about Brendan? Nothing.

"Sorry." He gave me an apologetic look, flushing slightly. "The taste of condoms—or maybe it's the texture—makes me hurl every time. Even the non-latex ones still . . ." He shuddered, his throat working as if resisting the urge to gag even at the thought. "I'm not exaggerating. I have humiliated myself all over a guy's junk making the attempt. But I tell you what, you test negative in another month or so, angel, and I swear I will *suck you dry*."

He put such a growly, hungry emphasis on those last three words that I arched in my seat and needed to adjust myself in my jeans.

"Jesus," I muttered, resting my head against the back of my seat and closing my eyes against the mental image. Recovering, I arched an eyebrow at him. "So, when do I get to see *your* test results?"

He grinned and made an ostentatious display of checking his wristwatch. "In about an hour and forty-five minutes, traffic permitting. Though, if you'd rather wait until I can return the favor, that's fair."

I thought about the sight of his cock, thick and dripping, and the feel of him in my hand, the scent of him, the taste of his pre-cum on my tongue.

"No. No, I don't think I'd rather wait."

"Oh, thank God." He laughed softly. "Anyway, the point of telling you about my ex–sugar daddy was to say: Give yourself a break for couch-surfing. It's not some scarlet letter on your chest, saying you're a deadbeat. People have sunk a lot lower to try to reach independence, and if you're a loser for sleeping on a friend's sofa, what am I for letting a guy I didn't even like pay my bills for five years in exchange for sex? If someone wants to help you, and if you know you're not just taking advantage of them, then let them help. Forget that voice that says you're a failure if you can't do it all yourself. Listen to the people who are saying you *can* for once, instead of all the ones who have told you that you *can't*. Think you can do that?"

I thought silently for a moment, then nodded. "I think I can try."

"Good."

Just like that, the atmosphere in the car shifted as he flashed his devilish grin and looked at his watch again. "One hour forty-two minutes . . ."

I let my head fall back and laughed.

CHAPTER TWENTY-SIX

If the wolves are hovering near your fragile heart
I'll do my part
And in time I know you'll learn
What you need to know
What you need to show everyone

— CASEY STRATTON, "THE WINDOW WILL CLOSE"

We didn't end up going out again after we reached Jace's apartment that afternoon, which was perfectly fine by me. I had no objections to staying in bed and taking advantage of the fact that I could go down on him without suffering the taste of latex. And he had taken a particularly evil delight in playing with my new nipple piercings. Not much—they were far too new for that. But every once in a while, he'd gently bump the end of a barbell with a fingertip, just enough to send a jolt of pain to tighten my body.

We came up for air when our cell phones chimed again, announcing that Zhen had been born healthy and beautiful—including a newborn shot of her in all her blotchy, wrinkled glory—and that Ling was doing great. We sent the requisite congrats and to celebrate, had Thai delivered, and snuggled on the sofa, pretending to watch a movie while using it as an excuse to make out (and it was some really fucking *good* making out; Lord, could that man kiss!). Then we went back to bed.

He had an impressive array of sex toys. By the time we crawled out of bed for breakfast Sunday morning, I was sore and exhausted from having a plug so thick I'd almost refused to consider it stuffed in my stretched, aching asshole. I'd struggled with it while he rode my cock and kept pulling me back from the edge of orgasm over and over again by tapping my nipple.

I didn't know what I'd expected from his apartment. Maybe I'd seen *Rent* too many times, and assumed he'd live in some unimproved industrial warehouse space covered in red brick and graffiti. Someplace that froze in winter and broiled in summer and always needed something repaired. Instead, he lived in a very ordinary, cookie-cutter condo, almost excruciatingly boring except for the paintings he'd hung on the walls.

"Where do you work?" I asked, seeing no signs of a studio.

"Right there." He pointed to his desktop computer, which was equipped with an elaborate graphics pad.

"I meant painting."

"Oh, I rent a space from another artist when I need it. I don't paint full-time. I do a lot of graphic design and digital art, with some set design work for local theaters on the side. I usually use the studio space on Saturdays, so I'm sure to paint once a week, and arrange for more time if I have a project I'm working really hard on."

"It didn't take you long to make those paintings of me."

He smiled softly. "No, it didn't. I was on fire when I was working on those. I was at the studio nearly three solid weeks, and I barely slept until they were done."

I didn't really know what to say to that. I'd known that night we'd spent together was incredible, but I hadn't realized the extent to which it had affected him.

I was afraid to ask why.

AT MY REQUEST, we went to see the theater for which Jace had been doing set design the first time we'd met. Afterward, we had lunch and fell into bed again. Truth be told, we spent quite a bit of that time napping because we were both exhausted from the past few nights, and we didn't crawl out of bed until almost dinner. When we were done eating, I did the good-guest thing I'd been brought up to do and insisted on cleaning the kitchen over his protests.

"Anything you'd like to do tonight?" he asked, leaning on his elbows on the table. "We've got a whole city to get into trouble in. We could head to Boystown, hit a club."

"Aw, damn!" I sighed in disgust, pausing in wiping down the counter. "I knew I should have brought something to wear clubbing."

"Not even the eyeliner?" He gave me a plaintive look, and I shook my head. "Okay, we're so going shopping. Club's on the agenda for tomorrow night."

I laughed and decided the expense might be worth it. When I resumed wiping the counter, my cloth bumped a shiny business card sticking out from under a stack of mail. It had a picture of a muscle-bound and presumably nude man.

"What's this for?"

He grinned, dropping me a wink. "Bathhouse."

"What? Are you serious?" I blinked at him in surprise. "I thought those all got shut down with the AIDS epidemic."

He nodded, pursing his lips. "A lot of them did. A few managed to rebrand themselves for the safer sex era. There are still some really seedy, disgusting ones, but others can be nice. They hand out condoms, discourage unprotected sex, even work with AIDS prevention organizations and offer on-site immediate testing. There are some new ones for the next generation, too, appealing to a younger crowd."

I waved the card. "And you've been here?"

"Are you going to freak if I say yes? Because I'll be honest, angel—until I met you, I hooked up *a lot*."

"What? No, no. I'm not gonna, you know, judge." Especially one particular part of me, which was quite interested in this conversation. I frowned, though, thinking of all the stories I'd heard about bathhouses being breeding grounds for disease. It didn't fit what I knew of Jace, as cautious as he was about such things. "So what's the appeal? Just a walk on the seedy side once in a while?"

Jace grimaced. "No, no. Look, I know the sort of rep those places have, and sometimes it's dead-on, but . . . it's part of our history, don't you get it?"

He looked so earnest that I sobered. "No, I guess I don't."

"Well, think about why it's there, angel. Why the clubs had back rooms." Jace leaned forward on the counter, his arms folded under him. "They're a remnant of a time—one not all that long ago—when most of us could never be ourselves at home. We couldn't be out, or have a lover, at least not one we acknowledged. Hell, a lot of us were married with kids, passing as straight. A lot of us still are, and if things had worked out differently with my parents trying to reprogram me, that might even have been me." He gestured at the card. "That's why those places exist. It's not just somewhere to go take a walk on the wild side. For a long time, places like that were the only places where we could be *us*. Anonymously, yeah, but still, for a moment we wouldn't have to hide who we were. So yeah, it sounds sleazy, but you need to respect the history that resulted in the bathhouses and saunas and back rooms."

"Wow. Heavy." I bowed my head a moment and let myself absorb his words. For as much as my life sucked, sometimes it was hard to remember that there was a time when things could have been much, *much* harder. Honestly, being a flaming princess was one of my less significant worries, at least now that I was out of high school, and as long as I avoided being alone in the wrong places.

"Sorry." Jace scratched his head with a self-conscious chuckle. "I got on my soapbox there. Anyway, I've got a lifetime membership to this one, free use of all the facilities. They have a weight room no one ever uses because most people are just there to fuck, so I go there to work out rather than pay for a gym membership. Sometimes I just play voyeur, or go to be social. A lot of old-school bathhouses consider conversation taboo, because it's supposed to be anonymous. But this one is more modern and relaxed, so you can chat guys up. And I won't say I've never hooked up there."

"How'd you score the membership deal?"

"I did their interior design when they remodeled a few years ago, including some of the murals on their walls. I design their promotional materials, too. It's definitely one of the nicer places, but you know, no matter how nice it is, you still have to deal with the fact that when it comes down to it, it's a meat market for anonymous sex. I'm not sure you'd like it."

I frowned. "Why not?"

He lifted an eyebrow. "Because you're young and gorgeous. You'd get a *lot* of attention there, much of it unwanted or unattractive, some of it even gross. Seriously. How would you feel about being groped by a handsy stranger?"

"You mean besides you?" I gave him an arch look as I rinsed the dishrag and hung it over the edge of the sink, then sighed. "Okay, yeah, you've got a point there. I don't know if I'd react well."

"It usually only takes a shake of your head or a 'no thanks' to tell someone to back off, and if that doesn't work, management will throw them out on their ass and revoke their membership. But I won't say some guys don't just go for the goods. When you go there, 'yes' is kind of assumed to be the default, unless otherwise stated. I can guarantee you'd get your ass and your package handled at least a few times."

"Ah." I frowned, turning the card over in my fingers. That didn't sound at all like my thing, especially with my personal space issues.

So why was I so tempted to say I wanted to go?

I admit, Jace's admonishment notwithstanding, some of it was probably just the appeal of seeing the seedier side of big-city gay life, the sort of thing I'd never find in the suburbs and on a college campus. I felt so sheltered and unworldly compared to Jace, who'd lived in Boston and Chicago and God knew where else. I wanted to know what he knew, see life from his perspective. Maybe if I did that, I could stop being so afraid and unsure and get a little bit of his confidence.

"Well, at least I wouldn't have to worry about what to wear." I shrugged, my heart racing nervously.

Jace gave me a searching look. "You're *honestly* considering this?"

"Yeah. Yeah, I am." I swallowed, then drew my shoulders back, straightening. "I want to go."

He stared at me for a long, questioning moment.

"Okay."

CHAPTER TWENTY-SEVEN

I slid myself toward the fire
But I'd never burn

— CASEY STRATTON, "OPALINE"

"So what is it you think you want to do here?" he asked on the car ride over.

I shrugged, my hands twisting nervously in my lap. "I don't know. Observe, I guess, to start. See what it's about."

"Are you wanting to hook up with someone?" His voice was neutral and his eyes were on the road. I couldn't tell from his profile exactly how he felt about that proposition, but it didn't matter. I shook my head quickly.

"No. No, I don't . . . I don't think so. That's not why— I don't want anyone but you."

The corner of his mouth curled up and he looked pleased. He liked that. He liked that a lot.

"Are you okay with watching others? Couples, even groups? Either in their rooms or sometimes in the public spaces?"

I drew a nervous breath. "I guess we'll find out. You like that, though, don't you?"

He nodded. "Sometimes. Depends on my mood. Sometimes I

get off, sometimes I just get ideas. You already knew I like observing people. It's the same principle."

"Yeah." I set my shoulders again, trying to shake off my nerves. "We'll just . . . see how it goes, okay?"

"Okay." He smirked. "For the record, your safeword is 'get me the fuck out of here.'"

I laughed, and how did he keep managing to make me do that when my stomach was in knots?

"I think I can remember that."

The first brush of a stranger's hand over my towel-covered dick convinced me that Jace hadn't been exaggerating. Supposedly there was a code where a closed towel indicated look-but-don't-touch, and an open towel was an invitation to help yourself, but not everyone followed it. I walked on, ignoring the brush, too nervous at being there in the first place to be all that skeeved out. Jace, however, turned to look at whoever it was and gave them a firm shake of his head. It helped that he had his hand planted between my shoulder blades, his body positioned close beside me to try to send the signal that my companion was already chosen. Of course, that wouldn't deter anyone looking for a group—and Jace was receiving every bit as much attention as I was—but it was a start.

He led me through a dimly lit maze of cubicle-sized rooms just like the one we'd rented. Some had men lying or standing in them with the door open, just waiting for any passer-by to take up the unspoken offer. Occasionally, I would see a gorgeous mural on a stretch of wall that made the paintings Jace had done of me look positively virginal. So far, seeing his works was the most amazing thing about the place.

The sounds of fucking were all around under the low pulse of club music, some of it coming from thin-walled rooms with the door shut, and some of it from rooms that were wide open. I couldn't bring myself to look at those, not yet. It felt wrong to gawk, even if they'd left the door open in an invitation to do just that—or possibly join in. And I could feel eyes upon me, upon *us*, from patrons both young and old—from muscle-bound gym rats to solidly built bears to saggy, middle-aged guys with wedding bands nearly embedded in their pudgy fingers. I kept my head down and let Jace wave off any attention that might be offered.

Maybe I was just too provincial for this shit.

And yet, despite my discomfort, I was at least a little turned on. Not fully; I wasn't more than half-hard under that towel (which, unless matters changed drastically, would remain firmly around my hips, thank you very much), but tension was winding tight in my nuts, sending pulses through my cock.

If I could have identified *what* was generating those pangs of arousal, I might have asked to pursue it. But I couldn't. Everything was a tumult of nerves and confusion and revulsion, mixed in with that almost-reluctant thread of eroticism.

We paused by a line of booths, some of which had men on their knees near the wall. Oh wow. Glory holes. I looked at Jace and he was gnawing his lip with that hungry look he got when he saw something he wanted.

"You like doing that?" I murmured to him.

"Don't know. Never tried it." He sighed deeply.

"Why not?"

"Because in that particular fantasy of mine, I'd really like to be the one on my knees."

"Why—" Then I remembered his little issue with the taste or texture of condoms. He couldn't live out that fantasy without taking a risk he'd rather not take.

Man, that sucked. So to speak.

I stood watching him watch the cocksuckers for a while longer, then I got a little brave.

"What about after I get tested next month? I mean, it won't be the same as a stranger, but . . ."

His eyes danced as he looked over at me and smiled. "I'm okay with role-play."

I smiled back, pleased to be able to offer him something he wanted and couldn't have from just anyone.

"Wanna go check out the hot tub?" he offered, and I nodded. I hoped the scent of chlorine would help cleanse some of the mélange of sweat, cologne, musk, latex, and cum that was assailing my nostrils.

The maze gave way to more open spaces. A glass-and-tile-enclosed steam room was off to one side, and further along was a lounge of some sort, but before that, we came to the Jacuzzi. I was glad Jace had advised me to wear the waterproof film over my new nipple piercings, because I wasn't sure I trusted anything, even the heavily chlorinated water, to be sanitary. It bubbled and foamed and steamed, the chemical fumes so heavy they burned my eyes. We laid aside our towels and sank into the water, claiming a space on the benches lining the sides.

For a hot tub, it was huge. There were only eight or so men in there now, but it could have easily seated twenty or more. Three of the men were in the far corner in a tangle of limbs, twined so closely around each other that only the occasional contrast in skin tone made it clear there were different people in that spot at all. Clouds of steam wafted up to obscure them, but their sounds rode over the low roar of the jets. Scattered around the sides of the pool, other men relaxed, ignoring them or watching unabashedly. Some even appeared to be stroking themselves underwater, and their attention wasn't just on the threesome in the corner. Speculative looks slid our way, and I thought by now that Jace's protective alpha-male vibe must have been pretty clear —or maybe it was just the way I was hanging on to him like I was going to be eaten otherwise—because when someone approached us, he leaned down, murmuring in Jace's ear rather than mine. Jace replied softly and turned his attention to me, speaking against my ear.

"This gentleman wants to know if I'd be willing to loan you to him. He thinks you belong to me. What do you think?" He punctuated the question by sucking on my earlobe.

I gasped and turned to him wide-eyed. Anyone who didn't know Jace's face as well as I was coming to wouldn't have recognized the hint of a smirk and the gleam in his eyes. He knew goddamn good and well I wouldn't be okay with that. He was just trying to wind me up.

And fuck me if it wasn't working. That coil of tension below my waist, the one tugging my nuts up nice and snug, got just a little tighter.

Two could play that game. For the first time, I let myself really look at another man here. He was in his mid- to late-thirties and very, very butch. He wasn't ripped, but there were slabs of muscle under a slight, beefy paunch; I had no doubt he was fucking *strong*. As in, he could break me in two, because he towered over me. He wasn't unattractive, especially if you liked bears, but he was a little scary and the erection that hung from his hips over the bubbling water was downright terrifying. He could break me in more ways than one.

Still, I let myself consider the notion, even if I already knew what my answer would be. And I let Jace see me do it, in case he decided to get too complacent in his role as my "owner," because that *so* was not what we were about, however out of my element I might be at the moment.

Jace's lips moved against my ear again. "If you agree to it, my one condition is that I get to watch. And *not* just to make sure everything is safe." To emphasize his point, he caught my hand under the water and pulled it into his lap.

Oh. Wow. Okay then.

It was more tempting than I would have assumed it would be when I'd walked in, especially when Jace dealt that little surprise punch, but I shook my head and managed a charming smile to the guy.

"Thanks, but not tonight."

He smiled back and walked away, and that was it.

When he was gone, I drew my hand off of Jace's cock, but let it remain on his thigh.

"Why did you even ask me? Why didn't you wave him off?"

He shrugged. "Because boundaries shift. What you thought you wanted in the car on the way here—which, to be fair, was pretty open-ended to begin with—might not be what you want now that we've been here a while. Plus, I wanted to see if subbing was your scene. I didn't think so, but you never know."

"Maybe a little bit when the mood strikes—you got pretty bossy on the Fourth, if I recall—but not really. I mean, I'm not quite as pure vanilla as Geoff and Robin, but I kind of fucking resent the idea that because I'm smaller, younger, pretty, and femme, I'm an automatic bottom or sub."

Jace's eyes widened, his gaze flying to my face in astonishment. His complexion turned an alarming shade of puce and his eyes bulged before I realized he was choking on laughter. Gasping, he leaned back against the wall of the hot tub and wiped his streaming eyes.

"Oh *Jesus*."

"What the hell is so funny?"

"Robin and Geoff, vanilla?" He dissolved into chuckles so hysterical he was damn near giggling. "Oh, angel, you have no idea."

"Seriously?"

He nodded. "You asked Geoff why he didn't have any tats the other day? He was giving you the family-friendly version. Truth is, he likes wearing marks of a different sort, if you know what I mean. Some pretty hard-core ones, too."

"Holy shit." I stared at him in consternation. With the exception of Robin's tats, Geoff and Robin seemed as white-bread suburbanite as they could get. I couldn't envision them being the least bit adventurous, much less— "Wow. I can't even— Right." I blinked a few times and tried to remember what I'd been saying. "Back to my original point about people assuming things about me . . ."

He laughed again, tightening his arm around my shoulders. "I nearly fell into that trap the first time, but you made damn sure I wouldn't again."

I smiled, *very* satisfied to hear that. "Good."

Then he dropped his voice to a seductive murmur. "I will say, I don't get my dom on all that often, but the idea that you're here with me and everyone else can look and admire, but *I'm* the only one who gets to touch, is pushing that button for me. This whole proprietary riff isn't just for your sense of security." His hand slid up my inner thigh, stopping just short of my groin. "I like these guys thinking I've got that much claim on you, even if it's only in their imaginations."

I shifted, lifting my hips off the bench, brushing his hand with my cock. My teeth seized my bottom lip, stifling my moan at the contact, and my eyes fell shut. "That, um . . . I have to admit, that sounds a lot better tonight than it normally would."

He drew in a breath, as though a surprising thought had occurred to him.

"Ah, so *that's* what's turning your crank tonight. Not the idea of seeing, but of *being seen*. Am I right? You want *all* these men, all of them, no matter how attractive or sleazy, just eating their hearts out over you, wanting you but unable to have you." He laughed softly as my cock jumped. "You little exhibitionist."

Oh shit. Suddenly I was *so fucking hard*. I groaned and buried my face in his neck, laughing at my own ego.

"Yes. Yes, okay? That's what I want. My vanity is ridiculous." In my mind, the whole riff about being an embarrassment and drawing attention to myself began to play out, and I had to make myself shut up before it put me in a funk. I shook my head and sighed. "Stupid, stupid, stupid."

"No, not stupid." He kissed my sweaty, steam-damp forehead. "That's terrific. I love that you know you're hot enough to pull something like that off."

He held me there a moment until my embarrassment began to fade, hastened by his reassurances. Then he took my hand and tugged me up out of the water.

"Come on. Let's go check out the steam room."

CHAPTER TWENTY-EIGHT

We were lost inside a scene
Where spirits called right out to me
And I could see them easily
For I was open to believe
There's a waterfall of what could be
If I would heal the tragedies
Of a life where nothing ever seems to be easy

— CASEY STRATTON, "I PROMISE LOVE"

With my towel once more tucked around my waist—though my junk was considerably more visible beneath its concealment than it had been when we'd arrived—I let Jace squire me into the steam room. Once inside, though, I stopped in my tracks.

Mr. Not Unattractive Bear was in there. Had Jace known that?

Apparently he had, because he climbed up to the highest tile riser opposite the guy and scooted back, patting the space between his thighs. "Come sit here, angel."

My pulse took up a nervous, unsteady flutter, and I think I was half a second away from bolting when I met Jace's eyes. They were understanding, but there was also promise in them. Promise that he'd make sure I got whatever I wanted. Promise that he'd stop if what he had planned was too much. Promise that he would make it worth my while if I trusted him.

Swallowing, I sat between his legs and leaned back when he drew me down against his chest, my head pillowed on his shoulder.

"Think you might be interested in a different game?" he asked, pitching his voice loud enough that it was apparent he was speaking to the stranger, who watched us intently. He wasn't the only one in the steam room, either. Someone was getting a blowjob on another bench, and another couple of guys were jerking each other off, their towels hanging open. A half-dozen or so others were just watching, a few caressing themselves idly. One was pretty attractive, most were middle-of-the-road, a couple were downright skeevy.

And quite a few of them began watching *us* after Jace spoke loudly enough to be heard on the riser across from us.

The anonymous bear gave us a good-natured grin. "I like all sorts of games."

"How about a round of look-but-don't-touch?"

That grin grew wider. "I like a good show, too."

Jace's fingers stroked down the side of my neck, making me shiver. "He's beautiful, isn't he?"

If it had been possible for my skin to get any warmer after the hot tub and steam, I would have flushed hotly. Instead, I just squirmed. Whatever Jace said about my knowing I was hot, hearing myself praised so baldly in public was as embarrassing as it was flattering.

"Yeah, he is," the stranger agreed. "Why do you think I wanted to get my dick in him?"

"I can't blame you. I can tell you from experience that he has the tightest, sweetest ass you can ever imagine fucking."

Holy shit. I should be taking exception to the fact that they were talking about me like I wasn't even there, objectifying me, but *fuck* if it wasn't turning me on. My skin was burning from a lot more than the steam. I moaned, closing my eyes and wriggling again. Beneath his towel, Jace was hard against my back. So fucking hard.

"See these?" Jace's fingers moved down to my sore, film-covered nipples, making me gasp even at their gentle pressure. "He had them done just a couple days ago while I stood there and watched. He sounded so good groaning and screaming, I just about creamed my pants listening to him. And he sounds even better in bed."

"You gonna make him scream for me tonight?" the stranger asked.

"I sure hope so." Jace played carefully with my nipples through the tape until I was whimpering, shuddering and hiding my face in his neck.

"Hurts," I whispered, writhing against him.

"I know it does, angel. But it feels good when it hurts a little, doesn't it? Maybe not a lot, but a little."

Why was it so fucking hot to have him blurt out that factoid to all these strangers? I moaned and nodded, still hiding my face.

"Make him look at me," the stranger demanded, his voice a little deeper and rougher now. "I want to see."

"You hear that? Show our new friend what it's doing to you, me playing with these."

I whimpered again, sharply, and drew my face away from Jace's wet neck, turning it out toward the room. I heard a groan that sounded too far away to be the bear we were playing with and nearly cried out at the thought of someone else, someone even *less* familiar than this complete stranger, watching me. Then Jace wriggled my sore nipple just a *little* bit harder and I did cry out.

"Fuck yeah," the bear moaned. "That's nice."

"You're a sadist?" Jace asked him conversationally.

"Oh yeah," he said with some relish. "Now I'm really wishing he'd let me take him for a ride, because I would have loved to make him scream."

"If you were going to try to hurt him, you'd have to do it with more than your dick." Jace sounded amused. "He takes that like a champ and comes back for more. Should have seen the plug I jammed up his ass last night. If it had been any bigger, I might as well have fisted him, and he was humping back on the thing like it was his favorite carnival ride until I got it all the way in, wailing the whole time."

"Oh Jesus!" I gasped, my spine arching, and holy fucking God I was *this close* to coming just from *words*.

"Greedy little cockslut, huh?" the bear asked.

"Is there any other kind?"

I turned my face back in to Jace's neck with a sharp groan, writhing in an agony of humiliated arousal. This was wrong. Wrong wrong wrong. How could I possibly want this, be responding to this?

But . . . no. I'd seen wrong. Done wrong. Been the victim of wrong. This was harmless. Fantasy. No one was being hurt here. We were all feeling good. So damn good. Why should it bother me that I was doing it? Why should I be ashamed?

"Look at our friend, angel. Open your eyes and look at him. Look at what he's doing. Then look at the rest of them."

Whimpering, I forced my eyes open to see the bear sitting across from us, stroking the massive erection tenting his towel. He looked *voracious*, as if given the slightest hint of an indication, he would bend me over this riser, ream me open, and stuff me full of his cock. And God help me, some shameful part of me had more than a passing curiosity about how it would feel if I let him do just that.

But the other part of me, the bigger part of me, thrilled at knowing he could never have me. Only Jace could. For the rest of them, I was unattainable.

Did I mention my vanity?

Looking around as Jace demanded, I realized we'd commanded pretty much every eye in the room. The two guys were still jerking each other off, but they were watching us as they did it. Even the one getting the blowjob, gasping and groaning, lifting his hips to fuck into the other guy's mouth, was watching us through heavy-lidded eyes.

I closed my eyes and hid my face again, not wanting to actually *see* them. I wanted to know they were watching, yes.

Admiring me. Wanting me. But I didn't want to see them do it. That was the point at which it started to tip over into too intrusive.

Jace seemed to get the message. He didn't demand I look around again.

"He has the prettiest cock, too," Jace said, picking up the thread again. At his tug, the ends of the towel slid loose around my waist. He drew the sides apart like a curtain, not just removing it, but *unveiling* me with deliberate showmanship. Moist air hit my cock, and I moaned. "Look at that. Just perfect."

"Oh God," I whispered as Jace's fingers skated lightly up and down my exposed dick. He didn't grasp me or try to stroke me, praise Jesus, because if he had, I would have blown like Mount Vesuvius. He did, however, drag his index finger through the pre-cum dripping down the head and feed it to me, thrusting it deep into my mouth. I sucked on his finger without being told, knowing that was what he was going for.

"And he's a world-class cocksucker. Just enough gag reflex to make it a little hard for him to take it all. I love to watch him struggle with it, and I've never fucked a tighter throat than his. Must be all those muscles from singing. If he were normally as submissive as he is just this instant, I'd feed him cum with every meal."

"Ah!" My hips bucked up at that image, which was a powerful one despite my complete lack of interest in anything more than idle submission. Jace knew how to spin a story, that was for damn sure. When the echo of my cry stopped bouncing off the tiles, I could hear the definite slap of skin on skin, someone, somewhere, jerking off hard and fast, moaning softly to himself. The voice was too high-pitched to be our friend, the bear.

"He's not?" Mr. Bear asked.

"Nope. In fact, you can be damn sure he's going to take this all out on my ass later."

"Guess I'd better enjoy this moment while it lasts then, huh?"

"Be my guest."

A low groan answered that, and I knew without looking that

the man's towel had come off and he was now getting his wank on with intent.

"Lift your knees, angel," Jace coaxed. "Show him that sweet asshole he's not gonna get to fuck."

The bear growled. "Oh, that's just cruel."

"We could stop," Jace said offhandedly, shrugging.

"Fuck no. Show me. Show me every bit of it."

That request took a bit more effort to meet. It was hard to make myself pull my knees up to my chest and brace my feet wide apart, giving him a perfect view down the alley to my balls and ass.

"More," he demanded, sounding a little breathless. "Show me that slutty little hole."

"Slide down," Jace said. I shuddered, but I obeyed, nearly lying in his lap. When I had, he hooked his arms under my knees and pulled them up, bending me in half and tipping the crack of my ass up into full view, pulling my cheeks apart with his hands.

"Like this?"

I writhed again, the humiliation almost too much, almost crossing that border. Too exposed. Too conspicuous. After the past couple days, my asshole was tender; I didn't know if it looked it, but it felt like it should be pink and swollen. Like anyone who looked should be able to tell just how thoroughly I'd been fucked recently. Jace's fingertip began tickling and pressing around my achy pucker and I was lost again, moaning insensibly, totally gone in the moment.

Then it pushed in, dry except for the moisture of sweat and steam, burning, and I cried out. A chorus of moans echoed me.

"That's it. That's it," Jace murmured. "He wants to hear you scream. Think we can give him that?"

I barely managed to whimper an assent, trembling, folded in half, exposed to the world with Jace's finger working in and out of my hole. Then he pressed in another finger, still dry, and I did scream. I thrashed in my nearly trapped position. The bear across from us grunted a full-throated encouragement.

"Need me to stop?" Jace asked.

232

"Oh God . . . Oh . . . I don't . . . No. No . . ." I finally managed to shake my head. "Just . . . lube . . ."

If I hadn't been quite so sore from that plug he'd bragged about, I probably could have handled it, but yeah, no, the dry thing wasn't happening this time.

"Okay." Jace eased his fingers carefully out and removed his arms from the backs of my legs, letting me stretch out again. He upended the small pouch he'd been carrying around with him since we'd arrived, with the condoms and little blister packs of lube in it. "Here."

He repositioned us so that I was on my hands and knees with my ass still exposed to the room, and he reclined nearly parallel to me, so that if he'd been under me, we might have sixty-nined. Instead, he just pulled his towel open. As he did so, I noticed his hands were shaking.

"Suck me off while I finger-fuck you." His mutter sounded a little urgent. "You don't know how fucking horny you're making me, doing all this. I'm about to explode. Just . . . give them a few good screams first. Make sure they really want you."

"Okay," I whispered, and then his fingers, slick with lube, thrust back into my ass.

I screamed again because they went deep, deep and hard, and I still ached, and it hurt and it was good and everyone could see it. I screamed for a million reasons, resting my forehead on Jace's thigh.

"Oh yeah," the bear moaned behind me. He'd been quiet during our logistical maneuvering, but obviously we hadn't lost his attention. "Yeah. Open that ass. Let me see it."

Holy fuck. Jace actually pulled his fingers out to push my cheeks apart and give the guy a full-on porn-quality gape shot, tugging at the edges of my tender asshole with his thumbs to spread me wider. I groaned abjectly.

Then Jace drove his fingers back in, not being gentle at all, and I obliged with another scream that wasn't even the slightest bit faked. Somewhere in the room, a shout followed, and I knew someone had popped.

I waited, letting Jace give them the show he'd promised,

moaning and wailing as he fucked me fast and hard with those fingers, pulling them all the way out and . . .

Oh shit, that was three.

Annnd then I had to bite my fist, hoping my sounds came across as arousal and discomfort rather than hilarity, because suddenly I had the most fucking *insane* image of my internal narrator sounding like the Count from *Sesame Street*, complete with bad Transylvanian accent.

Three! That's THREE fingers in my ass! Ha ha ha!

I nearly choked myself sucking down Jace's cock before I burst into giggles.

Fortunately the impulse to laugh was *very* short-lived, because those fingers went to work, and while my cries were muffled by Jace's cock, they were no less ardent. He tasted so fucking good: salt and sweat and a hint of chlorine. I could have sucked him all night.

I heard fapping from more than one direction, and one in particular sounded extremely close.

"You sure he won't let me fuck him?" the bear asked from almost directly above me. I stiffened and would have jerked away if not for Jace's hands, which suddenly became soothing.

"Angel?"

I shook my head emphatically and resumed sucking Jace's cock, though tension had crept in now, making it harder to take him deep.

"That's okay." The bear's voice, though ragged and full of need, still carried a note of kind understanding. The sound of his fist pumping up and down his own flesh quickened. "Fuck, you two are hot."

"Thank you." Jace sounded a bit strained himself. His fingers eased off inside me as he lost himself in the head I was giving him. His other hand stroked my hair.

"If our friend here comes right now, he's going to come on your back. You okay with that?" he asked gently. "Think we can let him have that, after he's been so much fun to play with?"

I went still, considering for a moment, half-repulsed and half-turned on by that very revulsion. I'd wanted to see the seedier side of gay life in the city, and this was it. Some anonymous stranger's cum painting my skin in a room full of other strangers.

Finally I nodded, and found my rhythm again, sucking Jace hard, tonguing, fucking my mouth on his thick cock.

Above me, the bear groaned and gasped, sounding more desperate with each passing moment, as did Jace. Tension quivered through Jace's legs and the hand on my hair, and he got harder, swelling in my mouth. Then there was a grunt and a scalding splatter on my back. I jerked and made a startled sound, despite knowing it was coming. That seemed to be Jace's cue to erupt, pulsing thick and bitter over my tongue.

I swallowed it down, still hard and aching from my own unrelieved arousal. When I was done, suddenly the mess on my back was unwanted, revolting. A step too far outside my comfort zone. I fumbled to yank one of our towels out from underneath us and Jace got the message, wiping me off and drawing me up against his chest, wrapping me protectively in his arms, where I trembled and waited for my confusion to pass.

I ventured an uncertain glance at our playmate as he wrapped his towel around his hips again, smiling at us quite kindly. He didn't look like some big, scary dom now. Just rather cuddly and friendly.

"Thanks, guys," he said with perfect courtesy. "I haven't had that much fun in a long time. Have a good night."

And with another amiable smile, he walked out of the steam room.

"Ready to go?" Jace asked gently, stroking my hair and shoulders. I nodded eagerly. Somewhere in the last few minutes of confusion, my boner had become decidedly less bone-like, but now my body was becoming aware of Jace again, naked and wrapped around me, warm and familiar. And as my brain quieted a little, my body decided it liked that situation quite a lot.

But not here. I was done with here.

JACE GAVE me the unsoiled towel to wrap up in and walked

unabashedly nude beside me, every bit as protective and solicitous as he'd been when we arrived, as he guided us back through
the darkened maze to our small room. When we were ensconced
within its private confines—no open door here, nope—he turned
to me, his eyes dancing.

"Okay, did you seriously fucking start *laughing* during all that?
Is that what I heard?"

Next thing I knew, I was curled up on the sheet-covered vinyl
mattress that barely deserved to be called a bed, laughing until
my stomach ached, until tears streamed from my eyes, until I
thought I might puke. Each time I thought I'd caught my breath
enough to try to explain, another wave of laughter took me. I
collapsed again, flapping a hand at him as if that would somehow
help.

"I can't . . . I can't . . . I can't even . . ." More helpless giggles. I
gave up trying to explain and just shook my head, wiping my
eyes. "Maybe I'll be able to explain later," I finally gasped.

He sat down on the mattress beside me, cupping a hand to the
side of my face and looking at me with a sobriety at odds with his
usual merriment. "Pretty sure I'm falling for you," he murmured,
completely matter-of-fact. "Just so you know."

Suddenly laughter was nowhere to be found. I felt such
tenderness toward him, such yearning for him, it ached, *physically*
ached. My heart raced inside my chest, terrified and ecstatic all
at once.

"Okay," I whispered. I wanted to say it back. It wouldn't be a
lie or meaningless reciprocation if I did. But the terror was still
too big, and I didn't even know what the terror was *about*. "I'm
scared."

"Don't be." His thumb caressed my cheekbone. "I'm not going
to make any demands. Not yet. Just let me be with you, as much
as I can be with me living here and you up in Michigan. Give us a
chance to see what this could turn into, okay?"

I closed my eyes and nodded against his warm palm, swallowing hard. "Okay."

He leaned down and kissed me then with an intimacy that

seemed inappropriate for this place. I lingered in it for a moment, then drew away. I didn't want to be here anymore.

"Take me home, Jace," I said softly, meeting his eyes. A few heartbeats of silent communion passed, communion where we said everything we needed to say, and then he stood and opened our locker to pass me my clothes.

CHAPTER TWENTY-NINE

I wasn't certain of anything then
I didn't know who I was just yet
Still a tiny light shone inside
It would lead me to what I had to find

— CASEY STRATTON, "RISING SUN"

G eoff texted again and said I didn't have to work until Wednesday, so Jace and I spent Monday doing a walking tour of downtown Chicago and spent the evening clubbing in Boystown. It was amazing to get to dance with Jace again, his body moving against mine with the beat of the music. It felt different than it had that first night at the Dunes, when we'd been unfamiliar, learning each other, vibrating with anticipation and drawing out the tension to just revel in it. Now that edge was gone, and yet it was still perfect. We moved together like our bodies knew each other, like we shared the same pulse. We were comfortable, but no less hot. Intimate, I guess, and a little needy, too. Tomorrow he'd be taking me back to Saugatuck and returning to his life in Chicago, and I think we were both grappling with that upcoming separation. I was pretty certain we'd see each other again, but there was an element of uncertainty to it, and not just because we'd miss each other until the next time. If this became a relationship, could we make the long-distance thing work? Would it even become a relationship in the first place, or would we discover that whatever we'd felt during these incredible few days had disappeared and things weren't the same anymore?

What if this was as good as it got?

We stayed up way too late after we got back to Jace's place, talking and making love. I had to admit, however much I would miss Jace, that my body might actually be glad for a day or two of reprieve, because keeping our hands off each other just wasn't an option.

The next day, after a late breakfast, we loaded my things into Jace's car and left for Michigan. We were uncharacteristically subdued; there was no talking or flirting or tantalizing caresses. I spent almost the first hour of the trip staring out the passenger-side window, and when I glanced at Jace he was shaking his head violently, blinking. "You okay?"

He smiled over at me. "Lack of sleep and highway hypnosis make for a bad combination."

"Want me to drive a while?"

"You've got to be pretty tired, too."

"Nah. Give me a cup of coffee and my music and I can go for hours."

He chuckled softly. "Okay then."

We pulled off at the next exit, hit a McDonald's drive-thru for coffee (desperate times and all), and traded off. Jace immediately reclined his seat, which made me pout jealously; I got carsick whenever I tried that. Then I scanned through my iPod, finally deciding on Casey Stratton again before merging back onto the interstate.

After a few minutes, Jace's hand settled on my thigh and I smiled. Even now, that compulsion to touch remained. We drove in silence, the music surrounding us, until I relaxed and added my voice to it, singing along.

When I glanced over at Jace, he'd fallen asleep with a smile on his face.

WE SPENT the afternoon catching up with Robin, Geoff, and Ling —interspersed, of course, with heaps of admiration and praise for baby Zhen. As the day wore on, though, I began to worry for Jace. He hadn't been able to get a room at the Dunes for the night, and all the B&Bs were booked up. If he had to drive home, he was going to have to leave soon, and even if he did, I still worried that he might be too tired. As Jace, Geoff, and Robin threw together dinner and Ling nursed Zhen in the glider-rocker, I hauled out my laptop, trying to find the nearest motel with a vacancy.

"What are you working on?" Ling asked, murmuring softly as Zhen suckled with weird, snorting little breaths and clicks.

"Just trying to find Jace a room somewhere so he doesn't fall asleep at the wheel on his way back home," I muttered, frowning at the search results.

She hummed thoughtfully. "I've been thinking. Why don't you stay at my apartment until you go back to school? I'm not going to need it for a few more months, so it's just sitting there. I didn't offer before because I didn't know you, but you've been around a while now and I think it would be all right. Just keep it clean is all I ask."

"Um . . . wow. Sure, that would be great, if I can afford the rent."

She waved me off. "I don't pay rent on it, except to help Geoff a little with the lease on the building. It's the space above his shop. It's got pretty much everything already except TV service, and really, who needs that when you have high-speed internet?"

And there it was, another solution to my financial situation just falling into my lap. Now that I'd had a couple paychecks from Geoff and Robin, in addition to what I'd made in tips playing at the coffeehouse—all of which was going straight into the bank and remaining untouched except for the occasional latte—it was looking like I might be able to cover at least most of the shortfall for next year. But only if I could continue to live rent-free, some- how. And here was Ling, offering that very opportunity.

Suddenly I was anxious and unsure again. Fuck. I hated being such an inconvenience to everyone. It seemed like no matter where I was, ever since I'd been in junior high and asking my aunt to drive me to choir practice, I was putting someone to more trouble than they ought to go to. Why did everyone else have to keep taking up my slack?

It was on the tip of my tongue to refuse, or insist on paying them something, when Jace appeared in the doorway, almost as though he'd picked up on my distress. My protest died unspoken as I remembered his words about accepting help when it was offered.

"Sure," I said thickly, swallowing. "Thanks, Ling. I'd appreciate that."

She smiled and that was the end of it. After we ate dinner, I packed up all my stuff, and Jace helped me move it to the cozy studio apartment in the office space upstairs from Geoff's studio. It offered a lovely view of downtown Saugatuck and Kalamazoo Lake. Now that I was in a space where I wouldn't disturb anyone else, I set up my keyboard and practiced awhile, banging my head against the brick wall of the impossibly complex piano part to "Opaline." Eventually I switched to more mellow pieces, and Jace began to nod off on the sofa.

We were both too exhausted to do more than fall into bed and go to sleep, but I awoke in the middle of the night, wrapped around him, the big spoon for once, and suddenly I needed him one last time.

Afterward, I lay with my head on his shoulder, listening to his heartbeat slow.

"I need to catch up on some work I've been neglecting." His lips brushed my hair. "I don't know if I'll be able to make it back up here this weekend."

I tried not to sigh tragically. "It's okay. I understand. Mo will be here anyway, and I've hardly gotten to see her in the last month, so I should probably try to give her my full attention."

"All right. The next weekend I'd really like to, though. If you want me to."

"Yeah," I whispered, turning my face up to him for a kiss. "I want you to."

And I really, really did. What was this ache in my chest at the prospect of not seeing him for nearly two weeks? Was this love, or at least the start of it?

I was pretty sure it was. Maybe not full-fledged—it was far too early for that—but there was definitely a seed beginning to sprout and take root.

I clung to him tighter and let it happen.

CHAPTER THIRTY

It's only your shadow
Said it's only an echo
So lie back down

— CASEY STRATTON, "WITHER AND DIE"

S trange. With all my issues, I would have imagined that living alone would be the least of my problems.

I guess it sort of made sense, though. Until that Memorial Day weekend when Mo had left on Sunday and Brendan had arrived on Monday, I had only ever spent two nights in a house alone.

The first time was one of my very earliest memories. I had been four years old. My mother had just rented a house with her latest "boyfriend" (read: guy she picked up at a bar who would feed her and buy her beer until he got tired of her and kicked her out). There wasn't even any furniture in the house, so I'd slept on blanket pallets on the floor with Colleen and Tonya, who were eight and two, respectively. Sometime in the middle of the night, we awoke to realize that neither Mom nor her boyfriend were there. To this day, I don't know where they went. To a bar, to the store to get beer, I don't know. It was so long ago, and I was so young that I don't even remember how it turned out—whether she came home while we were awake and searching for her, or if we eventually fell back asleep and found her there in the morning. All I remember was going outside into the darkened yard, scared out of my mind and sobbing at maybe midnight or 1 a.m., trying to find her.

It happened again a couple years later when I was in the first grade, shortly before child services took us away and placed us with our relatives. That time we awoke in the morning (probably on a school day) to discover she'd left sometime during the night. She didn't come back until that afternoon.

After the first incident, I began having what would become a recurring nightmare throughout my childhood and well into my teen years—the only dream I can remember having as a child, in fact. In that nightmare, my family had all become vampires and they were chasing me, trying to kill me while I did the whole silent-scream/want-to-run-but-can't-move thing.

That first night alone in Ling's apartment, I awoke from the vampire nightmare for the first time in years. Only this time, the vampires were Jace, Mo, Brendan, Robin, Ling, and Geoff. I lay there in the dark, gasping for breath, my heart racing and my palms sweating, trying to remember that I wasn't four years old, waiting for Momma to come home and make me feel safe again.

Blowing out a breath, I reached for my phone and sent Jace a text.

Hope you're sleeping like a sane person. Just thinking about you. Talk to you tomorrow.

A moment later, my phone rang. I smiled and answered it.

"Hey, did my text wake you?"

"No." His voice sounded tired, but alert. "I've been awake a couple hours. Went to bed early because I was exhausted and now my body thinks it's time to get up and start the day. I'll try to go back to sleep in another hour or so."

I nodded even though he couldn't see it, stretching out on Ling's ridiculously comfortable memory-foam mattress. "Okay.

I'd ask you how your day went or something, but I think we already covered that when we spoke before bed."

"So what are you doing awake?"

"I dunno. Just thinking, I guess. Restless." I didn't even know why I lied and didn't tell him about the nightmare.

Luckily, Jace didn't press for more. "Okay. Hey, can I pry a bit? Feel free to tell me to mind my own business."

"Sure, go ahead."

"When you were here, I noticed your prescription bottles were almost empty. Those are antidepressants you're on, right? How long have you been taking them?" I heard a sigh, as if Jace were settling back in bed. There seemed to be an edge to his voice, though I couldn't figure out what it might be for.

"Since my senior year in high school, when it became apparent that talk therapy wasn't going to be enough to make me right in the head." I laughed, trying to make a joke of it. "You got a bit of a basket case on your hands here. Sorry."

"That's three years." The edge grew sharper, and I could practically hear Jace frown. "Isn't there usually a time frame for getting off those things?"

I shrugged. "Yeah, for most people."

"So when are you going to be getting off them?"

"Probably never." Something about his tone was making my hackles rise defensively, and I could hear irritation creeping into my own voice. "Why?"

"I just don't like the idea that they've got you on drugs with no cutoff date. It's not good to use that shit as a crutch indefinitely. If your doctor isn't taking steps to wean you off them, then you need to find out why."

I pulled the phone away from my ear and blinked at it as though I could see Jace on the other end. "Excuse me?"

"What?"

"A crutch? Did you just actually say I'm using my meds as a *crutch*?" I scoffed. "Pardon me, Mr. Judgmental Asshole, can I please speak to the guy I just spent the last week with?"

"Hey, I'm not judging, I just know doctors can be—"

"Yeah, you *are* judging. 'Crutch' is one of those judge-y

words. And I'm telling you to step back and rethink your tone right the hell now." I sat up in the bed and drew my knees to my chest, which was suddenly tight and aching at the thought of fighting with Jace. But I was damned if I was going to let that shit pass.

"Fine," he snapped. "Then tell me why you don't have any plans to wean yourself off them, if your doctor is being negligent and leaving you on them indefinitely."

"You know what? I don't have to explain shit to you, asshole." My heart was racing, and I could barely draw a breath, my chest was so tight with anxiety. Panicking and unable to find any more words, I disconnected the call without even thinking about it.

Goddamn it. I'd already put up with that bullshit from my family, thinking I was just lazy and self-indulgent when I sank to a level where I could barely function. I didn't need Jace doing it, too.

My hand shook as it clutched my cell phone, regret for hanging up on him immediately assailing me. I shouldn't have done that, though in the moment, getting myself out of that conversation was the only possible option.

Fuck, what had I done?

The phone rang in my hand, and I stared at it a moment, my eyes burning. Wincing, I answered.

"Yeah?"

"You're right. I'm being an asshole."

The knot of tension in the center of my chest loosened a little. "Yeah, you are."

"Those drugs are a sore spot with me. I don't trust them. I *really* don't like seeing people on them."

"Yeah, well, too bad for you, because my meds aren't going anywhere."

He sighed, and I heard a rhythmic tapping that sounded like he was drumming his fingers on something. "Okay. Fine. I'd like to understand because it's sending up big red flags the way it looks from this end. I've got my reasons for being worried about that sort of shit, angel."

I fell silent, trying to wrestle down the sense of defensiveness and give him the benefit of the doubt that he actually did mean well. That he wasn't just being dismissive, like my family.

"Okay. You're right, antidepressants are meant to be temporary. Usually. But here's the thing: It's stress hormones that cause depression. They screw up your brain chemistry. And I was pretty much flooded with stress hormones my whole childhood. Ever since I was a baby. *My* brain chemistry is basically permanently fucked. I'm never going to be 'better.' The most I can hope for is to be functional, as opposed to being unable to drag my ass out of bed."

He swallowed audibly. "Shit. I'm sorry."

"Apology accepted. You don't know me well enough to weigh in on that sort of thing yet, Jace. And even if you did, you don't get to tell me how to manage my own health." I made myself relax a bit more. I'd have to remember this about Jace: that he could be a self-righteous, judgmental jerk without knowing the whole story at times. Good to know he wasn't perfect.

I took a few deep breaths and stepped back a little farther from the ledge. "You don't have to worry about me, though. I'm taking care of myself, making sure the meds I'm on are the right meds. My psychiatrist and I have worked really hard to make sure the side effects are minimal and I'm not on anything I don't need to be on. I still have a sex drive, I can still come, and I can even drink, so really, I'm not doing too badly. Mostly they just keep me from dropping so deep that I can't function. They keep me level. At least they will until I don't qualify for Medicaid anymore and have to pay for the fucking things. But hey, now at least I can't be denied health coverage for the preexisting condition, and insurance plans have to provide mental health coverage, so that's a win."

"And you don't think it's possible your doctor is using meds to shortcut other, more effective treatments?"

"I know she's not. I've been in therapy more than half my life, and it hasn't been enough. Things got bad for a while back in high school, and they got even worse this last year. I'm doing what I need to do to be healthy."

"How do you accept it so calmly?"

I shrugged, trying to settle in and get comfortable now that I was calmer. "I've lived with it my whole life. And really, it could be a lot worse. I could be self-medicating with booze and drugs. It runs in the family. My grandfather. My mom. My older sister went through period of *problem drinking*, and my younger sister didn't get to graduate with her class this spring because she'd missed so much school due to partying too hard." I snorted when I realized what I was doing. "Shit. Here I am talking about myself and my issues again."

"What do you mean? I brought it up."

I stretched out on the bed, trying to shake the feeling of being too conspicuous. Self-centered. Making everything about me. Drawing too much attention to myself, especially while airing dirty laundry.

"What about you?" I asked, trying to change the subject. "Going through what you went through as a teenager can't have left you as undamaged as you seem to be."

"Knock on wood." Jace chuckled weakly. "I think you can see why I don't trust shrinks and psychiatrists much. I was on those sorts of pills while I was in conversion therapy—high doses of pills that *did* decrease my sex drive. Obliterated it, really, and that was fully intentional on the part of my so-called therapists. I mean, hey, if I wasn't running around taking it up the ass, I wouldn't *really* be a fag, right?" He snorted. "Bigoted quacks should have their licenses revoked. Hell, I didn't even jerk off for over three years. Didn't want to and I couldn't come when I tried. *During high school.* Even when I was 'cured' enough to stop counseling, my parents insisted I remain on the drugs and in the support groups to keep me from 'relapsing.' It's why I was still a virgin when I got to Boston. I went through some really bad withdrawals when I left home because you're *not* supposed to quit those things without stepping down gradually. It was very dangerous."

"Jesus," I whispered, feeling a little nauseous.

"So yeah, I really don't care for the idea of those sorts of drugs much, though I guess I can see why it's a totally different situation for you. I seem to be okay functioning the way I am right now, so why mess with it?"

"That's good. You're lucky on that front, at least." I sighed, my mood still too unstable from my nightmare and the argument not to be left somewhat morose by the conversation. "I'm sorry they did that to you."

"Yeah, well, I'm sorry for the things that happened to you, too. It looks like neither one of us is coming into this without issues. I'm okay with that."

I plucked at the edge of the bed sheets with my free hand. "I'm jealous, to be honest. I wish I could be more like you." Well, that was one of my wishes. The other involved having this conversation snuggled up against him instead of over the phone, but that wasn't going to happen. "You know, functional without the pills and without feeling like my shit drags down on me all the time. I want to shake it off and be fucking *over* it, like it didn't matter and never will again. I don't want to spend all my time feeling sorry for myself, or *sounding* like I feel sorry for myself, because every single conversation somehow comes back to it all. It can't make me very fun to be around, and I don't want to use people to get my sympathy fix like my mom does."

I heard a rustle, as if he was moving. "Angel, your issues are a part of you. It's not feeling sorry for yourself to discuss the past as it relates to what's happening in the present. You're not asking for pity, you're trying to help me know you better. *After I asked.* You're never going to be able to completely divorce who you are now from who you used to be, and if I don't understand where you've come from, how can I ever understand *you*?"

"You do understand me. Better than anyone ever has."

"Yeah, I think I do. Which is why I wonder who told you that you feel sorry for yourself all the time."

"Aw fuck. Really? You're gonna do that?" I flipped over onto my stomach, propping myself up on my elbows. "I tell you I don't want to get bogged down in my shit so you ask me to bring more of it up?"

"You don't have to answer."

"Okay, then I won't."

"Doesn't mean I won't ask, though. Who told you that you can't tell anyone when something's hurting you? Who made you ashamed to feel what you feel?"

"Jesus, Jace, come on!"

"This shit comes from *outside*, Topher," he insisted. "It's like sometimes I hear someone else's words coming out of your mouth. It's not *you*. Someone gave you these messages, the same way they told you you're no good and would never be any good at the things you loved. And whoever those people were, I want to knock their fucking teeth in. I can't do that—at least not without getting arrested—so I'll do the next best thing, which is encourage you to say 'fuck 'em' and do the things they told you that you couldn't do. You want to be more like me? That's where you start. You say that, and then you do whatever the fuck you need to. So lay it on me. Tell me the shit they taught you it was bad to tell."

Goddamn it, now my eyes were burning again. I pinched the bridge of my nose. "Fuck. *Fuck*. Fine. It started in kindergarten, okay, with the stiff-upper-lip speeches. I'd burst into tears every time the bullies came after me, and they came after me a lot. When I tried to tell my family about it, they told me that if I didn't react, the bullies would get bored and go away. In other words, it was basically *my* fault that I was being bullied because I was a crybaby and a sissy. So then I had the shit the bullies were heaping on me, and the feeling that I was a failure every time I let it get to me."

"Okay. That sucks. Full stop. No pity here, and you're not asking for it, you're just telling me what I want to know. Go on."

I laughed without any real humor. "Well, when I moved in with my aunt and uncle in junior high, it got worse. Because *they* became the bullies. Every time I committed some sort of infraction, I got these . . . these *lectures*. They'd trap me standing up somewhere, like in a corner, or against the kitchen counter, and just browbeat me. And there were these unspoken *rules* about how I was supposed to act when they did this. I had to stand there, and listen, and be perfectly attentive. So getting away wasn't an option unless I physically pushed past them, and of course I couldn't do that. They'd go at me, sometimes for, like, two or three hours at a time."

I dragged a pillow under my chest, clutching it. "I don't know why they did it. Maybe it was a power thing. They couldn't feel they'd done their job until I had completely given in? I don't know. Anyway, every screw-up I made, it wasn't just a mistake or a lapse in judgment, it was a character flaw, you know? If I fucked up, it was because I was a *bad person*. I was selfish, or thoughtless, or irresponsible, or lazy. And they would hold grudges about petty shit and spring it on me out of the blue. Like, one time there was an earthquake in California, where some of our relatives lived. It happened while I was out at a play rehearsal, so I didn't even know about it. But the next time they got on me about something, I *also* got chewed out for not caring about anyone but myself because on that night, weeks before, I'd been humming a song from the play when I got home from rehearsal, instead of worrying about my relatives being in an earthquake I didn't even fucking *know* had happened."

I heard Jace sigh on the other end of the line. "Shit, angel. That's fucked up." But, like they had with Brendan, the words were coming in a torrent now, and I was desperate to make him truly *understand*.

"And my back and feet would start hurting because they kept me standing in one place so long, but if I slouched or fidgeted, I got reamed for not paying attention. If I let out anything sounding like a sigh, I was being rude. They would say the most awful, cutting, *unfair* things, but if I got angry at what they were saying, then I was ungrateful and disrespectful. If they saw tears in my eyes, they would accuse me of feeling sorry for myself. But if I started blinking or doing something to keep the tears back, then they accused me of *forcing* myself to cry in order to make them feel sorry for me."

Jace was silent for a long moment. His breath shook a little when he inhaled. Then, very calmly: "Okay. That sucks, too. Sucks a lot. But you're still not trying to play on my sympathies and get your pity fix by telling me. You're not manipulating me,

Topher. When they accused you of trying to do that, *they lied*. So tell me, are you feeling sorry for yourself?"

"To be honest, yeah. I'm feeling pretty fucking mopey right about now."

"You sure about that? Are you feeling sorry for yourself, or are you just *sad* because talking about that shit *hurts*? Because there's a fucking difference, and damn, angel, you are entitled to feel hurt about all that."

Suddenly I couldn't breathe. My heart started racing anxiously, the same way it had when Brendan had called what they'd done to me abuse. Why couldn't I challenge the concept of my aunt and uncle's infallibility, even when I knew in my head that they had been wrong? Every time I tried, something short-circuited and I began feeling panicky.

"I don't— I don't— I don't know," I stammered. "Isn't it the same thing?"

"No. No, it's not," Jace said tenderly. "You need to respect your pain for what it is. Stop beating yourself up for feeling it."

I shook my head violently, wiping my eyes on the pillow I clung to. "No, no. Stop. Just stop, Jace. This is *bullshit*. I *am* feeling sorry for myself. I mean, Jesus, throw me a pity party. It's not like they beat me. Hell, they didn't even torture me the way your family did to you. It's—"

"You think they didn't torture you?" Jace hooted. "What the fuck do you think you just described to me? If those were lectures, they were the fucking *waterboarding* of parental lectures. They tried to *break* you, Topher, break your soul, the same way my family and the doctors and camps and pastors tried to break me. Okay, so they didn't go about it the same way. Doesn't mean it doesn't count."

I groaned and closed my eyes. Once the torrent of memories was unleashed, they began replaying obsessively in my head, making me relive all the anxiety and frustration and anger and hurt. As it had with Brendan. I couldn't shut it off; it kept going and going.

"Fuck. If I'm not pitying myself, why does every conversation turn into this crap?"

"Because you know what they did to you was wrong, angel, so it eats at you, because it was *unfair*. Really fucking cruelly unfair. You're *justified* in feeling that you were mistreated. They've convinced you that everything you think and feel is wrong, and you've bought into it. If you could stop trying to convince yourself that they were right, you'd be able to put it into some sort of context and begin to move on." He sighed again on the other end of the line. "I mean, if your appendix was bursting, would you get better by telling yourself it wasn't happening and that the pain you were feeling was only you being sorry for yourself? Of course not. No one has ever healed by denying they were injured. Seems like your therapists should have made that clear along the way. Otherwise, I'm pretty sure you were missing the point of therapy."

That stopped me cold. Jesus, was that true? When I was a little kid, I had no idea why they started taking me to see a therapist. My family never explained, they just delivered me to the appointments, and then the guy asked me questions for a while. I'd assumed it was because of something wrong with me. Then when I was a teenager, I'd thought my aunt and uncle sent me to therapy to "fix" me rather than accepting that they might be in the wrong, too. I'd appreciated the opportunity to vent about what was going on in my life, but had I ever understood that I was supposed to be healing? And that I had to accept the pain as real in order to do so? I'd gotten good at talking about deeply personal stuff, but had I known I was supposed to be processing it? Had anyone ever *explained* to me why I was there?

There was a long pause while I digested that, and then Jace chuckled. "That aside, in the interest of fairness, I have to point out that not every conversation turns out this way. Some of them are about sex."

"I like those a lot better."

"Yeah?" I heard the mischievous lift in his voice and knew what was coming before he even spoke. "So, what are you wearing?"

And just like that, tears and frustration morphed into to

laughter and arousal. With something else to grasp, I was able to shut down the obsessive cycle of recollections.

"Same thing I was when I spoke to you before bedtime. My boxer briefs."

"Mm, love the way those look on you," he murmured. "They show off that tight, *tight* ass of yours. Think you might wanna take 'em off for me, angel?"

Jesus. Wow.

"Yeah," I whispered, pushing at my waistband. "Oh yeah . . ."

CHAPTER THIRTY-ONE

Funny me, so used to knowing what to say
I couldn't remain in
Something that would suffocate my passion
And kill my pride

— CASEY STRATTON, "PROJECTOR"

As horrible as it was to say it, when I saw Mo the following weekend, it was easier to live with the weight of my secret. Brendan, it turned out, had decided to go back to Lansing for the rest of the summer, so I wasn't in any danger of running into him again. I still didn't want to deceive Mo, but I also couldn't bring myself to out Brendan, so I just had to find a way to live with it.

It helped that we both had a lot to talk about, in the form of Jace and Cody the Archery Instructor. We pretty much spent the whole weekend drinking wine and comparing sex and is-or-isn't-it-a-relationship notes. Mo's opinion was that, yes, I definitely had a relationship going on with Jace.

Since I didn't really want to go back to that house where I'd been with Brendan, I invited her to stay with me at Ling's apartment, and we snuggled together and watched movies when I wasn't working. She admired my nipple piercings while simultaneously scolding me for not waiting until she was there to see me get them (though she thought the fact that Jace was there was quite hot, which it had been). She also just about passed out from incredulity when I told her the (somewhat sanitized) tale of going to the bathhouse in Chicago.

By the time she left on Sunday to spend one night in Big Rapids before heading back to camp, I'd decided my life didn't have to be completely ruined by the momentous screwup that was Brendan Gardner. Perhaps I didn't deserve a pardon, but it appeared I might have one anyway, so maybe I should just try to forgive myself and move on.

In short, life was actually looking better than it had since I'd arrived in Saugatuck at the beginning of the summer. Robin and Geoff paid me a more-than-fair wage, and now that Ling was on her maternity leave, I was getting more hours than ever. I wasn't certain I'd have enough money by the end of summer to cover what my scholarship didn't, but I'd be close. If I had to mortgage the first however-many-years of my post-graduate life with student loans, at least the amount would be minimal.

The week after Mo left was filled with anticipation, because Jace would be coming up on Friday to spend the weekend. It didn't seem to matter that we texted frequently and talked sometimes two or three times a day. It didn't matter that we were having so much phone sex (and one particularly memorable Skype video session) that we could start our own adult chat line. I ached to see him and touch him again.

At least until Friday afternoon, when Robin approached me as we were closing down the gallery.

"Have a seat, Topher," he said, gesturing toward the sofa upstairs in his office. "So, you probably noticed I sold that collection of paintings Jace did of you."

I squirmed, my face heating up. "Um, yeah, they weren't on display anymore, so I figured that was the case."

"Well, Jace informed me a few weeks ago that when they sold, he wanted the profits to go to you." He pulled a check out of his breast pocket and handed it to me.

"*What*? No. No! That's stupid." I gritted my teeth. "I didn't do anything. He did all the work, all I did was pose for some snap-shots! Jeez, is there ever going to be a guy I fuck who doesn't think he needs to pay my way?"

"It's not like that, Topher," he said sternly. "The fact is, under normal circumstances, he would have paid you a modeling fee. I suspect he didn't want to make it seem like he was offering to pay you for sex, but you do have something coming to you for your part in creating those pieces."

I looked at the check, and my eyes just about popped out of my skull. "*Fifteen thousand dollars?* You're telling me I earned that much for posing for him? Fuck, well isn't that a cushy gig?"

Robin's lips quirked. "Okay, no, your fee would probably only have been a few hundred dollars, but the paintings sold for five thousand each and Jace would like you to have it all. I haven't even taken out my commission like I usually do for consign-ments. So thirty percent of that is *my* gift to you. You want to accuse *me* of trying to pay your way because you're fucking me?"

"No, no, of course not, but—" I flailed, trying to find words, then my brain got caught up on the numbers. "Five thousand each? No fucking way!"

He shrugged. "You'd be surprised what people will pay for good art, especially in a town like this where wealthy, bored tourists have money to burn. I would have sold them separately for six or seven each, but the buyer wanted the collection so I cut him a deal."

I ran a hand through my hair. "I can't. I can't take this. I don't mooch off the guys I sleep with or expect them to support me. Not now, not ever."

Robin sighed. "Tell you what, don't decide anything until you talk to Jace. I'll keep the check, and if you decide you're comfort-able accepting it later, once you know where Jace is coming from on this, it's yours. Keep an open mind, okay? Give some thought to the idea that Jace doesn't mean it the way you think he does."

"Okay. Okay, fine." I grimaced and handed him back the check. "I'll talk to Jace, but this isn't happening."

"Give it a few days," Robin urged with a thin smile. "In the right context, it might feel different."

JACE and I had already arranged to meet at Ling's apartment when he arrived because, honestly, who were we kidding? We *had* intended to fuck each other's brains out the minute he got there. Needless to say, however, I wasn't much in the mood for sex after Robin had tried to offer me that check.

"Seriously, Jace? *Seriously?*" I demanded when I confronted him upon his arrival. "If I didn't accept money from Brendan to be his boy toy, what makes you think I'll take it from you? Damn it, I don't pick up guys, then expect them to support me. I'm not my useless whore of a mother!"

His eyebrows crept up at that. I think I would have totally lost my shit if he'd tried to make a joke or patronize me. Instead, he regarded me steadily. "Um, *useless whore?* You *do* remember how I got through art school, right?"

That set me back for a moment. "Shit. Sorry, yeah. I didn't mean you. I just— I pay my own way. I really don't want money shit messing up my adult relationships."

"So tell me you don't want to see me again."

That took me back a step. "What?"

"Tell me you don't want to see me again," he said simply but insistently. "I'll go right this minute, but I'll still want you to take it. There are no strings attached to this, Topher. I'm not doing it because I'm fucking you, or because I want to control you, or because I think I need to take care of you. Though, to be quite fucking honest, for once in your life maybe someone *should*, because from where I sit, you're about twenty years overdue for a little of that. I'm not even doing it because I feel sorry for you. It's not charity, it's not pity, and I'm not trying to be your sugar daddy. It's an opportunity. A leg up, because everyone needs one at some point in their lives."

I shook my head at that. "I appreciate the thought, but I can't be obligated to anyone, Jace. I'm trying so fucking hard to get free of all that—"

His mouth tightened, and now he was starting to look pissed

off. "Okay, what part of 'no strings attached' translates to 'obligated' for you?"

"There's *always* an obligation." I fixed my gaze on a spot on the floor, unable to look at him. I'd learned that lesson well. "No one does anything for anyone else without expecting something. Whether they insist you sit on their lap so they can play pocket pool with you, or stand there trapped in the corner while they ride you down until you feel absolutely fucking microscopic, or even just let them dictate your choices, there's always a cost when you let someone do something for you, even when they volunteer."

"Christ, Topher," Jace whispered, looking away. When he looked back, there were tears in his eyes, and suddenly I fucking *hated* myself. "Is that really how you see the world? How you see *me*?"

"Oh shit. No." I scrubbed my hands down my face. "No, Jace, no. Not you. Not you. I just—" No words would come to me. They were all lost in a formless maelstrom of fear and a yearning so powerful it ached. I wanted to rush to him and kneel at his feet and wrap my arms around his waist and let him hold me there against his belly until I felt *safe*. But I also wanted to tell him to go far, far away so I could rebuild all my defenses.

In the end, all I could do was stare at him, pleading wordlessly for understanding.

He looked back at me for a long moment, pain evident in his eyes. "Your whole life, not one single person you've loved or depended on has been worthy of your trust, have they?"

"Mo is," I muttered miserably. "Look what I've done to her, though."

"I honestly don't know what to say to convince you to give me the chance to be different. I can't even blame you for being afraid to try." He sighed, scrubbing his fingers through his hair almost violently. "Take the money, don't take the money, it's up to you. I was thinking I'd attach a well-intentioned condition that you use it to study something you love, something that ignites you, but after what you've said I won't even do that. Study something that pays the bills but leaves you empty inside, if that's what you feel you need to do. If you're still afraid of hidden strings, we'll call it a loan and you can pay me back someday. That way the obligation is out in front, nothing hidden."

God, he looked so *wounded*. I would have done anything to take that look from his eyes. Anything. But I stood there staring at him, as though I was trapped at the center of a labyrinth, looking in all directions but unable to decide which one was the way out.

"I'll level with you, Topher," he continued after a moment. "I'm absolutely head over heels for you, but I don't think I can do this knowing you're always on the alert, waiting for me to let you down. That's a fucking self-fulfilling prophecy there. I want to be the exception to the rule, to be the one who shows you it's okay to trust sometimes, but if you're not able to *truly* give me a fair shot, it's a waste of my time and yours."

Wow. Part of me wondered if this was some sort of record for length of time it took a maybe-relationship to crash and burn.

The other part of me just *hurt*.

"So here's what I'm going to do." He dropped his hands to his lap, letting them fall on his thighs as if they were too heavy. "I'm going to go get a room somewhere for the weekend, if I can find a vacancy. If not, I'll crash on Robin and Geoff's sofa until Sunday, then head back to Chicago. And I won't come back, though to be quite honest, I'll probably wait around a while for you once I'm there. But someday—and I don't know when it will be, so I'm not giving you a deadline—I'll have to give up hope and move on. In the meantime, if you decide you can try to trust me —*really* try—call me. Day or night. Anytime."

Overwhelmed by desperation, I opened my mouth to announce I was ready, but he held up his hand. "No. Not right now. Not to keep me from walking out. I want you to actually spend some time thinking about it before you decide. And what-ever you choose, that money's going to be with Robin indefi-nitely. It's yours whether you call me or not, whether or not we ever see each other again. If you want it." He looked away, his jaw tensing and his eyes shining. "Just try to be happy. That's all I ask."

With a sniff, he picked up his bags and walked out.

I<small>T TOOK</small> me exactly twelve hours to decide. Some of those were filled with tears. The rest were spent tossing and turning, unable to sleep as I asked myself, over and over, if I was willing to take the risk of letting someone have that much pull on me. If I was willing to make myself vulnerable to the way people treated you when you were indebted to them.

In the end, what sent me scrambling for my phone at four in the morning was that my fear of being without him, of never again feeling the things he made me feel, was greater than my fear of him hurting me.

Are you at the Dunes?

I typed the text, then pulled on my clothes as I waited for the answer.

Cottage 10.

I nearly broke land speed records getting there.

He opened the door almost before my knuckles even touched it, and we stared at each other a long, intense moment, asking questions and sending answers too complex to put into words. Then he stood aside to let me in and shut the door behind me.

A half-empty bottle of vodka sat on the bedside table, and his sketchbook was open on the king-size bed. Several sketches, only three of which looked finished, were scattered across the bedspread. Clearly, he hadn't been sleeping either.

Swallowing, I picked up the nearest one. A dark-skinned, pale-haired child with an angel's wings—too old to be a cherub, more like a small boy—stood in the middle of a dark forest, looking around in terror. His hand was outstretched, reaching for a shadow disappearing off the edge of the page, the unknown figure walking away from him, leaving him behind.

I drew a shuddering breath and picked up the next one. In this one, that same angel—now a willowy adolescent, his thin, maturing body draped in the ubiquitous short toga with strapped sandals wound around his ankles—stood with his shoulders hunched in the midst of a crowd of jeering figures. He held an ornate harp cradled protectively against his body, trying to shield it from further harm. Its strings were sprung, and its frame cracked and bent.

In the last one, an even more mature version of the angel—now a young man—knelt on one knee in another clearing in the woods. He was bruised and bleeding, his toga torn and stained. He held the bloody, tattered remnants of one of his wings, trying futilely to piece it back together.

My breath left me in an explosive gasp, nearly a sob, and I let the sketch fall back onto the bed.

Jace's arms slipped around my waist and he held me wordlessly, laying his face against the back of my shoulder.

"These aren't *me!*" I screamed in a whisper, two tears slipping down my cheeks. "Whatever you see, it's not me. I'm just a fuck-up who doesn't know anything, not even what he's doing from moment to moment. And I'm scared all the time, and I don't know how to be anything else, except maybe angry and sad."

His arms tightened around me. "I don't need you to be perfect. I don't need you to never make mistakes. I just need you to let me give you as much of myself as I can, and to trust that I will try as hard as possible never to hurt you intentionally. Can you do that? Can you let me love you?"

Jesus I was scared, so scared, *so fucking scared!* But I nodded and turned in his arms, wrapping myself around him. "Yeah. Yeah, I can do that."

I couldn't say how long we stood there, breathing each other in, letting the fear bleed away in the rightness of being together. Eventually, his lips found mine, salty and urgent, and I returned the kiss with equal desperation, clinging to him, trying to melt into him. He reached out with one hand and swept all the sketches to the floor. Then he pulled me onto the bed with him, and all the fear and sadness began to fade, flooded out by joy.

CHAPTER THIRTY-TWO

No chance to remain in
What was once my life
This has changed me

— CASEY STRATTON, "SHUT YOU DOWN"

T he next week, I changed the courses I had registered for in the spring. I also had a phone consultation with an adviser and applied to the music program for a Bachelor of Music Education degree.

"I'm going to be a private voice teacher," I announced proudly to Jace on the phone later that evening. "I'm going to put a heavy emphasis on vocal technique and music theory in my studies, so I can give my students the proper technical training. I'm going to take piano again, too, though I might see if I can find a self-study course for that since I don't know if I'll have room in my schedule. But this way, it won't matter if schools are slashing their music programs; there are plenty of parents always willing to pay for their darlings to have extracurricular lessons. So I'm going to help kids who are like I used to be—the ones with talent who just need dedicated personal training to make something of it."

"That's brilliant!" I could hear elation in his voice and beamed, thrilled with myself for coming up with the idea. "And it won't stop you from finding ways to perform if you still want to."

"No, it won't. In fact, studying technique, if I apply it and practice it myself, might actually get me a little of that training I missed out on, so I can step up my game. I might never be a star, but who knows, maybe someday I'll get more than a walk-on part in a community production."

"I'll be in the front row with an armful of roses," he said warmly.

I stared up at the ceiling, lying on the diagonal across Ling's bed. "The only thing is, I might have to add another year of study, since I was late declaring my major and I don't have some of the general credits I need. But with the money from the sale of those paintings, plus any I manage to earn working over the next couple summers, I should be able to afford it, even when my scholarship ends."

"So you're going to accept it, then?" If he sounded any more pleased, he was likely to start singing himself.

"Yeah. Yeah I am."

"Good."

I hung up the phone feeling extremely satisfied with myself. What sorcery was this? Was I *actually* beginning to get my shit together?

THE WEEKS that followed sailed by far more smoothly, full of more promise than I was accustomed to. Mo decided to spend her next free weekend in Big Rapids, so I drove down to Chicago after work on Saturday, since I didn't have to work again until Tuesday. The next weekend, Jace came up to Saugatuck, and the following Wednesday, I texted Mo to find out if she was coming down for the weekend.

Mom wants me to come to Ann Arbor Fri, she answered. *Will try to get there Sat.*

That Saturday I was working in the storeroom of the gallery, stupidly, stupidly content and unwary, when she stormed in.

"You *asshole!*"

Next thing I knew, I was on the floor seeing stars and wondering if she'd broken my jaw. *Fuck*, who knew she packed such a right hook?

Robin immediately rushed in and tried to subdue her, but I stared at her in resignation and waved him off.

"Don't. Don't, Robin. It's okay. I've earned this. Just—can you close the door, so we don't disturb anyone who comes in to browse? She won't damage the inventory, promise."

"It's not the inventory I'm worried about," he said tightly. "Whatever your reasons, Morgan, if you assault him again, I'm calling the cops, got it?"

She gave him a jerky, resentful nod, and he left, closing the door behind him. Then she went back to glaring at me. I looked back, not even bothering to pick myself up off the floor.

How had I let myself get so complacent that I'd forgotten there still needed to be an accounting for what I'd done back in June?

"Don't even *think* about telling me you're sorry, you fucking dick," she finally grated.

"I am, but I won't." I straightened up, though I remained seated on the floor, my knees drawn up in front of me. "Your dad told your mom?"

"Not about *you*, no." She crossed her arms over her chest. "He came out to her as bisexual, admitted to having an affair. He said that it might be better if they separated while he tried to figure out what that meant for him, but that he wouldn't blame her if she would rather just get divorced."

"Ah." I rubbed my jaw again, Damn, but that hurt.

I admit, I had started to think Brendan didn't have the balls to do it. I couldn't help but be a little proud of him, whatever the fallout might be for me now.

Her eyes gleamed with tears as she stared at me bitterly. "The fucking galling thing is, I didn't put it together, even after Mom told me he'd had an affair with a guy. There I was with that factoid in one hand and your fucking guilt-ridden confession about an affair with a married man in the other, and I was totally in denial." She sneered at me. "I spent the drive from Ann Arbor to Lansing thinking, *No way. Topher would never do that to me.* I figured what had happened was that after spending a couple months around you, Dad had some sort of revelation about himself, right? But then I got to his house and right there in his office, he had those goddamn paintings of you!"

"He *what?*" Oh shit. I was gonna puke. I was gonna puke. I put my head down, sucking in desperate breaths as a cold sweat prickled over my body and my head spun. I hated to say it, but for a moment Mo was *not* my first consideration. Seriously, what the fuck? "Oh no. Oh nonono . . ."

I was pulled out of my horror when her voice cracked.

"Goddamn it, Topher, why didn't you *tell* me? Why did you confess everything except that part? Why did you let me go on believing you were my friend when you'd—"

"I wanted to, Mo. I wanted to tell you everything. I didn't want to lie."

"Oh right! You know, I seem to recall standing there while you were spilling your guts, and somehow Dad's name never came up. Don't tell me you didn't have the fucking opportunity!"

"I know, but there were all those people there, and you just don't go around *outing* someone like that . . ."

"Yeah, well you just don't go around *fucking your best friend's dad* either, you prick!" For a moment I thought she was going to hit me again, but she pulled it back. "That's a fucking convenient sense of ethics you've got going on there, *girlfriend.*"

I winced at the disgust in her voice. She loomed above me, completely righteous, completely justified, and I couldn't muster a single defense. I didn't want to. I wasn't going to try to rationalize what I'd done, because it wasn't rational. I'd already told her back on the Fourth how horrible I felt about the whole thing, how wrong I knew it was and how little forgiveness I deserved. She knew all that already. She just hadn't known it was about her at the time.

She had every right in the world to hate me. I wasn't even going to try to take that from her.

Silent moments, filled with rage on her part and shame on

mine, pressed in on us. Finally she turned on her heel and stalked out, tossing over her shoulder, "Don't even fucking think about ever talking to me again."

And that was how I lost my best friend.

"I CAN BE THERE in three hours," Jace offered when I called him to tell him what had happened.

"No." I held an ice pack to my bruised jaw. "I had this coming. I just have to take my medicine. I think I'll spend the weekend brooding about what a shitty friend I am and mourning the loss of the friendship. I might have Ben & Jerry over to keep me company. Or maybe Ernest and Julio Gallo."

"Hey, no threesomes unless I get to watch."

I started to laugh, then winced. "Ow. No more jokes."

"Sorry. Okay." He sighed into his phone, the breath crackling in my ear. "You sure you're all right?"

"Yeah."

I was lying. Actually I wasn't sure at all. But I needed to talk to Robin about the other part of this whole thing. For some reason I didn't want Jace to know who had ended up buying those paintings. Maybe because I suspected he'd feel almost as violated by it as I did.

"Call me tonight?" he prompted when I'd been silent too long.

"Yeah, I will."

We murmured our good-byes and I turned off my phone just as Robin came upstairs to the office, where I lay on the sofa.

"Hey, need another ice pack?"

"No." I sighed and sat up to look at him. "Why did you sell Brendan those paintings? You had to have known I wouldn't want him to have them."

"What?" He blinked at me. "Oh shit. He must have used a buyer to get them for him because he knew Ling and I would recognize him. I swear, Topher, I would not have sold those to him, not for any amount of money. Jesus. That's creepy."

"Yeah, tell me about it." I shuddered. I didn't know if Brendan was just obsessed with me, or if he'd managed to fall in some slightly disturbing version of love with me, but either way I felt positively *sick* every time I thought of him looking at those paintings, not to mention the fixation that must have driven him to pay fifteen thousand dollars for them.

I ENDED UP TAKING BEN & Jerry *and* the Gallo brothers home that night, so it was a real orgy of self-pity, complete with BFF movies like *Beaches* and *Thelma & Louise*.

I went to bed with the sort of headache only low- to mid-grade red wine can give you, telling myself that I was absolutely, under no circumstances, allowed to text Mo. If she ever contacted me again, we'd talk, but if not, I would respect her wishes and keep away. I wasn't going to chase after her and try to grovel my way back into her good graces, though I would miss her.

She was under no obligation whatsoever to forgive me or give me another chance to be the sort of friend I should have been to begin with. I'd fucked up and I needed to accept the consequences.

If it wasn't for the headache and general grogginess that came from tossing and turning until you mope yourself to sleep, I might have had the presence of mind to send it to voice mail when a call came in from my sister at seven o'clock the next morning. Instead, I answered it without even looking at the caller ID, pain lancing through my temples too strongly to stare at the lit screen.

"Topher?" It took me a moment to place the voice. At first, I thought it was my mother calling; she and Colleen had very similar voices, and I couldn't always tell them apart at only a word or two.

"Yeah? Oh hi. Colleen. What's goin' on?"

"Did I wake you up?"

"Don't worry about it." Christ, my mouth tasted like the inside of a goat's stomach. I needed a shower and some coffee, stat. "I gotta be to work in a few hours anyway."

"Mom had an accident last night. She's in the hospital."

"What?" I sat up quickly.

"I'm sure she didn't know what would happen. She probably thought that if Grandpa had come back well enough after his stroke to drive even with his right-side impairment, why not her? She tried to go to the store by herself and had a wreck. Of course, she wasn't wearing a seat belt, because we all know she refuses unless someone makes her. She's got a skull fracture and two broken ribs, and she tore the hell out of the ligaments in her knee hitting the dashboard with it."

"Shit." I rubbed my aching forehead. I was too hungover right now to think things through and remember all the reasons I didn't go running when my family called. But just now, reeling from the loss of one of the two most emotionally significant relationships in my life, crawling home to the familiarity of Momma seemed like an appealing notion.

"I'll be there in a few hours."

CHAPTER THIRTY-THREE

I was there when your lips first said it
Shot me down I cannot forget it
You reduced me to nothing then
You produced a destructive trend

— CASEY STRATTON, "SHUT YOU DOWN"

The doctor happened to be in my mom's room at the Genesys Regional Medical Center when I arrived. I shook his hand and introduced myself, and he gave me a wry smile.

"Ah, hi. They said you're the pessimistic one."

I gave Colleen and Tonya a flat look. "I prefer to call it realistic. How's she doing?"

"Well, as I was just explaining to your sisters, right now we're monitoring her to make sure her lung doesn't collapse from the fractured ribs—which are fully broken, not just cracked, so I can't really overstate the danger there—and to assess any neurological trauma from the impact to her skull. The long-term issue is going to be her knee. It will probably take more than one surgery to repair all the ligament damage. She'll be on bed rest and crutches for months, and she'll need at least a year of physical therapy to strengthen the joint after it's repaired. This is going to impact her ability to function independently for a while. She's going to need some assistance."

I closed my eyes, feeling a trap spring closed around me.

Fuck.

The doctor continued describing the treatment my mom would need, and I listened, nodding attentively until he paused.

"Do you have any questions?"

I stared at my mother on the bed. The pale blonde hair that had left me with my Justin Timberlake 'fro had dulled, so now she colored it a much brassier shade that never managed to look natural. She had been twenty-one when I was born, but now, at forty-two, she looked closer to sixty. Nearly three decades of heavy drinking and smoking—and I meant that literally; she first began running away from home and partying at the age of thirteen—had ruined her skin and left her face bloated.

"Was anyone else injured in the accident?" I directed this more at Colleen, who shook her head.

"No, she hit a light pole, not another car. She doesn't have enough control over her right side to manage the accelerator and brake pedal, and it looks like she sped up going into a turn instead of slowing down."

I nodded and looked back at Mom, then to the doctor. Somehow, I'd ended up taking position against the wall, my arms crossed protectively across my chest.

"She's got a history of substance abuse and addiction. What's the plan to keep her from becoming dependent on the pain meds? I mean, I assume you're loading her up with narcotics for the time being?"

Apparently, no one had considered mentioning alcoholism as part of Mom's medical history when she was admitted, because the doctor was surprised by this.

"It's good that we know that. We'll try to wean her off the opiates as soon as possible, keep an eye on how much she's receiving, keep the doses to the minimum necessary for adequate pain management. However, that's going to be a bit of a challenge right now because with broken ribs, pain management is absolutely crucial. If it hurts too much, she might not breathe as deeply as she needs to in order to keep the lungs clear, which can lead to pneumonia. But we'll look for any warning signs that her reliance on the medication is increasing rather than decreasing, watch for drug-seeking behaviors, and so forth," he assured me.

"Okay. What was her blood alcohol level?"

"Topher!" Colleen glared at me, and Tonya rolled her eyes.

"She could have killed someone, Colleen!" I shot back, matching her glare for glare.

"I'm the one who's been running her errands, and I haven't bought her any alcohol."

"Right. And how do you know this is the first time she's tried to run an errand on her own? Maybe she's been getting her own beer."

"She doesn't drink anymore!"

"She's gone through periods of sobriety before and then relapsed."

Usually I was aware of when it happened because Mom always went for the phone when she'd been drinking, and she was an argumentative drunk. The last time, she'd called me while I was between classes my junior year in high school, and gone on one of her self-pity riffs. When I'd tried to tell her I had to get to class, she'd called me a little asshole and hung up on me. I'd been so shaken up that I'd gone home sick for the rest of the day.

I'd subsequently sent her a letter informing her that if she ever called me while drunk again, I would stop speaking to her entirely. Colleen and my aunt had been *furious* with me for it.

"Can you excuse us, Doctor?" Colleen asked, giving him her patented aren't-I-sweet-and-cute cheerleader smile. He nodded politely and left without ever answering my question, and Colleen whirled on me when he was gone. "If you're going to come in here and start making this all about your drama, you can leave."

"Oh, don't *even* tempt me!"

Tonya huffed and pushed herself away from the wall. "Whatever. You two duke this out on your own time. I've got to drive two hours to get back for my shift tonight. Mom and Dad will be here after they're out of work this evening."

Oh, yes, Tonya had been living with our aunt and uncle so long she considered them "Mom" and "Dad," which was why she could manage to treat issues involving our mother with so much detachment. She had accomplished what I'd tried so desperately to achieve; our mother didn't fill that space in Tonya's heart reserved for "Mom."

"Fine." I murmured. "Drive safely."

She gave me a hug, which I returned dutifully. My relationship with her wasn't nearly as contentious as the one with Colleen, though if there was a difference of opinions, she usually landed on Colleen's side of the fence. I was the black sheep in more ways than one. I didn't have the simpatico with either of them that they had with each other.

When Tonya was gone, I looked back at Colleen, who rubbed her forehead wearily.

"So, where's Grandma?" I asked.

"On a cruise to Alaska with her seniors' group. She won't be back for two weeks."

"Yeah, well, that's probably for the best, I suppose. Otherwise she'll freak out over money and we'll have to explain to her all over again that she won't be left on the hook for the medical bills if Mom dies, just like we had to last time."

Colleen nodded. "Yeah. Come on. Let's go down to the cafeteria, get some lunch and figure out what we're going to do."

On the way down the elevator, Jace called.

"Hey."

"Hey. Good morning. Sorry I didn't call until now. I was in conference with a new client and didn't get your messages. How's your mom?"

"She seems to be stable, but there's going to be some long-term issues we have to deal with."

"Let's see . . . Chicago to Flint is, what, five hours? Six? I'll be there this evening."

"You don't have to—"

"*I'll be there this evening.* Love you."

He hung up before I could answer, and I turned back to Colleen with a tense smile.

"So, how have you been? Work's going okay? How's your boyfriend—was it Gerry?"

"Terry."

I tended to steer clear of her boyfriends except when family functions absolutely required it, because a lot of the white residents of Flint were actually transplanted rednecks and hillbillies (including my family) who had moved there for jobs in the auto factories. None of them had ever gotten in my face, thank God. No, the problem was that—in the interest of keeping the peace and not embarrassing anyone—I was expected to let their ignorant (or sometimes subtly deliberate) racist or homophobic remarks roll off my back. If I called them out on it, everyone made me out to be the troublemaker.

For the next hour and a half, I listened and nodded attentively—with the occasional "hmm"—as Colleen told me everything that was going on in her life, a great deal of which seemed to involve drama with her boyfriend's ex. It was the sort of thing that really should have been left behind in high school, but even at the age of twenty-five, Colleen liked her catfights and jealous tiffs.

Most of our conversations went this way when we were getting along. She never once asked me what I'd been doing or how I was. She never even asked where I was living. For Colleen, everything was about her.

When her recitation about her latest weight loss endeavors had wound down (she was a size six trying to get down to a size four now that she'd had breast reduction surgery because "flat-chested women get to wear the cutest clothes!"), we fell silent, sipping our Cokes.

"She's going to need live-in care, Topher," she said finally.

"Well, luckily you're right here in town," I said brightly, knowing where this was going.

"You know I can't live with her. She and I fight all the time when we try to live together. You're the one she doesn't argue with. She likes you."

"She likes me because she knows she can get to me emotionally, and because I've never borrowed money from her and conveniently forgotten to pay it back. Multiple times."

Colleen huffed. "That is such bullshit. Families don't make 'loans' to each other. They help when someone needs help. She was never there for us as a mother, the least she could do was keep me from being evicted."

Month after month. I didn't say that part.

"Well, she did, and now the money Clay left her is gone and she's going to lose her house because she can't pay her bills living off disability. So yeah, however bad a mom she's been, I can see how she might resent that a bit."

"Whatever. I run her errands for her. She can suck it up about the money."

"Right, whatever." Yeah, that argument was a one-way street to a rant on how the world owed Colleen for her dysfunctional childhood. No matter what she did, my older sister always convinced herself that people were unreasonable for holding her accountable. Mom wasn't the only one she'd hit up for money. Every relative in the family had cut her off when she kept going back to the well.

"You need to move in with her, Topher. You're the only one who can. You heard the doctor. She's not going to be able to take care of herself for months, maybe years."

"No, I *can't.* In case you've forgotten, I'm enrolled in college."

"You can enroll at Mott or Baker—"

"Colleen, I have a *scholarship* at GVSU, remember? An actual university. An associate's degree from a community college is not going to get me the sort of career I need to make a decent living."

"Well, fine, apply at U of M Flint then. Jesus, Topher, you're such a snob. You don't *need* a degree to have a decent career, you know. I'm making a really good living selling blinds and wallpaper—"

Oh fuck. *Seriously, Colleen?*

"Really." The Condescending-fucking-Wonka meme had never smiled so blandly. "You go to people's homes to consult with them on those sales, right?"

"Yeah, I go out on calls so I can take measurements."

"Uh-huh. And how many of those people would let you in their homes for those consultations if your skin were the same color as mine? Would Blinds & More, or wherever it is you're working, have even hired you for that position to begin with if you looked like me?"

"Oh, come on! Not everything is about race!"

"Yeah, that's the knee-jerk reaction of people who never have to deal with racism. You bet your ass employment opportunity is about race. Don't fucking insult me by pretending the doors that are open to you would be open for me. I *need* that university degree to have a chance at earning more than a subsistence wage."

"You're only *half* black—"

"And I'll *absolutely* be sure to explain that to the employers who express interest in my pedigree. But most of them are just going to take one look at my skin and ask if I'm there applying for the job flipping burgers or mopping floors." I rolled my eyes. "So check your privilege, mmkay? That seventy-seven cents white women earn on the white man's dollar may be working okay for you, but without a university degree, I'll be making even less."

She gave me a disgusted look. "So what you're saying is, you're going to refuse to help our mother—who cannot function independently—because it means your future won't be quite as *glamorous* as you'd like it to be?"

I blinked at her. "*Glamorous?*"

"Look, we all have to make sacrifices to be part of a family."

My eyebrows crept toward my hairline. Ms. Open-Hand-Empty-Palm was lecturing *me* about sacrifice? Even worse, she was using that cajoling tone that said she thought she was imparting a lesson for my own good, not just attacking me.

"That's the problem with you, Christopher. That's why you have such a hard time getting along with everyone. You seem to think you should be able to do your own thing without pitching in. None of the rest of us get to do that."

That's when I snapped. When all the rage at being bludgeoned by accusations of selfishness year after year, all so I would feel bad enough to do things everyone else's way, just erupted.

"Okay, you know what? Fuck you, Colleen. Fuck you. *Fuck you.*" Out of the corner of my eye, the cafeteria cashier hovered with her hand over a phone, no doubt ready to call security because I was cussing out a white girl. I snatched up my backpack, dug through it until I found my checkbook, which I'd brought thinking I might need to pay some of Mom's bills while she was hospitalized. I scribbled a check and flung it in Colleen's face.

"There. You want my future, my education? Fine. Have it. Just fucking *have it*! I'll withdraw from my classes and go become a fry cook somewhere. Once you're done justifying the ways you're going to end up spending most of that on yourself—because, hey, I'm the only one in this family you *haven't* screwed out of money yet, and why should I be left out?—hopefully there will be enough left to hire a nurse or an aide or some shit to take care of Mom. Just don't ever ask me for a fucking thing again. Ever."

Well. At least I accomplished one thing: I shut her up. Colleen was still staring at the check in openmouthed awe, no doubt already imagining the shit she just *had* to buy with that money and rationalizing why it was perfectly okay for her to do so, when I stormed out of the cafeteria, wiping my face.

CHAPTER THIRTY-FOUR

I will not supply
What you need this time
I don't have any strength left
But you never see what is troubling me
You just turn the other cheek

— CASEY STRATTON, "SACRIFICE"

I went back to my mom's room. Where else could I go? I couldn't leave town if there were still medical decisions to be made, and my aunt and uncle would expect to see me there when they arrived in a few hours. She still wasn't awake—a fact which made me question the nurse.

"Well, she's on a lot of meds right now. It's probably for the best that she's resting, because otherwise she'd be hurting. She comes around for a few minutes every so often. Stick around, you'll get to say hi."

She smiled kindly and squeezed my shoulder.

Colleen didn't come back to the room until Aunt Blythe and Uncle Pete arrived that evening, at which point I was still steaming. I let her do the talking to explain Mom's condition to them, and then a doctor came by to check on her and answer more of their questions. While that was going on, I got a text from Jace.

I'm in the lobby. What room?

I directed him up to the third-floor room in the pulmonary wing while the doctor discussed his intention to put Mom on an oxygen mask.

"Her sats aren't what we'd like to see, and if they don't improve by tomorrow morning, we'll do more tests to see if there's a pulmonary contusion," the doctor was explaining. "The other possibility is that she might be developing pneumonia. Another problem we're struggling with just now is keeping her body temp stabilized. Her temperature keeps dropping, so we're trying get her warm."

I closed my eyes. Fuck. It was like her suicide attempt all over again. One problem cascading into another and another after that for weeks on end, waiting to see if she'd spiral down or pull out of it.

I swallowed. "She did that last time she was hospitalized, too, after her"—I slid a glance at Colleen—"*brain injury*. They said it might be because the trauma messed up her ability to regulate her body temp."

Actually, they'd thought it was because one of the drugs she'd taken had damaged some of those functions, but I didn't bother to add that.

The doctor nodded. "That's definitely one explanation. We'll monitor her overnight. I've called a pulmonologist to come examine her. If she's declined any more by tomorrow morning, we'll probably transfer her to the pulmonary ICU."

I nodded and closed my eyes again, steepling my fingers under my chin as I listened to him describe the knee injury and an upcoming consult with an orthopedic surgeon. A quiet knock at the door made me open them again.

Jace stood there wearing a friendly but cautious smile. Whatever the circumstances, he was, after all, Meeting the Family.

"Hi." I smiled back a little uncertainly. None of them even knew about Jace. Still, I held out a hand to him. "Come on in.

Aunt Blythe, Uncle Pete, Colleen, this is my boyfriend, Jace. Jace, this is my family—and of course, my mom." I gestured to the bed.

"Pleased to meet you." Jace bobbed a polite nod and walked calmly to stand beside me against the far wall, squeezing my fingertips briefly. Colleen's expression hardened, and I had no doubt that if she found the opportunity, I'd be hearing about the impropriety of "flaunting" my homosexuality in front of everyone and making them uncomfortable. She would accuse me of doing it to show off and make a statement.

Aunt Blythe and Uncle Pete didn't really react except to murmur courteous welcomes. They really *didn't* care that I was gay—in fact, they were both quite liberal, considering where they lived—as long as my unconventionality didn't embarrass them among their circle of acquaintances.

After the doctor finished his recitation, he left us alone.

"Well," my aunt said, nodding briskly. "I'll talk to a social worker while I'm here, start finding out about long-term care options and what your mom's insurance is going to cover."

"Talk to Colleen to coordinate that," I said dispassionately. "I've got to get back to my job in Saugatuck and won't have the time. We decided hiring a nurse would be the best thing for all of us, so I gave her some money to cover it. She'll be in charge of handling that since she's in the area."

Jace's head shot up and he stared at me in astonishment. I gave him a solemn look, silently begging him not to make an issue of it here and now. He seemed to get the message and didn't say anything.

Unfortunately, my uncle didn't pick up that same signal.

"What money?"

"Doesn't matter," I muttered, not meeting his eyes.

"Topher," my aunt insisted. *"What money?"*

"What I'd saved up for school, okay?" I said impatiently. "I gave her my college money."

Colleen's face went red, and I could just about see steam coming out of her ears. We both knew where this was going to lead. She'd probably been hoping I wouldn't mention the money I'd given her, so she could do whatever she wanted with it. Now that someone else knew, there would be an accounting. Which was exactly why I'd brought it up. I might be washing my hands of the situation, but at least this way someone could keep an eye on what she was doing.

"What?" Uncle Pete asked sharply. He was a tall man, quiet enough to be mistaken for soft-spoken, but he wasn't really. He didn't say much, but when he spoke, he did so with intelligence and authority, and got straight to the point. "Whoa, wait. No. That is *not* acceptable."

My aunt looked at me, aghast. "Topher! No. You need to keep that money for school."

I shook my head. "It doesn't matter. I'm not going to get an education if I'm stuck here taking care of Mom anyway, so it might as well go toward something that will help us all deal with this without completely fucking up our lives. I'll go to school part-time, stretch out getting my degree longer so I can work full-time. Or I'll get student loans, go into hock for the rest of my life like everyone else in the country."

My aunt's pinched nose flared at me cussing, and her dark blue eyes sparked. She was an absolutely beautiful woman except for that thin, hooked beak of hers; it was easy to see why she had been homecoming queen and always had so many friends. She was gentle and funny and entertaining—except when she had power over you and was pissed off. It was actually a bit disconcerting, a Jekyll-and-Hyde type of thing. Everyone liked her because they didn't see those moments. I could already see from Jace's reaction that my aunt and uncle weren't the ogres he was expecting.

"Colleen," she said tightly. "Give Topher his money back. We'll find another way to handle this *as a family*."

Colleen had a deer-caught-in-the-headlights look, and behind her eyes, the pathological liar within her, the one who took and took and took with no sense of obligation whatsoever, was spinning in circles to find a way to get out of this.

"I already deposited it at the ATM," she said at last. "I didn't want to risk anything happening to the check Topher threw at me until we had time to sit down and discuss this calmly, which I couldn't do because he was being so irrational. Now, I don't have my checkbook."

My uncle's jaw flexed, and my aunt reached into her bag and pulled out her own checkbook. "Well, when the bank opens Monday, Colleen, you can withdraw it and pay us back. With a *cashier's check.*" Colleen reddened, and I had to duck my head and bite my lip to avoid smirking and making a joke about locating the burn unit here at the hospital.

"How much was it?" Aunt Blythe pressed.

I closed my eyes, pinching the bridge of my nose with a tired sigh, refusing to answer. Fuck. Even my dramatic and liberating grand gesture had to be undermined, didn't it? I didn't know whether to be relieved or disgusted. On the one hand, I could afford school again. On the other, now I would never be free of this family and their guilt trips and manipulations.

"At least fifteen thousand dollars." Jace sounded pissed. Really, *really* pissed. I was definitely going hear about this when he got me alone. "*Right?*"

"Nineteen," Colleen snapped when my aunt stammered at the amount. I'd added the money I'd earned working for Geoff and Robin on top of the money from the paintings. "And just where the hell did you get that kind of money over the summer anyway, Christopher? What *exactly* have you been doing?"

Oh, no fucking way. I narrowed my eyes at her, then forced myself to shrug, batting my eyes disingenuously.

"Mostly running drugs," I chirped, beaming. "Also, rentboys go for top dollar in a rich town like Saugatuck. Then there were the porn videos." I gave Colleen a cheeky smile as she blustered. "I have a line on a few infants I can smuggle on the black market, but the buyers haven't come through yet."

"Topher." My aunt gave me a repressive look that I probably deserved, though she, too, seemed appalled by Colleen's insinuation. "Can we all try to get along?"

"It was from *me*." Jace quivered with outrage as he stared Colleen down. "I'm a painter, and sometimes my art sells in galleries. Topher did some modeling work for me this summer and I decided to share the profits from the paintings I sold to help pay *for his education."*

I flinched at the emphasis. The anger in Jace's voice was hot enough to blister. Colleen wasn't the only one who should locate the burn unit. *Ooh,* was I ever going to hear about this.

"Well, thank you, Jace," my uncle said quite courteously. The education bit at the end there had just earned him major credits with them. Aunt Blythe and Uncle Pete were the first high school and college graduates from their respective families, and, not coincidentally, the first ones to move out of the lower-class income brackets all the way to upper-middle class. They were big, *big* believers in higher education. Ironically, it was the one subject I was actually in perfect agreement with them on.

My aunt scribbled a check and pushed it at me. I didn't dare hesitate to grab it, because I was pretty sure Jace would lose his shit if I dug in my heels about this.

"Okay. Let's all go get some dinner and talk about this," Aunt Blythe said as I tucked the check in my wallet. "We'll figure out a solution that works for the whole family."

"We'd *love* to." Jace grabbed my arm, holding tight, his voice bright with false cheer.

What else could I do but smile gamely? "Sure."

"YOUR AUNT and uncle aren't what I expected," Jace said mildly as we searched for a decent hotel near the hospital. Once we were checked in, we'd be going back, because that was what my family did. When someone was in the hospital, we sat vigils.

After Aunt Blythe and Uncle Pete had treated us to a late dinner at their favorite Coney Island family restaurant, Colleen had gone home. My aunt and uncle went back to the hospital to check on Mom one more time before undertaking the two-hour drive back to Grand Rapids, so that they could be up for work in the morning. Before they left, we'd tentatively agreed that, if necessary, we would all pitch in—each as allowed by our respective incomes—to hire a nurse or aide if Mom needed one when she was out of the hospital. I was betting Colleen wouldn't have a dime to spare for the endeavor, though I was already mentally rearranging finances to stretch my degree out a little longer to be able to contribute.

While my attempting to pay for the whole thing myself hadn't accomplished what I'd intended, just the gesture might have done me one better. There had been something different in the way my aunt and uncle had spoken to me over dinner, as though they were conferring *with* me instead of dictating *to* me. By attempting to pay for the nurse, I'd moved myself into a different classification in their eyes. I'd demonstrated that I was self-sufficient. I was no longer a dependent, an unproductive drain on family resources like my mom and even sometimes Colleen. I was an adult, and someone who took his obligations to family seriously. It made them treat me with a new respect, and that respect was extended to Jace because obviously he, too, was a responsible and contributing citizen.

It was a little sad that in my family, you had to flash some cash before you could be regarded as an equal, but whatever. I'd take it.

"How's that?" I asked Jace, already knowing what he would say about Aunt Blythe and Uncle Pete.

"They're so . . . *nice.*" He looked at me in confusion. "Soft-spoken. Polite. I would have expected them to be a lot more . . . I don't know . . . rigid? Cold? Disapproving? . . . given what you've told me about them."

I nodded slowly. "If I met your family—and they didn't know I was gay and/or your boyfriend—what do you think I would see? Would they seem like monsters, or would they seem like normal, even nice, people?"

His mouth tightened. "Okay. Point taken."

"Sometimes when I remember the way they've treated me, it's hard for me to be objective, but really, no one's all good or all bad. Well, my sister sometimes challenges that idea, but even she can be fun when she's not being a raging bitch. My aunt and uncle are downright *wonderful* people about ninety-five percent of the time. That ninety-five percent makes it really hard for people on the outside to believe in the other five percent—the part you only see when you're living under their roof, under their authority. But that five percent can be pretty harsh."

He sighed and slipped his fingers through mine as we waited for the light to change. "Yeah, I can see that."

We fell silent for a moment, then he asked softly, "Why did you do it, Topher? What the fuck were you thinking?"

"It's family." I shrugged helplessly, tracing a finger in random patterns through the thin layer of oily haze that always seems to exist on the inside of car windows. "They make you crazy. They pull you in. No matter how much you hate them sometimes, you still go to Christmas dinner and try to love them. And there's always a part of you that tries to take care of them." I sighed, bowing my head. "My family has just enough redeeming qualities to make it really, really hard to cut myself off from them entirely, no matter how much they've fucked me up. Sometimes I want to, but if I tried, I'd feel like the bad guy. Colleen pissed me off enough today that I thought, if they took that money, I could finally do it. I could finally convince myself there was *nothing* in this family worth sticking around for. I could cut the last ties and maybe ditch some of the baggage that comes with them."

"Yeah, or maybe they would have just kept coming after you, expecting more. I meant for *you* to have that money, not your family."

"I know. I'm sorry. I just didn't know what else to do." I squeezed his hand. "I admit, also, that I might have been a little skeeved out by knowing who the money came from."

"Um . . . last I checked, it came from me."

"Wanna guess who bought those paintings?"

"Oh, are you *shitting* me?" He sighed. "Okay, now I just feel dirty."

"Yeah, that was pretty much my reaction. I don't know why it disturbs me, but it does."

"It disturbs you because it's fucking over the line. There's something very intimate about those paintings. It means he's not nearly as over it as you are, and that's kind of stalkery. I mean, really, who pays thousands of dollars for art of their ex-fling?"

I nodded. "I wouldn't have thought Brendan was that type. He was a normal guy, not like that at all. Now I wonder exactly why he came out to his family."

"You may need to take the initiative, nip any idea that you guys might get back together in the bud."

I blew out a slow breath as he pulled into the parking lot of a Holiday Inn. "Yeah. I'll do that."

"Okay. In the meantime"—Jace laid his fingers alongside my jaw and turned my face gently to look at him—"that money came from *me* to help *you*. He couldn't have known when he bought the paintings that I'd give the money to you. This isn't him trying to make you feel obligated or to control you. All right?"

"Right." I nodded once, resolutely, and Jace kissed me, then got out of the car to check us in.

CHAPTER THIRTY-FIVE

For a moment we all stop and look to you
Our lost one who
We will not forget
But we must keep moving through
The bitter truth

— CASEY STRATTON, "THE BITTER TRUTH"

M y mom was awake, if groggy and in a lot of pain, when we got back to the hospital.

"Hi, baby." She smiled happily when I took her hand and leaned down to kiss her cheek. Her voice was slightly slurred, but that was something that had begun to happen long before her suicide attempt and/or stroke—a reminder of the brain damage that came with long-term alcohol abuse.

"Hi, Mom," I murmured. Seeing her smile at me like that, knowing that—whatever her faults—she did love me as much as she was capable of loving anyone, and that being with me made her happy, made it very hard to remember all the reasons she wasn't good for me.

"How are you?"

"I'm okay." I smiled. "I brought someone with me. Mom, this is my boyfriend, Jace. Jace, this is Frederica, my mom."

"Nice to meet you, Mrs. Carlisle," Jace said very properly, and Mom squeezed my fingers, grinning.

"Kefler. I got remarried." Mom couldn't manage to lift her other hand to shake his without too much pain, but she grinned at me. "I like him. Very cute."

"So help me God, woman, if you say something inappropriate, I will smother you with a pillow."

I smiled to take the sting off my words. Jace's eyes widened, but Mom just laughed, or tried to, though her busted ribs made it impossible. She was, after all, the woman who had blurted things like *I'd like to lick his teeth!* to me about attractive men ever since I was a child. One time, when she was drunk, she'd told me that of all our fathers, Tonya's was the only one she'd actually loved, but she could never have remained with him because he'd had the world's smallest dick. It was from her that I'd learned the adage, *Men have two heads. One they think with, the other they use as a hat rack.* I think I'd been about ten or twelve when she'd dropped that one on me.

I might have been joking about the pillow part, but suspecting she might get inappropriate? Not out of bounds in the slightest.

"So, what have you been up to, baby?" she asked, not relinquishing my fingers. Her hand was too warm and puffy, the skin oddly smooth and shiny. Jace took a seat near the window.

I sat on the edge of her bed and held her hand and talked to her about my summer in Saugatuck, about the art gallery and the body art studio, about Robin and Geoff, Ling and Zhen, and how I'd picked Jace up on the beach.

"I thought I picked you up!" he protested, relaxing when he saw there wasn't likely to be any overt conflict here.

"So, you're going back to college?" she asked when I was done catching her up.

I nodded, meeting Jace's eyes. We hadn't yet discussed how things would change between us when I went back to Allendale. It was only about forty-five minutes farther away than Saugatuck for him, but still, we were going to have more of a separation between us.

"Yes, in a few weeks. I'm all registered for classes. I'm changing my major to music education."

"Music education?" She frowned. "Why not performance?"

"Because," I sighed tragically. "I have this unfortunate addiction: I like regular meals."

She gave me a narrow look. "Smart-ass. I don't know why you went to college to begin with. You should have gone to New York, gone straight to Broadway. Or at least gone to Juilliard."

I laughed, shaking my head. Yet another irony of my family: the only one of them who actually believed my talent to be worthwhile was my neglectful drunk of a mother, the one who didn't have a lick of common sense in her body. "Well. Maybe after I graduate."

"Damn right," she muttered, still looking displeased. Then she squeezed my hand. "Hey. You remember that Christmas play you had the lead in when you were in the sixth grade?"

"Yeah, of course I do." It was memorable not just because I'd had a leading role, but because Mom had actually attended. Something most kids took as a given had been momentous enough to catapult the memory to one of the happiest of my childhood.

She swung my hand back and forth. "I remember sitting there in that audience and hearing the other parents whispering, *My God, he's good!* I was so proud. You were meant to be a star, baby. You were always the extraordinary one."

I closed my eyes, willing away the sting. I didn't bother arguing that I wasn't good enough for the huge things she envisioned for me, however unrealistic it might be. She would have just insisted that her pipe dreams were perfectly reasonable. "Well, thanks. I'm glad you think so."

We stayed awhile longer, but she started to get drowsy when they dosed her with something for the pain again. Clearly it was the good shit, because she was in the clouds in minutes flat.

"I'll come see you tomorrow, Mom."

She slurred something in response as I kissed her cheek. And then, quite clearly: "I love you, baby."

"Love you, too, Momma," I whispered, and let go of her swollen hand.

Like I told Jace. No one is all good or all bad. Not even the woman whose screwups had made most of my life hell.

JACE WAS in the middle of giving me some morning sexin' when Colleen called, and let me tell you, you've never had an awkward conversation until you've tried to talk normally to your sister with your boyfriend's dick in your ass, because he flatly refused to move.

"Yeah, Colleen? What d'ya need?" I really didn't care if I sounded rushed. Let her think I was still carrying a grudge about her behavior the day before.

"I'm at the hospital. I stopped by to see Mom before going to work. They're moving her to ICU. She's developed an infection. They think it's just a bladder infection right now, but they're concerned about her breathing. She might be headed toward pneumonia."

"Fuck." Then Jace did move, rolling over to lie beside me, watching me with concern. "Didn't we go through all this last time?"

"She pulled through it last time, she'll pull through it again. Right now they're just being cautious. Tonya and Blythe should be here this afternoon, but I've got to get to work."

"Right." I rubbed my gritty eyes. "Um, let me take a shower and get some breakfast and I'll be up there in an hour or so."

I hung up with Colleen, and Jace drew me into his arms, down against his chest.

"Wow," I said after a moment of holding on to him for dear life. "Welcome to the worst three weeks of my life: the sequel."

"I'm here with you this time." His lips brushed my temple. "I can't change whatever is happening with your mom, but I can run interference, try to make everything else a little easier."

"Aren't you going to have to go home and work at some point?"

"I brought my tablet, so I can work here. The graphic processing on my laptop isn't quite as beefy as it is on my desktop, but I can manage for as long as necessary. If it becomes a problem, I'll upgrade the laptop."

"Thanks." I kissed his chest and pushed myself up as he discarded the unneeded condom. "I better go shower. Then I'll call Robin and Geoff and apologize for leaving them high and dry with Ling still on maternity leave."

"They'll be fine. I'll call them and give them the update while you shower. Then we'll get something decent to eat before going up to the hospital. There's a Bob Evans practically next door, and I haven't had their biscuits and sausage gravy in forever."

By NOON, Mom's temperature—which had been dropping so low they'd been worried about her the day before—had shot up. They had a weird, air-conditioned blanket thing laid over her to try to bring it down. Of course, each time they brought it down, it started to plummet again, so then they had to work to bring it back up. Apparently, whatever damage her (presumed) suicide attempt had done to her brain functions still made it difficult for her to autonomously control her body temperature whenever she was dealing with any other sort of trauma.

After making sure I'd be okay, Jace went back to the hotel to work, and I sat in Mom's room with my iPod and Android. I met the day nurse—a beautiful brother named Dominick Truscott—who would be providing dedicated care for her until the shift change at seven o'clock this evening. Dominick kept me company a little while he checked all the monitors and gizmos, asking about Saugatuck when I told him I was spending the summer there. Once I told him about the Dunes, he said he might go there on his next vacation.

Then I spent the afternoon shifting my attention back and forth between the muted TV on the wall and playing games on my phone. Finally, remembering my conversation with Jace the night before, I pulled up the information Brendan had entered into my phone when we were together and sent a message to his webmail address.

Brendan,

I just wanted to let you know that I admire the courage it took for you to come out to your family. I know that couldn't have been easy, but being honest about who you are usually isn't.

I also wanted to make sure you did it for the right reasons. Mo told me you have the paintings of me that were on sale in Robin's gallery. I hope you didn't come out with the idea that there could still be something between us, because that won't ever happen. We can't change the mistake we made, but it's over and we both have to move on.

I would honestly be more comfortable if you didn't have those paintings. Obviously it's your choice, but I'm sure you could put them on consignment with Robin again, and he could find another buyer. Even if you don't do it for me, consider how Mo will feel seeing them. Think about it, please.

Thank you for your friendship at the beginning of this summer. I'll always miss that.

Take care,
Topher

Sending the message made me unexpectedly sad. I thought I had come to terms with what had happened between me and Brendan, but there was still something bittersweet about saying it so plainly and deliberately. The rash, angry way I had broken things off before could have been excused and retracted, not that I ever would. This couldn't. It was final, which it really needed to be, and yet . . .

And yet I had cared for Brendan. There, I said it. I hadn't

loved him, but for a while this summer, something in me had connected to him emotionally. However it had ended, I couldn't be impersonal about it.

I drew myself up into a ball in my chair, my knees under my chin and my arms wrapped around them, and listened to my mother struggling to breathe. As the afternoon wore on, her hands, arms, and ankles swelled up with the edema I'd felt in her hand the night before, and then there were special pressure dressings to keep that under control.

Dominick told me they were encountering a little catch-22 with regard to her pain meds. One thing about being in the ICU was that they tried to be conservative with pain medication if possible, because it could alter some of the signs they needed to monitor closely, such as respiration. But as the doctor yesterday had pointed out, in the case of broken ribs, effective pain management was crucial. So they were damned if they did and damned if they didn't there.

Each bit of news that trickled in seemed a little more unpleasant.

I wished I still had the anger I'd had after I found her lying in a pool of vomit and scattered pills. The last time I'd sat in an ICU room like this one and watched her struggling to live, I had lost my ability to care about the outcome. A part of me really *had* been relieved at the prospect of her losing the fight. But I couldn't feel that now. All I could feel was scared.

I still resented her for all the ways she'd ruined my life, yes. I was still furious with her for all the times she'd turned my head around and mind-fucked me, yes. I was still *terrified* of getting drawn back into the black hole of her need for pity and validation, yes.

She had neglected me. Abandoned me to the care of people who had abused me. Manipulated and lied to me and left me a gigantic, walking, open wound, emotionally speaking.

But she was my mom.

I was ready to forgive and try to put our relationship on something resembling a functional level, if possible. Which, to be honest, it probably wasn't, but this was the cycle we had gone through since I was old enough to understand what the word "alcoholic" meant. Whether a healthy relationship was or wasn't a possibility, though, it was a fucking lousy time for her to consider dying, just when I'd finally reached the point where I felt strong enough to try again.

Apparently, God or Fate or whatever the fuck was controlling these things, however, decided my opinion on the timing was irrelevant, because when Tonya and Aunt Blythe arrived that evening, Mom was intubated, and a machine was breathing for her.

CHAPTER THIRTY-SIX

Tell me you might find your faith again
Give me a time, I'll see you then
I'll give this another chance

— CASEY STRATTON, "HIGHWAY"

For my money, there's nothing worse than that nowhere-land you find yourself in when it can truly go either way as you wait to see if a loved one will live or die. I think half of why I'd resigned myself to Mom's death the last time around wasn't just because I was over dealing with her, but because I couldn't handle the uncertainty, and needed to come down on one side or the other. It had left me confused and distraught when she managed to come through it.

As the week wore on, it looked like she might just pull it off again. Wednesday, she regained some lucidity and was breathing well enough to be extubated, which was when I got to deal with another special treat I'd faced before: ICU psychosis. It wasn't apparent to begin with while talking to her. She seemed perfectly rational until she looked at the doorway in alarm every time the nurse walked by.

"You okay, Mom?"

She grimaced. "She's the girlfriend of the Bad Guy."

"She's just your nurse. It's okay."

"No! No! She's meeting him in the parking lot of the South Flint Plaza tonight."

"Mom, the South Flint Plaza has been practically derelict since I was a kid."

"No, she's meeting him. He's the Bad Guy."

I blew out my breath and stopped trying to reason with her. When the nurse came in, I discussed Mom's physical condition with her and Mom started giving me angry looks.

Once the nurse was gone, she hissed at me, "Don't you talk to her!"

"She's all right, Mom. She's just taking care of you."

"No, they're the killers."

That night they had to put her in restraints. The next night, they loaded her to the gills on antipsychotic drugs. The following day, they inserted a chest tube because her thrashing and struggling in the midst of her paranoid delusions had caused her broken ribs to lacerate her lung, which subsequently collapsed. By Saturday, a week after her accident, she was under heavy sedation once more and her temperature was climbing with another infection, the source of which the doctors were having a hard time pinpointing.

I wasn't really in a frame of mind to appreciate how supportive Jace was that week, though he was absolutely amazing. He had to spend some of his time at the hotel working, but he tried to do it as quickly as possible so that he could keep me company at the hospital.

"Why don't you sing something for her?" he suggested one afternoon. "She'd like that."

"I can't." My throat tightened. I couldn't have found a song in that moment if my life depended on it.

Aside from him, I was alone with Mom a large portion of each day, though I sometimes had interesting conversations with the nurses, including Dominick, who was assigned to her on a couple more shifts. I became the hub of information dissemination, because I was the one who got the status reports from her doctors and nurses and conveyed them to the rest of the family in an endless cycle of phone calls. Colleen could only visit for a few hours in the evening because she worked all day. Tonya and Aunt Blythe tried to make the long drive from Grand Rapids as often as they could, but they couldn't do it every day with their work schedules. So it was Jace I had to lean on.

Thank God I'd accepted his gift of the money from those paintings, because there was no way I could go back to work myself. I was missing income opportunity for nearly the entire month of August, and I wouldn't have had enough to go back to school without him.

But it wasn't only the money. He brought me meals, shuffled me out of the ICU when I was clearly about to lose my mind if I didn't see something else for a while, and simply sat with me silently when I was too lost in my own head for conversation. One night I got back to the hotel to find that during the day, he'd made the nearly five-hour round trip drive to and from Saugatuck to collect more of my clothes, as well as my laptop and keyboard. That evening I sat fingering melancholy tunes on the keys, trying to find joy in it.

"Where do you go when you play?" he asked softly, lying on the bed behind me.

"I don't know. I don't know if I go anyplace so much as I just try to shut everything else out. I always have, even since I was a kid."

"Yeah?"

I nodded. "Yeah. I didn't have any friends, so when I was sad, I'd wander around alone—the backyard, neighborhood, playground, woods, whatever—and I'd sing, because singing always made me happy. Except that sometimes I was too sad for it to work, so I'd just end up crying while I sang."

His hand brushed down my back. "Play something happy now. Can you do that?"

I tried, but then the tears were too close, so I turned away from the keyboard and curled up in his arms instead.

Jace had also collected my mail, which contained the results of the test I'd had done at the beginning of August. The next night he managed to get my attention long enough to keep the promise he'd made to me that weekend after the Fourth of July. He was totally not exaggerating about sucking me dry, either. Afterward was the best night's sleep I got the entire time I was in Flint.

Sometimes, when I'd been quiet too long, he started asking leading questions to get me to talk and to remind me that I wasn't alone.

"Tell me a happy memory about your mom," he'd say.

"Um. One of my earliest memories—I was about three, I think —is when I'd been staying at Grandma's while Mom was away for some reason. It seemed like weeks or months. And . . . God, I can barely remember it, it must have been after Christmas, but in my mind, I *think* it was Christmas, you know? Anyway, one night I woke up in the middle of the night and she was there. She'd just arrived. And she lay down with me in the spare bedroom at Grandma's house and held me and I was just *so happy* to have Momma back."

Or I'd tell him about the times Mom, her late husband Clay, Clay's daughter, and I would sit around the dining room table and play euchre for hours on end. The next time Colleen and Tonya were both at the hospital with us, Jace hauled out a pack of cards and demanded we all sit around the table in the waiting room and teach him to play euchre.

As the second week of her stay in ICU aged, they put Mom on heparin because blood clots were beginning to form throughout her body.

Two days later, she stopped digesting the food they were giving her by means of an NG tube.

"Her organs are shutting down," her doctor told us gravely as we all sat together in a consultation room, which was considerably more comfortable than the waiting rooms. It looked like it was designed to be soothing, and I thought, *This is where they deliver the bad news.*

Grandma had arrived the day before, after the cruise ship she'd been on had finally made port someplace where she could book an emergency flight home. So we were all there, the whole dysfunctional clan plus one. I clung to Jace's hand, crushing it.

"She has an advance directive stating that she wants only palliative measures if it's determined there is no hope for meaningful recovery," the doctor continued. "This would be that point."

He left us alone then to discuss things, but there was nothing to discuss. Colleen sat with her head on Tonya's shoulder, her eyes rimmed with red, and we all agreed with almost no words spoken that we would honor Mom's wishes.

We signed the necessary papers, and they took her off the respirator that evening as we stood by her bedside and said our good-byes. I kissed her puffy, overly warm face one last time and then shrunk away to the back of the room, unable to watch. Twenty minutes later, she died.

That night, Jace had to stop holding me long enough to answer a knock on the door to our room and explain to the concerned hotel staff why they shouldn't call the cops about my hysterical sobbing.

MY AUNT RAN interference on a lot of the more mundane funeral arrangements, but eventually Tonya and Colleen and I found ourselves sitting with the consultant at the funeral home, discussing the service.

"Is there any music you'd like to have played or performed?"

I bowed my head and remained silent.

"Topher?" Tonya rose from her chair to come over and squat before mine so that she was in my line of sight. "Jace told me the other day that one of the last things Mom said to you before she went downhill was how much she loved your singing. Do you want to sing something for her?"

I immediately looked at Colleen, because she would be the one to accuse me of using Mom's death as an opportunity to showboat if she was feeling bitchy, but she didn't say anything. A fresh cascade of tears spilled down my cheeks, and I was half-tempted to refuse. How could I sing when I hadn't stopped crying for two days? But I nodded, bowed my head again, and said nothing else.

ROBIN AND GEOFF and Ling came to the funeral with baby Zhen. I got to introduce them to my sisters as I stood greeting and receiving every distant relative I never knew I had. Then I froze in my tracks, staring in disbelief as Jace approached with someone by his side.

"Mo."

She managed a trembling smile, wiping her eyes with the back of her hand. "Jace called me. He said he knew you wouldn't, but that if I thought I might be willing to ever talk to you again, I should consider being here."

I didn't dare fling myself into her arms the way I wanted to, not until she crossed that final step and embraced me. I didn't know how long I stood there clinging to her, whimpering abject apologies against her shoulder. Finally she stepped away.

"I'm still pissed." There was a catch in her voice. "I don't know if it can ever be the way it was before. But I'm here today."

"Thank you," I whispered, sniffling.

So she sat beside me, opposite Jace, and they each held my hands until the pastor called my name.

I kept it simple; I really didn't want to give anyone reason to accuse me of showing off. "There Lies the Answer" had never spoken to me before, but sometime in those days of preparing for the funeral, all the angry songs I had once associated with my mother had stopped feeling appropriate, and all I could think about was healing and forgiveness. I sat at the piano with my eyes closed, playing the music I'd learned by ear.

Underneath all the anger
There lies the answer

It felt surreal, to actually be sitting there playing at my mother's funeral. Was that really me? Was it really happening? It didn't seem possible. I'd imagined that same scenario a hundred times since I was a teenager, knowing it was an inevitability, but now that it was here, I felt odd and disconnected from it.

I can make it through
To do what I'm supposed to do
To come back to you

Perhaps the most unreal part of it was that the relief I'd expected to feel when she was finally dead, the knowledge that she was gone and would never be able to cause me any grief again, was completely absent. There had been moments—a lot of them—when I'd been entirely okay with the prospect of her death. Now it just hurt.

There's a path that forms for those willing to change
A tiny spark that can become a flame

I could hear sniffles from the mourners, and I knew tears were streaming down my own face. My voice quavered and hitched a few times, and I never once opened my eyes. Behind my eyelids, I saw the pretty young mother who had come home unexpectedly at Christmas and lain down and held me when I was almost too small to remember it. The mother who had come to my play in the middle of the school day and beamed with pride when I was in the sixth grade and had the lead. The mother who had always been convinced I could do anything, that I was talented and brilliant and beautiful. The mother with the razor-sharp wit that could sneak up on you and slip between your ribs before you even caught on.

There's a day that dawns when you can see through the night
A blindfold lifted to bring back sight somehow
I can feel it now
I can feel it now

When I returned to my seat, Colleen stood up, her face wet, and hugged me hard.

"That was beautiful," she whispered. "Mom would have loved it."

I hugged her back, all the bitter fights and cruel words forgotten, at least for the moment. I embraced her for being the sister who had also, in her own way, come out on the other side of everything that had been stacked against us as children. Who had been my playmate and caretaker when we'd been alone, stuck together in a situation neither of us could understand. Tonya had made it out early enough to be almost unscathed. But Colleen and I, for all our disagreements and personality conflicts, we were the survivors. I hugged her back and let myself remember that she was my sister and I loved her.

Then I sat through the rest of the service with my head on Jace's shoulder and Mo's hand clenched in mine, crying softly.

CHAPTER THIRTY-SEVEN

Connected to you like never before
Losing my fear as I reach your shore
For so many years I pretended I didn't need anyone
But I know that I need you now
I know that I need you now

— CASEY STRATTON, "STATIC INTO SOUND"

Jace and I went back to Saugatuck immediately after the graveside service. I didn't want to be there in Flint anymore, in that impersonal hotel or at my grandmother's house, surrounded by relatives I sometimes still hated as much as I loved them.

I wanted to be home.

Mo had said she would call me "sometime" as she left the funeral. I didn't know what "sometime" meant, but I wasn't going to press my luck. She would come to me in her own time. Or she wouldn't. Maybe our friendship still wouldn't recover. I owed it to her to leave the choice entirely in her hands. I'd forfeited all right to request anything of her.

To my astonishment, the paintings were back in Robin's shop. Robin hadn't accepted them on consignment from Brendan, he'd simply refunded Brendan's money. Which meant that Robin was temporarily out fifteen thousand dollars. I didn't even bother to offer to give him back the money he'd passed on to me or tell him he could pay me when the paintings sold again. Jace would have throttled me, and really, the game of Hot Potato with that fifteen thou was getting fucking ridiculous. Besides, Robin assured me, he would make it back as soon as they sold again, and they *would* sell, so I wasn't to worry about it.

Brendan had also left a very short note for me.

Topher,
I'm sorry.
Take care of yourself and be happy.
Brendan

The note caused my throat to tighten unexpectedly, and I found myself *missing* Brendan. Not the man I'd had the idiotic affair with, but my best friend's dad, who had befriended me and shown me a level of kindness and understanding I hadn't expected. The man who had been my confidant for a few peaceful weeks. I wished I could go back to the beginning of the summer and do it all over again, without the stupid mistakes, so I wouldn't have to lose him.

Robin and Geoff ordered take-out Chinese and we had a quasi-wake in their dining room. I spent most of it holding Zhen, who decided to mark the day by gracing me with her first-ever social smile. Holding her also turned out to be a better mood lifter than any antidepressant ever. I sat there copping sniffs of her warm, downy head and smiling responsively as the conversation flowed around me. If anyone minded that I didn't contribute much, they didn't say anything, other than to inform me that when Robin and Geoff ended up making their marriage "official" someplace where it was legal, I was on the hook to sing at the wedding.

It didn't matter that they were flattering me; I was still too much of a diva not to preen.

That night, snuggled together in bed in the apartment over

Geoff's studio, Jace hummed thoughtfully and kissed my shoulder.

"So. You move back to campus next week."

"Oh shit, don't remind me," I sighed, drawing his arm tightly around me. "Coach is gonna kick my ass. I haven't swum in weeks. I'm going to have to really bust my balls this season if I want to keep my scholarship."

"Are you going to move into the dorms?"

"No. I think I'm going to splurge and get my own apartment. I should have the money for it if I don't go overboard." I rolled to face him, a tension tugging at my nuts that hadn't been there much at all these past few weeks. "I don't want to have to deal with a pesky roommate when I want to fuck you on the sofa."

"Hmmm, that would simplify things," he murmured, smiling as I began to use my tongue to trace some of the elaborate swirls of tattoos that started at his neck and cascaded down his chest and arms. He gasped and arched when I reached his nipple, sucking and tonguing it with intent.

He seemed like he might be on the verge of adding something else to the conversation when my hand found his dick. Then it didn't really feel like we needed to say anything.

It was like discovering him all over again. I explored with my hands and mouth, nipping, pinching, sucking. We had hardly touched each other except for comfort purposes for weeks, and suddenly I was *starved* for the feel of his skin against mine. We scrambled out of our boxers like they were on fire, rolling together on the bed, sharing long, deep kisses, some slow and lingering, others hard and urgent. He got me onto my back and, *holy shit*, apparently my mind hadn't been entirely on the "suck you dry" distraction he'd given me that night in the hotel, because that gorgeous red mouth of his felt far more fucking incredible than I remembered. He brought me right to the very edge before I pushed him away.

"No! No . . ." I lay there and panted, pinching the base of my cock until it hurt trying to drive the orgasm back. "No. I want to fuck you."

Then there was more tussling and rolling, more hard,

desperate kisses full of tongue and teeth. I ended up lying atop him, sliding our cocks together in a complete inability to stop my hips from thrusting against him. He toyed with my nipple piercings, tugging firmly enough to capture my undivided attention. They were nearly healed now; the pressure added just the right amount of ache.

His thighs bracketed my hips and he jerked me down into another rough kiss. "Fuck me, Topher. Now."

Nodding, I drew away to rummage through the bedside table. I tossed the lube on the bed before reaching for the condoms, but Jace snatched them from my hand and threw them somewhere out onto the floor beyond the bed.

"Fuck me."

I stared at him, startled, but he just grabbed the lube and reached for my cock, slicking it, intent on his purpose.

"I love you," I blurted out of nowhere when the motion of his hand had stilled.

"Well, of course you do." He gave me a cocky smile, as if this was something I said to him every day, instead of for the first time. His eyes gleamed. "Tell me all about it later, or are you gonna leave me here holding my ass open for you all night?"

And just like that, there was *laughter* and *joy*. This thing wasn't scary, and I didn't have to mistrust it. I could just celebrate it.

"Smart-ass," I muttered, crawling over him. He chuckled, and it made him that much tighter when I pushed into him fast and hard the way he liked. Then there was no room for anything but panting and moaning and messy, openmouthed kisses where our tongues thrust at each other because we couldn't slow down long enough to seal our lips together properly. He was hot and tight and just fucking perfect in every possible way and *God*, I did love him and it was the most amazing thing ever.

Afterward, I collapsed, panting, atop him. My softening cock slipped out of his ass, wet and sloppy. Then he spoke again, stroking my hair while he caught his breath.

"Maybe you can get a two-bedroom apartment."

"Why would I want to do that?" Yeah, postorgasmic Topher's

higher brain sometimes functioned just above that of Cro-Magnon man, okay? Gimme a break.

"So I can have an office."

"You have an office at your place. Do you plan to spend that much time working when you come to see me?"

He blew a puff of air through his pursed lips, the breeze catching a lock of hair and blasting it away from his face. "Are you *really* gonna be that obtuse about this? Get with the program, angel."

"What? Oh? Oh!" Startled, I blinked at him. "But don't you need to be in Chicago?"

He shrugged. "Not all the time. That became pretty evident the past couple weeks. I would have to drive down once or twice a week to meet with clients, probably, and maybe sometimes stay down there short-term when I have another set or interior design gig, but it's workable."

"Allendale's practically a cow town, you know. It's pretty boring there."

"Yeah, and we got clubs in Grand Rapids we can hit if we want to go out, or there's Grand Haven, or Holland. Saugatuck's only, what, forty-five minutes away if we want to hit the Dunes? And there's no reason we can't go party down in Chicago when we feel the need." He chuckled, wriggling beneath me. "Besides, I'm pretty sure we can make our own fun."

Overjoyed, I began to laugh. "Oh yeah. Oh, hell yeah!"

EPILOGUE

A solace is coming
On the summer winds
No pain or disaster
I promise love

— CASEY STRATTON, "I PROMISE LOVE"

With Michigan still dragging its heels and marriage equality now law in Illinois, Robin and Geoff decided to have their wedding in Chicago the next summer. Zhen wasn't really old enough to be a flower girl, but she was walking by that point and pretty much drew all the attention away from the grooms. Not even my fabulous performance could compare. I was well and truly upstaged by a scene-stealing toddler.

I had to forgive her, though, when I realized she was warbling in something vaguely resembling the same tune I was carrying. She couldn't speak, and she wasn't even close to being on pitch, but her voice rose and fell when it was supposed to, and she could obviously recognize and anticipate the patterns in the music and try to mimic them. Clearly, she was a natural. And will I be making a star out of her someday? You bet your ass I will.

During the wedding, Jace watched me speculatively, but he

didn't make any romantic offers, and truth be told, I was okay with that. I knew I wanted to be with him forever, but at twenty-two, I was still too young and immature for marriage. I figured we'd revisit the subject after I graduated and started my career, especially since I was pretty damn determined we were moving to Chicago once I was out of school.

I mean, let's face it, I am just *far* too fucking fabulous for a conservative midsize town like Grand Rapids.

I would love to be able to report that my relationship with my family was magically all better after the ordeal of Mom's death bonded us together, but hello? Let's get real. The fact is, I don't have a damn thing in common with either of my sisters. Colleen is and always will be completely out for herself, for all that she does have the odd moment of likability. Tonya is a much better person, and I think if she could settle down, get an education, and stop partying so much, she might have a shot at a good life. But we'll never be besties either. Tonya likes things low-key, and I'm just too much for her. She thinks that I'm melodramatic and self-involved and maybe she's right. I don't know.

What I do know is that if I am a self-centered drama queen, I'm not a terrible person because of it. I've pretty much lost my ability to let my family make me feel inadequate. I like who I am, even if I'm not perfect.

Strangely, the relationship that improved the most was with my aunt and uncle. I won't say I don't still have moments when I resent the fuck out of the things they did to me when I was a teenager. Brendan was right. They *were* abusive at times while I was growing up. Maybe not constantly or catastrophically so on the great scale of things, but they were. They simply were. I can admit that now without cognitive dissonance making my emotions go haywire and throwing me into a fit of anxiety (did I mention I was in therapy again?).

The cognitive dissonance came in when I tried to cope with the fact that, while they were abusive, they're also, on the whole, good people. Good people with moments of horrifically bad judgment and anger and reactions, perhaps, but still. Once I realized they had recognized me as an adult and an equal, I didn't have to hate and be afraid of them anymore. They had no more power over me, and they could never hurt me again.

Does that mean they don't sometimes disapprove of my choices and try to nudge me to their (always, always, always inarguably correct, of course) way of living? Nah. And does it mean I don't still sometimes have moments of bitterness and resentment over the past? Of course not. But we've reached an armistice I can live with, without letting them make me unhealthy.

It's amusing to watch them try to figure out what to make of Jace, because his behavior doesn't match the assumptions they made when they saw his appearance. He throws all their assertions over the impracticality of frivolous pursuits like art and music—as well as the destructiveness of nonconforming behaviors such as, say, sporting multiple facial piercings and sheets of tattoos from the neck down—right out the window. Oddly enough, they seem to respect him more for that.

Brendan and Adele are getting divorced. Apparently after a few months of separation and some deliberation, Brendan decided he needed to explore the same-sex half of his bisexuality. I feel terrible for Adele, of course, but I'm actually a little proud of Brendan, both for having the courage to face up to who he truly is, and also for not using being bisexual as an excuse to cat around on his wife (well, his affair with me notwithstanding).

Now he's seeing a grad student from another department at Michigan State, and according to Mo, the whole thing smacks of a midlife crisis. As in, "Dad's having a midlife crisis; his name is Thom." Thom the Grad Student has Brendan acting like he's twenty-five again. New haircut, new wardrobe, new car. Hopefully Brendan will get his head right again before he loses everything.

And yes, if you're wondering, this does mean Mo is speaking to me. It actually took her months to do so after my mom's funeral. We'd see each other on campus once in a while, but we'd only nod and smile politely. I stuck by my resolution to let her determine if and how and when we started patching things up. Finally, the week before Thanksgiving, just as I was sitting on my hands to avoid texting her to wish her a happy twenty-third birthday, she sent me one instead.

I have to admit, girlfriend, I didn't think you'd be able to resist sending me a message for my birthday.

I smiled and immediately replied.

I almost didn't, but then I figured Cody the Archer was probably down from Big Rapids giving you all the birthday greetings you could possibly need. With his penis.

It took her a while to respond. *He was for a bit, but he's got an early class in the a.m.*

Then another message: *Thanks for not pushing me.*

I hugged my phone to my chest because I couldn't hug her.

Anytime. Anything you need.

Another long pause, which left me wondering if she was working or studying or what.

I'll be in Ann Arbor all winter break. Can we meet for coffee in January?

Okay, yeah, I cried then. I'm a big, blubbery baby. Like this is news.

Sure. Just tell me when and where and I'll be there.

We made an infrequent habit of those meetings, which became steadily more frequent through spring and into summer. We're still not back to where we were, but she doesn't despise me and that's about the best I can reasonably hope for. And now she's graduated, so the coffee meetings have ended. She'll be counseling at the summer camp in Traverse City again, and then she's moving in with Cody in Big Rapids as he does his post-grad work. It's entirely possible that once that happens, we'll drift apart entirely, except for the occasional tweet and Facebook poke. We'll have to see.

Jace is . . . God, where do I even begin? It's almost as though he's taken it upon himself to make up for all the support and opportunity my family never gave me. Like he has something to prove. I've told him it's not necessary and he needs to relax a little. Sometimes it makes me uncomfortable because, honestly, one man cannot possibly give enough love and attention to compensate for two decades' worth of neglect and abuse.

And he shouldn't have to. I certainly don't expect him to. I'm not Colleen, who insists the world owes her something for her shitty childhood. I just need him to be Jace, my sometimes judgmental yet incredibly sensitive, insightful, and sexy boyfriend. He needs to hold something back for taking care of himself, especially since it wasn't like his own upbringing fulfilled his every need. But maybe that was why he does it. Maybe giving me some of what he was denied fills the void left over from what his family did to him.

My biggest worry in our relationship right now is that he's going to burn himself out or start to resent how much he puts into the relationship if he keeps trying to do that. I admit, at least a little of this comes from the critical voices of my past telling me I never carry my weight, never give enough, that I'm never grateful enough. I worry that sooner or later, he'll feel things are imbalanced and that he isn't getting as much as he gives, and then where will we be?

Which is not to say that he isn't wonderful in every possible way. He really, really is. One day at the end of classes, I got a text message from him, asking me to meet him at a coffeehouse in downtown Grand Rapids. When I got there, however, he wasn't alone.

Casey Stratton was with him. Jace had taken it upon himself to make my teenage wish come true. Since Casey lived right there in town, Jace didn't see any reason why I *shouldn't* get to meet and talk with him. And it was a great time. Casey gave me a lot of encouragement and advice and we're going to keep in touch. He might not *quite* be my Yoda, and I'll never be in his league talent-wise, but having someone I can discuss music and the things we have in common with is nice; and when someone I admire that much says I can do more than I think I'm capable of, it really means something to me.

I'm starting to think I might try my hand at writing my own music, like he does.

For now, though, I'm meeting Jace at the pool. Since we stayed in our apartment in Allendale for the summer, it's easy for me to keep training for my final year on the swim team, and I'm making better times than ever before. And since Jace doesn't get to lift weights at the bathhouse anymore, he's taken to doing laps to keep in shape while I train. I still say he's got about a decade before he loses the struggle and becomes quite *cuddly* again.

And as far as I'm concerned? There is no fucking way I won't be there to see it.

THE END

ACKNOWLEDGMENTS

Thank you, Casey, for your generosity in letting me reference your music and for allowing me to give you a cameo in my book.

To purchase the amazing *Sea Change* (formerly *Saugatuck Summer*) soundtrack, please visit
https://store.caseystratton.com/album/music-from-saugatuck-summer

Risk Aware

SAUGATUCK BOOK 2

AMELIA C. GORMLEY

RISK AWARE

SAUGATUCK, BOOK 2

A Life Half-Lived No More...

Hemophiliac Geoff Gilchrest has lived his entire life swaddled in figurative bubble wrap, thanks to his overprotective mother. Now he's free of everything except the prison of his own mind, where forbidden desires war against crippling self-doubt.

Geoff is a masochist. He craves his sex with a side of pain and degradation. But when getting shoved against a wall could result in catastrophic brain injury and even a moderate flogging could leave him paralyzed—or worse—it's hard to find a dom willing to step up and give Geoff the experiences he's been longing for.

Robin Brady has doubts of his own. Still stinging from massive violations of trust on the part of his drug-addicted ex, he has retreated to Saugatuck to start a new life. But the yearning in Geoff's eyes calls to him, and he knows that, armed with a deft hand and foreknowledge, he can give Geoff what he's been seeking, without putting Geoff's safety at risk.

First, though, he's got to convince Geoff to trust him—not just with his well-being, but with his pride. Geoff's injured self-esteem and trouble with communicating what he perceives as weaknesses, could end them before they have a chance to begin.

STRAIN

In a world with little hope and no rules,
the only thing they have to lose
is themselves.

AMELIA C. GORMLEY

STRAIN

THE EROTIC, POST-APOCALYPTIC
THRILLER!

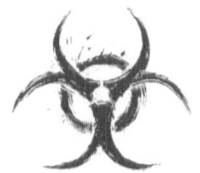

*In a world with little hope and no rules, the only thing they have to lose
is themselves.*

Rhys Cooper is a dead man. He's spent years hiding from the virus that
wiped out most of the human race, but an act of futile heroism has him
counting down his remaining days. The timely arrival of superhuman
soldiers offers some feeble hope—but only if Rhys can reconcile himself
to doing what is necessary to take advantage of it.

Sergeant Darius Murrell has seen too much death and too little
tenderness, seeking out survivors only to put the infected out of their
misery, or send the uninfected to a safe haven he and his fellow
Juggernaut troops can never enjoy. Rhys's situation is different, though.
Not only is there an improbable chance that Darius won't have to put a
bullet in Rhys's head, but he has somehow managed to get under Darius's
skin.

The virus Rhys must infect himself with is sexually transmitted, and
optimizing his chance of exposure requires him to submit as often as
possible to Darius—and the other soldiers. Though the boundaries of
morality have shifted in this harsh new world, what they must do has
them asking if their humanity is too high a price to pay for Rhys's
survival.

ALSO BY AMELIA C. GORMLEY

IMPULSE

Inertia

Acceleration

Velocity

SEASONS IN SAUGATUCK

The Field of Someone Else's Dreams

Sea Change (previously published as *Saugatuck Summer*)

Risk Aware

THE STRAIN TRILOGY

Juggernaut

Strain

Bane

(COMING SOON)

Player vs. Player

ABOUT THE AUTHOR

Amelia C. Gormley published her first short story in the school newspaper in the 4th grade, and since then has suffered the persistent delusion that enabling other people to hear the voices in her head might be a worthwhile endeavor. She's even convinced her hapless spouse that it could be a lucrative one as well, especially when coupled with her real-life interest in angst, kink, feminism, and pretty men.

When her husband and son aren't interacting with the back of her head as she stares at the computer, they rely on her to feed them, maintain their domicile, and keep some semblance of order in their lives (all very, very bad ideas—they really should know better by now.) She can also be found playing video games and ranting on Tumblr, seeing as how she's one of those horrid social justice warriors out to destroy free speech, gaming, geek culture, and everything else that's fun everywhere.

Blog: http://ameliacgormley.com
Tumblr: http://ameliacgormley.tumblr.com
Facebook: http://facebook.com/ameliacgormley
Twitter: http://twitter.com/ACGormley
Goodreads:
http://goodreads.com/author/show/6445292.Amelia_C_Gormley